A Glimpse of Eternity

The Story of Ariana's
Daughters

Books by Rachel Ann Nunes

Autumn Rain Novels
(Paranormal Romance)
Imprints
Shades of Gray
Final Call
Line of Fire
Blinded

Romantic Suspense
Eyes of a Stranger (Autumn
   Rain series prequel)

Women's Fiction
Flying Home
Fields of Home
Saving Madeline
Before I Say Goodbye
The Gift of Angels (novella)
A Greater Love
A Heartbeat Away

Huntington Family
Winter Fire
No Longer Strangers
Chasing Yesterday
By Morning Light
The Independence Club

Ariana Series (and spin-off)
Ariana: The Making of a Queen
Ariana: A Gift Most Precious
Ariana: A New Beginning
A Glimpse of Eternity (The
   Story of Ariana's Daughters)

Rebekka Series
This Time Forever *
Ties That Bind
Twice in a Lifetime

Mickelle Series
This Time Forever *
Bridge to Forever

Love Series (Christian Romantic
Suspense)
A Bid for Love
Framed for Love
Love on the Run

Romance
To Love and to Promise
Tomorrow and Always
Where I Belong
A Greater Love
This Very Moment
In Your Place

For Children
The Problem With Spaceships:
   Zero G
Daughter of a King
The Secret of the King

**Under the Name Rachel
Branton**
Tell Me No Lies
Your Eyes Don't Lies

Under the Name Teyla Branton
The Change (Unbounded #1)
The Cure (Unbounded #2)
The Escape (Unbounded #3)
The Reckoning (Unbounded #4)

* This Time Forever is the first
in both the Rebekka and the
Mickelle series.

A Glimpse of Eternity

The Story of Ariana's Daughters

RACHEL ANN NUNES

WHITE STAR PRESS

This is a work of fiction, and the views expressed herein are the sole responsibility of the author. Likewise, certain characters, places, and incidents are the product of the author's imagination, and any resemblance to actual persons, living or dead, or actual events or locales, is entirely coincidental.

A Glimpse of Eternity: The Story of Ariana's Daughters (Ariana, Book 4)

Published by White Star Press
P.O. Box 353
American Fork, Utah 84003

Printed in the United States of America
ISBN 13: 978-1-948982-49-8
Year of first White Star Press printing: 2025

For being there whenever I need you, TJ,
this one's for you.

Chapter One

The confrontation took place in the sitting room. Marie-Thérèse watched as a deep crimson flushed her sister's face. The color traveled from Josette's neck up to her brown eyes, where Marie-Thérèse imagined she could see fiery sparks leaping out, burning whatever they touched.

For a long moment their parents, Ariana and Jean-Marc Perrault, said nothing but regarded Josette quietly from their seat on the long blue couch. Marie-Thérèse could hear the tick-tock of the grandfather clock that stood near the window. She shifted nervously on the chair, her fingers drumming softly on the armrest. Outside the window, the twilight crept steadily on, enveloping the outside world with its diffused light.

"I tell you, I'm not going!" Josette repeated into the silence. It was the third time she had said that exact phrase in the past two minutes. "I don't want to leave France."

"Now is rather late to be telling us this," their father said. "Fall classes start in eight days." His voice was mild, but his face was set firmly in a way Marie-Thérèse recognized all too well. He would not compromise, no matter what.

"You can still get your money back," Josette protested.

Their mother rose from the couch and put her hand on Josette's arm. "That's not the point. You committed to go, and we all agreed it was best."

"But America is too far away. I'll die without Alphonse!" Josette stomped her foot like a small child and glared at Ariana. Marie-Thérèse thought how alike mother and daughter appeared. Of course, there were notable differences: Josette had long hair while Ariana's was short; Josette's curvaceous figure was taller and slightly fuller than her mother's; and Josette was deeply tanned by an active outdoor life. The biggest dissimilarity came from the twenty-four years separating them. Josette was hot-tempered and flighty, while Ariana's passion had been tempered by a difficult but fulfilling life.

"Die without him?" Their mother laughed. "Oh, Josette, be serious! You only met him a month ago."

"Alphonse is different."

"As was the boyfriend before this," Jean-Marc put in. "And he's not even a member of our church. You know how we feel about that."

"But Brigham Young University is so far away. Why can't I continue my education here?"

"You know very well why," Jean-Marc said. "Your mother and I both feel you need to gain some independence."

Josette turned to Marie-Thérèse, her face pleading. "Help me! They'll listen to you."

Marie-Thérèse wanted to help her sister, but she agreed with her parents. The twenty-year-old Josette needed a change in her life, and BYU just might be able to give it to her.

Josette herself had been the catalyst that had convinced Marie-Thérèse to side with their parents. Four months earlier, Marie-Thérèse had come home to find Josette and her latest boyfriend alone in the sitting room, making out. Or necking, as their parents called it. No one else was in the house. Josette's twin brother Marc was on his mission, André and Pauline were at a church activity, and their parents had taken their youngest brother, Louis-Géralde, to a birthday party. The only reason Marie-Thérèse had come home early from her college study group was because she'd forgotten her class notes.

She'd opened the apartment door with her key and had almost immediately heard the giggling behind the wooden screen that separated the sitting room from the entryway. Slowly, she had pushed the partition aside, already suspecting what she would find.

"Marie-Thérèse!" Josette had gasped from the couch. She pushed the boy away and sat up straight. "What are you doing home?"

"I should ask you the same thing."

Josette ran to her side. "Don't tell Mom and Dad, promise?" she whispered. "I mean, I'm twenty now, not sixteen. We were just kissing a little."

Marie-Thérèse glanced at the boy who sat calmly back against the couch, grinning at her. She recognized Marcelin Cuvier from one of her classes at the private college she and Josette attended, and knew his reputation. A little kissing was not the only thing on his mind.

He stood up and sauntered over to Josette, giving her a long kiss on the mouth. "I'd better go. Catch you tomorrow."

Josette's full lips went into a fake pout. "Okay, I guess." When he left, she turned back to Marie-Thérèse. "You won't tell, will you?"

"That depends."

"On what?"

"On if you leave him alone."

Josette laughed. "What do you mean?"

Her tone made Marie-Thérèse angry. "You know exactly what I mean. He's a spoiled rich boy who's only out for a good time." *Just like you,* she wanted to add, but refrained by biting her tongue. She had learned to think before acting—one of them had to be responsible, and Josette was almost never that.

"Well, what's wrong with having fun?"

"His fun is not our kind of fun," Marie-Thérèse retorted. "What about your values? What about a temple marriage?"

Josette crossed to the couch and put her feet up on the coffee table. "Goodness, I'm not sleeping with him, I'm just fooling around."

"You're playing with fire."

"What do you know about it? You hardly even go out."

"I do when I find someone worthy of what I want in my life."

Josette impatiently pulled her waist-length hair up and over the back of the couch. "Maybe it's time you stop being so picky. You don't want to end up an old maid, like Aunt Lu-Lu almost did." Her hair tumbled forward again as she picked up a magazine from the table and began to thumb through it much faster than she could ever read.

" 'Almost' doesn't count," Marie-Thérèse said, moving to sit beside her sister. "She found Jourdain and you know how wonderful he is. What if she'd settled for a nonmember and lost the chance of meeting him?"

"Is that what this is all about—my dating a nonmember? That's strange, coming from little Miss-I'm-planning-to-go-on-a-mission. What about repentance? What about me converting him? It does happen. Why don't *you* look at Aunt Lu-Lu?"

"Uncle Jourdain is different. Special."

"So is Marcelin." There was no flexibility in Josette's eyes.

"All right," said Marie-Thérèse. "What if I can prove that he's not special? What if I can prove he's only out for what he can get? What then? Would you promise to drop him?"

Josette's eyes narrowed. "How?"

"What if I can get him to ask me out? Or meet me somewhere."

Josette threw back her head and laughed. "Don't tell me you're interested in him. If that's the case, then—"

"I'm not interested in him," snapped Marie-Thérèse. "I've told you that I'll never let a man come between us. I'm just worried about you."

Her sister's laughter vanished. "I know you're worried. And you're right—no man is worth our friendship."

Marie-Thérèse knew Josette was remembering the first time they'd vowed never to let a man come between them. They'd been sixteen and the same boy had asked them out. At first they'd fought over him, but Pauline, then only twelve, had made them understand that sisters were more important than any transitory boyfriend. They'd both dumped the American boy, Kenny, and made the vow to never, ever allow a man to come between them.

"Then you'll let me do it?" Marie-Thérèse asked.

"Only if you'll agree to support me if he doesn't fail your test."

Marie-Thérèse hesitated only a second. "Okay. But I get a few tries."

"Three." They shook on the deal.

The next day, Josette amazed Marie-Thérèse by throwing herself into the plan. She styled Marie-Thérèse's hair, spraying and scrunching until it looked like a picture from a magazine. She even let her wear her favorite perfume. "Marcelin loves this," she giggled.

"You'd think you want him to fail."

"I want to be sure," Josette said. "No, not that blouse, wear this one. The green makes your eyes stand out. And this skirt." She pulled a tight-fitting emerald skirt out of their free-standing closet. "It goes with the blouse, and it makes you look sexy."

Marie-Thérèse rolled her eyes. "Oh, great." She studied herself in the full-length mirror near the closet. She was taller than Josette by about ten centimeters. Her shoulder-length hair was a lighter brown than her sister's and cut at varying lengths along her thin face to give it fullness and to emphasize the small, upturned nose and pixie face.

"You look a little like Aunt Paulette," Josette said suddenly, her eyes darting to a picture above Marie-Thérèse's bed. In it, Paulette Perrault held a baby Marie-Thérèse.

Marie-Thérèse nodded absently. Except for her nose, she did

favor her birth mother, who had died of AIDS when she was only four. They shared the same brown hair, the light-brown eyes, the lean body, and the many freckles. Marie-Thérèse's natural sister, Pauline, however, almost completely resembled their adoptive father. Marie-Thérèse often thought that her younger sister fit perfectly into her aunt and uncle's family—except for the fact that she had been born when her mother was sick and she was HIV positive. That didn't fit comfortably anywhere.

"I wish I was slim enough to wear that skirt," Josette said a little enviously.

Marie-Thérèse much preferred Josette's more womanly curves, but she did have to admit that she looked good today. She'd always considered herself plain against the backdrop of Josette's passionate beauty, but maybe she judged herself too harshly. Regardless, she hoped her looks would be enough for the task.

"What's your plan?" Josette asked as they rode the elevator down the five flights to the street. The May air was still cool this early in the morning, and Marie-Thérèse felt goose bumps rise on her bare arms.

"Well, Mom and Dad have plans tonight, and I've already given André and Pauline money to take Louis-Géralde to a movie. I thought I'd test Marcelin at our apartment."

"But I have a date with him tonight!"

"So I'm cancelling it. He'll come to pick you up and you won't be there. It's as simple as that."

"But I *will* be there," Josette said. "I want to hear for myself what he does."

Marie-Thérèse shrugged. "Fine by me. I don't want to be alone with him anyway. I don't trust him. If you're there, I won't have to ask one of my friends over to hide and watch." With effort, she formed a stiff smile. "And that way you can see what kind of a man he really is."

"Humph!" Josette tossed her long hair over her shoulder.

"*When* he passes your silly little test, I'm going out with him like I'd planned."

"Suit yourself. *If* he passes."

"He will," her sister insisted. "But I don't know why we went to all that work getting you ready this morning when he's not coming to get me until seven tonight." Josette's enthusiasm for the project had dimmed, but Marie-Thérèse became even more determined. Although her sister had agreed to give her three chances, she doubted there would be more than just this one. That understanding was the reason she had taken such care with her appearance this morning. Tonight she would make her move on Marcelin, but during the day she would lay her groundwork.

They walked the rest of the way to the metro in silence, and Josette didn't speak at all to Marie-Thérèse on the train. When they arrived at their university, she disappeared with a hasty wave of her hand. Marie-Thérèse stared after, loving her sister and wishing for the millionth time that she was a little more stable. *When had it happened? When had Josette changed?* Marie-Thérèse's eyebrows scrunched together as she fell into her usual habit of analyzing the world around her. Today she found no answer. Her sister still had the strong sense of love and responsibility she'd always felt for the family, but something else wasn't right.

Marie-Thérèse's plan came into play during the math class she shared with Marcelin. Both were finance majors, and in the same year. Since her childhood, Marie-Thérèse had wanted to follow her adoptive father's footsteps and go into banking. Marcelin was there to learn how to make his rich family even richer—or so he told anyone who would listen.

She arrived early to class, relieved to see that Marcelin hadn't yet found a seat. It wouldn't pay to be too obvious. The gathering students murmured among themselves, and Marie-Thérèse didn't miss the fact that Marcelin's companions were all young women— pretty young women. Ignoring her usual place in the front, she sat next to the chair Marcelin used each day without fail. The teacher entered, and the students quickly took their seats.

Without glancing her way, Marcelin settled into his accustomed spot. Marie-Thérèse felt her heart pounding so loudly that she was sure the whole class must hear. She waited until the teacher was well underway before pushing her pen off the desk with the edge of her book, praying silently that it would land near Marcelin.

It did. He leaned down and scooped it up, handing it back. *Now,* Marie-Thérèse told herself. She accepted the pen, but grabbed it farther up than necessary, touching his fingers.

"Thanks," she said with a smile. He grinned, and Marie-Thérèse noticed for the first time how good-looking he was. Her pulse quickened now for quite another reason. She purposely held his eyes with her own in the way Josette was famous for doing. He grinned and stared insolently back.

Well, at least he saw me, Marie-Thérèse thought.

"You look great today," Marcelin whispered.

She smiled and lowered her eyes. "Thanks."

"Hey, uh, I missed class the other day," he added. "Do you think you could give me your notes?"

This was way too easy. "Sure. You have a date with my sister tonight, don't you? You can get them then."

Marcelin blinked in surprise before his face blanked, and Marie-Thérèse knew he hadn't realized who she was, much less her relationship to Josette. She was nothing but backdrop, someone he'd never noticed before. Her face flamed, but she turned it so he wouldn't see.

Marie-Thérèse didn't dare look at Marcelin again. *Some femme fatale I am,* she thought with a silent sigh.

After class, Marcelin put his arm briefly on her shoulder. "See ya tonight."

"Tonight," she agreed, startling herself by giving him a wink. He grinned and strode out of the room, a picture of confidence, while she leaned against the wall until her knees were no longer shaking. "I'm no good at this," she muttered. "Even though I've had the best teacher." Josette had been adept at charming the opposite sex since she was five; it seemed to come naturally for her.

Later that evening, Josette changed hiding places four times before Marcelin came to the door. First she stretched out behind the couch in the sitting room. Second, she crouched behind the chair. Then she decided to stay in the kitchen and sneak out to listen at the folding wood partition which Marie-Thérèse would close after bringing Marcelin into the sitting room. At the last minute, she hid behind the couch again. "That way you won't have to remember to close the partition," she said.

From her flighty movements and quick speech, Marie-Thérèse could tell her sister was nervous, but that nervousness couldn't possibly equal the butterflies in her own stomach. She wished she could call the whole thing off.

Marcelin didn't arrive until ten minutes after the hour. Marie-Thérèse opened the door with a smile. "Come on in." She led the way to the sitting room and motioned for him to sit on the blue couch.

"I'm sorry to tell you this," she said, settling next to him a little closer than she would have normally liked. "But Josette can't make it tonight. She said she's really sorry and that she'll explain later."

"Oh." Marcelin looked disgruntled.

"I thought we could go over these notes, if you want. I use some abbreviations that might not be very clear."

"Sure." His voice was slightly sour.

Marie-Thérèse explained the meaning of her abbreviations as slowly as possible, catching his eyes and smiling often, but all too soon, she was finished. "Well, that's it."

Marcelin leaned back against the couch, one arm spread across the top, and stared at her lazily. "Thanks. I guess I'd better get going."

"I guess," Marie-Thérèse agreed reluctantly. What was she going to do? They'd been alone together a whole twenty minutes, and he'd been a perfect gentleman. She'd tried to make her pretend feelings for Marcelin obvious, so maybe Josette was right about him after all.

"How is it that you and Josette are the same age?" Marcelin asked. At least he didn't seem to be in too great a hurry to leave. "I thought she had a twin brother, not a sister."

"We're actually cousins. My parents died when I was young, and my aunt and uncle adopted my little sister and me. I'm four months older than Josette and Marc."

"Oh." Marcelin's face came suddenly close to hers. "I like you, Marie-Thérèse," he murmured. He kissed her, his lips plastering wetly on hers.

She pushed him away, trying not to show the anger kindling in her gut. "What about Josette? You're my sister's boyfriend."

"I won't tell her if you won't."

"You want to date us both?" Marie-Thérèse couldn't keep the incredulity from her voice.

"Why not? We'll keep it our little secret."

He tried to kiss her again, but Marie-Thérèse punched his chest and leapt to her feet. "I want you to leave."

Marcelin's face grew red. "I was under the impression you liked me."

His vehemence startled her into telling the truth. "I wanted to see for myself what kind of a man my sister dated. It was a test. And you failed."

Marcelin raised a fist. Marie-Thérèse became suddenly afraid, but she didn't flinch. "Leave," she repeated firmly.

To her relief, Marcelin dropped his hand and walked to the entryway. "It's your loss," he said. "You're too thin, anyway. I like my women to look like women, to be softer than dried up old bread." The comment stung, but Marie-Thérèse didn't let him see. "And forget about telling Josette," he added. "She'll never believe you. It's your word against mine."

"She'll believe me. We're sisters," Marie-Thérèse said, but she wondered if he was right. Would Josette have believed her if she hadn't heard for herself what kind of man Marcelin was?

"Cousins," corrected Marcelin. With that, he turned on his heel and strode out the door, slamming it behind him.

Utter silence filled the room. *Why doesn't Josette come out from behind the couch?* Marie-Thérèse made her way to where a small table with long legs and a gilt-edged mirror separated the wall from the couch. Josette lay under the table on her side.

"Josette, come out of there."

No answer.

Marie-Thérèse stooped down and reached tentatively toward her sister's hair. "I'm sorry," she murmured. She was. She almost wished she hadn't challenged her sister's relationship with Marcelin. Almost.

Josette looked up. There were tears on her face. "Will I ever find someone?" she whispered. "Someone who loves me for me?"

"When it's time."

Her sister scrambled from under the table and to her feet. "It's okay for you!" she shouted. "You don't care. You want to go on a mission and convert the world. I just want a family. What's so wrong with that?"

"You're only twenty"

The words spurred Josette to further anger. "I'm going after him! We didn't play fair. We tricked him! You tricked him!"

"It could have been anyone," Marie-Thérèse began.

Josette wouldn't listen. "I don't care what you say." With that she ran to the door.

Marie-Thérèse thought for a long time, and she knew what she had to do. When her parents arrived home, she told them what had happened.

Jean-Marc's eyes met Ariana's as though communicating some private message. "I think it's time," he said.

She nodded. "I'd hoped she'd settle down, but ever since Marc left . . ."

That's it! thought Marie-Thérèse. *It was when Marc left on his mission a year ago that Josette began to change.* Her sister had always been passionate about everything, but only in her twin brother's absence had she become uncontrollable. Josette had seemed to be the one to keep the impulsive Marc out of trouble, but apparently he had stabilized her as well. The twins had been very close—closer even than she and Josette, the cousin-sisters.

"What did we do wrong?" Ariana asked. "We didn't let her date until she was sixteen, and then only in group dates. How can she be so careless of what we've taught?"

Marie-Thérèse watched her father put his arm around her mother. "Ari, we did the best we knew how."

"I feel like she's drowning and I can't save her," Ariana said. "I haven't felt that way since André hung out with those drug pushers when he was twelve."

Involuntarily, Marie-Thérèse shuddered. A youthful drug addiction on her birth mother's part had caused her birth parents' AIDS all those years ago.

"I think BYU is a good option," her father said. "Apparently Josette needs some time to decide what she believes."

"But to send her away?" Ariana protested. "How can that be right? We won't be there to help her."

"Our prayers have been answered," Jean-Marc said gently. "Don't you think so?"

Marie-Thérèse saw the answer on her mother's face before she spoke. "Yes. This is our answer. But we can't send her alone."

As one, they turned toward Marie-Thérèse.

"What?" she asked warily. She had followed the conversation, but still didn't understand.

"We've decided to send Josette to Brigham Young University in Provo to finish college," Jean-Marc said. "We'd like you to go with her."

"But my mission."

"You won't be twenty-one until the end of November, and

you weren't planning to submit your papers until then anyway. It would only delay you a month or so. Do you think you could do that? Josette will need you, especially with Marc so far away."

Go to the United States? Marie-Thérèse had thought about going there for a vacation, but never for an extended period of time. She knew without a doubt that France was where she belonged. Still, she loved her sister, and the time in America would be a learning experience for them both. Her parents said that sending Josette was an answer to their prayers—shouldn't she be willing to do her part? "All right," she said. "I'll go."

The relief was evident on her parents' faces. "Good," her father said. "You can start filling out the papers right now."

"You have them already?"

"Yes," Jean-Marc said. "We've been in touch with the administration there. The missionary who baptized your mom already has things underway, in case we decided to go this route. He's a professor there."

Marie-Thérèse realized her parents had been aware of Josette's need all along and had been searching for some way to help her. "What if she refuses?" Marie-Thérèse asked.

"She's an adult," Jean-Marc said, "even if she doesn't act like one most of the time. We can't force her, but I think together we can convince her. Especially after what happened tonight."

Marie-Thérèse wasn't so sure. After all, Josette had gone after Marcelin. "Let me talk to her first, okay?"

Her parents smiled. "Thank you," Ariana said. "I knew you would help."

Marie-Thérèse was in the sitting room, filling out the application papers, when Josette came home a short time later. Josette said nothing but threw herself on the end of the couch. Her face showed no signs of tears. "Where's everybody?" she asked as though nothing had happened.

"In the TV room." Marie-Thérèse wanted more than anything to ask about Marcelin, but she didn't dare.

"What are you doing?"

"Filling out papers for Dad to fax tomorrow. I'm going to transfer to BYU."

"You're what?" Josette leaned closer, suddenly interested.

"It'll be good to get away," Marie-Thérèse said cautiously. "It'll be a whole new experience."

"But your mission."

"I'm only going to America until December. Then I'll come home."

Josette said nothing, but her expression was sad.

"How'd it go with Marcelin?" Marie-Thérèse asked softly.

Josette's luminous eyes met hers, and when she spoke the words came more slowly than Marie-Thérèse had ever heard them come from her sister. "He said you threw yourself at him, and that he had to fend you off."

"Did you tell him you were there?"

"No. I told him my sister would never lie. He denied it again, but I said he wasn't worth my relationship with my sister—that no man was."

Gratitude washed over Marie-Thérèse. Marcelin was put into his place, at least as far as they were concerned. "I'm sorry," she offered.

"I'm not," Josette said fiercely. "I hate him."

Marie-Thérèse stifled a laugh. Her sister hated with the same intensity that she loved.

Josette touched the papers on the desk. "Are you really going away?"

"Not without my sister." Marie-Thérèse brought out the second application from underneath her own. Most of it she had already filled out in her precise script.

A slow smile spread over Josette's face, making her more lovely than ever. Marie-Thérèse hugged her. "Come with me?"

"Okay," Josette said. "Whatever."

They told their parents together, both of whom expressed

pleasure in Josette's decision. "We feel this is an answer to prayer," Ariana said.

"For your own good," Jean-Marc added.

Josette acted as if she scarcely heard them. She threw herself into planning their move with the same passion she showed everything. "I'm going away to school in America," she told her friends. "And I might just have such a good time that I'll never come back! Maybe I'll even marry an American. I can't wait to get there!"

Yet things had abruptly changed again when Josette met this new boyfriend, Alphonse, a month before they were to leave for Utah. Since then, she'd been hinting about staying behind. Tonight, as they confronted one another in the sitting room, the situation had culminated in her blatant refusal to go.

"Marie-Thérèse, aren't you going to stick up for me?"

At Josette's repeated plea, Marie-Thérèse's pulled her thought back to the present. "I *want* to go to BYU," she said. "It'll be new and fun."

"I don't want to go!"

"Your grades slipped this past year," Jean-Marc said. "If you don't go now, you may never get in."

Josette's lower lip jutted out. "I don't care."

"You promised!" Marie-Thérèse said.

"But . . . Alphonse—"

"Will still be here when you come home for Christmas." Their mother put her hand on Josette's shoulder. "I trust you will do what's best."

Josette shrugged off Ariana's hand. "I hate it when you say that."

Marie-Thérèse smiled inwardly. Their mother knew only too well how to appeal to their sense of honor.

Josette glared at her, but Marie-Thérèse easily met her eyes. It had come to her just now what to say, a silent whispering of the Spirit. "Is Alphonse worth letting me down?" she asked. "Is he coming between us?"

Air whooshed out of Josette's lungs as though from an untied balloon. "Oh, dang it," she said. "Of course not." She faced their parents. "Okay, I'll go for one semester." She flounced to the door before turning and declaring, "But I'm going to hate every second."

Chapter Two

Elder Marc Perrault felt the old scars on his stomach itching. His "battle wounds," as he called them, had been caused partly by the kidney transplant he'd endured shortly after his sixteenth birthday and partly by the explosion in the metro which had caused his kidney failure in the first place. He'd been in the right place at the right time to help a stranger survive, but the cost hadn't been small. He thought of Danielle Massoni's beautiful gray eyes and knew it had been worth it.

As with old farmers who knew it would rain because of the aching in their bones, the itching warned Marc that the investigator he and his new companion were teaching wasn't focusing on what they were saying. She was about to break their hearts.

"You see," Elder Zachary Fields was saying in his Americanized French, "Being the perfect example, our Savior showed us the way back to our Father in Heaven." He spoke decent French for being in the country only three months. Of course, the younger missionary had studied two months at the Missionary Training Center in Provo, and before that in high school. He told Marc he'd always hoped he'd go to France on his mission.

"Even though Jesus himself was pure," Elder Fields went on,

"he was baptized, not only because it is a commandment, but so we would understand that everyone needs to accept baptism before they can return home to live with him."

Marc tried to catch his companion's eye to signal that something wasn't quite right, but Elder Fields didn't look his way. Marc wasn't surprised. They'd only been together a month, and it usually took longer to become accustomed to a companion's body language.

"That's so nice," Madame Legrand said as Elder Fields paused for breath. "You'll have to teach it all to my daughters when they come back from vacationing with their grandparents—they go there every summer, you know." They did know. She had told them each of the other two times they had come to call, once when they knocked at her door and the next day when they taught her the first lesson. That had been three days ago, and they had hoped to commit her to baptism during this second visit, but her mind was far away from spiritual matters. This discussion was quickly going nowhere.

"You'd like my daughters," Madame Legrand said. "They're right about your age, and they love anything to do with America." She winked at Elder Fields. "They both cook and know how to keep house. Oh, yes, I taught them, so they would make good wives. I bet they'd love to hear your lessons when they return home next week."

"What about you?" Marc asked.

"I always enjoy hearing about Jesus," she said absently. "Did I show you pictures of my daughters? They're very pretty."

Marc stifled his annoyance, praying silently. "You did, Madame Legrand, and they seem like . . . uh, like nice girls, but how do you feel about—"

"Then you'll come back and meet them? Maybe you could take them to see a movie."

"We don't date while we're on our missions," Marc said.

Her eyes narrowed. "What kind of religion is this? Can't go out with girls. You do like girls, don't you?"

Discouragement weighed heavily on Marc's heart. This woman's only interest in them was as sons-in-law for her aging daughters. He was about to make their excuses and leave when Elder Fields spoke, his blue eyes boring earnestly into Madame Legrand's.

"Your daughters are very important to you, I see," he said. "I know how you feel. My family is special to me as well. That's why what we're teaching is so important. What if I told you that you and your daughters could be a family forever? In our church, we believe that marriage is eternal, and that's why we have temples." He pulled out a flip chart and showed her each of the temples, explaining how sacred and important they were to him, and how the ordinances came about. "When I get married, it will be in one of these temples," he said. "Sealed forever. I want to know my family will be together forever, that the grandchildren I bounce on my knee will be as close to me in the next life as in this one."

Marc had opened his mouth to warn his companion not to skip too far ahead in the lessons, but stopped when he recognized the touch of the Spirit in the room.

"What a beautiful thing," Madame Legrand murmured, her eyes soft.

"I know these principles are true," Elder Fields said. "I've prayed about them and have felt the Spirit tell me so. How did you feel when you read from the book we left you last time? What did you feel during your prayer before you read?"

"Well, I . . .uh . . . didn't read it," she admitted, contradicting what she'd said earlier. "I was busy, and I felt kind of funny praying like that. I'm used to memorized prayers."

Marc felt a slight smile tug at his lips. No wonder she was not showing interest. When investigators failed to follow through, it almost always meant they hadn't understood the Book of Mormon's great importance. He took up where Elder Fields left off.

"Remember what we talked about last time, about how Heavenly Father always calls prophets to bring his word to the people?" Marc started from the beginning, explaining the many reasons why she should want to know for herself that the book was true. "If it is true," he added, "then everything we've talked to you about, including how families can be together forever, is also true. Do you see how important this book is?"

Elder Fields cast him a grateful smile, and for the first time Marc understood that the elder had been just as worried and frustrated as he had been. Marc was amazed at his junior companion's fortitude and his closeness to the Spirit. *I will learn from him and do better,* he vowed.

After bearing their testimonies of the Book of Mormon, the elders set up another appointment and left Madame Legrand holding her blue book to her chest.

"Whew!" said Elder Fields when they were outside the apartment building. "I was worried there for a minute."

"You did great." Though Marc had never considered himself short, he had to crane his neck to meet his companion's eyes.

"So did you. Remember, it was you who told me we had to care about what the investigator cared about before we could reach them."

"Yeah, but her daughters? In another minute, we both would have been engaged."

Elder Fields laughed. "We still might. The daughters come home next week."

"It'll be all right," Marc said confidently. "Once they go to church and talk with the members, they'll understand that we're off limits. At least *you* have nothing to worry about. After your mission, you'll go home to another country. They won't be able to follow you there."

"They could always go to BYU. Like your sisters."

"Yeah, that's right, they'll be leaving for America soon." As always when he thought of his twin sister, a warm feeling came to Marc's heart. The only thing he hated about being on a mission was being apart from her. She'd always mothered him somewhat, telling him not to do dangerous things, but she was as guilty of carelessness as he'd been. He hoped Marie-Thérèse was taking good care of her.

"Do you think they'd take a package to my parents for me?"

"I'm sure they would."

"She's a pretty girl," Elder Fields added.

Marc didn't have to ask who he was talking about. Ever since he'd shown him Josette's picture, his companion had been infatuated. "Of course," he said, "she looks like me."

Elder Fields punched him in the shoulder. "Right. Well, what should we do now?"

Marc considered a moment. The setting sun sent a hazy red light echoing over the sky, but there was still time for knocking doors. It was the least effective way of finding investigators, but they had nothing else lined up for the evening. He made a knocking motion with his hand and his companion immediately understood.

"How about that building over there?" Marc said. "We didn't finish knocking all those doors yesterday."

They knocked at each apartment with no luck, moving to the building next door and then the one beyond. At all the doors the people shook their heads and sent them away. One young man seemed interested, but his father quickly appeared in the doorway behind him and pushed the boy firmly out of the way. One glance at the missionary tags was enough for him. "Excuse me, excuse me, excuse me," he said and slammed the door in their faces so hard that Marc felt his short hair ruffle in the ensuing breeze.

He sighed. Some parts of missionary work he could definitely do without. Right now he would give almost anything for a bowl of his mother's vegetable stew and a soft bed.

They knocked on the rest of the doors with no better results. "We've got time for one more," Marc said, glancing at his watch. "If we hurry—it's almost curfew."

"I think we should try that pink building," Elder Fields said, pointing. "I've been wanting to go there for weeks." The building wasn't really pink, more of a dusty rose, but it did look incongruous among the other duller structures—perhaps some kind of a sign?

"Let's go." Marc knew enough to trust his companion's feeling. He was beginning to understand that Elder Fields was the most spiritually-attuned elder he'd yet served with in the mission field.

As they walked toward their goal, two mongrel dogs sprang out of a dark corridor between two buildings, their bared teeth looking huge and sharp in the dim light of the street lamp. The first was big and black and ugly. The other was big and brown and as ugly as the first. The mongrels growled deep in their throats.

"Run!" Marc yelled to Elder Fields. They fled back the way they'd come, the pink apartments forgotten, barely keeping ahead of the dogs. At last they spied their own apartment building. Elder Fields scooped up a few rocks and hurled them at the canines while Marc fumbled with the outside door key. They darted inside and pulled the lobby door shut as the dogs pawed on the outside.

"We've got to do something about those dogs," Elder Fields muttered.

Marc agreed. This was the third time in the last week these same dogs had chased them. "Tomorrow I'll talk to our landlady and see if she'll call somebody."

"Good idea," Elder Fields said. "This city has to have a dog catcher."

Uncharacteristically silent, they stumbled tiredly into the room they rented from the Vincent family, who were members of their congregation. It had been a discouraging month for both of them. In fact, the discussion with Madame Legrand had been the most promising they'd given together so far. Neither had seen a baptism in three months. For Elder Fields, that meant he'd never had the opportunity to baptize someone he'd taught.

"Can I see your sister's picture again?" Elder Fields asked.

Marc reluctantly handed it over, dreading the question he had been expecting the entire month. As expected, it came.

"I'd like to meet her someday. Do you think she'd write back if I sent her a letter?"

Marc quickly thought of an excuse. "I don't know. Her letters to me are rare enough, and I'm her twin. She might not make the effort for a stranger. She's really busy—she's usually got a lot of dates. And then there's school—"

"Yeah, you're probably right. But there's something about her. It's obvious you're taken with her—and she's your sister—so she must be a great person. Maybe I'll come visit you after my mission and sweep her off her feet. How would you like that?"

Elder Fields had gotten down to the crux of the matter, but it wasn't him Marc worried about. He knew Josette well—she was much like he'd been before missionary service changed him. She lived only for the presents people bought her, the expensive clothes, the glittering lights of the dance halls. His twin was warm, vivacious, and loving, but she was also light-minded and—Marc didn't like to admit it even to himself—frivolous. The spiritual Elder Fields could never love a woman like that, no matter how beautiful, and Marc wouldn't allow him to hurt her.

"You're not good enough for her," he said lightly. "Besides, she doesn't date younger men. You're a year younger than we are."

Elder Fields laughed. "Well, I guess I'd better work harder to impress you," he said. "The both of you. And I'm going to start with that pink building. Let's go ask Sister Vincent if she has any cayenne pepper. I've got a bone to pick with some dogs."

Chapter Three

Elder Zachary Fields left Madame Legrand's apartment feeling more content than he had in weeks. She'd read the Book of Mormon passages, and during the ensuing discussion she'd accepted the idea of baptism. "I'll want to pray about it, of course," she said, blushing slightly at her own words. "But if this is true, I'll eventually accept it."

Zack knew her reaction was a good sign, if not the complete conversion he and Elder Marc Perrault had prayed for. He felt good about her tentative commitment and hoped he would be in the area to see her baptism.

"Next time the daughters will be there," Elder Perrault said, making a face. "I hope they don't destroy her testimony."

Zack hoped so, too. He put on a confident face. "Maybe on Sunday we can fast to help her."

"Good idea."

"Now, how about knocking that pink building we keep wanting to get to?"

His companion grimaced. "Shall we make a run for it?"

Grinning, Zack pulled a small spray bottle out of his pocket. "I don't plan on running. I have faith the dogs won't like this cayenne mixture Sister Vincent and I whipped up the other morning while you were popping your kidney pills." He held up the bottle and Elder Perrault laughed.

They walked briskly down the cobblestone sidewalk, keeping watch for the giant dogs. Night fell quickly, and the missionaries jumped at each shadow. Zack's hand began to sweat around the bottle that had been in his pocket the entire day in preparation for this confrontation.

"I guess they aren't showing," Elder Perrault said with a nervous laugh. "We'll get to the pink building without a fight."

Zack knew it wouldn't be so easy; he had felt too strongly that they must visit the pink building. They went steadily on. Just when he was beginning to think his companion was right after all, the dogs jumped from behind a garbage bin, deep growls coming from their throats. Zack froze, and it seemed an eternity before he could talk his fingers into moving. The black dog circled, looking for a place to lunge, and Zack wondered how its canine mind understood that they planned to fight instead of run. Instinct, he supposed.

Elder Perrault turned with the circling dog, brandishing his scriptures like a sword. "Somehow I don't think this is what my sister had in mind when she bought these scriptures for me," he said in shaky voice. "Uh, Elder, don't you think you should spray them now? Any closer and they'll be eating my scriptures as an appetizer."

Zack pressed the nozzle and directed the stream toward the brown dog. It snarled ferociously, but as the water and cayenne hit its unprotected eyes, the growls quickly turned into yelps of pain. The dog bounded down the street, howling. Zack didn't have time to let himself feel the unexpected pity that rushed to his heart.

The black dog attacked, and Elder Perrault blocked the slobbering mouth with his scriptures. Strong jaws closed over the edge of the books as Zack again sprayed his potion. Immediately the dog released its hold and scuttled away, its whine filling the entire street.

Elder Perrault's face slowly regained its color. "Good timing," he said, pulling a tissue from his shirt pocket. Holding his scriptures gingerly, he wiped off the slobber left by the dog. Zack leaned over and saw the impressive teeth marks. "Good investment, those scriptures," he said. "They just saved you another operation."

Elder Perrault laughed. "That's one way to look at it, I guess. But next time, *I'll* do the spraying and *you* fend off the dogs."

"Deal." Zack turned his head toward the pink building. "Let's go find whoever it was we're supposed to find there."

"It better be someone very special."

"They will be." Zack felt the warmth of the Spirit confirming his thought.

On the third floor they met Pedro Leandro. He opened the door, his chestnut-colored face smiling. "Yes?" he asked with raised eyebrows.

"We're missionaries of the Church of Jesus Christ," Elder Perrault began, "and we have an important message to share."

"Do you believe in Christ?" Zack picked up on his companion's cue. As they spoke, dark head after dark head appeared behind the man. There were four children in all, and a grandmother.

"I do," the man said.

"Could we share our message with you?" Zack asked. The children clapped their hands at his accent and begged their father to let them in.

"It's just a message, isn't it?" he asked. "Without obligations?"

"Yes," Elder Perrault said. "We want everyone to hear for themselves about Jesus."

"Well . . ." the man said, vacillating.

"Are these all your children?" asked Zack. Most people in France seemed to have only a few children; but he'd also noticed that those of African descent, like this man, tended to have more—as if their desire for family took precedence over other goals.

"They certainly are." The man's words held a trace of pride.

He introduced each of the four children by name, and his wife's mother as well.

"Reminds me of my house," Elder Perrault said. "I have five brothers and sisters."

"I have four sisters," Zack put in, "and I sure do miss them."

"You're not from around here, are you?" one of the kids asked, tugging on Zack's arm.

Zack bent down to speak to the child on eye level. "I'm from America, and I miss my family. Maybe I can come back and play with you guys when we come to give your parents our message. What do you say?" He glanced up at their father.

"My wife isn't home right now," the man said. "But come back when she's here."

"How about Saturday at one?" Elder Perrault pulled out his appointment book.

"That'll be fine. But with no obligation, you understand."

"Oh, yes. See? I've written it right here." Elder Perrault held out the book.

"Without obligations," read the man. He smiled, showing a row of white teeth that seemed even brighter by contrast with his dark skin.

"Goodbye then." Zack waved to the children. "See you on Saturday."

They left the building at a brisk pace, heading for home to beat their evening curfew. Zack kept a look out, but the dogs didn't return.

"Without obligations," Elder Perrault said sadly as he undressed for the night.

Zack understood how his companion was feeling. Too many times he'd seen people react that way, and usually they wouldn't keep their appointment. But something was different about this family; Zack could feel it. He'd learned to heed those feelings.

"Remember the dogs," he said. "Monsieur Leandro will be there."

Elder Perrault's face brightened. "I hope so. I really liked the children. Especially the little girl—Sofia, wasn't it? She is so full of excitement and, well, innocent joy. She reminds me a little of my sister Pauline." He hit his chest near his heart, his voice becoming gruff with emotion. "I can't explain it exactly, but the idea that they might not accept hurts right here. Sofia deserves to know her Savior. They all do."

Zack put his hand on Elder Perrault's shoulder. "We're going to help them. I think these feelings we're having is the Lord's way of letting us know how important they are to him."

Elder Perrault's gaze shifted to the family picture on the dresser, and Zack felt his companion's homesickness as if it were his own. Zack missed his family, too, especially his little sister, Brionney, but strangely his thoughts lately had turned more and more to Elder Perrault's twin. She was beautiful, but there was something else in her face, some quality that called to Zack's heart and soul. He knew her name, but his companion was remarkably close-mouthed about anything else. Zack wished he could ask to see the close-up picture Elder Perrault carried in his wallet, but every time he did, his companion became defensive.

Zack shook off the thoughts and knelt with Elder Perrault for their companion prayer, reminding himself to focus on the task to which he had willingly pledged two years of his life. However potent, his feelings for this woman he had never met would have to wait.

Chapter Four

Josette stared at the array of clothing piled on her bed, mostly warm items. Six tall stacks to take, two smaller ones to leave behind. Her heart felt heavy as she lifted a handful of blouses and plopped them into the suitcase, blinking back the tears stinging her eyes.

I don't want to go! she thought. *Oh, Marc, where are you when I need you?* She felt angry and sad all at once. *Why don't I seem to know who I am when I'm not with Marc?* He'd been with her since their conception—was that why she hated being alone?

In front of the other single bed against the far wall, Marie-Thérèse's two suitcases were already neatly packed, ready for tomorrow's flight. Josette slumped to her bed and let her chin drop to her chest, but a rustling sound made her look up again.

Her little sister Pauline stood quietly in the doorway. She was almost exactly Josette's height, and her eyes and short hair were just as dark, but there the comparison ended. Pauline was infinitely thinner than anyone Josette had ever known. Her face was pleasant to look at, but it held obvious marks of the many illnesses she had survived. She was often sick, especially of late, and spent a good deal of time at the AIDS clinic. Her HIV wasn't yet officially

AIDS, but the line grew thinner each year. At sixteen, Pauline had already lived longer than the doctors had predicted at her birth. A miracle? Josette thought so.

Pauline walked over and began taking Josette's clothes out of the suitcase, repacking them carefully. "You don't want them to wrinkle," she said with her ever-ready smile. "I know how you hate to iron."

"Marie-Thérèse will be there," Josette said.

Pauline snorted. "She doesn't like to iron either."

"But she'll do it."

As Josette watched her sister pack, emotion overwhelmed her, and she put her face in her hands and started to sob. Pauline dropped the clothes and stepped in front of her, reaching to push Josette's hands away from her face. "What's wrong?"

"I can't do this," Josette wailed.

Pauline hugged her sister's head, pulling it against her stomach. Josette's arms came up around Pauline's thin body. "Can't do what?" Pauline asked.

Josette sniffed. "Go to America."

Pauline pulled away slightly to look down at her. "I thought you were excited to go."

"At first I was," Josette confessed. It was always easy to talk with Pauline. She was a light that lit up every room, and her quick smile always showed her love. "But I think . . . well . . ." Her voice lowered. "I was so ready to leave, but I'm a little afraid. I'm scared to leave my family."

"We'll be right here when you come back."

"Will you?" Josette sat up straight and gazed earnestly at her little sister. "Will all of you? Do we ever know?"

Pauline sat on the bed beside her. "I guess we don't ever know for certain, but we can't stop living because we're afraid. You know what I think? You're just missing Marc. If he were going with you, he'd have you laughing at yourself so fast, you'd forget you were scared."

Josette smiled in spite of herself. "He would, wouldn't he?" She sighed. "I guess I'm being stupid. I just keep wondering what it's going to be like. I mean, here I have lots of friends and boyfriends—even if most of them aren't in the Church. But there? I don't know what to expect."

Pauline's face lit up, and her laugh echoed through the room. "You're worried about guys? That's the real reason you don't want to go? That's funny!" If it had been anyone else, Josette would have been defensive, but Pauline's amusement lacked even the slightest trace of malice.

Pauline laid her head on Josette's shoulder. "Men will be men whatever their nationality, won't they? Those American boys don't stand a chance. You'll be a star with a hoard of worshippers in no time." She fingered Josette's straight hair. "You're so pretty. I wish I looked like you."

Josette hugged her sister, thinking that her inner beauty made up for the ravages of the HIV. "Thank you," she whispered. "I love you."

Pauline smiled. "So are we going to pack or not?"

Later that night as the family was finishing dinner, their mother brought out a square package and placed it on the table. "Will one of you have space for this?"

Josette eyed the parcel doubtfully, thinking of all the things she was already leaving behind. "What is it?"

"A package from Marc—or from his American companion. You know, the new one, Elder Fields. He sent it in the hopes that you'd have room to take it to his family in America. They live in Provo, he says, not too far away from BYU."

"I don't have a centimeter of room left," Josette said. "What does Marc's companion think we are, the postal service?"

Ariana's eyes closed, but before she could say anything, Marie-

Thérèse said, "He just wants to send his family some presents without it costing him his food money." She picked up the package. "I have room. It's not very big."

"Look, Elder Fields sent a picture of his family," their father said, handing a photograph to Marie-Thérèse.

"I suppose they want us to take the package right to their house," Josette grumbled. "And they'll probably want us to look at family pictures for hours."

Marie-Thérèse stared at the picture. "That wouldn't be too fun," she agreed. "Even if he is cute."

Josette grabbed the picture. A blond family stared out at her: parents, four daughters, and one son. She looked again. One very handsome son, tall, with broad shoulders, blue eyes, and brilliant white hair. "This is Elder Fields? Well, maybe looking at his pictures wouldn't be so bad. I could stand to look at him for a while, couldn't you, Marie-Thérèse?"

Pauline giggled, and seventeen-year-old André rolled his eyes. "And they say men are the ones who judge by looks," he said.

The buzzer in the hallway interrupted any retorts the girls might have come up with. Their youngest brother, Louis-Géralde, pushed back his chair and scrambled into the entryway. "I got it, I got it!" he squealed with all the excitement of a four-year-old. Josette followed him, hoping Alphonse had come to say good-bye. This would be their last chance to be together until Christmas.

Jumping onto a wooden stool that he kept in the spacious entryway for just such occasions, Louis-Géralde jabbed at the black intercom button with his chubby fingers. "Who is it?"

"Aunt Lu-Lu," came a crackly voice.

"Who?" Louis-Géralde said. "I don't have an Aunt Lu-Lu." He threw back his head and laughed.

Josette reached around his small head and pushed the button. Her brother jumped from the stool and landed on the polished wood floor with a loud crash. He opened the door to the hall and waited for the elevator to bring the visitors, dancing excitedly from one foot to the other.

When Lu-Lu arrived, she wasn't alone. Not only was her two-year-old daughter Mimi with her, but also her best friend Danielle Massoni and her two children, Raoul and Rebekka. Both women were striking, and Josette openly admired them.

"We've come to say good-bye," Lu-Lu said in heavily accented English. She had short brown hair dyed with red highlights, and beautiful green-brown eyes like Josette's father, who was her brother. Normally she was thin, but now her figure swelled with a new pregnancy.

"Thank you," Josette replied in the same language. Those two words at least came easily. Ever since she was small, she'd taken English at their private school and had practiced with the missionaries. She felt she knew the language passably well, though her French accent was much heavier than Marie-Thérèse's.

"Play!" Mimi tugged, freeing her hand from her mother's. She toddled toward Louis-Géralde, who motioned to Danielle's children to follow him. Though Raoul was twelve and Rebekka ten, they were his favorite playmates.

"Behave yourselves," Danielle called after them. Josette thought the warning useless because Raoul and Rebekka were the most well-behaved children she'd ever known, perhaps because their father insisted on strict obedience. Josette had never liked him, and she couldn't understand why Danielle put up with him at all—especially since he still refused to take the missionary discussions. At least he'd allowed his wife and children to become members.

"I'm so excited for you, Josette," Danielle said when the children had vanished. She was also slender like Lu-Lu, but her thick auburn hair fell mid-way down her back, almost as long as Josette's own. Her large gray eyes held an undeniable childlike quality, despite her thirty-three years. She had sculpted eyebrows that set off her eyes even further, drawing so much attention that one hardly had time to notice the stylish clothing she always wore.

"America! Ever since I joined the Church I've wanted to see it. Just think—you'll be able to go to the next conference and see the prophet in person! And the Salt Lake Temple. I'm so jealous."

Josette found herself being swept up in Danielle's enthusiasm. "I'll send you pictures," she volunteered.

"Would you? Thanks so much. But speaking of pictures"— she fumbled in her alligator skin bag—"I wanted you to see what Mathieu looked like, since he's going to pick you up at the airport in Salt Lake City. Oh, I can't find the picture."

"Don't worry about it," said Lu-Lu. "You cousin will probably be the only French man at the airport in Utah."

Danielle laughed. "You're right. Just remember that besides the dark hair, he looks kind of German. Our grandmother was from Germany. We named Rebekka after her."

"That's why you spell it funny," Josette said.

"The girls did meet Mathieu once before." Lu-Lu set her purse down on the small wall table in the entryway. "Don't you remember?"

"Oh, that's right," Danielle said. "At my baptism."

Josette remembered faintly. She had been sixteen then. Mathieu had been twenty-one and a new member himself. Danielle's bubbly eagerness to share the gospel had already brought fruits, even before her husband agreed to her own baptism. Mathieu had seemed nice enough to Josette, but had been gangling and awkward and too shy for good conversation. She'd given up on him after a few minutes for someone more interesting.

"Will you take this to him?" Danielle handed her a package the size of a large shoe box.

Josette sighed. "I guess so."

"So what are you doing out there?" Ariana called from the kitchen. "Come on in here. We have plenty of dessert."

Josette followed the women into the kitchen, where the children were already elbow-deep in huge bowls of bread pudding.

She handed the package Danielle had given her to Marie-Thérèse. "Could you squeeze this in? It's for Mathieu."

Marie-Thérèse made a face, but she set the package next to the larger one Elder Fields had sent.

Josette watched her family, feeling oddly detached. She didn't know how to describe the ache she felt in her heart, the hurt she'd been feeling for so long. There seemed to be no purpose in life, no joy she could hold inside forever. Was something wrong with her?

The only thing that chased the melancholy away was to keep busy, to have fun. But that glittering world washed away too easily when she was alone.

I miss Marc so much! She squeezed her eyes as the emotions washed over her. Such severe feelings of sadness hadn't overcome her since her brother had almost died in the explosion shortly before their sixteenth birthday. Marie-Thérèse was her best friend and confidante, but her twin brother was part of her soul. Could there be any closer bond? Even in a marriage? If the men she'd dated were any indication, Josette didn't think so.

To Josette's delight, Alphonse arrived before eight, and he took her out to dinner at a posh restaurant. She didn't confess that she'd already eaten earlier with her family. Besides, she'd only picked at the food to please her mother.

"Why so sad?" he asked as they finished their meal. He moved his thick eyebrows expressively as he talked. Josette enjoyed his dark good looks, but his nearness no longer made her tremble.

"I'm going to miss you." It was true, yet not quite.

"Of course you'll miss me. And I will miss you. We've had fun together. But we can't stop the rest of our lives for a little fun. If we're both still around at Christmas . . ." His comments made Josette even more depressed. She suspected he wouldn't be waiting around for her any more than she'd give up dating for him.

"Look," he said, bringing a hand from his pocket. "I brought you a present."

Josette clapped her hands together, the sadness vanishing. "Oh, Alphonse, you shouldn't have!"

He chuckled. "I know how you enjoy presents. Besides, now that I'm graduated and working at my grandfather's hotel, I can afford it."

She opened the small box to reveal a gold butterfly brooch, sparkling with diamond dust. "It's beautiful," she said, jumping up to kiss him lingeringly on the mouth. Heads turned their way, but she enjoyed the attention. For all the onlookers knew, Alphonse could have just proposed.

Why hadn't he? He had said many times that he loved her. Josette guessed it was not the marrying kind of love. Besides, what would she have said if he'd asked her to marry him? She knew she didn't love him—not that much. He was simply an excuse she'd tried to use to stay in France.

"I love it," she added, slightly more subdued.

"I know you do." He tried to fasten it to her dress. "It's the one we saw in the store last week."

"How wonderful of you to remember." He was right, she loved presents, and he'd bought her enough of them. "Here, let me do that." She wore her black, tight-fitting, column dress with the spaghetti straps, the dress her mother had not approved of, and his fingers were embarrassingly close to her skin.

When they left the restaurant and returned to his car, Alphonse kissed her hand repeatedly, then began working his way up her arm to her neck. "I can make you happy," he said, huskily. "And you can show me just how much you like your new present, and how much you're going to miss me in America."

"Don't," Josette said, pushing him back. He sounded more idiotic than a character in a poorly made film. Today she'd been crying about leaving him, but now she wanted only to get away. "I need to get home."

Alphonse's black eyes narrowed in anger, but he submitted to her request. "I don't understand you," he said as he dropped her off outside her apartment building. "One moment you're hot, the next cold. Are you simply playing with me?" Before she could reply, he went on. "I hope you have a good life in America. I hope you find whatever it is you're looking for."

Josette wanted to throw the pin at him, but it was so pretty that she restrained herself. *It's mine,* she thought. *And I don't owe him anything for it!* But she felt that she did. Was that the only reason he had given it to her—to make her feel obligated?

Feeling numb, she watched Alphonse speed off. It was always the same. Men treated her like a queen at first, but it quickly degenerated into what she would or would not do with them. She smoothed her dress. She knew she looked good—more than good. Why did she feel so empty?

"What is it I'm looking for?" she wondered aloud. "Alphonse doesn't know what he's talking about. I have everything I need. The only thing that's missing is . . . oh, I think I hate you, Alphonse."

She rode up the elevator and unlocked the door quietly, not wanting to disturb her family. There was a light in the kitchen and she approached it, driven like a moth.

"She shouldn't have left tonight," her father was saying. "She should have stayed here with her family. She didn't even say good-bye to her grandparents."

"They said they'd come by again tomorrow," her mother replied.

"They shouldn't have to. Josette needs to think more about others."

"She's young yet."

"So is Marie-Thérèse."

"Josette's not Marie-Thérèse. She has different problems and challenges."

"Well, I hope BYU straightens her out," her father said. "Her grades have been terrible, and it doesn't help that she keeps changing her major. She doesn't know what she wants."

Josette bit her lip and pushed the hair out of her eyes. Anger and humiliation spread through her heart. How dare they talk about her this way? She was an adult, not a child. She couldn't help it that Marie-Thérèse had always known exactly what she would do with her life—a mission, a finance degree, a home and children. Except for marriage and babies, Josette didn't see the joy in any of her sister's goals.

As for the rest of her siblings, they also had blueprints for their lives. André and Marc planned to go into engineering, Pauline wanted to work with people who had AIDS, and even Louis-Géralde said he was going to be a letter carrier. Her littlest brother thought it must be the "funnest" job in the whole world, and he met the mailman each day in the lobby of their apartment building to practice putting the letters in the boxes. As for Josette, she wanted to live, to . . . to . . .

She didn't know what she wanted. At BYU she'd signed up to learn about interior decorating. Maybe that would be her niche.

"Josette's going to BYU is the right thing to do," her mother said. "Some of us need a little extra push." Ariana's voice had a faraway quality. Josette heard a rustling, and she assumed her father was taking her mother into his arms.

"I'm so lucky to have you," her father whispered.

"We are both lucky."

The love in their voices made Josette want to sob. *That's what I want,* she thought. *Why can't I find it?* She'd dated at least a hundred guys, but not one had loved her like that.

Slowly, she walked back to the door to the apartment, opened it noisily, then slammed it for good measure. Her parents' faces appeared in the kitchen doorway, framed by light from behind.

"Your grandparents were here," her father said.

"I'm sorry I missed them." Josette hesitated, knowing what they wanted to hear, but not wanting to give in. "I know I shouldn't have gone," she forced out the words. "I'm sorry."

Her parents exchanged a pleased look, and Josette was glad she'd said the words, even if she hadn't meant them. Her father kissed her on both cheeks. "I'm going to bed," he said. "We all have an early day tomorrow." He grinned, and Josette felt herself smile back mechanically. "Not all of us will spend the day sleeping on a plane." He touched his wife's shoulder, letting his hand linger.

"I'll be there in a minute," she said.

He smiled and nodded, his hand dropping. With another smile for Josette, he walked down the hall.

Her mother put her arm around Josette's back, eyeing the thin spaghetti straps. "You're not taking that to America, are you?"

Josette didn't answer. "Do you ever miss your brother?"

Her mother watched her for several seconds in silence. "Come in here and let's talk about it," she said finally. "I'll make some hot chocolate." As Josette sat at the table, Ariana pulled out two mugs, filled them with milk, and put them in the microwave her dad had bought when Louis-Géralde was born.

"Ouch," she said, bringing the steaming mugs to the table. "Careful, it's hot." She put a spoon of chocolate in her milk before passing the container to Josette. "My brother was very much like your brother," she said after mixing her chocolate and taking a sip. "I loved him every bit as much as you love Marc—maybe more. You have other brothers and sisters, and I had only Antoine. But someday you'll find a relationship even better than the one you share with him. And he will also find one."

"Like you and Dad."

"Yes, but—" Her voice broke off as if she was uncertain how to continue. "But to find that, you have to remember what your destiny is. You are a princess, destined to be a royal queen."

Josette stifled a sigh. For as long as she could remember, her mother had told her these same words, but they didn't seem to have meaning in this life, only in death. Why would she want to think about death? She knew her mother's crusade had something to do with the death of Josette's half sister, Nette, the child born to Ariana during her first marriage before she joined the Church. Her mother wanted them to be righteous enough to be reunited with her one day. It was a worthy goal but so remote. An unattainable dream.

"You have to insist on being treated like a queen," her mother continued.

"Okay." Josette spoke dully, wanting only to wipe the anxiety from her mother's face. "I'll be good."

Ariana smiled. "I know. And I love you."

Josette wished she'd said she was proud instead.

She kissed her mother good night and headed for the room she'd shared with Marie-Thérèse since they were four. Her sister was sound asleep, and Josette undressed quietly in the dark. She smiled grimly, then rolled up the black dress and slipped it into the only spot left in her suitcase.

Inside, her hand touched the photograph of Elder Fields and his family, and she pulled it out. Though it was too dark to make out the faces, she saw his white hair and blue eyes vividly in her mind. He appeared so nice, not to mention good-looking. But appearances could be deceiving. Deep in his heart, was he like Alphonse? Or more like the stuffy young men in her stake, who couldn't seem to choose what socks to wear without praying about it?

She flung herself into bed, still clutching the photograph, but it was a long time before sleep came.

Chapter Five

A somber pall settled over the van, completely blotting out any joy—or at least Ariana thought so before she looked around and realized that it was only she and Josette who seemed to feel the gloom. Marie-Thérèse sat in the middle seat next to the brooding Josette, busily practicing her English phrases, a smile on her narrow face. André and Pauline were in the back, heads close together as usual, giggling and laughing. Louis-Géralde sat between them, enjoying their attention if not understanding everything they said.

Ariana found herself looking for her oldest son, Marc, before she remembered he was serving a mission. The army had rejected him for the year of mandatory service, but the Lord hadn't cared about Marc's kidney transplant, despite the immunosuppression medicine he took daily. For her part, Ariana was content that her son was serving in France so he would be close in case something happened.

Thank you, Jacques, she thought, *for saving my son. For giving him your kidney.* Briefly, Ariana wondered how her ex-husband and his new wife were doing. Since the birth of their baby boy in Nice three years earlier, she'd heard nothing. They had received the missionaries and his wife had been baptized, but had Jacques joined the Church?

Jean-Marc's hand reached out and caressed her arm. "It's all right," he mouthed. "We're doing the right thing."

She hoped he was right. Josette was floundering, and Ariana didn't know how to help her. *What did I do wrong?* she asked herself repeatedly. But Josette had to make her own choices, had to somehow develop her own testimony. Ariana had seen her decline, and she worried constantly that the passion and inconsistencies in her daughter would lead her to a life of sadness and despair. Each night she and Jean-Marc knelt and prayed fervently for help—and this was the answer. How could sending her away be the answer? *I must trust in the Lord,* she thought.

She kissed her daughters good-bye at the airport, not bothering to hide the tears in her eyes. "I love you," she whispered as she hugged them.

Then they were gone. André led the way back to the car with Louis-Géralde on his shoulders, both laughing. Pauline put her skinny arm around Ariana. "I love you, Mom." Her smile sent a ray of light into Ariana's heart, while at the same time bringing a dread.

"I still think we should have told them," Ariana said.

Pauline shook her head, her smile never dimming. "They wouldn't have gone."

She was right, but Ariana hoped Josette and Marie-Thérèse would forgive her later.

"Come on, Mom," Pauline said. "We always knew it would happen one day, didn't we? I'm not too sick yet. I don't want people waiting around and watching. When the time comes, we'll send for them." She squeezed Ariana's arm and bounded to catch up with her brothers.

Ariana stumbled, and Jean-Marc put his arm around her. She sighed and leaned into him. "She's wrong," she said softly. "I *didn't* know it would happen. I kept waiting for her to be cured.

For a miracle. You've heard the stories of the children born with AIDS, who months or even years later have no trace of the virus in their bodies. It does happen. I thought it would happen to her. When it didn't, I still kept praying." She broke off. "I've grown too comfortable with the postponement. I thought it was suspended forever, even without a full miracle."

Her husband's arm tightened. "I know exactly how you feel."

Ariana was grateful for his support. He hadn't been with her last month when the doctor had informed her that Pauline's HIV had become AIDS, that it was only a matter of time until the new tumor in her stomach would kill her, but he hadn't let her go to the doctor alone since. Still, it was as though the world ended that day, and they now lived in a strange suspension . . . waiting.

She wanted to scream and cry and yell. There was so much good in her life: Marc serving a mission, Marie-Thérèse doing well in college, André active at church, and her relationship with Jean-Marc growing ever sweeter. Now suddenly the joy was scrunched into a small place, locked away by the knowledge that Pauline was dying.

Ariana had known sixteen years ago, when she had first held a premature Pauline in her arms, that this time would come. She remembered vividly the undeniable bond she had shared with the newborn infant, along with the insufferable fear, the all-encompassing ache in her heart that came with knowing that she was setting herself up for this experience. Yet she'd taken Pauline into her home and had done the one thing that would cause her both the most pain and the most joy: she'd loved the HIV positive baby as her own.

How could she let Pauline go now?

A traitorous part of her recognized that at least the sword had finally fallen, the worst had been realized. There was some minuscule relief in knowing nothing worse could happen. Now she had to reach out to the Lord and into her soul to find the strength to face Pauline's impending death and the words to help her daughter be ready.

She'd done it before long ago with Paulette, Pauline's birth mother; it didn't get any easier with time.

Later that night Ariana awoke, hearing something that didn't match the usual night sounds. At first she thought Louis-Géralde might be having another attack of the stomach flu he'd suffered the week before, but the sounds came from Pauline's room.

"Jean-Marc!" Ariana called.

Without waiting for a reply, Ariana jumped from the bed and ran to the next room, her heart pounding. Switching on the light, she found Pauline sitting up in bed, heaving. Her frightened eyes blinked at the sudden brightness. Ariana rushed to the bed and put her arms around Pauline, who moaned softly. The sour smell of vomit wafted up to Ariana's nose.

"I'm sorry," Pauline mumbled. "I couldn't make it to the bathroom. My stomach hurt so bad. I couldn't move."

Ariana held Pauline's head against her breast, smoothing her hair. "It's all right. Don't worry. It'll wash." How easy it was to be nice to her. Ariana would gladly clean up after her daughter for a lifetime if that meant she would live.

Jean-Marc appeared in the doorway. "Are you all right?" He came toward the bed, his forehead creased with worry.

"I feel a little better now," Pauline murmured weakly.

"We'd better take you to the doctor first thing in the morning," Ariana said.

"It's just the flu, like Louis-Géralde had," Pauline said. "I'll be okay."

But Ariana knew a sickness like this could kill her daughter as surely as the cancerous tumor. With AIDS, nothing was minor. "It's just to be sure," she said lightly. Jean-Marc met her gaze, and his finger reached out and caught the tear on her cheek. Ariana pressed her face against his hand.

"Why don't you two get cleaned up?" Jean-Marc said. "I'll take care of things in here."

Pauline flushed with embarrassment. "Thanks, Dad."

Ariana found a new nightshirt in Pauline's drawer and helped her to the bathtub. When Jean-Marc finished cleaning her bed, he gave Pauline a blessing, and the three spent the rest of the night sleeping in the hall next to the bathroom so Pauline could throw up in the toilet when she needed. In the morning Ariana felt sick herself, but she wouldn't let Jean-Marc take Pauline to the doctor alone.

"We'll have to keep her in the hospital for a few days to be sure," the doctor said. "Even though she's not throwing up anymore, she's still losing a lot of fluids through her bowels. We have to make sure her body is getting enough liquids so she doesn't get too weak."

"Don't worry, Mom," Pauline said after the doctor left. "I'm going to be fine." Though she looked fragile, her face was its normal ray of sunshine. Despite the brave words and the smile, the way Pauline's hands clenched the thin blanket told Ariana how frightened she felt inside.

"Of course you're going to be fine," Ariana said. "But it's okay to be afraid."

"I'm not," Pauline insisted.

"Why don't you try to sleep? You need to gain some strength."

A shadow passed over Pauline's face. "Where will you be?"

"Right here. And Dad will stay too. André is with Louis-Géralde, so we don't have to hurry home."

Pauline settled obediently down in the hospital bed and closed her eyes. Ariana sat in the chair next to the bed and put her hand over Pauline's. With a silent prayer, she began a fast. When Jean-Marc brought her breakfast, she refused to eat, but by lunchtime she was shaking and could hardly think. Her muscles ached and her head felt light.

"You have to eat, Ari," Jean-Marc said, kneeling beside her chair. "You're not doing Pauline or any of us any good."

"I'm fasting."

"You're sick yourself. You've had little sleep in the past week, being up with Louis-Géralde and worrying about Josette. I don't think now's the time to fast."

Ariana bristled. "I have to get Pauline well." She darted a glance at the pale face of their sleeping daughter. "You know as well as I do that she could die from this. Why didn't I keep her away from Louise-Géralde?"

"You sent her to your mother's for a week. What more could you have done?" Jean-Marc grabbed her hand. "Don't do this to yourself, Ari. Your daughter needs you, and you shouldn't fast when you're sick. Let me and the rest of our family do it. Please."

Ariana looked at the food he'd brought from the hospital cafeteria. Though she couldn't tell what kind of meat lay next to the rice and french fries, it looked and smelled much better than any hospital food she could remember. Her stomach growled, and she hated herself for her weakness.

"The Lord will understand. You are only required to run as fast as you are able."

The logical side of her knew Jean-Marc was right. *Please forgive me, Lord,* she prayed. *I promise, I'll fast next week when I'm better. Please, help Pauline.*

After lunch, Ariana felt considerably better, but she worried that her lack of sacrifice would bode ill for Pauline. Then she chided herself, knowing the Lord didn't work that way. Besides, sending Josette to America had been right, and surely the Lord didn't mean for Pauline to die without her sisters there. Or did he?

Don't second-guess your inspiration, she told herself. Yet why did everything seem out of her control?

The next day Pauline was much stronger, and Jean-Marc returned to work. "The doctors said I could probably take you home tomorrow," Ariana said to her daughter.

Pauline hugged Ariana. "See? I told you. Thanks for staying with me, Mom."

"I'll be here whenever you need me," Ariana replied.

For a fleeting moment, Pauline looked sad, but she kept her thoughts to herself. "I know," she said with a bright smile.

Ariana laid her head on the pillow next to Pauline's, filled with gratitude to the Lord for the additional moments they'd been given. There was still time for a miracle.

Chapter Six

The flight to New York was long, but not very tedious. Marie-Thérèse kept busy studying her English dictionary, reading the American classic *To Kill a Mockingbird,* or simply watching the other passengers on the plane. Everything was new and exciting. She'd flown before, but had never been outside France except for traveling to either the Swiss or German temples to do baptisms for the dead.

At first she tried to talk with Josette, but her sister slumped morosely in the aisle seat, an ugly scowl on her pretty face. Marie-Thérèse left her alone, knowing that Josette's temper would fade as the miles passed below them.

Shortly before they arrived in New York, a young man walked down the aisle, and Josette perked up. Before Marie-Thérèse realized what was happening, he'd switched seats with the woman across from Josette, and they leaned over the aisle conversing in English. Josette had a fairly strong accent, and the words came slowly, but she improved with each try. Her smile flashed, bright like the sun, and her laughter made those around join in.

Marie-Thérèse shifted uncomfortably in the coach seat. Her flight bag and the package for Mathieu stuck awkwardly out from under the seat. There hadn't been space in her luggage, but she didn't mind taking the package. If only it weren't so cumbersome.

In New York they passed through Customs, and Marie-Thérèse had to open her luggage. As she did, she realized that half of one of her suitcases carried items that should have been divided between her and Josette—the goodies their mother had sent, the hangers for their clothes, the books on American culture their grandparents had purchased, Elder Fields' package, and finally the stuffed bear that Louis-Géralde had sent with them so they wouldn't miss him.

No wonder she didn't have room for Mathieu's package. She stifled the resentment before it built. Josette, completely oblivious, flirted with the man at Customs. He waved her along without opening her cases.

With relief, they finally checked their luggage and settled to wait for their domestic flight. "Maybe this isn't so bad," Josette said.

"Did you give him your address?" Marie-Thérèse asked.

"Who?"

"The boy on the plane."

Josette snorted scornfully. "He's too young. I wouldn't date someone younger than me. Besides, he lives someplace called Montana. It's not on my itinerary." She giggled. "But he was cute."

Marie-Thérèse sighed and looked away, wishing she could have stayed in France and prepared for her mission. Twice a week she'd been going on divisions with the missionaries, and she'd learned the lessons well. In her purse, she had a Book of Mormon the missionaries had challenged her to give away on her flight. Now who could she give it to?

"Hi again."

They looked up to see the boy from the plane. "Hi," Marie-Thérèse said. Could it be she was to give the book to him?

"Oh, Braden, how wonderful," Josette said. "I was just about to get something to eat. Will you join me?" She waved a hand at the fast food restaurants lining the wall. "Marie-Thérèse can watch our bags." She smiled sweetly. "We'll bring you something back."

"Don't be late," Marie-Thérèse said. It would be just like Josette to miss the plane.

The pair came back as their flight was boarding. "Just in time," Josette said breezily, shoving a carton of french fries at Marie-Thérèse. "Thank you so much for lunch, Braden."

"But—"

Josette kissed his cheek, picked up her single carry-on bag, and started for the gate. Braden's mouth stayed open and his face flushed. Marie-Thérèse had no doubt that he was considerably poorer than he'd been before meeting her sister, and he didn't have so much as an address to show for it.

"Here," Marie-Thérèse said softly, placing the book in his hands. "A gift for you." Embarrassed, she turned and fled the way Josette had gone, juggling her flight bag, purse, and french fries in one hand and her ticket and Mathieu's package in the other.

The flight was a repeat of the first one, except now the food served was American. Marie-Thérèse tried to sleep a little as it was bedtime in France, but Josette had come to life and there was no stopping the incessant words pouring from her mouth. Marie-Thérèse listened, even laughing occasionally. She loved her sister despite her lack of . . . She pushed the thought aside. It wasn't hers to judge, not really. Whatever made Josette happy was all right by her.

They arrived in Salt Lake City after ten, local time, and stumbled down the ramp searching for Mathieu, hoping they would recognize him. As the crowd of people cleared, Marie-Thérèse saw a young man with black hair and impressive dark eyes. He lounged in a chair, a relaxed smile on his face. "There he is," she said.

Josette stopped and stared, unmindful of the people who jostled past her. "I don't remember him looking that way. He's gorgeous!"

Marie-Thérèse laughed. Mathieu's lanky figure had filled out since they'd seen him last, but he'd always been good-looking to her. "Come on," she said to Josette, who surreptitiously checked her face in her compact. "You look fine."

"I'm a mess." Josette snapped the compact shut and popped it into her bag. "Hey, where is that package, anyway? I'll give it to him." She snatched the parcel out of Marie-Thérèse's hands and shot forward, a smile on her face.

"Mathieu," Josette said, leaning toward him for the customary kisses. "How good to see you again. Look what I've brought you from France. Or rather," she added when she saw Marie-Thérèse's face, "what *we've* brought you. Marie-Thérèse carried it most of the way."

Marie-Thérèse's annoyance ended with her sister's confession. Mathieu met her gaze, taking her hand and kissing her cheeks as he had her sister's, and she found his closeness affected her in a way she hadn't expected. Why did her heart beat so fast?

"Marie-Thérèse," he said, "I've been looking forward to seeing you again ever since our long conversation at my cousin's baptism. Tell me how you've been. Do you still plan on serving a mission?"

"Yes. I'll be putting in my papers soon. I'm excited to go."

"So was I. It was a wonderful experience."

"You went on a mission?" Josette asked, a slight pout to her lips.

Mathieu laughed. "Just got home last year, and I came back to BYU to finish my degree. This will be my last semester."

"You were here before?" Josette asked.

"Of course he was," Marie-Thérèse said, exasperated. "At Danielle's baptism he said he was coming to Provo to attend BYU."

"I had some time to kill before I could serve a mission," Mathieu said, picking up their bags. "I was twenty-one, but I hadn't been a member long enough to go on a mission at the time."

"That makes you what now?" Josette's brow furrowed as she did the addition. "Twenty-five?"

Mathieu's laugh was warm. "Guilty as charged."

"Wasn't it hard to come back to it after the interruption?" Josette asked.

"Wasn't exactly an interruption, just a different vein of study. I wouldn't change it for anything. My mission taught me things I could never learn in school."

Marie-Thérèse liked his easy confidence and the words he obviously meant. He didn't think of missionary service as having slowed his career, but rather having enhanced and prepared him for life, while at the same time giving him an opportunity to help people. That's exactly how she thought of a mission.

"I'm glad we came here to study," Josette said, surprising Marie-Thérèse.

"So am I," Mathieu looked at Marie-Thérèse as he spoke.

Her insides churned and suddenly her knees felt strangely weak, making it hard to stand. Not for anything could she tear her eyes away from his. "Let's go get our luggage, huh?" she said to break the spell.

Mathieu nodded and Josette hooked a proprietary arm through his, urging him on. Marie-Thérèse followed a step behind, feeling a loss she couldn't pinpoint. She was glad when Mathieu slowed slightly and matched his step with hers.

"Have you been waiting for us long?" Josette asked, gazing up at him with a captivating smile.

"Not too long," he said. "But I can tell you, it was well worth the wait."

Chapter Seven

Things are looking up, Josette thought as Mathieu drove them to the apartment he'd found for them off State Street in Provo. Not only was he great company, he was older and handsome enough to help her forget Alphonse.

"It's within walking distance of campus," Mathieu said after carrying their suitcases up to the fourth floor apartment. "I'll leave you to settle in, but I'll come around tomorrow and give you a tour so you'll be able to find your classes next week." He handed Josette a piece of paper. "Here's my number if you need anything. I just live a couple of buildings over. Your parents made sure there was a landline installed here in case you needed it."

Not the cell phone Josette would have preferred, but it would have to do for this one semester. "I'm so glad you're here, Mathieu." Josette gave him a hug. "What would we do without you?"

He grinned. "You'd think of something. For someone with your looks, I'm sure you could find a hoard of willing males."

Josette smiled doubtfully, uncertain whether he'd given her a compliment. "Hmmm," she said.

"As to the kissing cheeks, they don't do it here," Mathieu said. "Remember that, or people might think you're forward."

Marie-Thérèse laughed. "Did we scare you? Have you been among these Americans too long?"

"I thought Americans were warm-blooded," Josette said.

Mathieu chuckled. "I'll say they are. Wait until it gets cold and people are still wearing shorts and short-sleeved shirts to school. They're a bunch of nuts if I ever saw them."

"Dang, and I only brought one pair of shorts!" Josette felt like dancing. What had she been worried about? This was going to be a lot of fun—exactly like in the movies, only a little more Mormonized.

After Mathieu left, they made their beds with the linens from their suitcases and then talked far into the night, too pent-up for sleep. Noni and Rosellen, the other girls who shared their apartment, seemed excited to have foreign roommates.

"I've never even been out of Idaho before," confessed Rosellen, "and now here I am sitting with two exotic French women!" Her giggle bubbled up and over, making Josette smile.

"It's my second year here," said Noni from her seat on Josette's bed. She pulled her knees to her chest, revealing pink underwear sticking out from her high-cut shorts. One finger twisted the frizzy bleached curls framing her pretty face. "You'll love this place. It has an outdoor and indoor swimming pool, and so many people live here that something fun is always happening."

"What are you studying?" Marie-Thérèse asked Noni. The young and innocent Rosellen had already admitted to not knowing what her major would be.

"Me?" Noni laughed. "I don't go to school. I'm here to have fun. This is where all the smart single guys come."

A knowing look came over Marie-Thérèse's face—one Josette recognized all too well. "Don't," Josette said in French. "Don't start judging her."

"I'm not—"

"Good." Josette found herself admiring the tight-fitting ribbed shirt Noni had on, and she wanted to buy one for herself. She

wished she'd worked longer at the café where she'd begun working
when her father had temporarily lost his job. She'd dropped the
position when she entered college, unlike Marie-Thérèse, who had
continued working for two days a week. At least Josette still had a
bit of savings.

"Is something wrong?" Noni asked.

"Nothing," Josette said, stumbling over the *th* sound in the
word. "But I just love your top. Can you show me where to buy
one?"

The day after they arrived in Provo, Mathieu showed them around
as promised. Josette couldn't believe how large the BYU campus
actually was. And all that grass, with students sitting on it—
talking, reading, or simply soaking up the warm rays of the sun.
She insisted on stopping and taking off her sandals, spreading
herself out on the luscious green.

"I know," Mathieu said with a laugh. "I sit on the grass every
chance I get."

"The school doesn't mind?" asked Marie-Thérèse.

"Not unless everyone's cutting corners and using it as a path,"
he said. "In America, they like grass. They have parks full of it for
kids to play on."

"Very smart of them," Josette said. "I think I'll stay here
forever."

Marie-Thérèse laughed. "Listening to her, you'd never know that
I practically had to drag her to the plane, kicking and screaming."

"You're just mad because you had to bring the packages,"
Josette said. She turned to Mathieu. "So did you like the Swiss
chocolate Danielle sent?"

"Josette!" protested Marie-Thérèse.

"Just wondering." Why did her sister have to be so stuffy?

"We had to know what was in it for Customs," Marie-Thérèse

explained. "They still opened your package even after I told them what it was."

"They always do that to me, too," Mathieu said.

Josette watched his handsome face, feeling a flutter in her chest. She'd wait for a few weeks to see if anything more interesting came up, and if it didn't, maybe she would decide to date him. She settled back on the grass, feeling happier than she had since Marcelin had betrayed her with Marie-Thérèse. How lucky she was that she had seen through him in time.

"Speaking of packages," Marie-Thérèse said, "hadn't we better take the one Marc sent to the Fields?"

Josette yawned lazily. "Next week."

"What if we get busy? Tomorrow's Sunday, and school begins on Monday. If we take it today, we won't have to worry about it."

"Call and let them worry about picking it up," Josette suggested.

"What, and miss all the family pictures?" Mathieu laughed. "Why don't I take you, and then we'll go out to eat. My treat. They have a place nearby with tons of food, all you can eat."

"You'll spoil us," Marie-Thérèse said.

"Spoil you, nothing. You're worth it. Or, if it would make you feel better, we'll go dutch." Mathieu and Marie-Thérèse laughed, and inwardly Josette sighed. Leave it to Marie-Thérèse to protest a free meal. At this rate, Josette would use up her savings quickly. Her parents had made it clear that their monthly allowance was only for food—prepared at home—and necessities. Her father had agreed to an additional amount for spending, dependent upon proof of maintaining good grades. Josette had planned to let her dates pay for any meals she ate out, but what if all were as willing to let her pay as Mathieu seemed to be?

"Oh, all right," she said, jumping to her feet. "Let's get this over with already. Take us home to get that stupid package."

"Yes, your highness," Mathieu teased.

He waited in the car while they retrieved the package. "He really should pay for dinner," Josette grumbled. "It was his idea."

"It's not as if it's a date," Marie-Thérèse said. "I bet he'd pay if you asked him. What, don't tell me you've fallen for him already. That's a new record—even for you."

Josette smiled grudgingly.

"Are you ready?" Marie-Thérèse asked.

Josette glanced down at her shorts and her thin top. In a brief flash she recalled the picture her brother's missionary companion had sent her, especially the white-blond hair and blue, blue eyes of Elder Fields. "I think I'll change," she said. For some reason, one she couldn't even explain to herself, she wanted to make a good impression on the Fields family. "I'll just be a minute." She changed quickly to a purple rayon pantsuit her mother had bought for her last birthday, which set off her dark hair and eyes to perfection.

Marie-Thérèse's eyebrows arched, but she smoothed her camel skirt and said nothing. Josette glanced in the mirror, checking her makeup, and ran a brush through her hair. "Okay," she said at last.

"You look nice," Mathieu said to her in the car. "Older."

Josette grimaced. "That I could do without, I think."

"Nonsense. The older I get, the younger the older people seem. And I like older people."

Josette felt in her purse and pulled out the picture of the Fields family. Elder Fields stared back at her.

"They're all married except Marc's companion and his sister," Marie-Thérèse said, pointing over Josette's shoulder from her seat in the back. "Brionney, I think her name is."

"She looks like him," Mathieu said, starting the engine. "The little sister."

He was right. Except for a few too many pounds, Brionney looked the most like her brother. All the Fields family had blond hair, but only the two youngest had that remarkable white-blond color. Likewise, the eyes were all some shade of blue, but only Elder Fields and Brionney had the color of the sky on a clear day. It was all Josette could do to tear her eyes away. "I hope they're home," she said.

"You didn't call?" Mathieu asked.

"Elder Fields must have forgotten to include their number, and I couldn't find a phone book," said Marie-Thérèse.

"Well, no matter. We'll just throw it on their porch," Josette said, feeling better. "Then we won't have to look at family photographs." The others laughed, and Josette felt her own spirits soar. She couldn't help thinking that something important was about to happen.

They pulled up at the Fields' house in the foothills, and Josette felt taken aback by the beautiful landscaping. It wasn't the biggest house she had seen, not even close, but so well-loved that it seemed to welcome her. She practically skipped up the long, curving sidewalk, her heart pounding as they waited on the porch.

A chubby young girl answered the door. "Yes?" She looked at them questioningly. Her eyes were more startling than in the picture, and Josette thought her cute, even with the extra weight.

"You are Brionney?" Marie-Thérèse asked in English. "I recognize you from your picture. Your brother sent this package from France." She handed it to the girl.

The girl's face lit up. "You're from France? Yes, I can tell by your beautiful accent. How neat to meet you! You have to come in." She turned and called over her shoulder. "Mom, Dad, some people from France are here. They know Zack."

She ushered them into an elegantly furnished living room with gold shag carpet and a long green couch. Mr. and Mrs. Fields stood up to greet them. "I'm Irene," said the mother, "and this is my husband, Terrell. You've already met Brionney. She's our youngest."

"It's a pretty name," Josette said awkwardly. Would they even understand her English?

"Thank you." Irene indicated the couch. "Please, sit down. Tell us, how do you know our son?"

"We don't know him for ourselves," Marie-Thérèse said. "He's the companion of our brother."

"Your brother's companion," said Brionney. "How cool."

Marie-Thérèse grinned. "Yes, my brother's companion. You'll have to excuse us if we don't speak perfect English. We learned only in school and with the missionaries."

"You're doing just fine," said Terrell. "What would really be funny is to hear us speak French."

Josette laughed.

"Are you Elder Perrault's twin?" Brionney asked Josette. She pronounced the "l" and the "t" on their last name.

"Perrault," Josette corrected. "You do not say the last two letters. And yes, Marc is my twin."

"You look like him." Brionney sighed. "I always wanted to be a twin. But maybe someday I'll have them myself. Twins are special."

Josette nodded, unbidden tears stinging her eyes. "I miss Marc very much." But it went beyond that. It was almost as if a piece of her were missing.

Brionney's smile dimmed. "I miss my brother, too. I wish he could come home. Two years is a long time."

"Don't let her fool you," Irene said. "Zack teases her mercilessly when they're together. They fight like crazy."

Brionney shrugged and began opening the package in her lap. "Oh, look!" she exclaimed. "These are so cute!" She held up a long, tooth-shaped object dangling on a silver chain. "He sent a whole bunch of these."

"They're monkeys carved on a tooth," Mathieu said. "See? Hear no evil, see no evil, and speak no evil." Each monkey had his hands clapped over his ears, eyes, or mouth. "They sell these at all the flea markets. They're very popular with the tourists."

Also in the package were treats from France, a large stack of postcards, and a dozen small Eiffel Tower statues. "He must mean one for each of his sisters and the grandchildren," Irene said with misty eyes. "Thank you very much. It helps having you visit like this."

"So who are you?" Terrell asked Mathieu. "A brother?"

Mathieu laughed. "Oh, no. My cousin is a friend of their family. But since we're all members of the Church, we're like family."

Terrell's smile nearly split his face. "Oh, yes. I remember how it was in the mission field. I served in England, you know."

There was a brief, awkward silence. Marie-Thérèse slid forward on the couch. "I think we had better be going. We are glad you were home."

Josette felt an odd panic rise in her chest. "What about pictures?" she blurted. "Are you not going to show us pictures?"

Mathieu and Marie-Thérèse stared at her, their mouths open, but Brionney jumped to her feet and hauled a huge photo album from the bookcase. She settled on the couch next to Josette. "These are my parents when they were married. Here's their first baby—Talia. She has three boys now."

While Brionney and Josette pored over the pictures, Terrell and Irene Fields kept up a steady conversation with Marie-Thérèse and Mathieu, asking them about their families and school. Josette grew bored, but she knew she had no one to blame but herself.

On Brionney went, from Talia to Lauren and Mickelle, the other sisters. Finally, Zack was born. He was as cute a baby as Josette had ever seen. In each picture his eyes seemed to stare right at her.

"This was when Zack jumped into the pool to save me from drowning," Brionney said. "He was only six, but he knew how to swim like a fish. Mom was talking to a friend and didn't see me jump into the pool behind her. Dad saw, but he was clear across the pool and would never have gotten to me in time. Zack jumped in and pushed me to the side." It wasn't the only story Brionney told, and with every word her voice told of her love and admiration for her big brother.

"I can see he is very special," Josette said.

Brionney's eyes widened. "Hey, I have an idea. You could help me with my French. Would you? It's not my best subject, but I want to impress my brother when he gets home."

Josette hesitated. It was one thing to look at family pictures, but quite another to agree to teach Brionney. She'd come to BYU for fun, not for work.

"You could be her tutor," Irene put in. "We'd pay you."

"I guess so," Josette said, thinking of her small allowance. If they paid her, it might be worth it. "Let us try. Will Saturday mornings be okay? Not too early. Maybe eleven."

Brionney practically bounced on the couch with excitement. "Oh, yes! I would love it! I can't believe I'm going to learn French from a real French person!"

Josette smiled. Maybe it wasn't so bad having her own personal fan club of one.

"We must be leaving for dinner," Mathieu said, standing. "I'm taking these lovely ladies out for some American food."

"Please won't you stay and eat with us?" Irene asked. "I have plenty of food in the oven. And it's as American as it gets."

"Yes, do!" Brionney said.

"We do not want to intrude." Marie-Thérèse looked uncomfortable.

"It's no intrusion," Irene insisted. "Tell me, wouldn't your mother do the same if we visited?"

She would, Josette thought. *In fact, she would be hurt if they didn't stay.* There was also the fact that the dinner wouldn't cost a thing—Mathieu couldn't be trusted to pay after what he'd said that afternoon. "I would like to stay," she said.

So they did. Josette was amazed at how comfortable she felt there, despite the odd foods and unfamiliar atmosphere. The Fields were interesting and kind, and the love they felt for each other was apparent. Talk centered upon daily events, but everything was related somehow to the gospel. *It reminds me of home,* thought Josette, and the uncomfortable knot she'd felt in the pit of her stomach ever since leaving France relaxed.

When they finally left the Fields' home, darkness had fallen. Spotlights along the sidewalk lit both the bushes and their path to

Mathieu's old car. Brionney walked with them, and hugged Marie-Thérèse and Josette as they left. "I'm so glad to meet you," she whispered.

"I too," Josette said, meaning it. "We will see you next Saturday."

Brionney skipped back up the walk.

"You could have at least offered to do the lessons for free," Marie-Thérèse said once they were in the car.

"Why?" Josette asked. "I'm going to need the cash." She turned her gaze to Mathieu. "So where to now, oh-he-who-drives? Shall we go dancing?"

He shook his head. "No. I'm not sure what time your church starts, but mine starts early and I have a priesthood lesson to give."

"Do you go to a French-speaking branch?" Marie-Thérèse asked.

"No, I wanted to learn better English."

"So do I," she said.

"But the night is still young," Josette protested in disbelief.

Mathieu shrugged. "We could watch a little TV. They have a few good programs. But going dancing would keep us too late."

Josette sighed. She could have stayed in France to watch television. For all his good looks and charm, Mathieu was a little boring. She would have to fix that if they were going to date.

When they arrived at their apartment, Noni, dressed in a navy bikini, was leaving with a man. "We're going swimming," she said with a giggle. "Want to come?"

Josette eyed her companion. He wasn't good-looking in the same clean-cut sense as Mathieu or Elder Fields, but with his shaggy brown hair and the sharp curves of his face, he had a dangerous, impulsive attraction. He grinned, openly looking her up and down. "I'm Grady," he said, pushing his long bangs from his light-colored eyes. "Nice to meet you."

"He's my ex-boyfriend," Noni confided in a whisper. "But he's loaded and fun, so I still go out with him when he comes around. He lives a few buildings over. Come on, you'll like him."

Josette made a rapid decision. "I'm going swimming," she said to her sister.

"What time will you be back?"

"When they kick us out," Noni answered for her. "Now hurry up, Josette, and change."

Josette threw her one-piece suit on, wishing she had a two-piece like Noni. Finally, a woman who knew how to have fun!

She blew Mathieu a kiss before she left, and he winked back at her. "Have fun," he called. Did she imagine his voice was strained? *Good, it serves him right to be jealous,* she thought.

Grady put one arm around her and the other around Noni as they made their way to the pool. "You look great," he whispered in Josette's ear. "I'm sure glad we met. Say something so I can hear that gorgeous French accent. Maybe we'll dump yellow-head and get to know each other better."

All thoughts of Mathieu and Elder Zachary Fields fled from Josette's mind. *Now this is more like it,* she thought. *Maybe Grady is the man I've been searching for.*

The apartment seemed suddenly empty and small without Josette doing all the talking. Marie-Thérèse was all too aware of Mathieu's presence. She was glad Josette had deserted them. Mathieu had such great ideas, ones she would love to discuss without Josette's constant inane interruptions. On the other hand, she would now have to hold up her end of the conversation. What if he didn't like her? And why did it matter so much? She'd never cared before what a man thought.

She glanced at Mathieu from beneath her lashes to see what he was doing. He seemed to be waiting for something.

"I understand if you don't want to watch TV," he said.

Stifling an exclamation of surprise, Marie-Thérèse grabbed the remote and clicked it on. "I was just thinking about something else—sorry."

Mathieu sat on the couch and pulled out a coin from his pocket, tossing it to her.

"What's this?" she asked.

"For your thoughts."

Marie-Thérèse felt her face color and hoped he didn't notice.

There was no way she would tell him how glad she was that they were finally alone. "Uh, I was thinking about Josette," she said.

"She sure is lively."

Marie-Thérèse sat on the couch, a comfortable distance from Mathieu. "She's always been that way. She does everything with her whole self, that's for sure." She tossed the coin back to Mathieu. "Your turn. What are you thinking?"

He grimaced. "Do I dare say? I was thinking that I'd hate to be on Josette's bad side."

Marie-Thérèse laughed. "It's not pretty, I can tell you. But it passes quickly. She has a short memory for offenses—a good thing. And she has a sense of fairness. She's a pretty great sister." Marie-Thérèse clamped her mouth shut. Here she was alone with Mathieu, and all they did was talk about her sister. He must like Josette. The disappointment in Marie-Thérèse's heart surprised her.

"So are you, I can see that," Mathieu said. "Every sister as crazy as Josette should have someone to look after them."

"Oh, I know how to have fun." Marie-Thérèse didn't like the picture of the matronly chaperone his words painted.

Mathieu grinned. "I know—haven't I been with you all day? I haven't had this much fun since I don't know when."

Marie-Thérèse stifled the urge to ask if his enjoyment had more to do with her or Josette.

"Except for those pictures," he said. "I couldn't believe it when Josette wanted to look at them. We should have just dropped her off."

"We would have missed a good dinner."

"We could have found something else." Mathieu's eyes locked onto hers, and Marie-Thérèse swallowed hard. What were these feelings? Was this how Josette felt before she kissed a man?

The thought sobered Marie-Thérèse instantly. She wasn't like Josette and she wouldn't let herself get carried away, even if Mathieu was that type of guy—which he wasn't. She took a steadying breath. "Do you have brothers or sisters?"

"Not a one," Mathieu said. "My dad died when I was a baby, and my mom never remarried."

"That's crazy. What's it like to grow up without fighting for the bathroom?"

"I'll tell you if you can tell me what it's like to leave the house without your mom asking a hundred detailed questions."

They both laughed, and the tense moment was forgotten. They talked about their families and lives until the late show came on. "Can you believe how fast the time went?" Mathieu looked at the TV, shaking his head. "I didn't even see the movie."

"It was news, I think," Marie-Thérèse replied, though she couldn't say for sure.

"We'd better call it a night."

"Yes, we'd better."

Mathieu came to his feet reluctantly, and Marie-Thérèse walked with him to the door. "Thanks for staying," she said. "It was fun." The tense excitement in her stomach had returned, and she quickly opened the door to hide her feelings.

Mathieu paused in the doorway. "I'm glad you came, Marie-Thérèse. I think we're going to have a great semester." He leaned over, and for a moment Marie-Thérèse thought he was going to kiss her. She wondered what she would do. Would she back away and remind him of her mission plans, driving him away forever? Or would she kiss him back?

To her intense relief and frustration, Mathieu's kiss brushed first one cheek and then the other as any of her friends in France might do. It was the proper thing, but the fire in his touch was different from anything she'd experienced, leaving her oddly unsatisfied.

"Good night," he whispered.

She smiled and watched him leave, silently chiding herself for wanting something more. They hadn't been on a date, and even if they had been she would expect him to act like a gentleman.

She sighed and put her hands to her face where her cheeks still burned.

Chapter Nine

The small room was fuller than normal for the weekly AIDS support meeting. Everyone in the youth group had come, and Pauline noticed that two new members had joined the group. One of the boys was very young—perhaps between the ages of ten and twelve—and had his mother with him, but the second was older and sat alone, leaning back on his chair and staring at the others with a mocking smile. He had extremely short dark blond hair, hard brown eyes, and a lanky figure that often marked those with AIDS.

"Should I stay?" André said in Pauline's ear.

"No. Don't bother," she replied, fighting the constant tiredness that tugged at her body. "It's too crowded in here as it is. Go play your basketball game. I'll meet you there afterwards."

Her brother squeezed her hand. "Have fun, Dolly," he said, calling her by the old nickname only he still used.

Pauline flashed him her smile. "We always do, and there are new members tonight."

"Go easy on them, huh?"

"The sooner they realize that what they have won't go away, the better it will be for them." Her words were mild, but for an instant there was agony in André's eyes, quickly masked. Pauline laid her hand on his cheek. "I'm so lucky to have you as my brother."

"Don't go all mushy on me," André said flippantly, "or I won't come here with you anymore."

Pauline laughed. Her brother had been coming with her since they'd been old enough to use the metro alone. Originally he'd attended the sessions, but recently he'd taken to playing basketball in the connecting gym. She keenly noted the withdrawal but didn't blame him. Since she'd crossed the line between HIV and AIDS, he wasn't capable of staying with her; it hurt him too much.

He also hadn't agreed with her decision to hide her increasing illness from the rest of their siblings, but since his parents had agreed for the time being, he'd finally acquiesced to her wishes. "Get going," she told him, "or they'll start playing without you."

After he left, she smiled and waved at her old friends, feeling as comfortable here as she felt at home with her family—in some ways even more so. Here she could be blunt about her feelings of fear without worrying about hurting those she loved most.

"Where'd your boyfriend go?" asked a lazy voice as she sat down. It was the older boy she'd noticed earlier, except now he'd changed seats, apparently to torture her.

She cocked her head at the newcomer. "Boyfriend? Oh, you mean André."

"He's not your boyfriend?" Again the mocking smile.

"What if he is?" Pauline countered. She almost giggled, thinking that it was something Josette might have said.

"I'd say he was a wimp, leaving you here alone."

Anger flared. "My brother's been taking care of me ever since I can remember. If playing basketball in the next room helps him forget for a moment that I'm sick, then I want him to play."

For the first time the smile reached his eyes. "So he's not your boyfriend!" He held out his hand. "Hello, nice to meet you. I'm Emeri Fauré."

Pauline took his hand firmly. "I'm Pauline, and I'm glad you came. We have fun here."

"I've probably only got a few months left, according to the doctors," Emeri said carelessly, "so don't get too attached to me."

Pauline put a hand to her mouth and turned away. Something in his words hurt her very soul. While she'd come here to help others face their illness, the truth was that she hadn't faced the recent change in her own diagnosis.

Emeri touched her shoulder. "Hey there, now. I'm sorry. I didn't mean anything by it. I just wanted to get things out in the open. Isn't that what these sessions are for? I didn't mean to make you sad. Please, look at me."

He changed chairs again so he could see into her face. All traces of the mocking had vanished, and she saw a vulnerable young man who was afraid to die.

Like she was.

"It's not only you," she said. "I've had HIV since before I was born. I'm sixteen now. I've been on the border between HIV and AIDS for the past year or more, but last month they found a malignant tumor along with all my other problems. You know what that means. More than one opportunistic disease and the HIV is considered—"

"AIDS." He swore, making Pauline wince. "I know the drill. That's all I've heard for the past two years. Do you think I like this short haircut? My hair's only just growing back."

"I like it short." Without the hardness in his expression, he could have passed for a missionary. She swallowed hard. "I've had HIV for so long that I guess I figured I'd always have it, that it wouldn't go any further."

"Sixteen years is a long time," Emeri said. "I was diagnosed with AIDS two years ago. I didn't know before then."

"How did you get it?"

"I don't know. I tried some drugs once. I think that might have been it. I wish I'd listened to my parents."

"How does your family feel?"

He shrugged, his face dispassionate. "I left home when I found out. I never told them. I'm eighteen now, and I'm living with some buddies. They're nice, but they don't understand what it's like. That's why I finally came here. Dr. Medard recommended the youth group."

Pauline understood all too well. "That's why I come. I have to always be happy around my family. They love me so much, and I'm afraid to show any sadness because it'll hurt them." She stared at the carpet, wondering why she was telling her deepest thoughts to this complete stranger. "I'm not afraid, really. I know where I'm going after I die. You know why I'm really afraid?"

He shook his head.

"I'm worried about who's going to take care of my family. They need me."

Emeri laughed, a dry, hollow sound. "That's nice to know. When I die, no one will even care."

"I will," Pauline whispered, and found it was true.

Emeri stared at her for a long moment. "I know this may sound like a line, but I feel I know you. From the moment you walked in the door, I couldn't take my eyes off your face."

He took her hand and Pauline let him, feeling her heartbeat quicken in her chest. She knew exactly how he felt. Being with him was somehow like spending time with an old friend.

"Maybe we knew each other in the preexistence."

"The what?"

"Where we lived with our Heavenly Father before our birth."

"Don't tell me you still believe in God." The mocking smile was back and bitterness filled his eyes.

"Yes, I do. And I'd like to tell you why."

Emeri stared at her for a long moment without speaking. "Will you go out with me? I know a café by a park that we could go to. You know, to talk."

"Yes," Pauline said.

The bitterness in his gaze faded slightly, and Pauline knew now why she'd felt so strongly that she should come tonight, though she'd only wanted to go to bed early. She'd been led here to help Emeri Fauré.

Chapter Ten

When Pauline came home from her support meeting, Ariana immediately noticed something in her daughter's face. Beneath the weariness that had become a constant since Pauline's bout with the flu, there was an underlying glow.

"How'd it go?" she asked casually, lifting her cheek for Pauline's kiss.

Pauline sat next to her on the couch. "There were two new kids tonight."

"And she wants to go on a date with one of them." André slumped on the floor in front of Pauline.

"André!" Pauline slapped his arm, wincing as though she'd hit harder than expected. "It's not really a date. He's just a guy, and he's pretty nice."

"I heard everyone else saying he was rude," André said.

"Not to me. Abrupt maybe but not rude. He's having a hard time because he doesn't believe in God." She turned to Ariana. "Don't you see, Mom? How horrible would it be not to know where you go after this life. He's so sad. I have to teach him."

Ariana studied her daughter. Was there something more to

this glow than missionary work? With a flash she remembered the vision she'd experienced many years earlier—of Pauline kneeling at an altar in the temple across from a blond man whose face radiated love. Now Ariana knew Pauline would never live to see another birthday, much less live long enough to marry. The weakness in her body, the death in her weariness, reminded Ariana of Pauline's father a few months before he died.

"Couldn't you talk with him at the meetings?" Ariana asked. "Or send the missionaries?"

Pauline laughed. "Oh, Mom, right. There's no way he'd see the missionaries. Come on, I'm sixteen. I'm old enough to go out, even according to the prophet."

"But we don't know this boy."

"That's what I told her," André said.

"I'll let André go with us if you want," Pauline said. "I don't think Emeri would mind."

Ariana wasn't so sure. Pauline was thin and ill, but she was still a pretty girl. Her positive attitude and ready smile had been a beacon for more than one dying friend, several of whom had been boys who'd fallen half in love with her. But if Pauline felt she had the strength to help one more person, how could Ariana refuse? "I think that would be all right," she said finally. "But I'd like to meet him soon." Her heart rebelled as she said it. One more person to love and lose.

"Thanks, Mom."

"I don't know," André said grumpily. "The next thing I know, you'll want to go on *my* dates."

"Ha! Like you go on any." Pauline said.

"Well, that's 'cause I'm always with you!"

"What's going on?" Jean-Marc said, coming from the kitchen.

"I'll let Mom tell you." Pauline arose to her feet and kissed his cheeks. "I have to go to bed. But just so you know, I'm going on a date tomorrow. André's coming with me so I can show him how it's done." She glanced impishly at her brother, who chased her out of the room. Ariana noticed that André's motions were slower than normal in obvious deference to his sister's illness.

"She's going on a date?"

Ariana nodded and pulled Jean-Marc down to sit near her. "I haven't seen her this excited for a long time. I—I . . ."

"What?"

"I thought about that time when I saw her being married. I don't know. It gave me hope."

"That's something that's been in pretty short supply around here. This must be a good thing."

Ariana laid her head on his shoulder. "I wonder if he's blond."

Chapter Eleven

The next day Pauline brushed her hair very carefully, not wanting any more of it to fall out. Since she'd started chemotherapy a few weeks ago, she'd noticed a lot of loose strands in her brush. The doctor had said hers wasn't the kind of chemotherapy that would make her hair fall out, but that she would have some thinning. She'd thought she wouldn't mind but found that she did. What would she do if the doctor had to change her treatments and she lost all of it?

In her mind, she pictured Josette and her long, thick hair. Pauline had the same color and had been trying to grow it out, but it didn't look the same. Now, she didn't dare wash it for her date because she was afraid of losing it altogether.

"Mom, maybe I should get a wig," she said, coming from the bathroom.

"Oh, brother!" André moaned. "It's just a date."

Ariana smiled. "Let's watch and see if it gets any thinner. If it does, we'll get a wig. It'd just be until the treatments are over and your hair comes back in."

Pauline grimaced but didn't say anything more for fear of upsetting them. She looked at André. "Are you ready?"

"I guess," André mumbled. "We might as well get this date over with."

"Isn't this boy coming to get you?" Ariana's late morning cup of hot chocolate paused halfway to her lips.

"We're going to meet him in town, Mom," Pauline said.

"That sounds a little strange for a date."

"He's shy, that's all." Pauline waved her hands in frustration. "Besides, I keep telling you this isn't really a date. I'm going to teach him about the gospel."

"Yeah, and you spend so much time on your hair every day," André said.

Ariana laughed. "I think you're in good hands, Pauline. Your brother sees it like it is." She took a drink. "You'd better get going then, before your *student* wonders where you are."

Pauline and André left the house and headed toward the metro. Pauline's step slowed, and she noted with irritation that André slowed to match her pace. Tears stung her eyes. Why did her body have to betray her at every step? For her entire life she'd known she would die—but didn't everyone know that? The problem was that while she had long ago accepted her illness, it still held a quality of illusion. She had felt strong, mostly, up until this past year, and lately when she hadn't felt well, her father's blessings had seen her through. Was the end really near?

"Am I going too fast?" André asked.

Pauline smiled. "Not a chance. I'm just nervous, that's all."

"I didn't mean what I said about the wig," André said. "I think you'll look cute. You always do anyway."

André didn't hand out compliments readily and she was touched. "Thanks."

A short time later, they came upon Emeri lounging at a table in the appointed café. "Hello," he said to Pauline before thumbing at André. "What's he doing here?"

André bristled. "I've come to check you out, that's all. Pauline's *my* sister."

"Well, have a seat, watchdog, but I'm not paying for you. Only for Pauline."

Pauline put her hands on her hips. "That's enough right now, Emeri Fauré. If that's how you're going to treat my brother, I'm leaving right now."

Emeri shrugged. "Fine, I'll play nice. Please stay."

Pauline let her hands drop, but she didn't sit. "Well?"

"Well, what?" Emeri asked.

André grabbed the chair and pulled it out. "Here, Pauline. If he doesn't know how to be a gentleman, I'll have to show him."

Pauline saw a flash of embarrassment on Emeri's face. "You behave yourself, too, André," she warned, picking up the menu. From the look of Emeri's beat-up clothing, he didn't have much money, and she wondered if there was some way she could pay for their drink without offending him.

"So what'll you have?" Emeri asked.

"A lemonade, I guess. André and I love lemonade." Pauline kicked her brother under the table, daring him to defy her. The lemonade was the cheapest thing on the menu.

When Emeri ordered lemonade for them and a beer for him, she asked, "Couldn't you just have lemonade?"

"Why?"

"You'll live longer, that's why."

Emeri gave a bitter snort. "Like it will make a big difference."

Pauline again felt tears stinking her eyes, but she blinked so they wouldn't fall. "I don't like it when you talk that way."

Emeri studied her for a full minute. "Okay, fine. A lemonade. Why not? It's cheaper anyway."

He turned to signal the waiter, and André made a face that said, "What do you see in this creep?"

Pauline glared back. "You pay for the drinks," she mouthed. André shook his head. "Yes!" she emphasized silently.

"Am I interrupting something?" Emeri asked.

Pauline couldn't help but giggle. "Sorry. My brother's just stubborn. In a little while I'm going to send him home."

Emeri shot André a pleased look. "Okay by me."

"All right, all right," André said. "I'll be good. And in fact, I insist upon paying for all our drinks. But I'm staying."

Pauline grinned at him and said sweetly, "I think we should take him up on that, Emeri. What do you say?"

Emeri gave a wry laugh. "Maybe we should. That way he won't come next—"

"I love the clouds on days like this," Pauline interrupted. "See the big one up there? It looks like a teddy bear."

Emeri gazed up into the clouds. "Looks more like a shark to me."

"Hmm, I don't see that," she said. The silence grew long and deep, and under the table Pauline gave André a nudge. She'd never had a problem finding something to say. Why was it so hard with Emeri?

"So, where are you from?" André asked.

"I live not too far from the clinic with some buddies. I work for Dr. Medard."

Pauline had heard Dr. Medard had organized jobs at the AIDS clinic for many of the patients, but for all his gentleness in his practice, he was rumored to be a hard taskmaster. "He's a nice guy," she said. "He's been my doctor since I was born."

Emeri shrugged and gave her a charming grin. "I get along okay with him—as long as I do what he wants. I have to so he'll keep me in the program. I don't want to go back to public care. I like it here."

"Where's your family?" André asked.

Pauline waited for the answer, wishing she'd told André how Emeri had left them.

Emeri glanced at her and then back to André. "I don't know. They could be anywhere. Frankly, I don't care." He drank down the rest of his lemonade. "Are you guys about ready? I'm feeling restless. Let's walk a bit."

"Do you play basketball?" André asked.

Emeri shrugged. "When I get a chance. Hey, why don't we go over to the clinic now and shoot a few?"

"I don't know. Are you sure you're up to it?"

Emeri's face darkened at André's comment. "I may have AIDS, but I'm not dead yet. I'll run your butt all over the court." He added a couple of swearwords to emphasize his point.

Pauline stifled a sigh. Aside from his grin, she'd seen nothing appealing in Emeri by the stark light of day. Was this the man with whom she had shared her innermost feelings? Had his vulnerability last night and the connection she'd felt been only in her imagination?

André's face glowed an angry red. "I don't know where you came from, and it doesn't really matter, but I won't have you talking that way in front of my sister."

"Maybe you should use your energy for playing instead of talking," Emeri sneered. "Let's go play."

"Fine." André slapped his money on the tablecloth and vaulted to his feet.

Pauline had to hurry to keep up as they ran to catch the metro to the clinic two stops over. She'd made a big mistake in letting her brother come with her on this first date. How was she going to get close enough to Emeri to teach him if he and André were always at each other's throats?

During the basketball game, she noticed that André didn't cut Emeri any slack as he usually did when playing with other terminally ill opponents. He jumped, rebounded, and dribbled as though possessed. Emeri fought him every inch of the way until Pauline was sure he would collapse and die from the effort. His face was red, his chest heaving. At last he fell to the floor and didn't get up.

"So do I win?" André asked.

"Yes," Emeri gasped.

André shot Pauline a triumphant stare. She let her head drop into her hands and waited for what Emeri might do next. More swearing and bitterness? More hatred?

André held out a hand to the fallen figure. Emeri hesitated

only slightly before accepting help up. He slapped André on the back. "Thanks," he said. "That was the best game I've had in a long time. Most people let me win."

"Any time," André said. "You're good."

André headed for the door. "Pauline, I'll be waiting outside. Take your time."

Pauline stared, unable to believe her eyes. What had just happened? Were all men total idiots?

Though she didn't look in his direction, she felt Emeri coming to sit on the hard floor beside her. She glanced over to find him staring at her, his dark eyes searching her face, as if drinking in her presence. "He's a great guy, your brother. Wish I'd had one like him." The softer man she'd glimpsed last night had miraculously resurfaced.

"He's always been my favorite," she said tentatively.

Emeri lifted a hand as though to touch her arm, but let it fall to his lap instead. "Thank you for coming. I didn't expect that you would. It was fun."

She smiled. "Then I'm glad I came."

"Can we do it again?" Eagerness filled the words. "I promise I'll watch my language. You can bring your brother again too, if you want."

Pauline sensed that he had once again opened himself to her, fearing rejection but holding enough hope to risk it. She found that she would rather do almost anything than hurt him or see that devastating mask of anger and fear return.

"Sure," she said. "I'd like that."

Chapter Twelve

Brionney and Josette were in the front room, doing more laughing than practicing French verbs. In the kitchen, Marie-Thérèse tried to tune out their noise and concentrate on her math. She was finding the new concept difficult to understand, which was uncharacteristic for her, even though it had been explained in a different language.

They'd been in Provo for one month, and Marie-Thérèse was happy she had come. She enjoyed school, their new church congregation, and the many new friends she had met. She would much rather be with any of them than doing homework.

She flipped the math pages in irritation, and a thin sheaf of papers fell out. She knew what they were without looking. Last week, when Bishop Denney had extended her a calling as chorister, she'd told him of her mission plans and he'd given her several papers detailing some things she would need to do before completing the online application. "But I don't turn twenty-one until the end of November," she had murmured.

He gave her a patient smile. "That's less than two months away. If you're serious about serving, there's no reason not to submit your application in the next two or three weeks. Of course, there's always the chance that you'll meet someone special and change your mind."

"No way," Marie-Thérèse said, hoping he heard her conviction. "I've wanted to serve a mission for fifteen years. Marriage can wait."

Bishop Denney chuckled. "Can't fault you for that. Marriage will last an eternity. Many girls rush into it before they know what they want in a man."

Marie-Thérèse had kept the papers in her math book ever since but she hadn't really read them.

Her thoughts wandered to Mathieu, as they always seemed to when he wasn't around. She'd been with him a lot in the past weeks, but nearly always with Josette present. The few times they had been alone, usually studying or watching TV, the exciting tension she'd felt on that first night returned. Marie-Thérèse didn't know what to make of it, and apparently neither did Mathieu. He didn't try to kiss her, not even on the cheeks, and kept a physical distance from her that he didn't usually maintain when Josette was in the room. Marie-Thérèse didn't know whether to be disappointed or relieved. She did notice that Mathieu seemed irritated when she mentioned the papers the bishop had given her. Was his reaction the reason she hadn't paid more attention to them? *What am I waiting for?*

A knock at the door pulled Marie-Thérèse back to the present. She heard a male voice—another of Josette's many admirers. Though Marie-Thérèse wouldn't have dated the men her sister chose, she felt somewhat envious of her easy friendships.

"Some flowers for my French lady," the visitor said. "Now come and take a drive with me. The leaves are beautiful this time of year—I bet you have nothing like it in France. The mountains are a kaleidoscope of color."

"Kaleidoscope?" Josette asked.

"A whole bunch of colors mixed together. Come on, you'll enjoy it."

"No, I cannot go with you, Grady," Josette said. "Maybe another day. Right now I am helping Brionney learn French."

"I want to learn French too," Grady returned playfully.

Josette laughed. "Go away. I will see you later."

The door slammed, and the silence was filled by the girls' laughter.

"Oh, I wish I could be like you," Brionney said. "I wish I had a whole bunch of boyfriends who brought me flowers."

"And why should you not be? You are pretty."

"I'm fat," Brionney said. "That's always been my problem. Boys in America always like skinny girls."

"Then they are very stupid."

Marie-Thérèse rolled her eyes. A lot Josette knew about being less than perfect. Her sister had always been disgustingly stunning, and her flirtatious manner attracted everyone.

Even Mathieu?

Marie-Thérèse groaned. Why on earth should she care who Mathieu liked?

She put her fingers in her ears and concentrated on her homework so hard that her head pounded. Pages and pages of problems lay before her. How would she ever get them all done by Monday?

A movement in the doorway caught her attention. She looked up, expecting to see Josette and Brionney, but instead Mathieu gazed down on her. Today he was unshaven, and his face was darker where the short hairs grew. She loved it when he looked like that. What would it be like to rub her cheek against his? She felt herself color at the thought. "Hi, Mathieu," she said, pushing her hair from her eyes.

"I've come to see if you guys want to ride up to Salt Lake and see Temple Square. We've been planning on doing it, and since next week is conference, I thought we could scope out where—"

"Oh, I can't! I've got stacks of math to do, and I can't figure out what I'm doing."

Mathieu leaned over. "Sorry. Can't help you. We geologists don't have to go *that* far into math. But let me translate the directions into French, and maybe that will help."

Marie-Thérèse was glad to let him. Mathieu had a much firmer grasp on the English language than she had. She wasn't surprised that when he explained it in her native language, the concepts became clearer.

"I'm glad I only have to stay this semester," she said with a sigh.

"You're going home at Christmas for good?"

"You knew that."

"I thought maybe you would change your mind."

She shook her head. "No. France is the place for me. I only came here for Josette. As much as I'm enjoying America, I'd rather be with my family."

He grinned. "That's how I feel, but we're certainly in the minority. Many of the foreigners I know end up marrying and staying."

"Not me. Besides, I'm going on a mission, remember?" She touched the papers beside the math book.

Mathieu stared at her for a minute before picking up the papers and scanning them. "I thought maybe you would wait until your birthday," he said slowly.

She shrugged. "Why wait? I want to go more than anything."

His eyes met hers, searching, and Marie-Thérèse felt her senses reeling at his closeness. He bent closer . . . closer . . . then abruptly took a deep breath and pulled away. Had she imagined the moment? She looked down at her homework, blinking away the smarting in her eyes.

Josette flounced into the room with Brionney tagging behind. "I'm ready," she announced in English.

"You're going in shorts?" Mathieu asked, glancing down at his own casual slacks. "It's practically October."

"Why can't I wear shorts? All the Americans do."

"Yeah, I've see the kids waiting for the school busses in the morning," Marie-Thérèse said, glad for the interruption. "They wear shorts and jackets tied around their waists and shiver in the cold. Not exactly smart."

Brionney laughed. "Sounds like the kids I know. Fashion over comfort, you know."

"What about your French lesson?" Marie-Thérèse asked her.

"I'm going to Temple Square too," Brionney said. "I called my mom."

Josette tossed her dark head. "Don't worry," she said, switching into French, "we promised to speak only French, didn't we Mathieu?"

"If you change," he said.

Josette went up to him and touched his cheek with her hand. "Ooh," she squealed. "I just have to feel that with my face." Before Mathieu could object, she rubbed her cheek against his. "It feels like sandpaper," she said, giggling.

"You'd better go change, or I'll rub my face on your feet," Mathieu threatened.

"I might like it!" declared Josette, but she retreated a few steps.

Marie-Thérèse laughed with the others, but inside she felt miserable. *What is wrong with me?*

"Are you coming?" Josette asked.

"No, your sister has math to do, and then she's going to figure out what she needs to do before she submits her mission papers." Mathieu's voice lacked its usual warmth, but his face held no anger—or any other expression. A blank wall.

"Well, can I use your jeans then?" asked Josette. "The ones that are a bit loose on you?"

"Why not?" Marie-Thérèse said tartly. "They're in your drawer." Her only defense against her sister's borrowing tactics was her smaller size—and sometimes her good taste.

Brionney went with Josette, both oblivious to the tension between Marie-Thérèse and Mathieu. They waited in silence until Mathieu finally said, "You're sure you want to go on a mission?"

"I've wanted to since I was little. Don't you think it's a good idea?"

He sighed. "Yeah, I do. It was great. I just wish . . ." He stopped.

"Oh, never mind. If anyone should go on a mission, you should. I think you'll be great."

Marie-Thérèse didn't know whether to laugh or cry. "Thanks. That means a lot coming from you."

"What are friends for?" His smile was back, and Marie-Thérèse found she could breathe again.

"Okay, is this better?" Josette came into the room and twirled.

"Lots," Mathieu said. "But speak French, remember?"

She bowed, sending her long hair flying. "Yes, indeed, oh-he-who-drives. Let's go then." She hooked her arm through Mathieu's and glanced at Marie-Thérèse. "You really aren't coming?"

Marie-Thérèse shook her head miserably. She watched them leave the apartment, feeling somehow betrayed. *I hope Josette and Mathieu do fall in love,* she thought. *He's the only man she's gone out with that I approve of. Mom and Dad will be happy. I've done what I came here to do.*

Resolutely, she began to read the handouts the bishop had given her. "I'll start the online application as soon as I get a physical," she promised herself. At one time the idea had filled her soul with joy, but now the words echoed through the empty kitchen and back to her ears, sounding hollow and desolate.

You're not a missionary yet, she thought. She jumped up and ran from the apartment, plunging down the stairs and around the corner to the parking lot.

Mathieu's car was nowhere to be seen.

"It's just as well," she whispered. Her heart didn't agree.

Marie-Thérèse mechanically made a note in her planner to schedule a physical. Then she returned to her math.

Concentration escaped her. She remembered Mathieu's face, the expressionless mask that had fallen into place when she'd talked about a mission. What was he feeling? Why didn't he tell her?

"Oh, right," she said aloud. "It's not as if he wants to marry you. 'What are friends for?'—wasn't that what he said?" Still . . .

Resolutely, she put all thoughts of Mathieu aside and began to work.

Chapter Thirteen

"So you're saying that up in this so-called heaven of yours, you'll see your parents again." Emeri leaned back in his chair and gave a little chuckle. "I hope you give them a lecture about doing drugs."

"Emeri, this is not funny!" Pauline punched him in the arm. The weekly AIDS support meeting was over, and they were the only patients left in the room. She could hear the thumping of a basketball game in the next room.

Counting three support meetings, it was the seventh time she'd been with Emeri in the past two weeks. On each of the other four occasions they'd been together, André and Emeri had played basketball before going with Pauline for a quick meal or a walk in the park. A friendship had sprung up between André and Emeri, and she was glad for it, though Emeri never completely dropped his guard when André was present. Only in the rare moments they were alone did she see his true self. In those moments, it was as though their souls communicated. Only one thing continued to plague her; each time she or André tried to talk with Emeri about God or his missing family, Emeri would withdraw into his mocking shell. Or he would tease, which she could stand better than the bitterness, but it still frustrated her.

"Life after death? Well, it seems like one of those science fiction novels André's been telling us about. Speaking of that, why don't we go see that new sci-fi movie tomorrow? We could even let André come along, if you insist, though I think it's high time we go out on our own. Oh, come on, Sunshine, don't stick your lip out that way, or I'll have to—" Emeri leaned forward to kiss her, but Pauline drew away.

"Stop that. I'm mad at you. Besides André will be here any minute, and he'll see us."

"So what? I thought you tell your brother everything. Besides, it's just a kiss."

Pauline blushed. She didn't know if she was ready for their relationship to go beyond the friendship line. "Dang it, Emeri, you're changing the subject."

"Dang? Don't you think that's rather close to swearing?"

"This means a lot to me!"

Emeri put his face close to hers, suddenly serious. "I know it does, but I can't think about any of that right now. I'm just going to enjoy being with you for every second we have. I can't think beyond that. I can't." The urgency in his voice begged her not to continue, but Pauline couldn't let it go.

"If you listened, you might understand how much God loves you. You don't have to be afraid of dying. He has a plan."

Emeri cocked his head back to look at her. He shook his head very slowly. "Oh, Pauline, then why are you afraid?" His voice was calm and matter-of-fact, but Pauline felt the words knife into her heart.

"I'm not afraid."

Emeri took her hand. "Yes, you are. You said to me the night we met that your only fear is that your family wouldn't be able to get along without you. But that's not true. You're at least a little afraid of dying for its own sake, but you can't admit it. Your very life is a miracle to your family, yes, and they certainly expect you to live up to that grand idea. You have to be positive and happy every minute so you can spare their feelings. I've seen it in your relationship with André, and I'll bet it carries through to the rest of your family. That may be great for them, but for you it stinks. If you're afraid, you should be able to tell your family. They should comfort you." His voice lowered. "At least yours would try. They would never tell you to leave them alone."

Pauline felt angry at his words, but her curiosity ran deeper. "Did your family tell you to leave?" Emeri didn't answer, and Pauline knew from the look on his face that he wouldn't tell her more about his family, at least not today.

"What are you really afraid of, Pauline?" he challenged. "Tell me." He still held her hand and as she tried to pull away, he squeezed tighter. "Please."

A tear escaped and slid down her cheek. "God loves me, and things are the way they are for a reason. A sin has to have a consequence."

"Even on the innocent?" he asked bitterly.

"Yes. Because they will stand as witnesses, as testimonies against that sin. We've talked about this before. Yes, it does make me angry and afraid like you, but I know it's only for a little while. This life is short, but eternity is forever."

He snorted. "An eternity filled with glorious happiness and health." His voice became gentle, more so than Pauline had ever heard it. "If you believe that, why are you really afraid?"

She shook her head. "You don't want to know."

"You mean you don't want to tell me."

Pauline was touched enough by his perception to answer. "Okay, I will." She took a breath before rushing on. "I'm afraid because I know it's true and I'm not good enough. How can I go to heaven when sometimes I feel so angry at God for not healing me? For seeing my mother suffer each time she takes me to the doctor? But those feelings are wrong, Emeri. They're wrong because I know the gospel is true, and I know God's plan. But still I get sad and angry and afraid inside, and I know it's wrong, and so maybe I'm not good enough to go to heaven at all."

Emeri touched her face with his other hand, his eyes full of an emotion Pauline didn't recognize, but it made her heart pound. "Oh, Pauline. Dear, sweet Pauline. I can help you there. You're the most pure and wonderful person I've ever known. From the time I first saw you, I've felt that. I swear to you that if there is a heaven, you will go there. If there is a God, He'd know and understand and forgive all of your feelings—at least the God you've been telling me about would. Just because you believe your anger is wrong, doesn't mean your God won't cut you a little slack. If He won't, then I don't want to hear about Him. He wouldn't want to know me at all—not with all the hatred I have inside. Or is that what you're saying?"

Pauline knew Emeri was right. Each time she felt bitterness and anger, her Heavenly Father did understand. He had to! After all, she'd been allowed to contract AIDS, but she'd also been given spiritual experiences and blessings that equalled the agony. Blessings that included her family and Emeri. If God would forgive Emeri—and she knew He would—then He would also forgive her resentful thoughts.

"When Jesus prayed in Gethsemane, He felt our pain. Did you know that, Emeri?" she asked. "And He knew for himself what it's like to face death." She took her hand from his and wiped the tears from her face. She laughed self-consciously. "I'm sorry for being so emotional. I guess it's true we're always our own worst judges. You know what? I'm going to forget this stupid fear of mine and never mention it again."

Emeri frowned. "No, Pauline. We're dying. Dying! Whether you want to admit it or not, there's pain and bitterness in that. I want you to tell me everything. I don't want you to be happy and bright. I want you to be honest. Tell me how things really are. I want you to treat me with the same honesty I treat you. Will you do that for me?"

She met his unflinching gaze. "Okay, I'll tell you how I really feel, but I won't stop talking about God or my church. They're a part of who I am."

"I knew that already, Pauline, and I accept it. In fact, I wouldn't be honest if I didn't tell you there's a part of me that wishes you were right about this whole religion thing. It'd make things easier." He stood, took her hands in his, and pulled her to her feet. "Now let's go find that brother of yours before he works up another sermon on the evils of dating too young." He paused, his dark eyes dancing. "Or if you'd rather, you could give me a kiss."

"He'll walk in on us."

"At least his sermons would be more focused."

"All right." Pauline lifted her face and kissed him on the cheek.

"That," Emeri said, "was not exactly what I meant."

Pauline laughed. "Hi, André," she called, looking past Emeri. "We were just going to look for you."

Emeri shook his head and sighed.

Chapter Fourteen

I should have come here ages ago, Josette thought as she lay stomach-down on her bed in the room she shared with Marie-Thérèse. *I never knew BYU could be so fun.*

They were in the third week of November, the months of school having whirled by in a rush of dates, shopping, and occasional study. Mathieu had taken them to many tourist sights and numerous activities, mostly paying for them himself on his credit card, and Josette found herself liking him more than she'd expected. Except for his insistence on studying and going to bed early on Saturday nights, he was a lot of fun. During the evenings when he and Marie-Thérèse stayed in to study, Josette went out with her new American boyfriends—ones who saw life more like she did. Being a member of the Church didn't mean one had to be boring. Marie-Thérèse frowned each time she left, but didn't object as long as Josette told her where she was going and what time she'd return.

"She's getting to be as bad as a mother," Josette mumbled aloud to the empty room. She stared at her English book, realizing she'd read the same passage several times without understanding anything. Tomorrow she had a test, and if she wanted to keep the spending allowance her parents had promised, she had to get reasonable grades—either that or fall back on her own dwindling resources. Luckily, she had a good memory, and learning was generally a matter of reading the material a couple of times. She felt bad for Marie-Thérèse, who had to study harder to internalize each lesson.

Josette's other classes were easy. She'd finally found something she was good at. Interior design came as naturally to her as shopping for clothes.

Yawning, she rose from her bed and stumbled to the kitchen. It was early for dinner, but she might be able to find something to snack on while she forced herself to read the dull material.

She waved to Marie-Thérèse as she passed the small front room where her sister sat on the couch with several books spread around her, frowning in concentration. Her hair looked great, and Josette wondered why she'd bothered when they didn't plan on going anywhere this Thursday night. Was she hoping someone would drop by? She smiled. If someone did drop by, it would most likely be for her, and not for her sister.

The doorbell rang, and she heard Marie-Thérèse answer it. She hoped it was someone who could manage to drag her away from the grind of studying. Maybe it was Ben from next door, who always gazed at her as if he couldn't live without her. Or maybe the dangerous Grady, Noni's ex-boyfriend, who took her to expensive restaurants and teased her about her French accent.

She heard Mathieu's voice and dropped her half-eaten apple onto the counter, her daydreams vanishing. Mathieu was better than all of them, and she thought maybe he was starting to love her. He'd be a man her parents would approve of, and he seemed to indulge her whims and flirtations with other men. What more could she ask for?

"I thought you might want to go with me," Mathieu was saying as she entered the front room.

Marie-Thérèse stood near the door, a silly smile on her face. "I've been wanting to see it."

"Where are we going?" Josette asked. The other two looked uncomfortable, and for the first time Josette noticed that Mathieu held only two tickets in his hand.

"Uh, it's just a musical I happened to get a couple of tickets for at the last minute," Mathieu said. "I knew Marie-Thérèse was interested in going, and I was going to get them next week for her birthday, but tonight they practically fell into my hands—my roommate's date cancelled on him and he decided not to go. I didn't think you would be interested, Jose." He called her by the nickname only her twin brother Marc used, and for some reason it rankled. "It's really not your style, but if you want to go, take my ticket. I'll even drive you both there and come back to pick you up."

Marie-Thérèse's smile dimmed slightly. "Oh, no, you and Josette can go. There's still time for me to get tickets. It'll be on for two more weeks."

"I don't know." Mathieu looked at Josette, waiting.

Josette swallowed the lump in her throat. All this time she'd thought Mathieu was interested in her, and yet he'd come tonight to take her sister out. How many times had they gone out alone? Why hadn't Marie-Thérèse said anything? Josette felt her heart wilting, but she forced anger to replace the hurt.

"I don't like musicals," she said stiffly. "But thanks anyway." Her sister and Mathieu exchanged a hopeful look, twisting the knife in her heart. "Besides," she added, "I have a test tomorrow, and I have to at least read through the material. Good-bye. Have fun." She stalked down the corridor, silently hoping Mathieu's car would break down before they could leave the parking lot.

Marie-Thérèse came after her. "You can go. I've got studying to do, too."

Josette whirled on her sister. "He asked *you*."

"That's only because he knew I wanted to go. It's not as if he likes me or anything."

"You like him."

Marie-Thérèse's cheeks burned a bright red. "No, I don't. I-I . . . We're just friends. We study together, that's all. You know I'm going on a mission. I'm not interested in a relationship."

"Well, I am." Josette dove onto the bed. Her book flipped shut and her notes went flying.

Her sister bit her lip and then cleared her throat. "You can have him," she said in an odd voice. "Remember our vow? No man to come between us—ever."

Josette softened. "I want a relationship, but I didn't say with Mathieu. You go ahead. I really don't like musicals. You know—all that singing. Besides, Mathieu isn't very exciting."

Then why do you want him? a silent voice mocked inside her head.

Marie-Thérèse pursed her lips, but didn't speak for a long moment.

"Go," Josette encouraged. "Go have a little fun before you sentence yourself to eighteen months with no men." She shuddered. "Yuck!"

Marie-Thérèse began to rapidly change her clothes. "If you're sure," she said, sounding almost pathetic.

Josette could see that she wanted to go more than anything, and not only because of the musical. "I'm sure." Josette picked up her papers from the floor and arranged them again on the bed.

Marie-Thérèse touched her shoulder. "I'll be home by ten, maybe sooner. I'll call if there's a change."

I'm not your mother, Josette almost said, but refrained. She wanted her sister to return early. The thought of her alone with Mathieu upset her more than she would admit.

When her sister was gone, Josette read the English passage, forcing herself to look up the words she didn't understand. "This is so awful," she said. "I hate English. I really, really hate English."

"Josette! Are you here?" came an urgent voice from the hall.

"Yes!" Josette bounced from the bed.

Noni appeared in the doorway, her tanned face flushed by

the four-story climb to the apartment. "Some of the girls and I are going dancing in Salt Lake. Wanna come? I saw Rosellen downstairs, but you know how she is—too scared she's going to miss her beauty sleep or be late to a class. Come on! Get dressed."

Josette was changing before she realized what she was doing. Tight-fitting black Levis with a form-flattering ribbed turtleneck in bold horizontal stripes were perfect for a night on the town. She glanced at her book and papers on the bed, but their call wasn't as loud or demanding as Noni's—and certainly not as enticing.

As she left the apartment, she thought fleetingly of leaving Marie-Thérèse a note to explain where she was going and what time she'd be back. Then she remembered her sister's desertion. "With my boyfriend!" she mumbled in French.

"What?" asked Noni.

"Nothing," she said in English. "I am ready."

Chapter Fifteen

Mathieu opened the car door for Marie-Thérèse and helped her inside as though they were on a real date. She admitted to herself that it seemed like a real date—more so than studying or watching a film. The drive to the theater was short and the silence comfortable.

"I heard from my Mom," Mathieu said. "She can't wait until I get home for Christmas. I'm looking forward to going. I've been away too long."

Marie-Thérèse knew what he meant. When she thought of her family, especially Pauline, she longed to be home. "Well, there's not much time left," she said brightly. "I mean, before we go back."

"No." His voice sounded sorrowful. "There's not much time left." Before Marie-Thérèse could ask what was wrong, he added, "Here we are. Let's hurry so we get good seats."

Marie-Thérèse didn't wait for him to open her door but jumped out and bounded across the sidewalk. "I'll race you!" He laughed and ran with her to the building.

The musical was everything Marie-Thérèse had expected. She and Mathieu laughed during the humorous parts and watched solemnly as the characters passed through their trials. It seemed only natural for Mathieu to take her hand.

They continued to hold hands as they left the theater and walked slowly to the car. The entire area was dark except for the moon and stars overhead and the weak lights in the parking lot. There was no snow on the ground, but Marie-Thérèse expected it any day. Their breath made warm clouds in the cool night air.

Mathieu paused when they reached the car. Instead of opening the door, he stepped closer to her. She looked up, an odd pounding in her ears. "Marie-Thérèse, I—" He stopped talking and kissed her.

Kissed her!

Marie-Thérèse responded, enjoying his closeness as the passion swept through her body. Until she remembered that falling in love—even with Mathieu—didn't fit into her plans. With both hands she pushed at his chest. "Stop." It was a weak protest, but Mathieu drew away.

"I'm sorry," he said. "The night . . . I don't know . . . forgive me." His face creased with anger, but none of it seemed directed toward her. With precise movements, he opened the car door and helped her inside.

He started the engine and drove home more quickly than usual. Marie-Thérèse felt guilty. Mathieu had apologized for kissing her, but she knew it was just as much her fault. She'd wanted to kiss him. Her chin rose in defiance. *What was wrong with that?*

"So, did you submit your application?" Mathieu asked with nonchalance, as though nothing had happened.

Marie-Thérèse started. "No, I didn't. Yet."

He relaxed visibly. Or was it her imagination? "That was some show," he said. "We should catch another one. Would you like to?"

"I'd love to. It was a lot of fun." Marie-Thérèse made a mental note to pay for the next one they attended. If they were just friends, it was only fair.

Just friends, just friends, just friends. That was all they were.

Tonight they had simply been carried away by the romance in the musical. Nothing more.

Mathieu walked her to the apartment. "It's early yet. Would you like to stay?" she asked.

He hesitated. "I should say no because I have an early class, but I would like to for a while. Maybe Josette would like to come and sit with us. We could help with her homework."

Given what had happened in the parking lot, Marie-Thérèse thought maybe having her sister around was a good idea. "Come on in then, and find a TV channel you like. I'll go get Josette."

But Josette was nowhere to be seen, and Marie-Thérèse began to worry. Where could she be? Her sister always left a message if Marie-Thérèse wasn't home when she left. They both did. Was Josette angry about not going to the musical? Was something wrong?

"She's not in our room," she told Mathieu. "And there's no note. That's not like her. I'm a little worried."

"We'd better go look for her, just in case," Mathieu said.

"Good idea."

He held open the door. "Don't worry, she's probably next door." Mathieu seemed as relieved as she was to leave the empty apartment.

Just friends, her inner voice taunted. She was willing to bet that Josette wouldn't draw such firm lines.

Chapter Sixteen

Noni took Josette to a club she'd never been to before. The fact that Josette couldn't pronounce its name in English didn't stop her from dancing every dance with one admirer after another—a dozen in all. They loved her French accent, her wit, and her long hair. Josette rode a wave of approval until the drive home, when she felt abandoned and empty.

"You're a hit," Noni said. "We'll have to come back."

"Why?" Josette asked flippantly. "I gave to them my phone number."

"All of them?" Noni giggled.

"Why not? I like them and they like me." *Or what they think is me,* she amended silently. The thought left her hurting. Was that the sum of who she was—a beautiful face men enjoyed looking at but never wanted to marry? Was she as empty-headed as Noni appeared to be? Josette wasn't sure she wanted to hear the answer.

She pretended to sleep on the way home, while Noni and the other two girls who'd gone with them chattered endlessly. For the first time, Josette found nothing appealing in their conversation.

She stumbled sleepily into the apartment after Noni opened

the door. Marie-Thérèse rushed up to her. "Are you all right?" she asked in rapid French, for once ignoring politeness.

"Of course I'm all right."

Her sister's freckled face flushed as anger overcame her concern. "Where have you been? I've been frantic! I've been all over these apartments, looking everywhere for you. Everywhere! Mathieu is still searching. I called all your friends, even that grungy Grady, and no one knew anything!"

Josette's own fury burst to life, filling the emptiness of earlier. She welcomed the warmth. "You're not my keeper, and I don't answer to you!" She stalked down the hall to their room, slamming the door behind her.

Marie-Thérèse followed. "You're my sister, for heaven's sake. Of course I'm going to worry about you!"

"Well, I'm a big girl, so get over it. You had your date and I went dancing. Big deal!"

"You could have at least left a note!"

"You're not my mother!"

Marie-Thérèse sat down on her bed, breathing heavily and regularly, as if counting each deep breath. The scarlet slowly faded from her cheeks. "How would you feel if you were me?" she asked, her voice abruptly calm. "I got home at nine-thirty, and there was your book and papers, just like when I left. Your clothes were all over the floor, but there was no you. I was worried."

"I'm a big girl. I can take care of myself," Josette insisted.

Marie-Thérèse stared up at her. "Of course you can. I know that. And I can take care of myself. That's not the point."

"We're not at home. We don't have to check in."

"Is that why you think we tell Mom where we're going?" Marie-Thérèse shook her head. "That's not why at all. It's because we respect her and because we know she'll worry if she has no idea where we are. Don't you understand? It's common courtesy. Yes, it's also so that if we're too late, she'll know where to look for us in case we're in trouble, but the main reason is respect. Look, I don't want to keep track of your every move, but I also don't want to waste three hours worrying that you might be hurt and dying in some gutter. Wouldn't you be upset if I'd been missing?"

Josette's fury abated at the love in her sister's voice. "Okay," she said reluctantly, sitting on her own bed. "I guess you're right. I'm sorry. I didn't mean to worry you. I was just in a hurry when we left." For a while they didn't speak, and then Josette asked tentatively, "So do you think you could spare a minute to help me with this English?"

Marie-Thérèse frowned at the clock. "I suppose. But first we'd better find Mathieu and let him know you're okay."

Hope surged through Josette. "He was worried?"

"Of course he was, silly. We both were."

Josette smiled. Maybe the night hadn't been a total waste.

Chapter Seventeen

The next morning after her first class, Marie-Thérèse went home to get the mail at the same time she always did. She wondered if Mathieu would be there. For weeks they'd both been coming to get the mail at the same time after having accidentally run into each other at the mailboxes. Marie-Thérèse tried never to vary the time she went because she enjoyed seeing Mathieu alone each day, if only for a few minutes. But would he come today after what had happened between them the night before? Had their kiss ruined their friendship?

"How are you?"

Marie-Thérèse nearly jumped as he came up behind her. "Mathieu!"

"Were you expecting someone else?"

"No, you just startled me."

He grinned. "Good. I like to keep you on your toes."

Marie-Thérèse felt relieved. They were still friends, even after last night's fiasco. She didn't know what she would have done if he hadn't been here.

They opened their mailboxes and scanned through their mail. "So how's Josette?" Mathieu asked.

"She was sleeping when I left this morning. I hope she got to her first class all right."

"Well, she seems to enjoy design, so I'll bet she went."

Marie-Thérèse nodded absently as she focused on the letters in her box. "Hey, a letter from Pauline!" She tore it open and scanned the first line. "Listen to this!"

" 'Things are going better here than you might guess. I have to confess—I think I'm in love. His name in Emeri Fauré, and he has blond hair and a smile that makes me want to laugh. I met him at the AIDS clinic. He comes for the support group like I do. He's not a member of the Church, but I'm working on him. We talk a lot about God and dying, but it doesn't make me sad. I just realize how lucky I am to have been born in the Church and have the truth of the gospel. Emeri is so afraid of dying, but I know where I'm going after this life. It makes a huge difference.' "

"How lucky she is?" Mathieu commented quietly. "How can she be so positive?"

"She's always that way." Yet Marie-Thérèse also wondered how Pauline could always be so happy. If someone asked her to describe her little sister in one word, she would say *sunshine*.

"I'm glad she found someone," Mathieu said. "She deserves it."

Marie-Thérèse found herself agreeing. It was good to have a relationship with a man who had common interests and challenges. Like with Mathieu. She swallowed hard and felt her face coloring, but he didn't appear to notice.

"Here's the rest," Marie-Thérèse said, focusing on the letter.

" 'Emeri and André play basketball a lot, and we've taken to going out to eat afterward. André insists on coming with us and we let him. I think he likes Emeri. I haven't introduced Emeri to Mom and Dad yet. He doesn't have any contact with his own parents, and he's nervous about meeting mine. I'm also worried about what they might say when they learn that he's more than just a friend. He doesn't get along well with most people, but he's very special to me, and I think they'll see that—if he finally agrees to meet them.

Well, since I'm mailing this early, you should get this letter and card long before your birthday. Hope it's a nice one. We'll see you next month. Say hi to Josette for me. Love, Pauline.'"

"I can't wait to meet her again," Mathieu said. "When I saw her at my cousin's baptism, she was just a little thing, but full of life, if I remember correctly. Wasn't it she who—"

"Threw the punch on Marc?" finished Marie-Thérèse with a laugh. "Yes, but he deserved it—he kept tying her ponytails in knots. That really was funny." She sobered. "There's something different about her letters now, but I can't really pinpoint what."

"Because she's in love?" Mathieu suggested.

"I don't think it's that. It's more of a resignation."

"Do you think she's become sicker?"

"I worry about that. I mean, all she ever talks about in her letters is her support meetings and the family. She doesn't even mention school or hiking or any of the activities she used to be involved in. If she's pulled out of all that now, it wouldn't be a good sign."

Several girls came to the mailboxes, and Mathieu took her arm and led her down the sidewalk. "You don't think your parents would hide anything from you, do you?"

"Not really, but then they've also been worried about Josette. Perhaps they're balancing out the two. You know, seeing where I'm needed the most." Marie-Thérèse sighed. "Pauline's one of the reasons I'm so anxious to get home."

"What about your mission?"

Marie-Thérèse's step faltered. "I don't know. I have to believe she'll be all right." She gazed at Mathieu and saw concern in his face. "Thank you for caring," she said, her voice falling to a whisper. "I've never told anyone before, but that's one of the things that really bothers me about serving a mission. I need to be there for Pauline, if something should happen. The rest of my family is important to me, but Pauline is all I have left of my real parents—I mean my birth parents." She shook her head impatiently. "It always bothers me when I hear adopted people talk about their 'real parents.' I mean, real parents are those who've sat up with you when you were sick, who explained the gospel and life, who took pictures when you went on your first date. You know what I mean. But despite all that, Pauline is my blood sister, and I feel a special bond with her."

"I think I understand a little," Mathieu said. "I always wished I had someone like that. A brother." Mathieu put an arm around her. Marie-Thérèse knew it was meant for comfort, but her heart betrayed her with its rapid thumping.

"I wish everyone would just say what's really going on and not try to protect anyone," she said.

Before the words came out, she didn't realize they were partly meant for Mathieu. Why didn't he tell her how he felt? But then, what did she expect? She'd made it all too clear that she wanted to serve a mission, and he could do nothing but respect her wishes. That was the kind of man he was. So maybe the real question lay with her. What did she really want?

Chapter Eighteen

"We need to try a different series of treatments," Dr. Medard said. "What we're doing isn't working anymore."

Pauline had known it would happen, and the words shouldn't affect her so strongly, yet they did. She brought her hand up to her hair, and Dr. Medard saw the motion. "Yes, I'm afraid this time you'll lose your hair completely."

"It'll grow back," her mother said. "What's important is that this treatment gets rid of the tumor."

All Pauline's fears came to the surface. She leapt to her feet. "My hair won't ever grow back! It won't! I'm not getting better!" Her voice changed to a quiet desperation. "Why won't either of you admit that?" Without another word, Pauline ran for the door. She made it down the hall past the nurses and to the bathroom before she crumpled into a sobbing heap. *Emeri*, she thought. *I need you!* He at least would be honest.

After a while, she heard someone come into the bathroom and knew without looking that it was her mother. Ariana said nothing, but came and sat on the floor next to Pauline. "Can I help?"

"I'm sorry, Mom." Pauline gulped for air. "I didn't sleep well, and I didn't eat much breakfast. I—"

"It's all right." Ariana put her arms around Pauline and held her tightly. "You don't have to pretend around me, Pauline. I know you're afraid. I'm afraid, too."

Pauline pressed her face into her mother's chest. It felt so good to be held and rocked as though she were a baby. In her mother's arms, nothing could touch or hurt her. Or it seemed that way.

"Sometimes I wish I could just die and get it over with," Pauline said. "I'm tired of seeing you hurt, of feeling my body so weak. I'm tired of . . ." Her voice trailed off.

"Of being afraid."

Pauline hiccupped. "You knew?"

"Of course I knew. How could you not be afraid?"

"Oh, Mom!" Pauline poured out her heart to her mother, telling her all the things she'd only told Emeri. Ariana didn't try to push her fears away or explain them, she simply listened. It was exactly what Pauline needed. Pauline already knew the answers. What she needed from her mother was love and understanding— and to be held and comforted.

"I love you so much," Ariana whispered.

Pauline smiled. "I love you, too."

Pauline leaned against the wall surrounding the edge of the Eiffel Tower, feeling the light breeze blow through the hair sticking out from under her hat. Below, she could see the Seine River and tiny people who seemed almost inhuman as they scurried about their daily activities. Beside her Emeri was silent, caught up in his own thoughts.

It was their first outing completely alone. Emeri had been urging her to go with him for some time now, but she'd been afraid. Of what? Her feelings for him? Of needing him too much? Both concerns were moot because she already needed him. She already cared.

She glanced over at Emeri and saw the vulnerability in his face. No one else could see it, except André, perhaps, and only then on occasion. She stepped closer to Emeri until her arm touched his. He smiled and she felt content. His features were so familiar to her that she could shut her eyes and recall every detail. His hair had grown longer but was still short enough to please even her parents if he would agree to meet them. His eyes made her want to stare at him forever.

Without warning, Emeri stroked her hair. He hadn't tried to touch her since the support meeting when she'd confessed her fears, and the act surprised her. "It's good to be alone with you," he said in a low voice.

Pauline winced as she saw a few strands of hair come away in his hand. Her hair had thinned so much in the past week that she'd self-consciously begun wearing a hat every time she saw Emeri. He twirled the dark hair in his hands, refusing to meet her eyes.

"I'm getting a wig," she said brightly, gently tucking the rest of her hair up into her hat.

"Cancer!" Emeri spit the word out like a bit of phlegm.

"AIDS," she corrected automatically. "The cancer is just one of the opportunistic diseases." She felt stupid as she said it. Emeri knew the process as well as she did.

Emeri grabbed her and pulled her close, holding her so tightly that she found it difficult to breathe. He didn't say anything, he simply held her.

"I'm sorry, Emeri. Say something. Are you okay?"

She felt his chest heave several times before he spoke. "I didn't care about dying. I didn't care about any of it." There were rough, unshed tears in his voice now and self-disdain as well. "Until I met you. I lived in the dark, but you're like the sun. Oh, dear God, there's no reason to this insanity!"

Pauline felt the pain in his words and wondered how long it had been since anyone had loved him as she was beginning to. She hugged him back with all her strength. "I know this doesn't make much sense now, but I know God loves us both."

He drew away, blinking quickly, his face drawn tight. "How can you say that? After what He's done?" He beat his fists helplessly at the low wall in front of them.

Pauline forced herself to answer calmly. The fact that Emeri was talking about God as a real Being was progress from the abrupt denial he'd expressed at that first support meeting. "We've talked about this before. He didn't do this to me. My mom made a bad choice when she was young, that's all. She tried to make amends. She even gave up months of her own life so I could be born."

"Into this?" Emeri scoffed. "What kind of a life is this?"

"Well, I've enjoyed a lot of years. I'm glad she didn't abort me." Pauline made a sweeping motion around her. "Emeri, there's so much more to life than what's here. Sure, there's a lot of pain and sadness where you and I are coming from, but we can still enjoy this life and plan for the next."

Emeri clenched his teeth. "I can't believe that. I won't."

"Why?"

He said nothing for a long time. "I don't want to hurt you, Pauline, but I believe religion is a crutch for people who can't face reality. Life is bad, so we'll wait for the next one. What a da—what a joke! Well, I don't want to wait for some pipe dream, Pauline. I want to act now! I want to feel! I want to . . ." He broke off and pulled her close again and kissed her, long and searchingly.

Pauline didn't have time to be surprised at her own reaction to this, her first real kiss, or to worry that she wasn't doing it right. All she wanted was for Emeri to keep kissing her. His mouth turned gentle, caressing, spreading a sweet warmth throughout her body. No wonder her parents had cautioned so strongly about physical intimacy. She was flying!

Emeri stopped kissing her, but he didn't remove his arms. They stood, cheek to cheek, ignoring the tourists who'd also come to see the Eiffel Tower. Pauline felt dampness on her face and knew that Emeri was crying.

"Oh, Sunshine," he whispered. "I want to live. Before I met you, I thought I didn't care. But now I want to live."

"So do I." Tears squeezed out of Pauline's eyes and trickled down her cheeks.

"Is something wrong?" her mother asked when Pauline arrived at the apartment. Emeri, of course, had refused to come up in case he might run into her parents.

"It's Emeri." Pauline saw the concern in Ariana's face and hastened to reassure her mother. "I think he's beginning to see that maybe I'm right about God, but I don't like seeing him hurt. Why would believing make us—him, I mean—feel bad?"

Ariana took her hands. "The truth does that sometimes. When you realize, for example, that love can be eternal, it becomes more important than it was before. So much more hinges on working thing out, on growing and changing together. Hope can be painful without real faith. It's like seeing a treasure in front of you but never being able to hold or use it."

Pauline frowned. "I wish Emeri could believe. It's so easy."

"No, it's not, Pauline," Ariana said. "If Emeri has to admit that you're right, he'll have to let go of years of bitterness and pain. From what you and André tell me, I think that's what he's hiding behind. That can be pretty scary for anyone."

"So if he gets rid of that, he'll have to face the truth straight on? Like we do. Knowing that God loves me and still can let me . . ." Pauline saw the sadness in her mother's eyes and couldn't complete the sentence, despite the new openness they shared. She wondered if her mother's hope was something akin to the wall of bitterness Emeri had built around himself. But no, hope was not a surrender to the inevitable. It was a strength, a catapult to faith. Pauline felt like crying again. "Did you ever see something in someone that nobody else did?"

Ariana's eyes took on a faraway look. "Oh, yes."

"Did he change?"

"Yes, but it took a long time. And it was much too late to affect our relationship. But that doesn't have anything to do with what might happen to Emeri. Your life has been full of miracles, and I have no doubt they will continue."

Miracle baby. Miracle child. Miracle healing. If that was true, then her Heavenly Father would at least guide her to help Emeri. "Thanks, Mom." Pauline went to her own room and lay on her bed. With relish, she recalled each detail of her afternoon with Emeri. For the first time in her life, she knew she was in love.

Chapter Nineteen

The day of Marie-Thérèse's twenty-first birthday came with bright sunlight and no gray clouds. Outside, the air was crisp and clean. She pulled off her mittens to open the mailbox with the tiny key. Inside was a small stack of letters. Eagerly, she searched through the junk mail and found two more birthday cards from friends and a letter from Marc.

She looked around for Mathieu, missing him. Why wasn't he here? It had been more than a week since their kiss, and things had seemed to return to normal—if you could count how his presence affected her as normal. Occasionally one of them would miss their daily two-minute rendezvous, but surely he wouldn't have made other plans on her birthday. She lingered for a few moments before walking back to the apartment alone.

"Josette, get up!" she called as she walked in the door of their room. "Marc wrote to me."

"It's Saturday," Josette whined. "Even Rosellen is still sleeping."

"Is not. She went to the library this morning. It's almost eleven. Brionney will be here for her lesson."

Josette pulled herself to a sitting position, her hair spilling everywhere. "Marc hasn't written me for two months."

"Well, when's the last time you wrote to him?" Marie-Thérèse ripped open the envelope. Inside was a birthday card and a hastily written letter. Josette scooted close on the bed to read with her.

Dear Sisters,

I'm writing to you both even though you've neglected me horribly. What's going on at that university anyway? Do you both have too much homework or too many boyfriends that you have to ignore your poor, hardworking brother?

Can you believe we're finally going to have some baptisms? Six to be exact. My first in over six months of diligent work and lots of prayer. After hearing so many times about a golden family, we actually found one ourselves. Incredible! I was beginning to think golden families were a myth, something they only told us about in the MTC to keep us going. I was wrong. By the time you get this letter, they will have been baptized—a dad, a mom, three boys, and a grandmother! There's one more, little Sofia, but she's too young to be baptized yet.

But I'll tell you, even though they're golden, it has been a rough seven weeks. Pedro lost his job, their car broke down, and Sofia had to have an emergency appendectomy. Instead of these trials having weakened their faith, they've only caused the Leandros to grow closer to the church members and to the Lord. When we were at the hospital giving Sofia a blessing, Pedro said to me, "You know, even if the whole world were destroyed and there was no branch of the Church in France, I would keep studying the Book of Mormon in my home with my family." Can you believe that? I can't even tell you how much it meant to me and how much I love them. The Lord has blessed me by letting me be part of their conversion.

If there is to be any credit to us for finding this family, it should go to my junior companion, who's a spiritual giant, so to speak. Elder Fields is incredible, and I'll be sorry when we're separated. It should be soon, because he is more than ready to be a trainer himself.

Well, I don't have anything else to say, except behave your-
selves. Oh yeah, my companion is glad you're teaching his sister
French. He got a letter one of you must have helped her write,
and it was all in French. He says he's going to start writing to
her in French, too. By the way, she writes him every week—
which is a lot more faithful than two sisters I know.

Take care. I love you both. I'll try to write at Christmas.
Love, Marc

After she finished the letter, Marie-Thérèse found herself
looking forward to her own mission with a fervor she hadn't felt
since Mathieu's kiss. How wonderful it would be to help people
find the truth. To make an eternal difference in another person's
life. Yearning filled her soul.

"I'm going to finish filling out my mission application online,"
she said, deciding suddenly. She had the physical and everything
else she needed. What had she been waiting for? This letter was
certainly the answer to her prayers.

What about Mathieu? a voice inside her asked.

What about him? she thought. *He knows I've always planned to*
go on a mission. He understands. It's not as if we're in love or anything.
We're just friends.

Forcing thoughts of Mathieu aside, she said to Josette, "Just
think! By January I could be serving a real mission. Maybe I'll
even be called to the same mission as Marc, and get to serve a few
months with him before he finishes in April."

"That's great." Josette sounded bored. "Mom and Dad will be
proud of you both." She arose and wandered into the kitchen.

Marie-Thérèse thought of her birth parents, and knew they
would also be proud of her decision. Her father had faithfully
filled two years of missionary service, setting the example for
his younger brother and sister who later served missions of their
own. As a convert, her mother hadn't had a chance to go on a

mission, but after her marriage she had helped many people join the Church. Marie-Thérèse could almost feel her presence near, as she had at many times during her life. She had no doubt who her guardian angel was.

"Marie-Thérèse," Josette called from the kitchen. "Marie-Thérèse, how many times do I have to call you? Marc's letter isn't good enough to sit and stare at all day. Hurry up! Mathieu's on the phone. He wants to borrow some flour. He says he's in the middle of a project and wants to know if you'll run it over. I can't because I've got to wait for Brionney."

Marie-Thérèse jumped to her feet and ran to the kitchen, vaguely recalling something Mathieu had said last week about a project. "What's this I hear?" she said into the phone. "You want to borrow something, *and* you want me to bring it over?"

"Please," Mathieu said, amusement thick in his voice. "I'm right in the middle of a project, and I can't leave. Just bring as much flour as you've got."

"Okay, lazybones, I'll be right there. But you owe me."

"Anything you want."

His voice this time came across gruff, devoid of any lightheartedness, and Marie-Thérèse didn't know what to say. "Uh, g'bye."

"Wait! Got any salt?"

"How much do you need?"

"All of it. I'll replace it. Please, hurry!"

"Aye, aye, captain." Marie-Thérèse hung up the phone and gathered the items in a plastic bag.

"What about your mission application?" Josette asked.

"I'll do it when I get back, but would you call the executive secretary for me? Please? Just this once? The bishop wanted to meet with me one more time before he sends my application on to the stake president."

"The executive secretary? He's the one with the cute new haircut, isn't he?"

"Yes. Will you call him? I want an appointment for any time tomorrow if the bishop has time."

"Sure. Better get going. Mathieu sounded desperate."

With a wave, Marie-Thérèse hurried to the door where she met Brionney. "Bonjour," Marie-Thérèse said.

"Bonjour." Brionney's round face dimpled. She twirled a set of car keys on her hand, announcing to the world that she was finally a driver. Her sixteenth birthday had been the month before, but Marie-Thérèse knew that today was her first time driving alone to her lesson.

Marie-Thérèse hid a smile, remembering when she'd received her own driver's license at eighteen. She'd been excited—until she realized that Paris wasn't exactly the easiest place to drive a car. Now she preferred using the metro.

An incredible disaster confronted Marie-Thérèse when she arrived at Mathieu's apartment. Flour sprinkled the floor, and bits of a doughy mixture were ground into the linoleum by Mathieu's bare feet, which were also covered with flour. Behind him, the sink was full of dirty pans and bowls containing remnants of different colored doughs.

"I thought I had enough stuff," Mathieu said sheepishly. "But I spilled a little flour . . ."

"A little?"

"And it's taking more dough than I thought. Come and see." He shut the door and ushered her in. Now she saw the "project," which sat on the floor in the place of the oblong table that usually graced that part of the kitchen. The foot-high structure was three feet long and two feet wide. He stared at it with reverence.

"What is it?" she asked.

"What do you mean?" he said, feigning hurt. "Can't you see that this is one land mass here, and this is another? The plates they're on are colliding, and this land mass is being pushed under and turned into a liquid because of the intense heat. These new mountains are forming because of the pressure. See? Well, you will.

As soon as I get some more dough cooked up. Meanwhile, see what you can do to straighten the mountains before they dry." He pushed at the lopsided mountains with his dough-caked fingers.

"Here, let me do it." Marie-Thérèse sat on the floor and began to shape the mountains, using a picture from a book Mathieu had propped up against the wall as a model. Now that she studied it, she could see Mathieu's project was very detailed. He'd painstakingly portrayed layer upon layer of geologic time, and in different colors to show the contrast. All that was really missing was the landscaping on the top layer and the budding mountains.

"So much dough," she muttered.

"Not really. The middle has a Styrofoam base." He stared at her oddly, but Marie-Thérèse didn't understand why. She turned back to the mountains. There was something strange about the one closest to her. It was as if it had something hard inside—perhaps dried-up clay. She squeezed hard and felt it break away.

"You've got someth—" She stared at the shape, her heart nearly stopping. It was thick and round with a hole through the middle and a large, dough-covered gem sticking out from one side. Joy burst through her like a firecracker exploding in the dark. Mathieu loved her. *Her*!

Marie-Thérèse remembered to breathe. Involuntarily, she twisted toward Mathieu who stood at the stove, his clothes dusted white, an enigmatic expression on his face. Neither said anything for a long moment, and then Mathieu approached and sat beside her on the floor.

"I know you want to go on a mission," he said. "But I want you to know there's another option. Like you said last week in relation to your parents and Pauline, I think it's long past time that I stop fooling myself and tell things like they really are."

With his words, reality set in. "But—"

He put a gentle finger to her mouth, and she smelled the dough on his hand before he pulled it away. "I've tried to distance myself," he said. "I've tried to date other women. But I love you,

Marie-Thérèse. Only you. I think we could make something of our relationship. Won't you think about it? Pray about it?" His face was earnest and so utterly loving that Marie-Thérèse would have given almost anything to fall into his arms and accept his proposal.

Almost anything.

"I care about you," she said, "but I need to go on a mission. All my life I've dreamed about going, about making an eternal difference in someone's life."

"You'd be making that kind of a difference in my life."

"You know what I mean. You've been on a mission. You've seen people's lives change."

"I have," he agreed, "and I had never felt more joy in my life—until I fell in love with you."

Marie-Thérèse's mind was a mass of confusion. His love exhilarated her, but . . . there was that little word between them. She cared about Mathieu—she wouldn't admit even to herself that it might be love, because then she would commit herself—*but* all her plans pulled her in another direction.

"I could wait for you, if that's what you want."

Marie-Thérèse was tempted, but was that fair to Mathieu? He'd talked many times of having a family, and she knew he was ready to move on with his life. She had no right to encourage him unless she could pledge her love and forego her mission. "That's not fair to you."

He inclined his head, showing he understood and even agreed. She believed he loved her, but without time to develop that love, another woman might be able to take her place. In fact, it was all too likely. She'd seen it over and over with the members of her stake. If she went on a mission, there was no guarantee Mathieu would be available when she returned. He would find another woman, and she would have to find another man. She'd always believed there were many good companions to choose from with whom she could find equal happiness—but then why did her heart hunger so for Mathieu? What if what they had was the once-in-a-lifetime kind of love?

Love? Was that what it really was? The kind her parents shared? Why did she feel like crying and singing at once?

"You don't have to answer now," he said, seeing her indecision. "Talk to the bishop, if you want. Pray about it."

Her tongue ran over her lips, tasting the trace of salt his finger had left. His eyes followed the movement, and for a moment she thought he might kiss her. When he didn't, she offered him the ring, still partially covered in dough.

"Keep it," he said, coming to his feet, "until you decide for sure. It was my grandmother's diamond. I had it set in a new band after my mission. I felt I came to BYU to find my wife, but I have to admit I was a little reluctant because I didn't want to end up staying here." He chuckled softly. "Little did I know I'd meet a French woman. I guess I should have asked you all those years ago at my cousin's baptism. Did you know I had a crush on you then?" She shook her head wordlessly. "Well, it's true. But you were only sixteen and I told myself I was too old for you." He watched her for a silent moment before sauntering back to the stove where the water boiled madly.

Marie-Thérèse turned back to work on the mountains, clutching the ring between the palm and the two smallest fingers of her right hand. She'd been completely taken with Mathieu when she was sixteen. If she'd known he had felt the same way, things between them now might have been very different. She would have had the last four years to write to him, to get to know him, and to become accustomed to the idea of being a wife instead of serving a mission.

But I want to serve a mission! she insisted. *I won't give that up.*

A short time later, Mathieu returned to her side with a batch of the salty dough. He divided it into two, added green and brown coloring, and began to landscape the hillside. "I have some little trees I bought," he said, waving at the counter top. "You want to put them on?" His voice sounded normal, as if nothing had occurred between them, but his brow furrowed every time he glanced her way.

"Okay." First she went to the sink and washed the ring he had given her. It was beautiful, catching the light from the kitchen window and reflecting it in every direction. Without thinking, she slipped the thick band of gold onto her ring finger. It was slightly large, but its beauty made her reluctant to take it off.

"There's a box for the ring inside the cupboard," Mathieu said without turning from his project.

Firmly, she put the ring in the box and snapped it shut. Placing it on the counter, she picked up the package of trees.

They worked for another hour before Mathieu was satisfied. He sat back on his heels and sighed. "Thanks. I couldn't have done it without you. Those chocolate shavings really look like fallen bark, and the green coconut for grass works better than the clay. Where do you learn those things?"

She shrugged. "Around. Your mountain looks great. I like the cave you added."

"I hope it all gets a good grade." He glanced at his watch. "I didn't realize it was so late. I'm sorry I kept you so long."

"That's okay. I had nothing else to do." She remembered his proposal and felt her face color. With all her freckles, her cheeks must look like brown and red splotches. Whatever did he see in her?

"If you'll give me a chance to change, I'll take you out to lunch."

She glanced down at her own flour-spotted jeans. "I need to change too. How about I meet you in fifteen minutes?"

"It'll only take me five," he said quickly. "Wait for me, okay? I need to talk with Josette anyway."

Marie-Thérèse wanted to ask why. Was he preparing to court her sister if she didn't accept his proposal? Or was he going to tell Josette about their relationship?

What relationship? her mind said.

Mathieu darted into his bedroom. Marie-Thérèse scarcely had time to put the ring box in her pocket before he returned. She forced a smile. "You have dough in your hair."

"You do too." They began to remove the clay, but abruptly stopped, their hands falling to their sides. They stood close together without moving. Marie-Thérèse's breath quickened and all sorts of crazy ideas raced through her head.

Making a monumental effort, she turned away and said lightly, "I'll race you." She was out the door before she'd finished, with Mathieu not far behind.

They arrived laughing at her apartment door, their chests heaving. Mathieu bowed. "I concede the tie to you," he said, motioning for her to open the door.

"Concede, nothing! I beat you fair and square." She turned the knob and pushed into the apartment.

"Surprise!" Shouts echoed through the room as Marie-Thérèse stared into the many faces of her friends.

Josette beamed. "Happy birthday, my dear sister." She glared at Mathieu. "You took long enough. We were just about to start thinking that you—how do you Americans say it?—yes, eloped or something!" Her expression showed she was joking, but her guess was too close for comfort.

Josette put one of her arms through Marie-Thérèse's and the other through Mathieu's. "Come on, your cake is in here. Sandwiches, too. Brionney and I had a busy morning."

It was a wonderful surprise and the best birthday party in a long time. Only one thing marred Marie-Thérèse's enjoyment. As she opened Josette's gift, the triple combination she'd been wanting, her sister cocked her head and announced in awkward English, "These are for Marie-Thérèse to use when she goes to her mission. I purchased some for my brother before his mission and now for her. Guess what? She is going to submit her application today, and this morning I made appointment with the bishop—for her!"

Everyone clapped and gave their congratulations, but Marie-Thérèse saw the misery in Mathieu's eyes. She wanted to strangle Josette. Too bad she spoke English well enough to be understood at all.

"There's one more present," Mathieu said, pulling something out of his pocket.

"But—"

"This is your birthday present." He thrust the little oblong box in her hand.

Of course—the engagement ring wasn't her present, but something else altogether. She tore off the wrapper. Inside the box was a thick herringbone bracelet in 14 karat gold. "But Mathieu, you can't afford this!"

"Don't worry about it. My credit is good and I'm working. I wanted to get it for you."

"Mathieu is almost graduated," Josette added. "Then he will make lots of money. Say thank you and be happy."

"Thank you," Marie-Thérèse echoed. "It really is beautiful."

"It's for you to remember me," he said in French, so low that only Marie-Thérèse heard the words.

Josette fingered the bracelet. "I like it very much, Mathieu. You come to my birthday next year in France, no?"

Everyone laughed again, and Josette swaggered with the attention. The cake and other goodies were nearly gone, but Josette had an idea. "What if we go swimming? The pool is fixed, I think."

"It's fixed," said Rosellen. "I went yesterday."

"After we can get videos to watch," Noni suggested. "Let's make a whole day of it."

"Good idea!" shouted Josette. "Everybody go to the pool. Tonight—more party!"

"Bring your favorite snack for tonight!" Noni added as the guests filed out the door.

"I'll go pick up the videos now," Mathieu said. "We'll have a better choice if we don't wait. Any suggestions?" Almost everyone had some. Two guys decided to go with him to help choose.

Marie-Thérèse watched everyone leave. "Aren't you coming?" Josette asked.

"I'll be down in a minute," she replied. "I just want to put my things away."

Josette nodded and was gone. Marie-Thérèse laid her head on the kitchen table and shut her eyes, uncertain how she should feel. "Are you all right?" asked a voice from the doorway.

She lifted her head. "Brionney. I thought you'd gone with the others."

The younger girl made a face. "I don't like to swim much. I feel too awkward. Fat, I guess."

"You're very pretty," Marie-Thérèse said.

Brionney shrugged and remained silent. Marie-Thérèse arose from the table, feeling uncomfortable under her stare.

"It's Mathieu, isn't it?" Brionney said.

Marie-Thérèse sat down again. "How did you know?"

Brionney sat down next to her. "I see the way he looks at you. I've known for a long time how he feels about you going on a mission. He goes quiet every time anyone mentions it."

"He never said anything."

"Lots of things don't need to be said."

Marie-Thérèse retrieved the ring box from her pocket. "He asked me to marry him."

Brionney opened the box and exclaimed. "Oh, how beautiful! And big. I didn't think college students could afford stuff like this."

"The diamond was his grandmother's."

The girl squealed. "How romantic. Why don't you wear it?"

"I haven't accepted." Marie-Thérèse felt her face droop. "I want to go on a mission. I've wanted to since I was very young. How can I give that up?"

"Your first duty is to get married." Brionney's face clearly showed she didn't understand Marie-Thérèse's priorities.

"But I have felt so strongly that I should go on a mission." *I've planned for it,* she added silently. Was rigidly adhering to a lifetime plan a sin?

"What if you don't marry him?" Brionney asked, looking glum.

"Then he'll marry someone else." Marie-Thérèse's heart ached at the thought. "I can't ask him to wait for me. It wouldn't be right."

"I'd ask," Brionney said, trying on the ring.

Marie-Thérèse sighed. Brionney was young and there was no way she could understand. "There are many worthy people to choose from," she said.

"Maybe, but Mathieu's special. I wish I were older and skinnier. Maybe he'd like me."

"He likes you now."

"As a friend," groaned Brionney. "The story of my life."

Marie-Thérèse took the ring from her, avoiding the temptation to put it on her finger. She placed it gently in the box and snapped the cover shut. "I'm going to change into my suit," she said, pushing her chair back from the table.

The rest of the evening, she and Mathieu had no time for private talk. Marie-Thérèse felt torn between relief and agony.

"What's up?" Josette asked after they kicked everyone out just before midnight.

"I'm nervous, I guess," she said, surprised that her sister had noticed her anxiety.

Josette pulled her nightshirt over her head and fished her hair out of the back. It had grown longer than Marie-Thérèse had ever seen it, nearly long enough to sit on. "About your mission? Well, don't worry. I know you'll be great at it. You're good at anything you set your mind to. And I'm proud of you."

Josette's display of faith only made Marie-Thérèse feel worse. She felt as if she were on a seesaw, constantly wavering back and forth between her planned future and the enticing surprise she'd found in Mathieu.

"Do I love him?" She asked the question of herself and the Lord many times that night, falling asleep on her knees as she prayed against the side of her bed.

The next afternoon, Bishop Denney awaited Marie-Thérèse with a warm smile. "I expected you before this. You were so anxious to serve a mission."

"Well, I cannot go until January," she said, taking the seat he indicated.

"That only leaves a little over a month and often you won't actually leave for up to three months after receiving the call. But I looked over the application and everything seems in order. You'll need to meet with the stake president, of course. I've already told him about you, and he's expecting your call."

Marie-Thérèse thought he seemed too jovial for the turmoil inside her. She started to speak but found she had no voice.

"Is something wrong?" he asked.

Marie-Thérèse said nothing. Bishop Denney waited, but when she volunteered no information, he spoke again, "Are you sure about wanting to go on a mission? Has something changed?"

She lifted her eyes from the gray marbled carpet and met his probing gaze. "I want to go on a mission," she said, choosing her next words carefully. "It is just that . . . a man I care about wants to marry me. His name is Mathieu, and he is from my country."

The bishop chuckled, though she could see no amusement in the situation. "Is he a member? Can he take you through the temple? Do you love him?" She nodded at the first two questions, but hesitated at the last.

"I don't know!" She stood and began to pace. "How can one decide to be married for the rest of eternity? That is so . . . so scary! What if things don't work out?"

Bishop Denney's eyebrows knit in concern. "As long as two people love each other and put the Lord first and then each other above all else, a marriage will be successful. Most of it's give and take . . . and talking problems out before they become unsurmountable.

I feel you're a person who would work hard to make your marriage work. Is Mathieu?"

He was . . . or at least Marie-Thérèse thought so. "But this is the only opportunity I have to serve a mission while I am young," she said. "My whole life I have dreamed of it." She paused before rushing on, knowing that in her distress, her French accent made her English difficult to understand. "You said I could make a marriage work. It does not have to be with Mathieu, no? I could wait."

The bishop inclined his head gravely, but a small smile played on his lips. "I think the question here is what does the Lord want you to do? Are you willing to accept His counsel?"

"Oh, yes. But I do not get an answer. At least one that I understand." She sat back in her seat. "What do you think?"

"Only you can decide."

Marie-Thérèse looked up at the ceiling. "I wish I didn't want to marry Mathieu so much. Or that I didn't feel I should go on a mission. I don't know which to choose! I wish there was some way to know for sure. I wish I could go somewhere special and ask the Lord."

"You can go anywhere to ask Him those questions. As a daughter of our Heavenly Father, you deserve to receive revelation in any quiet place you seek it. You can know for sure."

Marie-Thérèse felt tears coursing down her cheeks. "But I am not feeling anything. All night I prayed in my room. I have walked outside alone, asking Him over and over. Today, I stayed in church and prayed. For more than a month I have been struggling with submitting my application. I have not done it before now because of Mathieu, but I did not want to admit it even to myself. I do not know what to do! This decision will affect the rest of my life, and Mathieu's life as well. I need help. Please?" Marie-Thérèse could barely form the words through her sobs. In a rush, she continued, "Last night when I was praying, I kept thinking that if only I could go to the temple, I would be able to hear the Lord there."

"You can hear the Lord anywhere," the bishop said gently, handing her a tissue from the box on his desk.

"I know that, but . . . the temple is sacred. Maybe there I could separate my carnal feelings and listen only to the Spirit. Please, is there any way I could go through the temple?"

Bishop Denney thought for a long time. "Maybe," he said slowly, "there is a possibility. I'll have to talk it over with the stake president. Normally we don't give recommends to people unless they are getting married or going on a mission—"

"But I am planning to get married or go on a mission."

"I realize that. Since you are serious about doing one or the other, I think perhaps we can make an exception in your case and let you go through. I mean, if the stake president sent your application along to Salt Lake, you would get your call in a couple weeks and go through the temple anyway. Regardless, going even such a short time early should not be taken lightly. Once you make covenants in the temple with the Lord, there is that much more danger should you fail to keep the promises made there. There is nothing Satan loves more than to cause someone to break their temple covenants."

Marie-Thérèse's tears had ceased with the hope of attending the temple. "All of my life I have been taught how important the temple is. I would rather die than betray any covenants I will make with the Lord."

The bishop smiled. "I know that. I wouldn't even be considering letting you go through if I hadn't come to know you so well these past months. I believe you've prayed as fervently as you say, and perhaps this is the beginning of an answer for you."

After discussing the temple in much more detail, Bishop Denney went with her to see the stake president, who was interviewing down the hall. Marie-Thérèse left them with a temple recommend secured tightly in her hand, silently thanking the Lord for the opportunity to visit His house.

Darkness had fallen during the hours she'd been with the

bishop and stake president. She'd called from the bishop's office to tell Josette she would be late, so she knew her sister wouldn't be worried or waiting up for her. She certainly didn't expect to find Mathieu pacing outside her apartment building.

"I talked to Josette," he said without preamble. "She told me where you were. Did you . . . I mean . . . your application . . ." His face showed anxiety mixed with hope.

"The bishop's going to hold on to it for a while before sending it on to the stake president. Until I make a decision."

The trepidation in Mathieu's eyes decreased. "Then I guess I'm still in the running."

"Oh, Mathieu, don't say it that way. If I would marry anyone now, it would be you. I just have to be sure." She held up the recommend. "I'm going to the temple to help me decide."

"Can I go with you?" he asked.

She smiled through her tears. "I would like that."

He hugged her briefly before quickly stepping away. "I'll try to behave myself, Marie-Thérèse, but you are so beautiful that I want to kiss you and never stop. But I'm not going to even give you a small kiss until . . ." He backed away as he spoke. "It's hard enough as it is." With that he turned and faded into the night. Marie-Thérèse watched after him, feeling better than she'd felt in months.

Chapter Twenty

Ariana listened on the phone as Marie-Thérèse explained the situation between her and Mathieu Portier. *My little girl's in love!* Ariana thought. She could hear it in her voice and in the way she tried so hard to deny it. Ariana also knew she needed to encourage her daughter without making her choice for her. The only way Marie-Thérèse could find happiness was to know for herself that what she was doing was right.

"Going to the temple is a good idea," Ariana said. "I would really like to be there to go through with you, but I can't leave right now."

"Oh, I didn't expect you to come all this way, but I wanted your blessing."

"You have it, of course. I just wish I could be there."

The silence lengthened before Marie-Thérèse asked. "Is it Pauline?"

Ariana bit her lip, grateful Marie-Thérèse couldn't see her expression. "Yes," she said carefully. "She's been sick, but don't worry too much. We've got her on a new program that seems to be working. We'll keep you informed. Meanwhile, you work on making your decision. Your father and I will be fasting and praying for you. Everyone here will."

"I'd actually like this to be kept kind of a secret, if you don't mind," Marie-Thérèse said. "You can tell Dad, of course. But either way I decide, I'd like to break it to the family myself."

Ariana laughed. "We know how to keep a secret. We won't tell."

When she hung up the phone, Ariana recounted the conversation to Jean-Marc. "I can't believe it," he said. "If any of the children served a mission, I would have thought it would be Marie-Thérèse."

"Exactly what I thought. But you should have heard her voice. She really likes this Mathieu."

"I think I'll call her myself," Jean-Marc reached for the phone. "I still need to ask her the questions I ask about all Josette's dates."

Ariana smiled. "Good idea. You do that. But don't talk her out of getting married, if that's what she wants to do."

Jean-Marc summoned a wounded look. "What? Getting married was the best thing I ever did."

She kissed him. "And don't you forget it."

Leaving him to his phone call, Ariana went to check on Louis-Géralde. She found him sleeping in his bed, arms spread out in typical four-year-old abandon. She sat beside his inert figure and stroked his soft cheek, loving the feel of healthiness that radiated from him. So different from Pauline.

Should she have told Marie-Thérèse about Pauline's cancer? Maybe it was time. Tomorrow she would try to convince Pauline.

Chapter Twenty-one

Zack Fields was proud of the Leandro family and the progress they were making in the Church. Already they had callings, and the children thrived as their spirituality increased, as if their souls had found the place where they belonged. On the other hand, Madame Legrand and her daughters still vacillated.

Brionney's letter came again in French, and Zack wondered about the woman who helped her write it. The letter was friendly, so typically Brionney, and yet there was another flavor to it that he could not exactly describe. A zest for life? A longing? A vulnerability? It was all of these and more. He studied the curve of Josette's face in the picture on Elder Perrault's dresser, reaching out his finger to trace it. Instead of live flesh, it was only the slick feeling of the glossy photograph paper, which was vastly unsatisfying.

A snort behind him showed that his action hadn't gone unnoticed. Reluctantly he flipped off the light and went to bed.

When Zack slept, he saw Josette, but she was far away, almost out of sight. He felt sadness, though it was only a dream, and when he awoke in the night, the feeling stayed with him. Self-consciously, he prayed: "Please help her, Father. Please be with her."

The next day he wrote to Brionney, "Please keep an eye on Elder Perrault's sisters." He wrote in English to be sure she understood. "I have an uneasy feeling about something."

Chapter Twenty-two

"I wish I could go with you!" Josette said Tuesday afternoon after her last class.

Marie-Thérèse squeezed her arm. "I wish you could, too."

"Don't you feel awkward going without Mom and Dad?"

Her sister nodded. "I always thought I'd go through the temple with them, but this will save us the trip to Switzerland or Germany before my mission or whatever, since our temple isn't yet built."

Mission or whatever? Josette didn't understand the reference. Of late, her sister had been more reticent than usual.

"Besides, they agreed that I should ask Brionney's parents to take their place," Marie-Thérèse added.

Josette felt irritated that Marie-Thérèse had called her parents before telling her. Once they'd shared every secret, but now there seemed to be an unbridgeable gulf between them.

Brionney and her parents arrived shortly, and Marie-Thérèse ducked her head in greeting. "Thank you very much for coming, Irene."

Irene gave her a big smile. "I feel very honored to be invited, Marie-Thérèse." The way she said Marie-Thérèse's name showed she'd been practicing the pronunciation. "Terrell will be meeting us at the temple."

Brionney sat on the couch. "Well, have fun. I guess I'll hang out here since I can't go to the temple yet either. Is that okay with you, Josette?"

"I don't mind," Josette said. At least spending time with Brionney would be more fun than being alone.

"Oh, and we saw Mathieu across the way," Brionney added. "He'll be here any minute."

"He's going too?" Josette asked, not sure how she felt about that. Even as she spoke, Mathieu arrived, his gray eyes more intense than usual. He didn't greet anyone, but looked at Marie-Thérèse silently.

"What is this?" Josette quipped in what she knew was awkward English. "It is not a funeral, no?" Everyone smiled, but the mood—at least from Mathieu—didn't change.

"Happy bunch," Josette muttered as they left.

"Well, it would be a happy time," Brionney said. "If only your sister would come to her senses."

Josette tensed. "What do you mean?"

"I'm saying that poor Mathieu has a right to be worried. If Marie-Thérèse goes through the temple and still feels she should go on a mission, he knows he'll have lost her for good."

A sick feeling came to Josette's stomach. Brionney's words brought everything into sudden focus—Marie-Thérèse's strangeness, Mathieu's subtle stares and abrupt silences. He loved Marie-Thérèse, wanted to spend the rest of eternity with her, and once again Josette was just another pretty face.

She struggled valiantly for control, but Brionney gazed up at her anxiously from her seat on the couch. "Is everything okay? Didn't you know?"

"Of course I knew," Josette lied.

"Well, you'd have to be blind not to notice. How did you like the ring? That's really something."

"Yeah," Josette agreed faintly.

"It's so sweet that the diamond belonged to Mathieu's grandmother," Brionney added with a long sigh. "I wish it were me."

Josette made an unintelligible noise.

"What's wrong? You look funny," Brionney said.

"Nothing. I just have ache in my stomach." That much was true.

Brionney's brow creased with concern. "I hope you're not getting sick. You don't need that, with school and all. Maybe you should go to bed."

"I think so." Anything to get rid of peering eyes, so she could let down her guard.

"Do you want some juice or something?"

"Not really."

"Okay, then. You get some rest."

When Brionney was gone, Josette went to her room, her steps resembling those of a sleepwalker. In her mind she reviewed the conversation, refusing to believe. Yet in her sister's top drawer, tucked behind her underwear, she found the ring box. The ring fit her hand as if made for her, and she held it out to catch the light. It was large, expensive, and surely something meant for her, not Marie-Thérèse. How she would love to wear this, to show it to her friends.

An idea came to her. Maybe Mathieu turned to her sister because he thought Josette wasn't ready for marriage. "But I am," she said aloud. "And I would give up all my other boyfriends for him." She clenched her jaw. "And Marie-Thérèse wants to go on a mission. He has no right to make her give that up."

I'll show him how I feel, she thought. *Then he'll leave my sister alone, and we'll be together.*

She tried to believe her plan was good, that she wasn't considering it for selfish purposes. *Marie-Thérèse would do the same for me. She did, in fact, when we were testing Marcelin. Well, sort of.*

For a long moment, she stared at the ring on her finger. At last she put it back in the box and tucked it in Marie-Thérèse's drawer, out of sight.

Marie-Thérèse came home much later, her eyes sparkling. "Oh, it was so wonderful!" she said, sitting on the edge of her bed. "I feel like I'm fully dressed for the first time in my whole life." She met Josette's eyes. "The Church is true. I know it with all of my heart!"

Josette tried to be happy for her sister, but she resented the fact that Marie-Thérèse now held even more secrets from her. "Did you get the answer you were looking for?" she asked, as if her sister had confided in her all along. "I mean, regarding Mathieu?"

Marie-Thérèse didn't seem surprised by the question, making Josette wonder fleetingly if her sister had tried to talk with her about the choice she had to make. "No," Marie-Thérèse said with a sad smile, "but I'll go again. Maybe every day. It's so peaceful there, like heaven. I almost imagined I could see Jesus. I wish I had."

Her attitude convinced Josette that her plan was sound. Not only did her sister need to go on a mission, she would be a wonderful missionary. She couldn't let her sister marry Mathieu, only for her to regret it for the rest of her life.

The following Friday turned out to be the perfect day for Josette to enact her plan. Rosellen had gone home for the weekend, and Noni had to work. Even Marie-Thérèse made it easy for her by going to the temple after her last class.

"I'll be doing a couple of sessions this time, but I'll be home by nine or so," she said. "I've got to finish some homework."

Josette felt a twinge of guilt as her sister left the apartment, bundled up against the cold walk to the temple. "What about coming home?" she asked.

Marie-Thérèse waved the concern aside. "I have a ride."

"Mathieu?" Josette asked anxiously.

"No, Irene. She's meeting me there later."

Josette made preparations for an intimate dinner, but waited an hour before calling Mathieu to make sure her sister was really gone and that it wasn't too early to eat. The phone rang three times before he picked it up. "Oh, Mathieu," she said breathlessly, "you're home."

"Sad, isn't it? And on a Friday night, too." His voice sounded unhappy.

"Me, too. Want to have dinner with me? My treat."

He laughed. "That really would be a treat. Did somebody die and leave you a bundle?"

Josette giggled, though she was too nervous to find it funny. "No, though my test scores are good enough to convince my parents to send my allowance. Besides, you always take us places and pay."

"I'll be there in a few minutes." Mathieu hung up before Josette could tell him what she had in mind.

She changed hurriedly into the black column dress with the spaghetti straps. The sheer material hugged her body, making her feel feminine and alluring. Above her right breast, she fastened the butterfly broach Alphonse had given her that last night in France. She piled her long hair on her head, leaving a few strands down to soften her face. With mascara, she lengthened her already long lashes and used blush to enhance her cheekbones. In the mirror, her eyes peered back at her large, dark, and innocent. Mathieu didn't stand a chance.

The doorbell rang and Josette swept to the door, as regally as any noble queen. *If only Mom could see me now,* she thought.

When she opened the door, Mathieu stared around the candlelit room in surprise. "What's up?" he asked cautiously. His eyes focused on her dress and his jaw dropped.

"Like it?" She twirled for his benefit, noticing with disappointment that he wore faded jeans and a sweatshirt.

"Don't you think it's a little cold to be wearing that?"

"Not if we're staying in to eat," Josette said. "We're alone." Taking his hand, she drew him into the room.

"I thought we could go out for this," he said, shoving a coupon under her nose. BUILD YOUR OWN SPUD, it read in bold letters.

Irritation flared in Josette's heart. Didn't this idiot know when a girl was trying to create a romantic evening?

"Come on in," she invited. "I made dinner."

"Jose, I think you should change and we should go out for something," Mathieu said with a trace of panic in his voice.

She smiled. He was nervous, definitely afraid of letting her know how he felt. Well, she'd put an end to that right now. "Don't worry Mathieu." She pushed herself against him, guiding his arms around her back.

Mathieu stiffened. "I think we'd both feel better later if—"

"I love you," she blurted, sliding her arms up and around his neck.

"Marie-Thérèse—"

"Is at the temple, praying about becoming a missionary. We both know how you feel about me, so leave her out of it. I'm here, and I love you." She kissed him long and deep on the mouth, breaking off when she realized he wasn't returning the kiss. Mathieu took her arms from around his neck and pushed her gently but firmly away from him.

Shock flooded her. She'd been so sure he'd want her over Marie-Thérèse. "I'm more beautiful!" she wailed, not caring how it sounded. She lunged toward him, thinking if she could only kiss him again it would make everything right.

He held her back easily. "Stop! Think what you're doing."

"You love me," Josette insisted.

"Not that way."

"Yes, you do! I know you do. You just didn't think I was interested. Well, I am."

"But I'm not!" He paused before adding, "Look at you, all

made up like a woman in some film. Yes, you're beautiful on the outside, but inside you have no substance. You have idea who you could be—who you were meant to be. Marie-Thérèse is beautiful in here, where it counts." He thumped his chest.

"She wants to serve a mission. She won't marry you!" Josette yelled, wishing the spite in her voice could dig into his heart as his words had pierced into hers.

Mathieu snorted. "That's how little you understand. I want to marry your sister, but even more than that, I want a woman who loves the Lord—before me—whatever choices it leads her to make. I want a woman I can trust to raise my children to be responsible adults, not spoiled children who live only to have fun. Grow up, Josette! It's about time that you do."

He turned on his heel and left the apartment, slamming the door after him. Josette threw herself on the sofa and sobbed violently. Mathieu didn't love or respect her. He thought she was empty inside. The hurt and humiliation were too deep to bear.

After a long time, her tears slowed and eventually ceased. She sat vacantly, wondering how she would ever face Mathieu again.

A burning smell reached her nose: the dinner she'd so carefully planned. Slowly, she stood and went into the kitchen to turn off the stove, not bothering to look inside. She moved down the hall to the bathroom, where she washed her face repeatedly with cold water until the redness and swelling eased. The ache in her heart didn't go away.

Before she contemplated her actions, her hand lifted the phone and began dialing. "Hello, Grady?" she asked as a voice answered at the other end.

"Hi, my little cabbage," Grady teased. Josette laughed in spite of herself; the French term of endearment didn't translate well into English.

"Are you doing anything tonight?" she asked, trying to muster her confidence. "I'm all alone, and I thought of you . . ."

"I was thinking of you, too," Grady said. "I was just going to call you." A part of her recognized his lie, but the wounded part of her drank in the glib words. "I'll be right over," he added.

Josette reapplied her makeup while she waited. A few more strands of hair had escaped the pile on her head, but it looked as though she'd planned it that way. Her eyes showed almost no redness, only a melancholy that she imagined made her more dramatic.

Grady gave a long, low whistle when she opened the door. "You look wonderful." He took her hands and kissed her cheek. "You smell great, too."

Josette basked in his attention. Now here was a man who appreciated her.

"You look too good for my eyes only." The eyes in question were blue like his dark sweater, but not the clear blue of the sky that Brionney and her brother shared. Why did she think of them now? She pushed the thoughts away.

"What is spud?" she asked, remembering Mathieu's coupon.

Grady laughed. "That's what I love about you. Everything is so new. A spud is a potato. You can say 'a spud' or 'the spuds,' but not just plain 'spud.' Here we bake 'em, open 'em up, and put stuff on top—whatever you want. Kind of like a salad bar."

"Do you want to eat one?"

He shook his head, his eyes traveling over her dress. "Not with you looking like that. I know just the place we can go. We'll have to stop by my apartment so I can change, but I'll only be a minute."

He helped Josette on with her good coat. "Wait," she said. "I have to leave a note for my sister." She was tempted not to leave a note to punish her for Mathieu's rejection, but she knew it wasn't Marie-Thérèse's fault and she didn't want her sister to worry. *Went with Grady,* she scrawled on the message board in French. *Be back by ten. Call if later.*

Grady shuffled impatiently at the door, and Josette hurried to not keep him waiting. At his apartment building, she waited in the car, its motor running, while he changed. He came out a few minutes later with his shaggy hair slicked back behind his ears, wearing green dress pants and a blazer made in a darker shade. He looked handsome—certainly more the proper companion than Mathieu with his jeans.

He drove past American Fork to a place called The Garden Wall Restaurant at Thanksgiving Point. Josette immediately loved the rich atmosphere but gasped at the prices. On the budget her parents allowed her, she couldn't afford spending thirty or forty dollars for a complete meal. Grady grinned. "Don't worry about it," he said. "You're worth it."

For a moment, Josette felt she was.

They had an appetizer while they waited for the main course to arrive. Grady chattered easily, and with his attentiveness, Josette all but forgot Mathieu's rejection. When the waiter brought their non-alcoholic drinks, Grady slipped a small bottle from the pocket of his blazer, opened it, and poured something into his cup. "Want some?"

Josette knew it was some kind of alcohol, and for the first time, twinges of unease stirred in her stomach. "I don't drink."

"Neither did I—until I realized what I was missing." He stuck the bottle back in his pocket, not forcing the issue.

"Aren't you a member of the Church?" Josette felt stupid that she didn't even know if he was a member. It had never come up in their conversation before now. She'd just assumed he was.

He shrugged. "I was baptized, I guess."

Josette felt oddly disturbed by his answer. His drinking also bothered her, but she didn't understand why since many of her boyfriends in France enjoyed wine with dinner. Maybe it was because Grady was a Mormon. There were a lot of things she would do, but drinking wasn't on that list—even feeling as depressed as she did over Mathieu's rejection.

They finished the meal, talking about anything that came to mind, and Josette forgot her uneasiness. Grady acted like a perfect gentleman.

While they waited for the waiter to bring their check, another waiter behind them dropped a full tray of plates onto the floor, breaking them. When he went down on one knee to begin the cleanup, his shoulder bumped a tray of ice water and glasses balanced on a folding stand. The tall glasses crashed to the ground and shattered. The waiter grimaced and continued his cleanup.

Grady laughed. "A chain of events. You can't stop it."

On the drive home, Grady was strangely morose. Could it be from the alcohol? Josette watched carefully, but he seemed to drive as well as ever. "How about a video at my apartment?"

Josette nodded in agreement. Anything was better than facing Marie-Thérèse. What if Mathieu told her what happened? Josette needed more time to come up with a plausible reason for her behavior with him. She glanced at her watch. It was nearly ten. She'd have to call soon so her sister wouldn't worry.

What excuse could she use with Marie-Thérèse? The more she thought about it, the more worried she became. She'd have no choice but to make up a story. Her conscience screamed in protest, and she tried not to listen. She had to do what she had to do. But what if Marie-Thérèse believed Mathieu over her own sister? "No, she promised a man would never come between us," she mumbled.

"What's that?" Grady turned off the engine and turned to her.

"I said no hunky-punky," Josette said sweetly.

"That's hanky-panky. You're so cute, Josette." Grady leaned over and kissed her briefly on the mouth. He smelled like musk.

He opened her car door and led her into his apartment. All the lights were out and Josette could tell no one else was home. The disquiet in her heart returned. "Maybe I should go home," she said.

"It's too early. Come on, just a little longer." He crossed to the VCR and put in a tape before settling himself on the couch.

"I need to call my sister then." Josette sat beside Grady, but she made no move to borrow his phone. It was her parent's fault really. If they had sprung for a couple of cell phones, she could have simply texted her sister that she'd be late and not have to worry about explaining what had happened with Mathieu.

They watched the video in comfortable silence. Josette began to feel sleepy, and she didn't mind it when Grady cuddled up to her. She settled into the circle of his arm and laid her head on his shoulder. The video went on, but she was unaware of what was on the screen.

Grady was kissing her before she had a chance to object. "You're so beautiful," he murmured. "I love the way you always look."

Josette enjoyed the compliment. At first she responded to Grady's kisses until he pushed too far. "Stop," she said, trying to get up. Everything was happening in fast-forward. She needed time to think.

"No," Grady said, pushing her back onto the couch.

Fear came through, giving Josette the power to escape his grasp. "Take me home," she said, jumping up. "Please. I'm tired."

He took her in his arms again. "It's too early, and it's about time you stopped playing with me."

Josette raked her nails against his cheek in an effort to escape, but the act only inflamed him further. He backhanded her, sending her reeling to the floor, pain shooting though her head and neck.

In the next second his weight was on top of her. She kicked, punched, and bit him, fighting for all she was worth. *If only Mom could see me now.* The thought was as tormenting as Grady's punches.

She freed herself again and ran blindly away from him, down the hall and into a bedroom. It had a lock, but Grady pushed open the door before she could turn it. In a moment he was on her again. She heard the ripping of her dress.

Please, dear Father, she prayed. *Help me!*

Chapter Twenty-three

Marie-Thérèse enjoyed her time at the temple, her fourth session since Tuesday. The first time she'd gone through the temple, she'd been nervous and everything had been too new for her to concentrate on her problem. "Don't rush it," Irene Fields had said to her. "Give yourself time."

Since then, she'd been able to ponder the possibilities of her future and the choices she had to make. In the temple, the cares of the world were of little importance, and for the first time she glimpsed the real meaning of life. Amidst all the white clothes, friendly smiles, and hushed voices, she could envision what heaven was like, and an indescribable joy flooded her soul.

Irene squeezed her hand. Today, Marie-Thérèse had attended her first session alone, but Irene had met her for the second. It helped to have someone more experienced to talk to about her choices.

"I do love Mathieu," she admitted to Irene as they talked in the celestial room after the session, whispering to maintain the reverent atmosphere. "But when I think about how much the Savior has done for me, I want to do my part and serve a mission. Why can't Heavenly Father just tell me what to do?"

Irene laughed. "That would be too easy. We have to do some of the work ourselves. How did you feel when you prayed about marrying Mathieu?"

A flush spread over Marie-Thérèse's cheeks. "I felt good." More than good, tingly even, but she had also felt good about going on a mission.

Irene must have read some of her feelings in her face. "Maybe in your case, either choice is acceptable to the Lord. Maybe you have to decide what you want most."

"I want both." Marie-Thérèse stared down at her hands, clenched in her lap. Except for the dark freckles, they were almost as white as her temple dress. "I . . . it would be easier to marry Mathieu, I think."

A wide smile covered Irene's face. "Are you afraid of taking what appears to be the easy way out?"

"I guess so."

"Well, I can tell you that a mission can be hard, but it can't begin to compare to a life of marriage and raising children. I know, because I've done both. What you might also be forgetting is that as a mother you *are* doing missionary work. Each child you raise up to believe in the Lord is every bit as important as someone you find and baptize. Ours is a continual mission."

"They say women are supposed to get married, if they have the chance."

It seemed to Marie-Thérèse that Irene was trying hard not to smile again. "That they do," the older woman said. "I guess what it boils down to is if you can chance losing Mathieu." She held up her hand to prevent Marie-Thérèse's reply. "Oh, I'm not saying there won't be another man. But when there is, it won't be Mathieu. Will you be happier with one, or with the other? That I can't say. You can't know, either. What you have to determine is what's in your heart right now."

Deep down, Marie-Thérèse had known this all along. She

pictured Mathieu—his tall, lean frame, his dark hair, the way his dancing gray eyes stared at her. Her heart was full of tenderness and a kind of ache. Could she risk losing him?

"He said I would be making a difference in his eternity," she said, almost to herself.

"And in your children's. But you have to do it willingly. I mean, he could find someone else, just as you could. Or he could wait for you."

That wasn't an option Marie-Thérèse was willing to consider. How could she give her whole effort to the Lord on a mission if her heart was with Mathieu, continually worrying that she might lose him to another woman? How could she bear to be apart from him at all?

Irene pulled up her sleeve and glanced at her watch. "They'll be closing up soon. Are you ready to leave?"

They drove in silence to the apartment complex. "Thanks, Irene," Marie-Thérèse said. "You will never know how much I appreciate your coming with me."

"I'm glad to be here for you. I hope that if my daughters are ever away from me, someone will be able to help them. I only wish I could see into the future for you."

Marie-Thérèse gave a short laugh. "Me, too. Or that there could be two of me for a while."

Irene put her hand on Marie-Thérèse's shoulder. "There isn't a woman alive who hasn't wished that at one time or another. Think of all the housework I could get done—with plenty of time to do what I really enjoy."

They continued to talk until the cold forced Irene to restart the car. Marie-Thérèse waved good-bye and walked stiffly to her apartment. The sky was clear and black, and the stars winked down on her benevolently. She stopped at the base of the stairs and lifted her face to soak up the beauty, experiencing again the peace that had filled her at the temple. She felt close to an answer.

Reluctantly, she climbed the four flights of stairs. Noni lay on the couch facing the television. "Hi," she said without taking her eyes from the screen.

"Hi," said Marie-Thérèse.

She went to her room, shedding her coat as the heat in the small apartment seeped into her flesh. The room was empty, but the jeans Josette had borrowed from her earlier lay in a heap in the middle of the floor. That meant her sister had gone out.

Marie-Thérèse retraced her steps down the hall and into the kitchen. On the message board she saw Josette's scrawled message saying she'd be home by ten. Instinctively, she glanced at the clock. It read fifteen to eleven. *Did Irene and I talk that long? Where is Josette?*

Marie-Thérèse hoped her sister hadn't become worried about her and gone looking. She chided herself for being so preoccupied with her own problems that she hadn't thought to call.

"Noni, have you see Josette?" Marie-Thérèse asked, going into the front room. "Her note says she should be home by now."

The girl dragged her eyes from the television. "I haven't seen her. I've been here since ten or so."

"Were there any messages on the machine?"

"Yeah. Mathieu called. He wanted you to call him as soon as you got in."

Where was Josette? Marie-Thérèse found it suddenly hard to breathe past the growing consternation in her chest. She dialed Mathieu's number quickly, hoping he knew something.

"Have you seen Josette?" she asked when he answered.

"What? No. Hi, how are you? Just 'Where's Josette?' "

Marie-Thérèse wasn't in the mood for games. "She's missing. It's not like her to be late without calling. Since we fought about it, she's been more regular than the clock. I'm worried. Her note says she's with Grady."

"I don't like that guy. We'd better go look for her." His voice was grim, stoking Marie-Thérèse's fear. "Something happened earlier,"

Mathieu added. "Something you should know. With Josette . . . but we'd better find her first. She might need us."

What did that mean? But Marie-Thérèse was too worried to puzzle it out.

She met Mathieu in front of her apartment. Together they checked the pool and the common areas of the apartment complex. "I know where Grady lives," Marie-Thérèse said. "We'd better check there."

In the car, Mathieu put his hand over hers. "Everything's going to be all right."

"Then why do I feel so awful?" Marie-Thérèse stared intently ahead, as if doing so would make them arrive more swiftly. "Hurry, Mathieu."

At Grady's apartment building, they jumped out of the car and ran up a flight of outside stairs. Marie-Thérèse banged on the door, and after a long time a sleepy-looking man opened the door. "Whatcha want?" he asked.

"Is Grady here?" Marie-Thérèse asked.

"No," the man said with obvious irritation. "He lives upstairs. Darn idiot makes too much noise. Tell him to shut up." The door slammed, but Marie-Thérèse was already bounding up the second flight, with Mathieu close behind. A dark cloud floated across the moon's surface, blotting out the dim light. Marie-Thérèse pushed on.

Once again she banged on a door. There was no answer, but she heard a scream, abruptly muffled. Marie-Thérèse tried to peek in the lighted window, but blinds blocked her view. She turned helplessly to Mathieu. He beat on the door with his fist, but behind the door, everything was still.

"She's in there, I know it!" Marie-Thérèse said.

Mathieu removed his coat and wrapped it around his hand. He punched his fist through the window, breaking the glass. Then he laid the coat over the sill and wiggled through. Marie-Thérèse followed close behind.

"There's no one here," Mathieu said.

"Look." Marie-Thérèse pointed to Josette's coat, which lay crumpled on the floor by the couch. The coffee table was overturned and magazines were strewn everywhere.

"Her shoe!" Mathieu pointed down the hall. Marie-Thérèse tried to push past him, but Mathieu held her back. "Follow me," he whispered.

In a few seconds they were down the hall, flinging the doors open. One was locked. Mathieu held his breath and threw his shoulder against the door. On the second thrust, Marie-Thérèse heard the door splinter and silently blessed whoever had made it so flimsy.

Inside the room, Josette lay on the floor struggling wildly. Grady was on top of her. Fury engulfed Marie-Thérèse. "Get off her!" she screamed.

Mathieu grabbed Grady by the neck and hauled him to his feet. Josette sobbed in relief, holding her arms across her chest. Marie-Thérèse knelt by her sister, gathering the trembling body into her arms. The spaghetti straps on her dress were missing and the silk was ripped under Josette's arm to her waist. Bruises and scratches covered her face, neck, and arms.

Marie-Thérèse covered her sister with her coat. "It's okay now," she murmured, pulling Josette's dress down over her legs, bare except for ruined nylons.

Josette pointed an accusing finger at Grady. "He—he tried to rape me." She turned her face into Marie-Thérèse's dress and sobbed.

Grady struggled, but Mathieu kept a firm grasp on him. "She asked for it!" Grady said. At that Josette lunged for him, but Marie-Thérèse held her back, fearing for her safety. Grady laughed and stuck out his chin. "She's a tease."

"She asked for it, did she?" Mathieu muttered. "Just like you asked for this." He pushed Grady back and slugged him in the stomach. Grady doubled over and fell to the ground.

Josette pulled away from Marie-Thérèse, jumping to her feet to hover over Grady's body. She kicked him. "I hate you! I hate you!" she screamed.

Grady's eyes showed red, but with Mathieu standing above him, he didn't dare fight back.

Josette crumpled again. Mathieu wrapped her tighter in Marie-Thérèse's coat and swept her up in his arms. "Let's get her home."

"It's my word against hers," Grady called as they started down the hall. "And everyone knows she's a tease."

They ignored him.

"We have to call the police," Marie-Thérèse said in the car. She sat in the backseat with her arm around Josette. "We have to."

Josette had her eyes closed tight and didn't answer.

"Of course we do," Mathieu said. "But we're only three minutes from home. We'll do it there."

Josette began to shiver. Marie-Thérèse rubbed her back and arms until her hands ached.

When they arrived at their apartments, Mathieu reached in to carry Josette. "I can walk," she protested, momentarily rousing from the apathy she had lapsed into.

"You don't have your shoes."

There was something odd between them that Marie-Thérèse couldn't pinpoint. Mathieu's words of earlier returned to her. What was it he wanted to tell her? Was it about them? Had he decided he didn't want to marry her after all? How did Josette work into the equation?

In that moment, Marie-Thérèse knew she loved Mathieu and wanted to be with him forever. A mission was important, but not as important as marrying the right man at the right time.

How interesting that the revelation about Mathieu didn't come in the temple as she'd expected, but near her own apartment while talking with Mathieu and Josette. The bishop had been right all along. The temple experience had helped her understand so much about life, but personal revelation did come to those who needed it—no matter where they were.

The apartment appeared deserted, and Marie-Thérèse thought Noni must have retired.

"This is partly my fault," Mathieu said as he laid Josette on her bed.

"Why?" Marie-Thérèse cradled Josette's head in her lap. An ugly bruise had formed on her left cheekbone, in the shape of a man's fingers, and blood dripped from a deep scratch near the bruise. Josette touched it gingerly, and Marie-Thérèse saw that three of her sister's beautiful fingernails were broken.

"Your sister and I had a talk," Mathieu continued, "and I'm afraid I wasn't very nice to her."

Josette lifted her head. "You tried to kiss to me!"

Mathieu blinked. "What? No way!" He looked at Marie-Thérèse. "She came on to me, and I refused to play her little game, whatever it was."

A deep flush stained the undamaged part of Josette's face, and Marie-Thérèse knew Mathieu told the truth. Relief rushed through her—relief that it was Josette who'd tried to betray her and not Mathieu. There was a time when she would have wished it to be the other way around. With any other man, she still would, but not with Mathieu.

"That's not true!" Josette cried, sitting up. "You can't believe him over me!"

"Can I talk to my sister alone?" Marie-Thérèse said to Mathieu. She smiled to show her belief in him, and he nodded once, sharply, but the concern didn't leave his face.

"Okay, but don't clean off any more blood. The police will want pictures for the report. I'll go wait for them." Mathieu leaned down and kissed Marie-Thérèse's forehead, and a familiar warmth spread through her, subduing her anger at her sister.

"Why did you do it?" Marie-Thérèse asked when he was gone.

Josette froze. For a long moment she stared at Marie-Thérèse with her brown eyes wide and sad, her bruised face crying out for help.

"I was testing him," she said finally. "Like the way you tested Marcelin in France."

"You agreed to that," Marie-Thérèse said. "And there was a reason."

"There was a reason here, too." Josette stared at the quilt on her bed, plucking at the yarn ties. Her fingers were red and scratched. "I—I liked him. I wanted to know if he had any feelings for me."

Marie-Thérèse's anger built. "So you tried to steal my boyfriend because you liked him? For heaven's sake, you have so many men interested in you—why him? Why the only man who cares about me?"

"He's different," Josette said. Marie-Thérèse understood what she meant, but was surprised her sister had noticed. "And he's not the only man interested in you," Josette continued. "A lot are, you just don't know it. And they're all like Mathieu." She held her palms to the sides of her head as if it ached. "Why can't a man like that want me?" She collapsed onto the bed and sobbed as if her heart were breaking.

Marie-Thérèse gathered her sister in her arms. "You will find someone as good as Mathieu one day, but first you may have to change a few things about your life."

Josette pulled away. "I can't change who I am! I like me. I like me." Her head dropped once again into Marie-Thérèse's lap as she dully repeated the phrase over and over, as if trying to convince both of them.

Marie-Thérèse stroked her sister's hair. "Shhh," she said softly.

Josette's sobs gradually subsided. When she'd been quiet for several minutes, she twisted her head to gaze into her sister's eyes. "You're not giving him up for me, are you? Mathieu's coming between us, isn't he?"

Marie-Thérèse knew what Josette was asking. Both had kept the pledge—until now.

"He's not just a man," Marie-Thérèse said slowly as her mind searched for words to voice the feelings she hadn't fully understood until now. "He's far more than that. He—he represents eternity. In the back of my mind, I think I always knew this day would come, only I thought it would be you first. But here we are. I love Mathieu, and I want to marry him . . . forever. That bond is stronger than ours, whether we like it or not." Tears slipped down her cheeks now, dribbling off her chin and mingling with the tears on her sister's face. "I'll always be here for you, Josette. Always. But please don't make me choose. I don't want to lose you."

Josette sat up and hugged Marie-Thérèse, pressing her cheek against her sister's, wincing slightly but otherwise seeming to ignore the pain of her wounds. "I won't," she whispered. "I'm happy for you. I really am." The desolation in her voice ripped at Marie-Thérèse's heart, but there was nothing she could do to change it. Her course was clear; she loved Mathieu.

Rapid footsteps sounded in the hallway, and the door burst open to reveal Brionney and Irene. "We just heard!" Brionney's blue eyes were wide with worry. Her head shook back and forth, making the light reflect off her white tresses. "Mathieu called us."

"You poor thing." Irene settled herself on the bed and took Josette's hand. "He didn't . . . I mean, did he succeed in . . ."

Josette shook her head. "Marie-Thérèse and Mathieu stopped him." She started to cry again. "But he almost did, and it was awful! I kept fighting and pushing, but he was too strong. I couldn't do anything."

Irene put her arms around Josette's shaking body. "You did enough. Hush now. Everything will be okay." She waited a few seconds before adding, "The police are here. A couple of them are going after Grady. Others will be interviewing you and Marie-Thérèse. They feel it would be best to question you separately, but they said I could stay with you."

Josette sighed in relief. "Thank you."

Marie-Thérèse gave a last squeeze to her sister's arm and left the room. She met a woman police officer in the hallway. "Be gentle," Marie-Thérèse said to her.

The woman flashed her a smile. "Don't you worry. Will she need any translating?"

"I don't think so. She does well enough."

Marie-Thérèse answered a male officer's questions quickly as he wrote on a pad. "So you definitely can identify the suspect," he said.

"Absolutely. We pulled him off her."

The officer nodded grimly, flipping his book shut. "We'll get him. It's just a matter of time. We have officer's staking out his apartment. We think he may be connected to several on-campus rapes. Your sister was very lucky."

Marie-Thérèse had to agree.

Noni stuck her frizzy head out of the kitchen. She wore long pajamas and thick, fuzzy slippers. "I'm sorry," she said, hesitantly. "I feel it's my fault. I introduced her to Grady."

"You know him well?" the policeman asked.

"Yes."

"Did he ever attack you?"

Noni colored. "Not like that. But one night, we'd been drinking and we . . . that was a long time ago. I knew what I was getting into." She shook her head. "Josette didn't. She's basically innocent."

"Do you know where he might go?" the policeman asked.

Before Noni could answer, Marie-Thérèse cleared her throat and asked. "Do you know where Mathieu Portier is—the man who called you?"

The policemen nodded. "He asked me to send you downstairs when we were finished."

"Will you let me know when you're done with my sister?"

"It'll probably be a while. Then we'll have to go down to the precinct to file a formal complaint. We'll need pictures, too."

"I'll go with her."

"Of course." The man's eyes showed approval.

Marie-Thérèse excused herself and sprinted down the steps in her apartment building, slowing as she reached the bottom.

She found Mathieu sitting on the cold cement sidewalk with his back against the red brick of the apartment building. He stood, shivering in the cold, his breath billowing in warm clouds.

"Marie-Thérèse." He said nothing more, but opened his arms in a silent plea.

She went into them, feeling the coldness of his clothes through her own. She lifted her lips to his. He leaned forward, but at the last minute pulled back with a groan.

"I love you," she whispered.

A grin spread hesitantly over his handsome features. "Does that mean . . .?"

"Yes, I want to marry you."

"Are you sure? No regrets?"

She met his earnest gray eyes, loving the way he was willing to be sure. "The only regret I think I would have is if I let you go."

He hugged and kissed her until she gasped for breath. They both laughed, and a few tears escaped as well.

For a moment they said nothing as they drank in the newness of their love. Marie-Thérèse rubbed her cheek against his, feeling the prickling of his beginning beard. It did feel like sandpaper, as Josette had once said, but she loved it.

Mathieu whispered in her ear, "You've made me the happiest man in the whole world. I promise to make you every bit as happy—if it takes the rest of my life."

"The rest of eternity, you mean."

"That too." He kissed her again.

Chapter Twenty-four

Pauline and Emeri walked hand-in-hand down the cobblestone sidewalk of the busy street. They moved slowly, stopping whenever they needed to rest. For Pauline, the frequent stops were a necessity. If it hadn't been for Emeri, she wouldn't have left the apartment at all. But she had to see him.

Her head was mostly bald now, after the hair had dropped out in bunches. At first she'd tried to wear a wig, but both André and Emeri had laughed at the result, and the wig itself had been so hot and itchy that Pauline had given it away. Instead, she shaved her remaining hair and constantly wore a hat.

"Look! Some Christmas cards," Pauline said, stopping at an outdoor display. "I need to get a few." She thumbed through the cards, picking out the ones with the brightest colors. "Don't you want to get some?"

"I don't have anyone to send them to, and my friends and I don't exchange anything."

Pauline placed a card in his hands. "What about this one? For your parents."

Emeri glared at her. "That's ridiculous. I'm not sending them a card."

"Why not? It'll be Christmas soon. You said yourself they don't know where you are. Wouldn't that be a nice gift for them? To know their son is okay?"

"What'll I say? 'Hi, Merry Christmas. I'm dying of AIDS. Hope you're happy for kicking me out in the cold.' Is that what you want me to say?" He shook his head. "No, Pauline, don't go there."

Pauline would have laughed if not for the seriousness in Emeri's voice and expression. She had suggested sending the card without any real hope, but now she realized he needed to send it as much as his parents might need to receive it. Whatever had gone on between Emeri and his parents was far from over, and she became determined to help them open a channel of communication. One way or the other, Emeri needed closure.

"Well, that's not exactly the sort of information you should send in a Christmas card," she said lightly. "But we could call them or visit. I'll go with you."

"No way. Get that out of your head right now. I'm never going back there. Never! And I'm not writing them."

Pauline knew he meant what he said. "Very well, then, *I'll* write the card. You just give me the address." Before Emeri could object, she grabbed the card from him, dug in her purse for a pen, and began writing.

"There. It says, 'Just wanted you to know that I am fine. Hope you have a good Christmas. Emeri.' " She had debated writing "Love, Emeri" but felt that might be going too far.

"I'm not sending that card."

"You're not, but I am," Pauline insisted. "Look here, Emeri. I've been cutting you a lot of slack in your refusal to meet my parents, even though I don't agree. That's because I really care for you. But if you don't let me send this card, I won't go out with you anymore. I mean it. Your parents may not be wonderful people, but they deserve to know you're okay."

"I'm not okay," he said sullenly.

Pauline frowned at him. "I'm waiting." She hoped he wouldn't call her bluff. The truth was, she didn't think she could go more than a day or two without seeing him. When he wasn't with her, she felt that a part of herself was missing.

He scowled, and Pauline impulsively leaned forward to kiss him. It took a few seconds before he relaxed enough to kiss her back. Pauline giggled and drew away. "So what's the address? Or at least the last place you know they were living last."

Shaking his head in disgust, he told her. When she was finished writing, she bought the card and some stamps and slipped it into the nearest mailbox before he could change his mind.

Emeri stared silently at the mailbox for along silent minute. Then he put his arms around her and pulled her close. "Would you have really refused to go out with me?" he asked softly.

"No."

"I never knew you could be so sneaky."

"I learned a few things from Josette."

"Well, sending a card is one thing. Just so you don't get it into your head to call them or something."

Pauline winked at him. "I'm making no promises."

"You'd better not."

She gave him an enigmatic smile and took his hand. They strolled once more down the sidewalk, comfortable in their companionship, the argument forgotten.

"Oh, look at that!" Pauline pointed to a small musical merry-go-round with tiny unicorns moving up and down as they circled. She laughed. "How adorable!"

Emeri stared at it. "Unicorns are supposed to be magical, you know."

"Then let's make a wish."

He grinned. "I don't know if it's that kind of magic. I think it has something to do with healing properties. If you touch them, or something."

"All the better. We could both use some of that magic. Come on!"

She tugged on him and he followed her into the store. There was a long line and only one clerk. Pauline sighed and leaned against Emeri.

He looked at her worriedly. "Maybe we should come back later. You're looking a little pale. Do you want to sit down?"

"I'm always pale," Pauline objected. But then the room flickered and she grabbed onto him. "Maybe I'm not feeling so well. I think I'd better go home."

He caught her as she fell. From far away she heard him call a taxi and give the driver the address to the clinic. In a short time Pauline lay in the examining room, listening as Dr. Medard assured them that this sort of fatigue was a normal symptom of the cancer. "I think you've overexerted yourself today," he said. "Why don't you rest right here, and I'll go call your parents."

"Thank you," Pauline murmured.

When the doctor left, Emeri paced the room, his anger showing through the mocking exterior he had put in place for Dr. Medard. "I'm the one who's supposed to die first—not you!" She knew the fact that his cancer had responded better to chemotherapy than hers ate at him constantly.

"That's not for us to say," she said, trying to keep her voice steady. More than anything, she had to help him face what would happen. "It could be worse. One of us could have been hit by a car, and then we'd have *no* time."

Emeri crossed to the bed and grabbed her hands. "Marry me, Sunshine. Please! I love you, and I want to spend what time we have left together. I want to be with you every second of the day and night. To see your smile. I want to go to the mountains with you, and to the beach. Everywhere. I want to hold your hand when you're scared or sick. I want to take care of you."

Pauline almost laughed. For so long she'd dreamed of such a

day as this, but without any real hope, considering her illness. She knew that she loved Emeri, more than she'd ever thought it was possible to love another human being.

"Only in the temple," she said. "I love you, but I'll marry you only in the temple."

Anger flashed on his face but was gone again just as quickly. "I can't go there."

"Not yet. But there's still time. Why don't you come over and meet my parents and the missionaries?"

Emeri's mouth drew tight. "I love you so much. Ever since that day at the Eiffel Tower, I've known that I love you. But that doesn't change the way I feel about God. I won't listen to your missionaries."

Sadness threatened to overwhelm Pauline, but she pushed it away and smiled. "One day you'll realize how much Heavenly Father loves you, and when you do, you'll understand that we can be together forever."

He said nothing, but his dark eyes brooded. She tightened her grasp on his hands and pulled him down to kiss him on the cheek. "I love you," she whispered. "That will never, ever change."

"I don't want to lose you." He kissed her on the mouth.

"Am I interrupting something?" said a voice at the door.

Emeri straightened, his mocking smile back in place. "About time you got here, André. Some brother you are, coming after the crisis is averted."

"I only just heard," André said. "Mom's here too, but she's with Dr. Medard. Dad's on his way."

Emeri looked uncomfortable. "I'd better get to work anyway, now that your family's here to take care of you," he said to Pauline. "Dr. Medard has a whole room of files he's making me go through. When I finish, I'll call you."

"Or come by?" It was a question she always asked, but he'd never taken her up on it.

"Maybe." With a wink he was gone.

André walked over to the bed and kissed her cheeks in greeting. "How are you feeling, Dolly?"

She pointed to the hat near her pillow. "A little bald, if you know what I mean."

"You look cute." He ran his hand over her bare head.

She laughed. "You are such a bad liar."

"Really?" He kept his face serious. "Darn—I like to be good at everything I do."

She curled her fist and punched his shoulder, though there was barely enough force behind the blow to make itself felt.

As usual, André pretended not to see her weakness. They fell into an easy conversation, but Pauline found it hard to concentrate.

"What's wrong?" André asked finally.

"Emeri asked me to marry him." It felt good to tell someone.

André held perfectly still. "And?"

"I told him I would—in the temple."

André frowned. "That means he'd have to be baptized and wait a year. Maybe if you really love him you should marry him now." His eyes didn't meet hers, and she knew he referred to the obvious fact that they might not have that long. "I mean, I wouldn't suggest it under other circumstances. And . . . well . . . I really like Emeri."

Pauline sighed. "I can't do that—even if Mom and Dad agreed. Don't you see? I really love him, André. I need him to find the truth so we can be together forever. I don't want him just for this little bit of time." She struggled to sit up. "Promise me you'll keep working on him, no matter what. Please!"

André was silent for what seemed too long. Pauline knew he didn't make promises lightly, and she started to fear that he wouldn't agree. At last he nodded slowly. "I will. If it's the last thing I do."

Pauline smiled at him, her happiness returning. "Thanks. But don't say anything about Emeri asking me to marry him, okay?

Mom's worried enough about what happened to Josette in Provo. I don't want to add to her worries any more than I already have."

André saluted. "Yes, Mademoiselle. Whatever you say."

Pauline giggled. "Then go find the doctor, so you can take me home. I'm feeling much better now."

"I've already talked to the doctor," their mother said from the doorway, her expression somber.

Pauline's smile faded. "I can go home, can't I?"

Ariana came to sit on Pauline's bed. "Yes. But you have to promise to take it easier."

"I promise."

Ariana hesitated a moment before adding, "Perhaps we should call the girls home from college."

André looked away from them, his face pained. Pauline's own fear twisted inside. "The treatments aren't working, are they?" she asked softly. It wasn't the first time her mother had made the suggestion.

Ariana's eyes brimmed with unshed tears. "Not as well as we'd hoped. The tumor hasn't grown since we started the new treatments, but it hasn't become smaller either."

"I'm feeling fine," Pauline said. "They only have two weeks left or something like that. I'm not . . . I'll be here. Please, Mom. I don't want them to hover over me. I don't want them to be sad. Besides, in her last letter, Marie-Thérèse said Josette was doing so well in school. Give them just a few more weeks."

Ariana studied her for a long moment without speaking. Then she appeared to make a sudden decision. "All right. I'll have to talk to your father about it, of course, and see how he feels. And we'll need to pray. But one more episode like this, and I'm calling them to come home. It isn't right to keep it from them anymore."

"Okay." Pauline answered, but in her heart she rebelled. She wasn't going anywhere—yet. She would fight for every second to be with Emeri.

A few days later, Pauline felt well enough to go to the group meeting at the clinic; at least that was what she told everyone. To herself she admitted that she should stay in bed, but nothing could keep her from Emeri. André had brought him to the house the day before when her mother was out shopping, but lying in bed all today without seeing him had been much too long. She had to take every chance she could to be with him. When he was with her, she felt . . . well, if not good then at least better than before.

Emeri waited at the door for her. He grabbed her in a bear hug. "I've missed you so much."

"You just saw me yesterday," she said with a grin. But she knew exactly how he felt. An entire night was too many hours to be separated from each other. She almost began to doubt the wisdom of her insistence on a temple marriage. Yet she couldn't let herself give up the blessings of eternity for a fleeting joy on earth. Pauline felt convinced that Emeri would never accept the gospel if she gave in. *This is a sacrifice we both must make, even if you don't realize it,* she thought.

He kissed her briefly before pulling off her hat and holding it out of her reach.

"Emeri, stop that!"

"Okay." He plopped the hat onto her head. "But you look cute bald."

"Shiny, you mean." She adjusted the brim so she could see him better. "It's a wonder you want to be seen in public with me now."

"If you haven't looked around, a good third of those here tonight are missing hair."

He was right about that much. She was in good company.

The members of the group began to gravitate toward the chairs. Beside her, Pauline felt Emeri stiffen. She looked over and saw a man coming through the door. "He shouldn't be here," Emeri grated. "That's why I joined this group instead of the adult one. I couldn't stand being with him and his kind." Emeri's hands clenched at his sides.

"That's Renard," Pauline says. "He comes here sometimes. He's okay."

"No, he's not. He's gay, and I don't like him. No, that's not strong enough. I detest him."

"Emeri!" Pauline didn't condone homosexuality, but she didn't share Emeri's hatred toward Renard. She knew he suffered now every bit as much as she did.

"They're to blame for what's happening to you," Emeri said, his voice bitter. "And to me and all the others who have AIDS. But they don't take responsibility. Don't you see? They're the perfect political machine, with no children and all their money. They started the AIDS epidemic with their lifestyle, but you'll never see Renard with his lovers on posters to raise money and sympathy of the public. No, instead they use innocent women and children. All to get a few more dollars for research to save their lives—which is wrong when their so-called free lifestyle of bar-hopping and sleeping around caused the disease in the first place."

Pauline tried to speak but Emeri ran over her words. "Oh, I know you got AIDS from your mom and she got it from using drugs, but the bare truth is that if you traced it back, she got it from one of those guys, and they're still spreading it. They don't want the freedom to be with one person of the same sex. They want to fall in the sack with anyone who's willing. They don't care about you or me. They only care about satisfying their lust."

Emeri hadn't kept his voice down, and the others were gathering around where they stood. Pauline sensed resentment in almost everyone present, but more exuded from Emeri than from everyone else combined. Renard stood alone by the door, a devastated expression on his face.

"He's right," said the mother of the youngest boy in the group. Pauline knew the child had contracted HIV from a blood transfusion. "They keep asking for money—billions of dollars for research—but if they'd just be moral and stay with a single partner, the epidemic would be over. Everyone who has AIDS would die out, and no more people would be infected. But they don't. They keep hurting others, and they'll keep on hurting others."

"The gays want the lifestyle," a teen added, "but then they cry because they get AIDS. What do they expect?"

"They've successfully convinced people that AIDS is a women's and innocent's disease," another parent said acidly. "According to them, homosexuals have no responsibility at all. But any way you look at it, they are to blame for the spreading of AIDS to women and drug users—and to children." Murmurs of assent rippled through the group.

Pauline worried what might happen next. The crowd stared angrily at Renard, urged on by their fear and helplessness. Pauline knew that Emeri and the others told the truth, that the horror of AIDS would never be conquered unless anonymous promiscuity in the gay community ceased. She also believed that hatred would not solve the problem.

"Emeri," she said, fighting the weariness in both her body and soul.

"Don't tell me you condone their actions." His voice was full of revulsion that she knew was not directed toward her.

"I don't condone it, but . . ." She waited until she had everyone's attention. "But there is a difference between compassion and condoning." She crossed to stand beside Renard. "I know Renard here, and he suffers with his sickness as much as we do."

Renard lifted his bowed his head. "Emeri is right," he said, surprising Pauline. "For many years I believed the lies they told me, that I was born this way and that I needed to fulfill all my desires to be complete. They were wrong. I've never been happy, not really, and I know that kind of life will never give me the relationship I crave. Before I die, I want to change. That's why I'm here. I want to know what a normal life is like. I want to face God with a clear conscience." He turned to Pauline. "Can I be forgiven, do you think? Can I become whole again?"

She blinked back the tears. "We have to forsake our sins to know God. If you do that, yes, I believe He'll forgive you."

The mood of the crowd had changed, and people wandered back to their seats, their conversation turning to less volatile matters. Emeri drew Pauline aside. "I still hate them," he muttered.

"I know."

He watched her for a moment and then said slowly, "I love you, Pauline. I would do anything I could to save you."

He touched her cheek, and she placed her hand over his. "Loving me is enough. Love can solve just about everything." She motioned to where Renard was talking with the mother of the youngest HIV victim. "Even with him."

Emeri didn't seem convinced, but in her short life Pauline had seen people make drastic changes because of love. Renard was proof of that. Loving Emeri was all she could do for him. That and pray. Someday he would find the truth for himself.

She saw now that she was right not to marry Emeri. He still had a long journey ahead of him before he found happiness. At least as long as she or André were alive, he wouldn't be alone.

Chapter Twenty-five

Josette felt the swing of Grady's fist, and then he was on top of her again. "Tease!" he screamed as she tried futilely to escape. She heard the rip of her dress and felt the cool air against her bare skin.

She sat up in bed, breathing heavily as the dream faded. She'd pushed the blankets from the bed in her sleep and goose bumps covered her flesh in the cold morning air. She crossed her hands and rubbed them on the opposite arms to bring the warmth back to her body. An old T-shirt was all she wore, though her discarded jeans lay on the floor. She didn't remember taking them off after her late night of study, but she must have.

Pulling them on again, Josette glanced at the clock. It was ten already, and Brionney would be arriving for her Saturday lesson since she'd asked to begin an hour earlier today.

The mirror on the desk captured Josette's attention. Her face looked thinner than she remembered it from two weeks earlier, before that fatal date with Grady. Her eye no longer hurt, but the bruises still carried traces of green. The hurt inside would take longer to heal. Because of the counseling Marie-Thérèse insisted she attend, she was beginning to understand that while she could have done a great deal to prevent the attack, she was not responsible for it.

Am I a tease?

The question haunted her. She refused to go out on any more dates—no matter how good-looking or rich the guy happened to be—and threw herself into her studies with renewed determination.

"Not all men are like Grady," Marie-Thérèse had said after the sixth night she'd stayed home to study.

Josette knew that, but for now she wasn't ready to take another risk. Grady's attack had frightened her beyond words, and there was no way she'd place herself in a position to repeat that dreadful night.

Something's wrong with me, she concluded. No one seemed to want her for herself, and she was sick of men liking her for how she looked. She played down her makeup—if she wore it at all—and her long hair that people so admired was worn in a severe ponytail down her back. Her head often ached with the concentrated weight, but Josette considered the pain a part of her sentence.

She put on a sweater and checked the heat. The dial read seventy-four degrees Fahrenheit so she shouldn't be cold. Did the ice come from her heart?

In the kitchen she found a note Marie-Thérèse had left on the message board: *Went shopping with Mathieu. Be back by two.*

Mathieu had been good to her after that night, and in fact last week he'd apologized. "I shouldn't have been so abrupt. When someone says they love you, you shouldn't act the way I did."

"It's nothing," she'd insisted, but she felt mortified every time she thought about it.

Mathieu made a noise in his throat. "No matter what you feel right now, you're a daughter of God and He loves you. He has a great future planned for you. You just need to figure out what it is."

"Let's just never mention this again, okay?"

He agreed, the relief on his face almost amusing.

Marie-Thérèse had also been kind. All the irritation she might have felt at Josette's attempted betrayal was swallowed up in her newfound love. Josette had never seen her sister so content, and she loved her enough to be happy for her. She felt sure Marie-Thérèse had made the right choice.

On the other hand, Mathieu and Marie-Thérèse were so caught up in each other that it was easy to feel left out.

Like today.

Deciding she wasn't hungry, Josette went into the front room to wait for Brionney. On the coffee table, she spied the butterfly broach Alphonse had given her in Paris. The police had found it in Grady's apartment and brought it back to her in a plastic sack. She picked up the plastic and let the pin slide into her hand. The diamond dust glittered in the weak sunlight coming through the window panes. One of the wings was bent, and she straightened it with a tug. It looked as good as new. No sign of the ruin she felt.

When Brionney arrived, Josette was still staring at the pin. "Thanks for letting me come early," Brionney said. "I just know if I don't supervise the decorations for our school Christmas dance, it won't get done right."

"Didn't you have a dance a month ago?" Josette asked.

Brionney shrugged. "Homecoming, like you guys had here. But that's a formal date thing, and I didn't go."

Josette had gone to the Homecoming at BYU, though she could barely remember the face of the student she'd gone with. It hadn't been as fun as she expected, and she almost wished she'd stayed home with Marie-Thérèse and Mathieu. Was that the night they'd begun to fall in love? Did it matter?

"Whatcha got there?"

Josette handed her the broach.

"It's beautiful."

"Keep it," Josette said. Even to her ears, her voice sounded distant.

"Oh, but I couldn't! It looks so expensive."

"If you don't, I'm just going to throw it away." As she had the black dress. She'd cut it into tiny pieces before dumping it in the trash.

"But—"

"I wore it that night. It reminds me."

"Oh." Brionney pushed up her sweater and pinned the broach on the shirt she wore underneath.

Josette gave a sigh of relief. "Besides," she said in a lighter tone, "it'll give you something to remember me by."

Her friend frowned. "You're not coming back next semester?"

"I was thinking about it, but now . . ."

"I'm going to miss you," Brionney said, her voice uneven. "You're my best friend, you know."

Josette smiled—her first real smile in two weeks. She put her arm around the younger girl. "Getting to know you has been the best part of coming to America," she said. "I don't know what I would have done without you these past few weeks."

Brionney removed the thin rope chain she wore around her neck. A yellow-gold charm fell off into her hand. It was half of an inch-high heart, cut in a precise zig zag on one side where it had been separated from its other half. She handed the charm to Josette.

"What is this?" Josette asked.

"It's half of a heart," Brionney said. "When put with the other it says, 'The Lord watch between me and thee while we are absent one from another,' or something like that. My brother Zack has the other side, so I haven't read it for a while. I gave it to him before he left on his mission. I want you to have this half."

"But it's special."

"I know, silly. That's why I want you to have it."

"What will your brother say?"

"He'll understand. It'll make me feel good knowing the two people I love most have something from me. Besides, I can always go and buy another pair and have a side to match both of you."

Josette hugged Brionney. "Thank you," she whispered. The sundered heart was exactly right for how she felt. It would remind her to never let another man hurt her. She unfastened her own necklace—a fine byzantine chain her parents had given her when she graduated from high school. The thickness barely allowed for the charm to slip on.

"So, how are the two lovebirds coming along?" Brionney asked as she brought out her French book.

"Lovebirds? Oh, you mean Marie-Thérèse and Mathieu."

"They're so cute together. I can't wait until I fall in love. Do they still stare at each other with goo-goo eyes?"

Josette laughed, though she wasn't sure what goo-goo eyes meant. "They really are funny. I never saw Marie-Thérèse act this way." She raised her voice in imitation. "Oh, how did I ever breathe before I met him?"

"And how did the world rotate before I met her?" Brionney lowered her voice to sound like a man, speaking with an exaggerated French accent. She giggled. "Maybe they both should see a shrink."

"Why? They aren't too tall."

They fell onto the floor, laughing so hard they almost missed hearing the phone ring.

"Hello?" Josette asked a bit breathlessly.

"May I speak with Josette Perrault?"

"This is she."

"This is Officer Blaine Ewell, and I'm calling to inform you that yesterday we picked up Grady Ladd. I thought you'd want to know. Also, we've had several charges added to yours by some women in his apartment building. He's planning to plead guilty, so there'll be no need for a trial."

"Thank you for calling," Josette said, her knees suddenly weak. She was glad she didn't have to face Grady again. She replaced the receiver and sat down on a chair, realizing again that the experience could have been a lot worse.

Instead of cheering her, an ominous feeling seemed to hang over her, like the dense fog that occasionally shrouded Utah Valley.

If only Marc were here, she thought. *I miss him.*

Chapter Twenty-six

"I just don't get it," Elder Fields said to Marc. "Why don't you want me to write your sister? It must be me, because she's absolutely beautiful. I can't imagine her not being perfect. From the way you talk about her, I think I'd like her. After all, I like you."

"She's not like me, really," Marc said.

"How can she not be? You're twins, and raised in the same family."

Marc hesitated, torn between his friendship with Elder Fields and the love and loyalty he felt for his twin sister. Josette won out. There was no way he would tell his companion that the sister he adored probably wasn't worthy of him. "It just wouldn't work," he said. "Trust me. I know her and I know you, and it wouldn't work."

Elder Fields must have heard the sincerity in his voice, because he didn't persist. "If you say so, Elder. Well, I guess you'd better get going. The cab's waiting." He stuck out his hand and the young men shook solemnly. "It's been good serving with you," Elder Fields continued. "I'll visit you before I leave France. My parents are coming to pick me up, so we're going to stay a week or so."

Marc grinned. "Seventeen months is a long time away, but I

might still remember you. I'll even show you around. You're going to love my family."

Elder Fields didn't speak for a long time, then a slow smile spread over his face. "That's what I've been trying to tell you, Elder. I'll love all your family, including Josette."

Marc snorted. "You never give up."

"If we gave up, we'd never baptize anyone."

"Madame Legrand is taking her time." It was Marc's one regret in being transferred from the area.

"I'll keep working on her," his companion said confidently. "She's almost there. Her daughters being baptized next week should help."

Marc clapped him on the back. "If it were anyone else, I'd be a lot more reluctant to leave this area. But I have faith in you."

"Even if I'm not good enough to be family?" Elder Fields' voice was light, and his tone told Marc he was teasing.

"I'd better get going."

"Hey, maybe you should forget about being an engineer and go into real estate with me. My dad will make an opening for you."

"And leave France? I don't think so. Besides, my brother's counting on me to go into business with him when we finish college."

"Well, if you change your mind . . ."

Marc left, sad to bid his favorite companion farewell but also anticipating the new area the president was sending him to open with a greenie from America. It would be hard work, but Marc felt up to it. Already it was nearly Christmas, and he had only until the end of April before he'd leave his mission behind him.

When he arrived at the mission home to collect his new companion, the mission president called him into his office for a private interview. He was a tall man, big without being fat, and full of suppressed energy. In place of his usual kind smile, he wore a frown and his face was tight with concern. "I'm afraid I have some bad news about your family."

Marc listened in numbed silence as the president explained.

"I'm so sorry, Elder." The president's arm went around him. Gradually the shock subsided, released by a clean flood of tears.

Chapter Twenty-seven

They'd been studying in the library for nearly two hours. Marie-Thérèse glanced over at Mathieu, whose nose was buried in his book. Her face felt raw. She loved it when Mathieu left his beard for a few days, but it played havoc with her sensitive skin when he kissed her. They seemed to do a lot of that nowadays—kissing. She gave a short laugh. Never in her life had she been tempted to break or even stretch the law of chastity—until now. It was one thing to be morally clean when you were waiting to find the right person to marry, but quite another thing when you finally met the man you planned to love for eternity. Suddenly, staying morally clean took on a whole new light. A difficult one.

In a week classes would be over. The end of this week and part of next would be full of exams, and then they'd go home—together. Marie-Thérèse pictured the surprise on her parents' faces. She and Mathieu were waiting until they were back in France to surprise them with the news of their engagement.

May would be the best time for the wedding because Marc would be home, but Marie-Thérèse wished she didn't have to wait. Four and a half months had never seemed so long.

Mathieu looked up and caught her gaze. "I love you," he mouthed.

Marie-Thérèse grinned. At this rate, she'd never finish her studying.

"Let's go back to my apartment," she said, gathering her books. "I'd like to check on Josette. I feel bad leaving her alone so much."

"She's not the same. I miss the old Josette. Parts of her, anyway."

Marie-Thérèse agreed. She didn't miss Josette's flightiness, her questionable boyfriends, or her selfishness, but she did miss the bright laughter and her sister's exuberance for life. Somehow the vitality had left Josette, leaving an empty shell as though there was nothing left to fill her inside. "Give her time. I think she'll bounce back now that Grady's been caught. She and Brionney were laughing at church yesterday."

"That girl is good for Josette," Mathieu pulled on his coat and hefted his backpack. "She's got her head on straight. You can tell her parents raised her right."

Mathieu tried to take her backpack, but Marie-Thérèse slung it over her shoulder. "Just because we're getting married doesn't mean I'm suddenly weak."

He laughed and put his arm around her.

Outside, snow fell in large, puffy-looking flakes. Marie-Thérèse stopped and stared. It rarely snowed in Paris, and since she'd been in Utah the snow hadn't stayed long on the streets and had been rather slushy. She scooped some up in her hand. It felt like powder . . . tingly powder that burned her hand with its icy sharpness. Instinctively she brought it to her mouth, tasting the coolness with delight.

They stared at the blanket of snow that had layered the walks and grass while they were inside. Students made footprints in the snow, but they were quickly filling up again. The trees and bushes held inches of snow, as did the rooftops. Everywhere Marie-Thérèse looked there was white.

"It's beautiful," she murmured. "I'm glad I got to see it this way."

"Now you know what the people here mean by a white Christmas." Mathieu took her hand. "I never understood that before I came to Provo."

When they arrived at the apartment, Marie-Thérèse noticed immediately that all was not well. Brionney sat on the couch, comforting Josette, while Irene hovered nervously nearby. Marie-Thérèse twisted the engagement ring on her finger. Mathieu had sent it to be sized so it fit properly, but she still wasn't accustomed to wearing the thick band.

"Marie-Thérèse," Josette wailed, jumping up. "It's Pauline! She has cancer! We have to go home before it's too late."

Marie-Thérèse hugged her sister, her breath coming faster as the shock set in.

"Your mother called me and asked me to come here to talk to you," Irene said. "She didn't want you two to be alone when you heard."

"My mother called you?" Marie-Thérèse asked, feeling slow and stupid.

"Well, one of the missionaries serving in your home area, actually. They translated for her. For the past hour or so we've been arranging with your professors to have your tests done today or early tomorrow morning. Two of them said they'll accept the work you've already done as full credit—I guess you have enough points in those classes already. In the others you may have to send in any assignments you haven't finished. Anyway, I've booked you on a flight tomorrow. Right after you finish your tests."

Marie-Thérèse wanted to jump on a plane that instant, but the logical part of her knew they shouldn't give up nearly four months of hard work.

Irene wrung her hands. "Your mother wanted to wait until you went home for Christmas, but she was worried that you might not have the chance to say good-bye."

"But Pauline was doing so well." Josette had stopped crying, but her face was streaked with tears.

"Are you ready for your tests?" Marie-Thérèse forced herself to ask calmly. Her insides churned with emotion she wouldn't let herself feel. How could she have been so wrapped up in her own new love that she hadn't recognized that her sister was gravely ill?

"I don't care about the stupid tests. I just want to go home."

"The flight isn't until tomorrow so we might as well get the tests over with," Marie-Thérèse said.

She felt Mathieu's arm around her shoulder. "I'll be there as soon as I can," he said.

She nodded but didn't speak, fearing the tears would come seeping through. There was no time for that—not yet.

The next twenty-four hours passed like a bad dream—slow and torturous in some parts, surrealistically swift in others. They went to the testing center to take the tests available there, and later that night they each took an exam with separate professors. Marie-Thérèse slept little as she packed and studied for her one remaining test, to be taken at six the next morning. She called her parents to find out about Pauline's condition, but there was no answer at their apartment.

On Tuesday morning, Mathieu took them to the airport at nine. Brionney and Irene accompanied them. "Let us know," Irene said.

"We will." Marie-Thérèse accepted her hug.

Brionney threw her arms around Josette. "Write to me."

Marie-Thérèse didn't hear Josette's response because Mathieu took her in his arms. Desolation at leaving him overwhelmed her, hurting almost as much as the fear of losing Pauline.

How could I have ever thought of not marrying him?

Much later, after the flight attendants had served lunch and Josette snored softly in the seat next to her, Marie-Thérèse put her head under the tiny flight pillow and cried.

Chapter Twenty-eight

When Jean-Marc brought the girls home from the airport Wednesday morning, Ariana rushed to meet them at the door. Both Marie-Thérèse and Josette looked tired, and their faces were red and splotchy. Josette's hair was rigidly drawn back in a long French braid, making the new sharp planes in her face jut out unbecomingly. She'd become as slender as Marie-Thérèse, but the thinness didn't complement her as it did her sister. Ariana made a mental note to talk with her daughter and make sure she was all right. Josette had seemed to recover from the attack in Provo, but obviously she was still suffering.

"Where is Pauline?" Marie-Thérèse demanded. "Why isn't she in the hospital?"

"She's in her room," Ariana said. "Resting. There isn't anything more the doctor can do for her. She wanted to come home, and we agreed."

"How—how long does she have?" Marie-Thérèse's voice was less forceful now.

Jean-Marc set down the two suitcases he was carrying. "The doctor doesn't know. It depends on a lot of things. We thought having you here would help. Marc's here, too."

Tears slipped down Josette's cheeks. "Why didn't you tell us sooner? I—I'm so furious with you for not telling me!" Silence filled the entryway as Josette glared at them, but instead of the customary fire in her eyes, there was an icy sadness.

"We thought it important that you finish your semester, if you could." Ariana had expected a little anger or resentment from both her daughters, but Josette's coldness took her by surprise.

Josette tossed her head. "I don't care about school—and I hate Provo. Pauline's way more important."

Ariana tried to reach out to her, but Josette stepped away.

Jean-Marc pushed past Ariana and firmly put his arms around their daughter. "Pauline wanted it this way," he said. "We had to respect her wishes as well as do what we thought was best for you. We told her the last time she collapsed that if it happened again, we would need to call you home. She agreed."

"She collapsed?" Marie-Thérèse asked.

"Yes, from exhaustion." Ariana glanced toward the hall, but of course she couldn't see that far down to Pauline's room. "The first time last week it wasn't bad. She was out with a friend and he took her to the clinic. She was up and walking again in a few days. This last time it wasn't a collapse exactly. She simply woke up without the energy to get out of bed. We took her to the doctor, but there's nothing more he can do except give her medication if the pain gets too bad." She put her hand on her upper stomach, beneath her breasts, in the same place where the tumor grew inside Pauline's body. "Mostly, she tries not to take the medication because she wants to be aware of what's going on."

"I want to see her," Marie-Thérèse said.

Josette nodded in agreement. "Me, too."

"Well, she's been waiting for you." Ariana held up her hand. "Try to be positive, okay? Pauline may be the bravest person we know, but she's still afraid."

Josette started to cry again. Ariana held out her arms and this time Josette accepted her comfort. "What should I say?" Josette asked. "What if I say the wrong thing?"

"Tell her how much you love her. That will be enough."

They went to Pauline's room, and Ariana saw the girls' expressions lighten when they heard Pauline's tinkling laughter. André was on the floor, lumbering around on hands and knees with Louis-Géralde on his back saying, "On horsey, get going! Oops, I'm gonna fall off." The two fell to the floor. Marc, sitting on a chair next to the bed, leaned over and tickled the small boy.

Louis-Géralde noticed them first. "They're here!" He jumped off the floor and launched himself first at Marie-Thérèse and then at Josette, chattering as fast as his four-year-old mouth would allow.

Pauline's eyes brightened. "You look so different, Josette. You're skinnier than Olive Oyle. Marie-Thérèse, I love your hair." The sisters hugged and tears flowed down their cheeks. "It's so good to see you," Pauline added.

Marc and André hovered near the bed, awaiting their turn to greet their sisters. Josette hugged Marc tightly, and Ariana saw her whisper something in his ear. Her twin smiled and pressed his cheek against hers.

Ariana felt Jean-Marc's hand in hers. She looked over at him and read her own thoughts in his green-brown eyes. All of their children together again—full of smiles and joy. For this peaceful moment, at least, the realities of life were set at bay and Ariana was happy.

Chapter Twenty-nine

Marie-Thérèse stayed with Pauline that night when everyone else had gone to their rooms. "Marie-Thérèse," Pauline said, waving a thin hand in front of her sister's eyes. "Hey, Marie-Thérèse, you're about a million worlds away. What is it?"

Marie-Thérèse started guiltily. "I'm sorry, Pauline. I just was thinking."

"You looked like you were dreaming. Your face was all soft and . . . Marie-Thérèse, I can't believe it. You're in love!" Pauline pushed herself farther up on her pillows. "You can't hide information like that, you have to tell me. Who is it? Not an American—it can't be an American! Mom couldn't take losing you right now, not when . . . Spill everything, right now!"

Marie-Thérèse found herself telling Pauline all about Mathieu. "I knew going to America was going to be good for you," Pauline gushed. "Oh, I can't believe it. I'm so excited!" But she started to cry.

"What's wrong?" Marie-Thérèse stared at her sister, hardly knowing how to comfort her.

"I'm not going to see the wedding. I won't be there to see your babies. I—" Pauline stopped and swallowed hard. She closed her mouth and pinched her lips together as though to keep herself from sobbing.

Marie-Thérèse held her sister as she had when she was small and had skinned her knees or had been teased by the other children for having HIV. "I'm so sorry," she mumbled, hating the inadequate words.

"I know you're sorry. Everybody is sorry."

"It doesn't change things, does it?" said Marie-Thérèse. This was a side of her sister she had never seen. "What can I do? How can I help you not be afraid?"

"I'm not afraid," Pauline whispered. "I was once, but I'm not anymore. I just think that when I'm in heaven, sometimes I'm going to look down and wish I could be with you. I know they say this life is but a blink in all of eternity, but right now it seems like an awful big blink."

"To me, too," Marie-Thérèse said. "Oh, Pauline, I love you so much."

Pauline wiped the tears from Marie-Thérèse's face. "Please don't be sad. I want more than anything for you to be happy."

She pulled away and reached under her bed for a battered bundle that Marie-Thérèse recognized immediately. "That's the baby blanket Mom made for you before she died, the one you keep Dolly in."

Pauline nodded. "I don't think I ever thanked you for giving Dolly to me."

"You were only a baby."

"I know, but she's always been my favorite. I should have told you."

Marie-Thérèse fingered the worn blanket, still covering the doll. "You didn't need to. I knew. You never went anywhere without her."

"Dolly and the blanket were the only real connection I had with our mother," Pauline said. "I remember lying in my room sometimes at night, wondering where Mother was and how she'd felt when she made Dolly." She paused and added softy. "I used to talk to her."

"So did I," Marie-Thérèse admitted. "I think she heard. Dad too." She tried to unwrap the doll, but Pauline put her hand over hers.

"Do you think they'll look just like they did in the video tapes?" Pauline asked. "Will they come to meet me? Will I know them?"

Marie-Thérèse began to cry again at her sister's questions. "Yes. They loved us so much, and they will be so glad to see you."

"Then maybe I won't miss you as much as I think," Pauline said with a watery smile. "Now stop that crying. I'm trying to give you a present. Remember how Dolly used to look? With only one embroidered eye gone and her stuffing coming out? Well, look at her now." Pauline opened the blanket and revealed the treasure. The rag doll had been carefully patched and wore a new set of clothes. She had two eyes and new yarn for hair.

"I fixed her these last few days, lying here," Pauline said. "Mom helped me. I want you to have her back and keep her for your first daughter. I know she'll treasure her as much as I do."

Marie-Thérèse hugged the doll to her chest. "Thank you. It's the best present in the whole world."

Pauline grinned, but her face showed the effort their exchange had exacted. Marie-Thérèse touched her sister's arm. "Look at me, keeping you up so late. I'm afraid I'm still running on American time, and they haven't even eaten dinner yet. Come to think of it, I'm hungry."

"Don't leave," Pauline said. "Stay with me a little longer, until I fall asleep."

"Okay, if you don't mind."

Pauline smiled and held her hand, her eyes drooping. With her free hand, Marie-Thérèse turned the lamp to a lower setting. "Sing me a song," Pauline said. "Daddy's song."

Marie-Thérèse knew immediately what song she meant. It was the one their father had sung to them each night before he died.

Pauline had been too young to remember, but Ariana and Jean-Marc had captured the song on film. Marie-Thérèse didn't know where the song had originally come from or even if her father had used the right words, but for years after his death, she had insisted on singing parts of the song to baby Pauline so she wouldn't forget.

> *Tell me why life is so beautiful.*
> *Tell me why life is so happy.*
> *Tell me why, dear Mademoiselle.*
> *Is it because you love me?*

Four times through, and Pauline was asleep. Marie-Thérèse watched her sister's face, its contours sharpened by the shadows. So thin. So fragile. So guileless. Marie-Thérèse recognized the look, though it had been years since her parents had died. For a brief second, the pain in her heart was too terrible to bear.

She kissed Pauline's cheek and left the room, still clutching Dolly, and found her mother waiting for her in the hall. Without speaking, Ariana held out her arms. Marie-Thérèse went into them and the pain in her heart lightened—just as it had when Ariana had opened her heart and home to her as a child.

"Thank you so much," Marie-Thérèse whispered. "Thank you for loving Pauline—and me."

"I've received more from you two than I've ever given," Ariana said. "Never once have I regretted having either of you in our family."

"Not even during the hard times?"

"No. Never." Ariana paused. "But I was worried you were still angry at me. You were when you arrived."

Marie-Thérèse sighed. "I thought you should have told me about the cancer before. But when I was unpacking this afternoon, I found all the letters Pauline wrote me while I was in Utah. I'm so grateful for them now. Seeing her this way . . ." Marie-Thérèse brought a hand to her heart. "It hurts so much. But it's strange,

Mom. Sometimes when I think about her going to see our parents and all that, I feel an almost happy hurt because I know she'll be so excited to see them. Then I feel almost sad again, because I don't know if I want her to be happy without me." Marie-Thérèse started to cry. "I mean, I want her to be happy, but I'll miss her so much."

"I feel the same way," Ariana said.

For the first time, Marie-Thérèse noticed the worry lines in her mother's forehead. Ariana had buried her first child at eight months old—how must she be feeling now to watch a second daughter die? Pauline's death would be harder on her than anyone else.

Marie-Thérèse gently said goodnight and went to her room, silently vowing to do everything she could to help her mother. Only then did she realize that Ariana hadn't questioned her about her decision regarding Mathieu. *Well*, she thought, *that information can wait.*

She lay on her bed and let her thoughts drift to Mathieu.

Chapter Thirty

The next morning, Josette crept into Pauline's room to make sure she was all right. Her sister had the phone in her hand and looked up, guilt written on her face.

"Gotta go. I'll call you later." With effort, Pauline leaned over and hung up the phone.

"Who was it?" Josette asked. Pauline with something to hide? What an amazing thought.

Pauline shrugged a thin shoulder. "A friend, that's all."

"Tell me." Josette sat on the bed.

"It's Emeri."

"You mean the boy you wrote us about? Well, is he coming over? I can't wait to meet him."

Pauline shook her head miserably. "He won't come—not while Mom and Dad are here, and they won't leave me now."

"But why won't he come? That's so strange."

"It's something to do with his own parents," Pauline said. "He had a falling out with them. He won't tell me exactly, but I think they kicked him out of the house. It was right when he found out about his AIDS."

"Did his parents know?"

"That he was sick? No. I don't think so. I bought a Christmas card and made him send it to his parents. I kept a copy of the address, and I was thinking about going to see them, but I'm hoping they'll come looking for him, that whatever happened can be worked out." Pauline looked at Josette with pleading eyes. "Oh, Josette, I need to see him! Can't you figure some way to get Mom and Dad out of the apartment for just a little while so André can bring Emeri over? Please? If I ever wanted anything from you, it's this. Can't you figure something out?"

"You really care about him this much?"

"Yes, I do." Pauline spoke softly, but the look on her face told Josette more than any words ever could.

Josette straightened, her mind already working out the possibilities. "I may not be able to get Mom and Dad out of the house, but I'll bet a nice little outing in the fresh air would do you some good."

Pauline frowned. "I can't walk now, I'm too weak. I've tried, but it's no use."

"A chair! You should have a wheelchair."

Pauline brightened. "Of course."

"I'll be right back." Josette ran from the room, feeling more useful than she had in weeks. She found her parents in the kitchen and blurted out her idea.

Jean-Marc shook his head. "I don't think you realize how sick your sister is. She can barely sit up."

"But she's horribly bored!" Josette exclaimed. "We can't let her stare at the wall until she dies. Don't you see how much she hates that? This way she could just lie back in the chair, and I could take her for a walk down the street or to the swing sets to watch the children play."

"It's winter," Ariana said. "She shouldn't be out in the cold."

"The sun's out and it's almost warm. She can wear a jacket and a mound of blankets. Please. She really wants to go."

Ariana and Jean-Marc discussed the options. "It may make her weaker," Jean-Marc said.

Ariana glanced at Josette. "But it will make her happy."

In the end, Josette won, and she drove with her father to pick out a wheelchair. They arrived home shortly before lunch with the coveted chair.

"Dad wanted to buy you a better one," Josette told Pauline, "but I insisted on this one because they had it in stock."

"I'm so glad." Two rosy spots appeared on Pauline's pale cheeks.

Ariana went to the bed and checked her forehead for fever. "You'd better eat something first."

"But I'm not . . . okay, I'll eat."

When Ariana left to make lunch, Josette grinned. "So did you call him?"

Pauline nodded. "Yes, but I have to call back and tell him what time. I was so afraid you wouldn't get the chair."

"Well, call him." She started to hand her sister the phone, but André and Marc came into the room.

"I see Josette got her way as usual," Marc teased.

"That's right," Josette said. "And Pauline is going outside as soon as she eats."

"So where are we going?" André asked.

Josette looked at Pauline, and when Pauline nodded, she explained about Emeri.

"I should have known," André said. "Why don't you just leave it to me? I'll have Emeri down at the swings in, say, an hour."

Pauline touched his hand. "Thank you."

Ariana came in with lunch for Pauline and while she ate, Josette waited in the TV room with Marc. "I can't believe little Pauline's old enough to fall in love," he said.

"Well, she isn't," Josette returned. "But she's had to grow up fast." Before she could help herself, tears flooded her eyes and she hid her face in her hands.

"Are you all right?" Marc asked.

"I don't know. I don't know if any of us will ever be all right again without Pauline."

He put an arm around her. "We'll get through this together."

Her heart ached. Her own problems seemed so insignificant in the face of Pauline's impending death. A part of her didn't care if she was ever happy again. "I'm so glad you're here, Marc," she said. "I don't want to be without you now. I've missed you so much."

"I've missed you, too. It must be all that shared amniotic fluid or something."

Despite her mood, Josette smiled. She was about to reply when their mother came into the room. "Pauline's ready for you."

As her father placed Pauline's limp body into the wheelchair, Josette had second thoughts. Pauline was more frail than she'd imagined. Would this outing do more harm than good? But she couldn't bring herself to take away Pauline's happy smile.

As promised, André waited for them near the swings. With him stood a thin, angry-looking boy about André's age. His dark-blond hair wasn't long but not as short as Josette expected. He wore faded jeans and a long-sleeved T-shirt.

"This is Emeri," André said.

"Of course it is." Josette put out her hand. "Nice to meet you."

But Emeri knelt next to Pauline's chair, ignoring Josette completely.

"Be nice to him," André murmured in her ear. "He doesn't mean to be rude. He's anxious to see Pauline, that's all. And he can't help what he's wearing. None of your snobby college boyfriends will see you with him anyway, so don't make fun."

Josette glared at him. "I don't care what he's wearing," she mouthed. André looked surprised, but before she could think why, Emeri spoke to them harshly. "Please, could you leave us alone for a minute?"

They stood some distance away, watching but not close enough to hear. Emeri knelt on the cement in front of Pauline, her hand in his. His face was pleading.

"He's trying to talk her into marrying him," André said.

Marc frowned and took a step forward. "I don't know if I like that."

André put a hand out to stop his brother. "He's all right. Give them another moment. Pauline's a smart girl. She knows what she is doing."

Pauline shook her head gently and said something in reply. She lifted her arms as if to hold Emeri, but they fell back to her lap before she could complete the action. Josette bit her bottom lip and tried to hold back her tears. *Poor, Pauline. She's so weak, she can't even hug him.*

Instead, Pauline leaned her head down and forward until it met his. For a long moment they stayed that way, touching and yearning. Then her eyes went to them and they knew it was time to go.

"Goodbye, Emeri," Pauline said.

"No, Pauline, no," Emeri moaned. "I can't live without you! I don't want to."

A tear slid down her cheek. "Oh, Emeri. I don't want to be without you, either. Please—you know what you have to do."

Emeri's face tightened, but he didn't respond except to say, "I'll walk back with you."

Pauline looked content now, but Emeri's misery seemed to grow with each step. André tried to talk with him, but when they reached their building, Emeri shrugged him off and darted down the street.

"What did you mean when you said he knew what he had to do?" Josette asked Pauline when they were once more in her room alone.

Pauline acted as though she hadn't heard. "Will you help him, Josette? He's a good person—he's just had a hard life."

"I'm willing to do whatever I can, but he didn't even look at me."

"I know he was rude. You can forgive him that, can't you? For me?"

Josette blinked back the tears. "Of course, I will. I'm glad to.

I'm just sorry I haven't been the kind of sister I should have been all these years. I know I haven't been a good example."

Pauline titled her head on the pillow. "You're different now. What happened? Was it that boy?"

Josette had avoided talking about that terrible night, except with her counselor, but Pauline had always been special. "When he tried to rape me . . . it's just, well, one part of me thinks—I feel I deserved it."

"No way! You should never think that."

"But I'd been doing a lot of things I shouldn't have. If I'd been better, I would have been a lot safer. I should never have gone out with him." She shook her head. "That's all behind me now. I'm going to be the person I should have been all along. And you can be sure that I'm never going to trust a stupid man again."

Pauline slipped her thin hand into Josette's. "One day you'll find someone good, I know you will."

"I don't want to, Pauline." Tears stung Josette's eyes. "It hurts too much, and I'm tired of making the effort. I could never be sure he loved me for me and not just my looks. Oh, that sounds so conceited, doesn't it?"

Pauline smiled. "Kind of. But I know you'll find someone when it's time. Until then, you should focus on something else. Like maybe helping people, or teach them the gospel. You could start with Emeri. I'll bet you could charm him into listening better than I could. If he could feel the Spirit, I know he'd change."

"I'll help, but I'm through trying to charm anyone. It only makes things worse."

Pauline looked at her gravely. "If there's one thing I've learned in my life, it's that everything has a purpose. It's how we look at it that makes the difference."

Grady's attack had a purpose? The idea was a new one for Josette, but it bore consideration. *Maybe this is how the Lord intended things to be.* If she and Marie-Thérèse hadn't gone to BYU, Marie-Thérèse might not have met Mathieu, and Grady's attack would never have happened. Whether she liked to admit it or not, both Mathieu and Grady had made an impact on her life, urging her to reevaluate her priorities.

"Thank you, Pauline," Josette said. But her sister was already asleep. Josette tucked the covers around Pauline and settled back in her chair to think.

Chapter Thirty-one

During the days that followed Pauline's outing, the weather was too stormy for her to go out again, but she didn't seem to mind. She lay in bed listening to music or watching her siblings who stayed with her almost constantly, even during the long hours she slept. There was a resigned contentment in her manner that Josette had never seen before. Only when they talked of Emeri did Pauline look unhappy.

Three days after seeing Emeri, the home care nurse who visited Pauline began to come twice daily. She explained that the end was near. Pauline ate and drank little as her body prepared to shut down. They asked about an IV to prevent dehydration, but the nurse explained that the IV would only prolong Pauline's pain.

On Sunday, Josette found her mother in the kitchen sobbing as though her heart was breaking. Fear cut into Josette's stomach. Josette wanted to run away from her mother's pain, but Jean-Marc, Marc, and Marie-Thérèse had gone to church, and André and Louis-Géralde were with Pauline, so she was the only one available to help.

Josette patted her shoulder. "It's okay, Mom."

To her relief, André galloped down the hall with a grinning

Louis-Géralde on his back. She motioned quickly, and Louis-Géralde jumped down from André and climbed onto Ariana's lap, laying his head against her chest and patting her cheek with his chubby hand. Ariana's sobs stopped, but the tears still leaked from her eyes. Josette had never seen her mother so upset, not even when Marc had nearly died in the bomb explosion that had damaged his kidneys.

"I saw her getting married," Ariana said, drawing a deep breath. "I never told anyone except your father this, but years ago I had a dream. I saw Pauline smiling like she always does, as bright as the sun. She was dressed in white and kneeling at an altar in the temple. Across from her, I saw a man with blond hair. They were both so happy." She wiped a hand over her eyes, clearing them of tears. "I guess I started to believe it would really happen. I mean now, not in heaven." Her voice broke. "I wanted to believe. I'm sorry, children, forgive me. I just don't want to lose her. She has always reminded me of little Nette."

Nette was the daughter Ariana had lost when she was in her first marriage, before she had met their father. Josette had seen pictures, and the baby didn't look much like Pauline, except for the dark eyes and ready smile, but there was no logic to feelings. She hugged her mother, wishing she could take her pain away.

"It will still happen," André said. "Pauline *will* get married."

"I know that," Ariana replied. "And I am so grateful for that knowledge. How blessed we are to have the gospel—to know that she will live on, and that we will get to be with her again. I don't know how we would cope if we didn't have that assurance. But . . ." Her voice drained away. "I just wanted to meet him, I guess. I wanted to go pick out the wedding dress."

"I know who he is," André said.

She looked up at him with remorse. "Oh, I'm so very sorry," she murmured, wiping her face with both hands. "I'll be all right. You don't have to try and make me feel better."

André laughed, and the sound shocked Josette. André and

Pauline had always been inseparable, and she'd thought he would be the most affected by her decline. "I mean it," he said. "There's a guy at the clinic. The one Pauline has been dating. He asked her to marry him."

Ariana stared at him. "Emeri. It has to be him."

"That's right," Josette said, excited now. "She wrote us about him. She said she was in love. Marie-Thérèse can show you the letters."

"She really loves him?" Ariana looked more concerned than happy at the prospect. "It's not like Pauline to keep such a secret from me. I thought they were just friends. I've never even met him. I kept asking, but she kept avoiding me."

"She wanted to tell you, but Emeri refused to meet you and Dad." André's face was earnest. "I think he's afraid you'll send him away or something. Maybe not let him see Pauline. But I was with them during most of their dates, and Pauline never did anything for you not to be proud of."

"When she talks about him, she glows," Josette said. "And she misses him now."

André shot a thankful nod in her direction. He added nervously, "I wanted her to marry him right now, but she said she would only do it in the temple. He's a great guy, Mom."

Ariana smiled, and Josette felt her insides relax. "I want to meet him," Ariana said. "He should be here."

André headed for the door. "I'll go and tell him." He hesitated. "He has no family of his own. I'm afraid he might do something to himself when—if—Pauline . . . well . . . I'll be back as soon as I can."

Josette's eyes met her mother's. The tiny wrinkles surrounding them seemed lighter now. "Everything is going to be all right, Josette. The Lord has his plans; sometimes we're just too stubborn or wrapped up in our own feelings to understand them. Now, let's get back to Pauline. We've left her alone too long."

When André arrived at the clinic where Emeri was working on Dr. Medard's files, Emeri was sure he'd come to tell him that Pauline was dead. He was engulfed in an all-encompassing emptiness that left him unable to speak or move.

Instead, André smiled at him gently. "Pauline needs you to come to the house."

"I can't."

André snorted. "I won't take that excuse anymore. My parents aren't your parents. I don't know what happened in your family, but that has nothing to do with Pauline. Either you're coming or I'm carrying you."

"But your parents—"

"Want you to come. Don't you see? They need you."

"They don't even know me."

"Whose fault is that? Pauline may forgive you for not being with her now, but I won't. My parents aren't going to forbid you to see her—and what difference would it make if they did? At least you'd have tried for Pauline."

Emeri watched André's face deepen to a dark shade of red. "You're a coward, Emeri. A coward! Now, are you coming, or do I go home to my sister and watch her die without the man she loves?"

André stared at him for a full minute before turning on his heel, shaking his head in disgust. Emeri couldn't let him go. The last three days without Pauline had been the worst hell he could imagine. "Wait," he said. "I thought you were going to carry me." No matter the risk, he knew he had to see her.

André smiled. "Come on, then."

They were silent all the way to the apartment. Emeri felt a mixture of anticipation and dread. He'd been to the Perrault apartment building each day, yearning for the courage to knock on her door. Why was he such a coward? An ache grew in his heart that had nothing to do with Pauline. Had his parents received his Christmas card? Did they even care, or had they thrown it away?

His heart pounded furiously as André opened the door and led him into the entryway and down the empty hall. Inside a room, he saw Pauline lying in bed with her eyes closed. Others surrounded her, but Emeri couldn't take his eyes from the beautiful older woman who sat next to Pauline.

Pauline's mother, he thought.

He stiffened, steeling himself against the anger and rejection he knew he would read in her eyes. She wouldn't want him here; he didn't belong. He was dirty both physically and spiritually, well-deserving of the ultimate punishment God had bestowed upon him.

"Emeri." Ariana's eyes held his. "Thank you for coming. I needed you here." Emeri didn't understand why she should need him when she had so many of her own children around her, but he knew she spoke the truth.

"Emeri?" Pauline's eyes opened.

"Yes, Sunshine," he managed.

She held out her hand. "I knew you'd come."

All that day and the next, Emeri stayed by Pauline's bedside. Often she would open her eyes and watch him, and he could see the gratitude she felt for his presence. Sometimes she would smile and talk to him or to her family, but occasionally the pain would be too great and the nurse would give her medication to help her rest.

Emeri was never alone more than once or twice with Pauline. Ariana and Jean-Marc rarely left their daughter's bedside, and when they did, there was always one of her siblings present. As they sat around the bed, the family relived past adventures, and though he felt apart from them, Emeri enjoyed the stories and the feeling in the room. There was a spirit of comfort he'd felt before only when alone with Pauline.

Jean-Marc and Marc gave Pauline several blessings to deal with the pain. Once, Emeri prayed with them in his heart, wishing God really lived and that He had the power to heal her. But the blessing gave no such promise. *A fantasy. A crutch. A lie*, he thought. But sensing the family's serenity, he wished he could believe.

On Monday evening, Pauline opened her eyes. She tried to move, but grimaced with pain. "Would you like something?" Ariana asked.

"Marie-Thérèse," Pauline said.

Marie-Thérèse came to the bed, her eyes anxious. "I'm here, Pauline."

"Your little boy is going to be just fine. I'll help look after him."

Marie-Thérèse wrinkled her brow in confusion. "Thank you."

Pauline's words made no sense to Emeri. "A dream," he murmured. The nurse had warned that the medication could cause hallucinations.

Pauline smiled at him faintly. "My Emeri, always the critic. But this time I know what I'm saying." She swiveled her head to André. "Remember your promise. It means more to me than anything."

They both glanced at Emeri. "I will," André said.

Emeri felt Pauline was talking about him, but he didn't know what she meant. Did André understand the message, or was he patronizing her as Marie-Thérèse had done?

Early the next morning, Pauline was much weaker. Several times they tried to give her water, but she refused. During breakfast, Emeri was alone in the room except for Ariana.

"Emeri?" Pauline said.

His throat constricted. "Yes?"

"I love you."

He glanced at Ariana's face, but he didn't see resentment or hatred as he half expected. "I love you too, Sunshine," he whispered.

Ariana touched his shoulder before moving to the bed to sit next to Pauline. She stroked her daughter's hair, humming a song Emeri didn't recognize. Pauline grinned up at her. "Daddy's song," she said. Then she closed her eyes and slept.

Two hours later Pauline died, surrounded by her family and friends. Emeri was nearest the bed when her breathing shallowed and stopped, almost an imperceptible change. He gave a cry and put his arms around her. "No, Pauline! No!" He shook her gently before hugging her to his chest.

Ariana was sitting in a rocker with a sleeping Louis-Géralde in her arms. She gave the child to someone and rushed to Pauline's bedside, with Jean-Marc close behind. Soft sobbing began in the room around the bed as the family turned to one another for comfort.

Only Emeri was alone.

He stared at the people around him, mostly strangers he'd seen lingering for two days, but whose names he'd never bothered to learn. An older, silver-haired man said, "She's happy now. I'll bet she's with her parents."

"No!" Emeri roared, jumping to his feet. "No! No! No!" André tried to reach out to him, but Emeri shoved him against the wall. "I curse you all!" he shouted. "And I curse your God!" He turned and ran from the room.

Torment like he had never known wracked his thin body. He ran and ran in the cold streets until he had no strength left. He fell and lay on the road, motionless, wishing he could turn back the clock. He'd known Pauline was dying, but had thought that with him holding her it would be easier. It wasn't.

He heard squealing brakes on a car. "Is something wrong?" someone asked. "Are you hurt?"

Emeri ignored the voice and continued to lie on the blacktop, dry-faced and voiceless. There was too much agony in his heart to give in to the release of tears. People continued to talk to him, but he didn't notice them or what was said. All thoughts focused on the brief glimpse of paradise he'd shared with the only woman he would ever love. *No one could ever take your place,* he told her. He felt this as strongly as he breathed air.

He recalled her face, her shining smile, her ready laughter, and the few kisses she'd given him. His whole being ached with the need he felt. "Oh, Pauline," he groaned. Something inside him broke, and he began sobbing and screaming, pushing away the strange hands that tried to offer comfort.

Someone called the police, and they took him home. As it was late morning, his roommates were gone to work, and the apartment was empty. "You gonna be okay?" one of the policeman asked, seeming genuinely concerned.

Probably afraid of having to clean up after another suicide. Emeri managed a grim smile. "I'll be fine," he grunted.

Alone once more, he lay on his bed. The policeman had read his intentions correctly, but Emeri didn't need drastic measures; he would simply neglect to take his medication. Given a little luck, he'd die within the month.

He knew Pauline wouldn't be pleased, but she would never know. How could he go back to the horror of his life without her to soften his fears? Without her to give him hope? He hit the wall with his fist.

Why hadn't she married him? Then he would have had more special memories and the added dignity of mourning a spouse. She'd loved him! She had! And now there was nothing.

If only it was true, he thought. *If only I could see her again like she believed.*

Emeri turned his face to the pillow and wished he were dead. When darkness came again, he heard his friends in the next room. They knocked once on his bedroom door but didn't enter. He waited until their noises ceased before creeping to the kitchen for something to stop the gnawing in his belly, feeling disgust at himself for having to eat at all. How long did it take for someone to starve to death? He threw the bread in the garbage and returned to his room. From under his pillow he drew out the lock of Pauline's hair, the one he'd kept since their outing at the Eiffel Tower. Clutching it in his hand, he fell into a fitful sleep.

Chapter Thirty-two

The next two days were not lonely ones for the Perrault family. Their apartment filled with fresh flowers, plants, food, and condolence cards as people came to share their grief. After the first day Josette didn't cry anymore, because every time she became sad Marc would find some way to chase away the tears. Josette clung to him, grateful to have her twin—her other half—at her side.

Sometimes Josette felt Pauline wasn't gone at all, but just where they couldn't see her—a constant invisible presence.

At the moment of Pauline's death, things became clear in Josette's mind. Mathieu had said that she didn't know her own value or where she was going in life, and his words had been true. Now, as she pondered the gospel principles, she understood with a surety she'd never felt before that they were true. There was an afterlife, and Pauline would be happy. A warm rush of feeling confirmed her realization. But Josette wasn't sure that the life she had been living would bring her to the same place her sister had gone.

I'll change, she vowed. She didn't know where to begin, but felt Pauline would lead the way . . . somehow. Her little sister had always been the one to bring perspective to their lives . . . and so much joy.

For some reason, her thoughts turned to Emeri. She remembered his fevered exclamations on the day Pauline had died, how his brown eyes had stared into space with no apparent will except to die. There had been something so aching and defenseless about him that Josette felt the wall she had built around her heart soften. He was someone who loved her sister as much—perhaps more—than she did. He wouldn't be looking for a good time, or for anything at all from Josette, and yet, maybe she could help him as Pauline had asked.

Maybe she could finally do some good.

Chapter Thirty-three

Wednesday passed in a pain-filled haze. Emeri thought he could feel no worse, but Thursday morning brought André and a renewed agony. He wanted to tell his friend to get lost, and yet at the same time he yearned to throw himself into André's arms and cry.

"Come on, get up." André told him.

"No." Emeri's voice was muffled by the pillow.

His friend sat on the bed. "It's Pauline's funeral this morning. I'd think she'd want her fiancé there."

Emeri turned. "Her fiancé?"

"Yes. She told me about you two. She tells me everything. We're almost as close as you were."

Despite his resistance, André's words made Emeri feel better.

"I told her she should marry you right away—even being only sixteen," André added, "but she said she was going to do it right. She can be pretty determined."

"Tell me about it." Did that sharp chuckle come from his own mouth? Emeri couldn't be sure.

"My parents know how she felt about you. My sisters and

brothers, too. You need to go to the funeral. Besides, Pauline will want you there."

Emeri pasted on a smile, the sneering kind he'd mostly stopped using around André and Pauline. "She's not going to be there."

André's voice was steady. "Yes, she will. And more importantly, her family is, and we need you. You're part of us."

"I'll never be a part of your family. Pauline's dead."

"So? Does that mean we all give up on life? Didn't you listen to anything she taught you? Emeri, please come. If not for Pauline, then for me. I need you to come—we all do."

Emeri felt the naked pain in his voice, and he knew André suffered as much as he did. Perhaps there was some way he could help his friend before he died. "Fine. I'll go."

André helped him out of bed and pushed him toward the bathroom. "Hurry and shower. There's not much time."

The funeral was held at a church house because there wasn't enough room to hold all the guests at the mortuary. Emeri felt out of place, but he knew it had nothing to do with the poor way he was dressed. How different he would feel if Pauline were with him. Nothing else mattered but her love.

The chapel filled to overflowing with friends and relatives. The immediate family kept together near the front, holding tightly to one another. As Emeri and André entered, a beautiful girl with incredibly long brown hair separated herself from the family and swooped down on him. He knew he'd met her before, but until now he hadn't paid attention to her beauty. Josette was whole and vital, much like he imagined Pauline would have been without the sickness.

"Thank you for coming," she said, leading him up the aisle. He almost believed she meant it.

"Glad you're here, Emeri," Marc said to him as they approached. His eyes were red, but his manner calm. This was the one Pauline had called a missionary; he looked like an older version of André.

Pauline's father, Jean-Marc, held out his hand and shook Emeri's firmly, nodding in greeting. Ariana turned from a white-haired woman, and without a word of reproach for the way he'd acted at the house, she put her arms around him and pulled him close. She was shorter than he was, but he felt the comfort in her arms as though he were an infant. For the first time since Pauline's death, he cried. Ariana continued to hold him until the tempest calmed, her own tears joining his.

When he drew away, she smiled and spoke. "Come and sit by me."

Throughout the service, Emeri was aware of Pauline's family. They mourned her, but each talked about Pauline as though she was among them, listening in. He almost expected to see her, and several times caught himself searching the chapel for her bright face. An unusual calm came over his heart. Could there be something to Pauline's claims? Could it be that he hadn't lost her forever?

The thought was too good to be true.

Chapter Thirty-four

Marc sat next to Josette during the service. Despite the circumstances, he thought how good it was to be back with his family. His appreciation for them had grown on his mission; and now, with Pauline's absence, everyone felt a renewed determination to be worthy to see her again. Marc felt even more gratitude toward the Savior and the sacrifice that made eternal families possible. This helped stem the ache of missing his sister.

Josette surprised him. She was different somehow, though he couldn't pinpoint exactly what had changed. Her laugh rarely came, but that was to be expected during this time of mourning. She smiled and talked to him as usual, but she wasn't quite the same.

He gave up wondering and followed his family from the chapel, nodding at friends who'd come to comfort them.

"Marc!" A little body followed the words, coming at him like a missile.

"Rebekka!"

Danielle's ten-year-old daughter hugged him as tightly as her slender arms allowed. "Oh, I missed you! I tried to come and see you before, and Mom wouldn't let me go again. I'm so glad you came back."

"She's been talking about nothing else since she heard you were here," Danielle said, coming up beside them. Marc felt a leap inside him as he always did when he saw the beautiful Danielle, the woman he'd risked his life to save when he was fifteen. Not once had he regretted the act. He admitted to himself that he cared deeply for her, though he knew nothing more than friendship would ever come of it; even if she hadn't been fourteen years older than he was, she was completely dedicated to her husband.

"How great to see you," he said. "Mom told me you came by the house yesterday, but I wasn't home."

The little girl in front of him hugged him again. "You did miss me, didn't you, Marc?" Rebekka had gray eyes, high cheekbones, and auburn hair like her mother. From her father she had her firm jaw and her height. The little girl had been his faithful admirer from the age of five. Two years ago, she'd asked him to baptize her. "You're not going back to Nice, are you?" she continued. "I can't lose both you and Pauline!"

Her eyes glistened with tears, and her utter sincerity made Marc take notice. She was too big for him to kneel down and scoop her into his arms like he once had, but he leaned down and met her tearful gaze. "I am going back, but I'll write you like always. At the end of April, I'll be home for good. It'll go fast, you'll see."

Rebekka held his hand. "Promise?"

"I promise."

"Hey, I thought missionaries weren't supposed to hold hands." André tweaked Rebekka's ponytail.

"Sisters don't count," Marc said, straightening. "Rebekka's practically a sister. Besides, she's too young to worry about."

That must not have set well with Rebekka, because she promptly dropped his hand and drew herself to her full height. "Well!" she huffed and stalked away.

After the internment, most attendees left to go about their lives, but family and close friends returned to the church where the Relief Society sisters had prepared a luncheon. Little Rebekka sat next to Marc on one side; Josette sat on the other. Next to her was Emeri, looking slightly more happy than when he'd first come—if that mocking smile on the hard face could be called happy. Rebekka chattered endlessly, forgetting Marc's earlier comment, and he tried to give her his full attention. Danielle sat opposite them with her husband, Philippe, and Marc didn't like to watch them together. The way they sat comfortably close, with their shoulders touching, and the way their eyes occasionally met and held showed their obvious love. It bothered Marc that Philippe wasn't baptized, and that Danielle still could love him so completely. What did she see in that guy?

Grandfather Géralde had just offered the prayer when a young man Marc didn't recognize burst in the door, his head bobbing back and forth as he searched the small crowd. Marie-Thérèse gasped and jumped to her feet. It took her only a few seconds to throw herself into the man's arms and begin kissing him with a passion previously unseen in his reserved sister.

Mouth open, Marc tore his gaze away from the spectacle to see shock and surprise on all the faces around him. Only Josette and Emeri weren't interested and talked together in low voices.

"It's Mathieu, my cousin," Danielle said in her velvet-soft voice. "The one I sent the package to."

"That must have been some package," Marc muttered.

Rebekka laughed, her tinkling voice seeming to break the spell.

Marc followed his parents to where Marie-Thérèse stood with the stranger. "Marie-Thérèse, is there something you'd like to tell us?" Jean-Marc asked.

Marc saw that his father was trying very hard not to smile.

Marie-Thérèse's face and neck turned a bright red, but the man with her laughed confidently. He had the same color eyes as Danielle and Rebekka.

"This is Mathieu, my fiancé." Marie-Thérèse's flush deepened, but she didn't let go of Mathieu's hand. "I meant to tell you before, but there hasn't been time."

"I'm glad to see you again," Mathieu said, proffering his hand to Ariana and Jean-Marc. "We met at Danielle's baptism."

"Yes, I remember you," Ariana said, smiling.

"I hope you're not disappointed," Marie-Thérèse said. "I know you thought I was going on a mission. It's just that"—she glanced at Mathieu—"the Lord called me on a different one."

"Of course we're not disappointed." Ariana hugged her daughter. "We told you that when you called us from Provo before you went through the temple. As long as you do it right, I'm happy for you."

"We'll be married in the temple," Mathieu said. "And I'm going to spend the rest of my life making her happy."

"See that you do," Jean-Marc said with a wink. "Welcome to the family."

"Oh yeah, the ring." Marie-Thérèse fumbled in her purse and drew out a dark box. She opened it, and Mathieu took the ring and slipped it on her finger.

"There, it's official," he said.

A contented smile graced Ariana's face. "I guess I'm going wedding dress shopping with one of my daughters after all."

Until Rebekka giggled, Marc hadn't known she'd followed him. Somehow it reminded him of Pauline and how happy she'd always been. Only a short time before they'd all said good-bye to Pauline, yet already their family had increased by two—if they included Emeri. Marie-Thérèse's face shone with happiness, and she and Mathieu could hardly tear their eyes away from each other. Marc was fiercely glad that she'd become engaged now; it was just what their mother needed. What they all needed. How like Marie-Thérèse to change the tone of the day.

Marc almost laughed aloud. *Only Mormons could celebrate a funeral and an engagement on the same day,* he thought, shaking his head.

Rebekka tugged on his hand, her feet dancing excitedly on the shining wood floor, her eyes happy. "I wish it was our turn, Marc," she said.

This time Marc did laugh aloud. "I told you before," he said to her as they returned to their table. "By the time you're old enough to marry, I'll be an old man and you won't have anything to do with me." He'd told her that repeatedly since she was five years old and thought she'd finally given up the idea.

"No way," she said. "I'll always love you."

Marc sighed.

Chapter Thirty-five

"Are you taking your medication?" Josette asked Emeri early the next morning. One of his roommates had let her in, but Emeri was still in bed. She walked farther into his room and opened the blinds.

"Go bug someone else," Emeri said with a moan. But he let her bring his pills and a cup of water.

Josette worried that there wouldn't be enough time to save Emeri. Marc would only be staying until after Christmas, which would come in four days. Could they teach him everything in that short time? As an ordained missionary, Josette felt sure that Marc could help Emeri better than she could. Not that she wouldn't give it her best try. Why else would she wake up so early on a Friday morning, when normally Marie-Thérèse had to drag her out of bed?

She knew her self-appointed role as Emeri's savior helped her deal with her own loss, but there was something more. He exuded a helpless desperation she found appealing.

"You are invited to lunch at the house," she said. "We all want you there—will you come? Please?"

He groaned. "I guess. If you promise to let me sleep in tomorrow."

"Maybe."

At her family's apartment, Josette was afraid to leave him alone for a minute, and she was glad André felt the same. In fact, the whole family, except Marie-Thérèse, who was in a sphere of her own with Mathieu, went out of their way to make Emeri feel more comfortable.

Lunch consisted of a variety of foods brought by the Relief Society. There was plenty for even the pickiest eater to choose from, but Josette noticed that Emeri ate little.

Afterwards, he slipped out of the house while Josette was in the bathroom. "Why did you let him go?" she demanded from André.

"I couldn't tie him down." Seeing her frustration, he added, "Don't worry, he promised to meet me at the clinic in an hour. We're going to play basketball."

While André was gone, Marc showed Josette how he would conduct a real missionary lesson, and Josette marveled at its simplicity. She was still studying his manual when André returned home late that evening.

"Did he seem all right?" she asked anxiously.

André's face was serious. "For now. But I'm scared he won't make it. He doesn't want to try."

"The gospel's the answer," Josette said. "It has to be. Let's go teach him now."

"Tomorrow. I left him in his underwear. He's going to bed."

"All right then."

That night Josette prayed harder than she'd prayed in a long time. "Please, dear Father, let him feel the truth."

Early the next morning, she insisted on going to Emeri's apartment. "He may need us," she told André. "Come with me or I'll go myself."

"I promised Pauline I'd take care of Emeri, and I will," André said. "Even if it means protecting him from *you*."

Josette heard the laughter in his voice and decided not to take offense.

Marc rubbed the sleep from his eyes. "I'd better come as well."

The drive to Emeri's was silent. One of his roommates answered the door sleepily and motioned them to go on in to Emeri's room. "I thought I got to sleep in today," Emeri groaned when they knocked and entered.

"Ha!" Josette said. "From the dark circles under your eyes, I doubt you're doing anything resembling sleep. Take your pills. Here's water."

Emeri rolled his eyes, but he accepted the medication and the water. After gulping them down, he asked, "Now can I go back to bed?"

"I thought we could talk a little," Marc said.

Emeri scowled. "I'm not listening to your missionary lessons. I've told André before."

"We're just going to talk," Josette said.

"Fine, let's talk." Emeri sat Indian-style on his bed and folded his arms loosely on his lap. The others settled themselves around the room, Josette on a low table, Marc on a chair, and André on the floor.

Josette used every opportunity to slip the principles of the gospel into the conversation. She became impatient when Emeri didn't understand or didn't agree with her perceptions, and she had to continually make an effort to curb her sharp tongue. She wished she possessed Marc's control and ability to express himself.

A few hours later, she and Marc left Emeri with André.

"Sometimes I want to put my hands around his throat and choke him," Josette said to Marc in exasperation as they drove home. "Then he'd know I was telling the truth because he'd die and see heaven. How can you be so patient with him?"

He laughed. "It's the mission. You learn very quickly that unconditional love gets you a lot further than force. If you can get the investigator to feel and recognize the Spirit, most of your work is done."

"So how can we help Emeri feel the Spirit?"

Marc looked at her strangely. "I didn't think you'd want to learn this. You're . . . different somehow."

Josette snorted, but she knew he spoke the truth. Emeri's salvation had become the most important thing to her, more important than anything money could buy. She'd grown to love Emeri in the days she'd known him. Not as she'd thought she loved Mathieu, but more like the love she might have for a sibling . . . like she felt for Pauline, or perhaps Louis-Géralde. Already she felt as though Emeri had been her friend for a long time, and thoughts of him rejecting the gospel made her want to cry. The hard exterior he showed was nothing more to her than a transparent mask.

"I have to make him see how important it is," she said to herself.

Marc's eyebrows knitted as he concentrated on his driving. "You can't *make* him do anything."

"Then how can I help?"

"Pray, fast, bear testimony, and pray some more. And just be his friend."

Josette had begun to do all that. It had been a long time since she'd completed an honest fast, but tomorrow she would succeed. Silently she vowed to fast again each Sunday until Emeri accepted the gospel. At every opportunity, she would pray long and hard.

Being friends with Emeri proved to be the most difficult of Marc's suggestions. But Josette wasn't going to take no for an answer. On Sunday morning she awoke early and headed for the metro, this time leaving her brothers behind.

"What do you want from me?" Emeri asked irritably when she arrived at his apartment. He threw himself on his bed, stomach upward, and put his thin arms under his head.

"I want you to come to church later with me today. There's still a few hours before it starts."

He shook his head. "No, really. What do you want?" His smile mocked her.

Josette thought for a moment. "I want you to be happy."

"I can never be happy without Pauline," he said flatly.

The insinuation that he cared more for Pauline than she did infuriated her, but she stifled the stinging retort that first came to mind. "That's also why I'm here." Josette sat across from him on a hard-backed chair. "Because I love Pauline. My sister loves you, and she wants to marry you."

Emeri stood, his face flushing. "Then why didn't she? I'm so sick and tired of you and André talking like Pauline's just gone to the store to buy some bread. She's dead, gone, kaput . . . a drop in the cup of milk that is the universe, so to speak. I hate you trying to make me feel better. I *want* to feel bad. If you loved her as much as I did, you'd feel the same way."

He shook his fist between them, and instinctively Josette recoiled. As in her dreams, she saw Grady's face and felt the terror of the night of his attack. She must have cried out, because Emeri dropped his fist and stepped to her side. "I wouldn't hurt you," he said. "Heck, you're probably stronger than I am. Don't cry. Please, I'll behave."

Josette took a shuddering breath and took full advantage of his remorse. "It's Christmas Eve tomorrow. Mom's expecting you for Christmas dinner at midnight. Will you come?"

His cheeks rippled as he clenched and unclenched the muscles in his jaw. "I'll be there," he said without inflection.

Josette let her smile cover her face. "Thank you, Emeri."

"I—I don't have presents." The slight stutter told Josette of his insecurity as he could not.

"You won't need them. Just yourself is enough." She hesitated. "Besides, you know what we want—all of us."

"I can't believe something just because you want me to."

"No, but you could ask the Lord."

"When I know He doesn't exist? That's pretty silly."

"Maybe. Then again, think of it this way. Was Pauline an idiot?"

"No, of course not."

"We'll neither am I, and neither is André or my parents, and we believe."

Emeri mumbled something about mass delusion, but Josette thought he sounded less certain than before. "I'll come for dinner tomorrow night," he said. "But don't expect presents—of any kind."

Josette arose hastily. "Just come—that'll be enough."

"Tell André he doesn't need to come see me tonight," Emeri said. "I won't be here."

"He won't listen to me." Josette knew André would come, and Emeri would be waiting. The boys shared a bond forged by Pauline in life and made stronger by her death.

As she left the metro and neared her apartment on foot, shivering in her leather coat, she saw André waiting for her in the street. "Come on," he said jubilantly. "I've found it! It was in my drawer—one of the places you thought she might put it. I've been waiting for you so we could go."

"Tell me about it on the way. Oh, but first I'd better tell Mom where we're going. I don't want her to worry."

"I already told her." His nose was red from the cold, and his warm breath made a cloud in the cold air.

"You're freezing. How long have you been out here?"

He shrugged. "Not long."

They retraced her steps to the metro. "Dad said we could take his car, but we have to go get it at the church."

A honking horn drew their attention. "It's Alphonse," Josette said, her heart beating more rapidly than before.

The car pulled up to the curb in front of the entrance to the underground train. "Josette, it *is* you."

"Hi, Alphonse," she said faintly, staring at her old boyfriend. She pulled her foot back from the stairs that led down into the metro. Embarrassment spread through her to be caught using public transport like an average working person. She should have begged her mother to take her in the van instead of braving the discomfort of the hard-seated train—especially in such cold weather. She could usually get her way if she tried—and that would have prevented the humiliation of this meeting.

"Do you want a ride?" Alphonse's black eyes stared at her lazily, making Josette suddenly aware that she wasn't wearing any makeup. And he had never seen her with her hair tied back so severely. Why hadn't she at least worn her hat?

"We could go out to breakfast," Alphonse suggested.

Josette felt an urge to jump into the warmth of Alphonse's car, to tell him to take her home and wait for her to get ready. She rubbed her gloved hands together. Being with him would be like old times. Fun. Not to mention warm.

"I can't. I'm going somewhere important." *And it's Sunday*, she added silently.

"You don't sound too sure," drawled Alphonse. "Besides, what can be more important than having fun with me?"

Josette glanced at her brother and saw that he watched her with guarded eyes. Regardless of what she chose, he would go on and their mission would be accomplished. He didn't need her.

Something inside her rebelled. This outing had been *her* idea, and it was much more important than spending time with a playboy like Alphonse. She stared at him with new eyes. What had she ever seen in him anyway? Sure, he was good-looking, wealthy, and knew all the latest fads, but would that help her get to heaven where Pauline waited? Would he be able to take her to the temple? No. More than likely, he would lead her to more heartache than Grady had ever wreaked upon her. The things Alphonse craved meant so little—why hadn't she understood that before? This realization forced an embarrassing thought into her mind: *What did people see when they looked at me?*

"I can't go," she said. "I'm sorry."

Irritation flashed over his features. "Okay then. See ya around."

"Yeah, see ya around." Her last words went unnoticed in the squealing of his tires on the cold blacktop.

"Thank you," André said quietly. "I didn't want to go alone. You're better at meeting strangers."

"I need to go," she replied. Then she grinned. "Besides, when Emeri gets his surprise, I can't let you take all the credit."

André sighed. "I just hope it works out—and that he doesn't hate us."

"Me, too." Josette was all too aware that their plan could be a horrible mistake.

They rode the metro to near the chapel where their father was attending meetings. "Are you sure about this?" he asked them.

Josette nodded in assent, though she wasn't really sure. "We have to try, don't we?"

"Yes, I guess you do."

"Besides, it was Pauline's idea," André added. "She was the one who really found them."

"Good luck, then." Jean-Marc flipped Josette the keys to the car. "Try not to be too late. Your mother will worry if you don't show up for church."

"We'll try to make it back in time."

As he slid into the passenger seat, André asked, "What if they really don't want to see him?" André said.

Josette chewed her lip thoughtfully. "Then we'll never tell him. I wish Marc was with us. With his missionary training, it would be easy for him."

"Somebody has to go to church with Mom and Louis-Géralde. Besides, he promised to go invite Emeri."

That brought a smile to Josette's face. "I already did, and he didn't seem too anxious. He said for you not to bother coming tonight."

"He always says that."

Their conversation drifted to other things—mostly to memories of Pauline. Josette was surprised that she could laugh again.

The hour drive went all too quickly. They found themselves in the countryside far away from the bustle of Paris, and here they could see small groups of houses instead of towering, closely packed apartment buildings.

André peered at the map. "Turn here. Go straight until we get to the end of the road, then turn right. The house number should be easy to find."

It was. Josette brought the car to a full stop and killed the engine. She met André's nervous gaze. "Okay," she said. "Let's go."

They opened the freshly painted white iron gate and walked up the cobbled path. The stones were bigger than Josette was accustomed to seeing in most places in Paris, but she thought them pretty. Everything looked immaculate and well cared-for. How could people like these throw away their son?

Footsteps responded almost immediately to their knock at the door. Josette's heartbeat quickened. *Is this how Marc feels when he knocks on doors as a missionary?*

A woman about her mother's age answered the door without peeping through the spy hole or asking who was there. Her blonde hair was swept into a roll at the base of her neck, the strands streaked with a lighter gray that fit naturally with her fair complexion and kind eyes. "May I help you?" she asked.

André looked at her, saying nothing, and Josette wished again that they'd brought Marc to do the talking. "Are you Madame Fauré?"

"Yes." The woman's brow wrinkled. "Why do you want to know?"

Josette took a deep breath. "It's about Emeri."

Madame Fauré paled. "Oh," she said, bringing an open hand to her heart.

"Who is it, dear?" a man's voice came from somewhere inside the house. She turned to answer, the light catching her face and emphasizing the fine lines around her blue eyes.

"They know Emeri."

A tall man came into view in the hall behind Madame Fauré.

Josette could see from the wide set of his brown eyes and the square face that he was Emeri's father. Unlike his wife, who was thick in the waist and legs, he tended toward leanness.

"Is this true?" he asked. "You know my son?"

Josette nodded, afraid to trust her voice.

"He's our friend," André said. "He dated our sister."

Monsieur Fauré looked them over, as if searching for visible flaws. What he saw must have pleased him because his face relaxed. "Please, come in. Leave your coats here and we'll talk in the sitting room." He gestured to a coat tree behind the door. Josette would have preferred to keep her coat, as she felt it insulated her nervousness, but she obeyed.

The couple led the way to the sitting room. Its furnishings were simple: couch, rocking chair, coffee table, bookcase, and the typical family pictures. A younger Emeri smiled out at them, but with none of the mocking that was so prevalent in his manner now. He looked confident and in control.

Josette and André sat on the couch, while Emeri's mother settled into the rocking chair. Only Emeri's father stood, his hands plunged into the worn pockets of his rough pants.

"Where is he?" Madame Fauré asked.

"He's in Paris," Josette said. "Didn't you know?"

The older woman shook her head. "We haven't heard from him since he left two years ago. We weren't sure where he was. Except for this." She picked up a Christmas card on the coffee table. It had a nativity scene on the front—a glittering-robed Mary cradling a tiny Jesus to her breast. "This came in the mail a few weeks ago." Madame Fauré handed Josette the card, opened so she could read what was inside.

"Just wanted you to know that I am fine," Josette read. "Hope you have a good Christmas." She looked up from the card. "That's my sister's writing."

"Pauline bought the card," André explained. "She made Emeri give her the address, and they mailed it together."

"Then it wasn't from him." Monsieur Fauré's voice was bitter.

"But it was," Josette said earnestly. "At least as much as it could be. Emeri gave Pauline the address, didn't he? He wanted you to know he was all right."

"Two years without contacting us." Monsieur Fauré began to pace. Josette could feel the power and frustration in the tight strides. "Two years of worry, of wondering if he was even alive." He stopped abruptly. "Tell me, would you do that to your parents?"

Josette shook her head and opened her mouth to speak. Madame Fauré beat her to it. "I tried to find him at first," she said. Her husband's stare focused angrily on her, but she shrugged it aside. "I did, but he wasn't anywhere. I think he knew I would look." She swallowed hard. "Then I just prayed that he'd come home and we could work things out. He's a good boy at heart. Really."

Josette glanced at André for explanation, but he shrugged.

Monsieur Fauré saw their confusion. "Emeri was a smart child," he said. "He knew all the answers in school, and we had real hopes that he'd grow up to be something, not just to lay cobblestone like his old man." He gave a short, mirthless laugh. "When he got older, things changed. Suddenly he didn't like to show how smart he was, and he flunked classes. I see now that we probably pushed him too hard, but he's our only child, and we wanted him to do something with his life." Monsieur Fauré's eyes pinned hers and Josette knew the worst was coming.

"He started running with a crowd of misfits," Monsieur Fauré continued, "and they did things we didn't approve of. Finally, we told him he had to change . . . or leave. The next morning he was gone. He didn't even leave a note."

"But do you love him?" Josette felt stupid even as she asked the question. Emeri's mother clearly had love in her eyes, and his father's love was there too, if buried deeply beneath the hurt and anger.

"We love him," Monsieur Fauré said, "but I still meant what

I said that day. I won't have him turning this house upside down with his selfishness, or let him hurt his mother again. If he wants to come back, it'll have to be on our terms."

Emeri's mother was crying. "Is that what he wants?" she asked. "To come home?"

Josette wanted to weep at the hope in her face. "Emeri doesn't know we're here. We came because he needs you, but he won't come himself."

"I think he's changed," André put in.

"How?" the couple said together.

Josette closed her eyes, praying silently that the couple would open their hearts to Emeri and his situation. Pauline had known Emeri would have to face them one day, and that was why she'd paved the way for this visit. For all their sakes, Emeri needed to make peace.

Chapter Thirty-six

Josette is so pushy. Yet even as Emeri thought the words, he knew she and André were all that stood between him and death. They brought him food, friendship, money, and made him take his medication.

Why was it that when they were near he could feel Pauline?

He went to the dresser where he kept his few clothes, most given to him by friends or bought with the paltry sum he made at the clinic. The top of the dresser was completely bare, except for the box he kept there. Inside this was the musical merry-go-round he and Pauline had seen in the shop that day, complete with the mythical unicorns. He'd intended to give it to Pauline for Christmas to remind her of their hopes and dreams. At first he wanted to buy her a ring, but she'd been adamant.

"When we're ready," she had said with a beautiful smile. For some reason, the memory didn't seem so painful now.

Emeri wound the base on the merry-go-round and set it turning. Music filled the room, and he was amazed to find he was smiling. "Can it be true, Pauline?"

The music told him anything was possible, but Emeri was long used to disappointments. AIDS, cancer, other opportunistic illness, and even his parents proved that. Once he'd believed they would find him and say they loved him despite the illness he knew he'd brought upon himself—perhaps even deserved. Yet never once in two years had he heard from them. Maybe Pauline was right that he should have called them first.

Regardless, his parents weren't like hers. He would have gone with Pauline to meet her parents much earlier if he'd known how the family would treat him. The way Ariana had put her arms around him reminded him of his own mother when he was small.

Emeri sat down on his bed, still watching the white unicorns bob up and down on their gold posts. He'd been wrong refusing to meet Pauline's parents. Was he wrong about other things as well? He'd tried so hard to keep his perspective, to reject anything that could let him down or cause him pain. Until he met Pauline. She'd changed him, and now he was afraid because there was nothing to hide him from the truth—whatever it turned out to be.

The unicorns continued in their circle and the music urged them on. Emeri stood and turned it off.

Chapter Thirty-seven

The package was still in Pauline's top drawer, where she'd left it before taking to her bed. It was addressed to Emeri. Ariana placed it beneath the tree with the other presents awaiting midnight on Christmas Eve.

She and Marie-Thérèse had gone through Pauline's belongings, storing some things for keepsakes and giving the rest away. There was only one special item Ariana couldn't find, but perhaps Pauline had given it to Josette or André for safekeeping. She would remember to ask them later.

"Is it time yet?" Louis-Géralde danced from foot to foot. "Is Father Christmas coming?"

She smiled. Christmas was so much more exciting through the eyes of a small child. Her youngest son brought back memories of other Christmases when her older children were small.

The guests began to arrive, and a subtle energy filled the air. Their apartment had been created from two smaller ones joined together, making the kitchen twice its former size and a perfect setting for a special Christmas dinner. Jean-Marc put the leaves in the table, and Marie-Thérèse set it with the best china. Louis-Géralde laid out the silverware that had once been Ariana's grandmother's.

"We're back," Josette said from the entryway. She came into the kitchen with the outside cold clinging to her coat. Her nose and cheeks beneath the large brown cap were rosy and her eyes bright with suppressed excitement. "We brought Emeri."

André and Emeri came in behind her. Louis-Géralde ran up to them. "I'm glad you got here before Father Christmas," he said. "He might not know where to leave your presents."

"So are we eating yet?" asked Grandma Simone.

"We have to sing first," Marc protested, "or it won't be Christmas."

They gathered in the sitting room before the small tree that nestled in a corner of the room. Ariana scanned the beloved faces of her children, her parents, Jean-Marc's mother, his sister and her family, and Grandma Simone. Everyone she loved gathered in one place, plus the two new additions, Mathieu and Emeri.

"I never imagined it would be Marie-Thérèse to get married first," Jean-Marc said in her ear.

Ariana smiled, snuggling closer to her husband on the couch. Marie-Thérèse and Mathieu were so wrapped up in each other that little seemed to penetrate their world. She knew the Lord had timed Marie-Thérèse's romance perfectly to offset the loss of her sister.

"Poor kid." Jean-Marc's voice was full of sympathy. Ariana turned her head to see him watching Emeri. The boy's eyes were wide, taking in the atmosphere around him. How long had it been since he'd had a proper Christmas? How long since he'd been included in a family?

"Pauline always did have a soft heart," she whispered.

"He's a good boy," Jean-Marc said.

The buzzer rang and Josette, who'd been hovering by the door, darted into the entryway. "I'll get it," she called over her shoulder.

"But everyone's already here." Louis-Géralde jumped up from his place by the presents under the tree. "Maybe it's Father Christmas!"

Josette reappeared in the doorway a short time later. The family was singing and Emeri sang with them, his eyes glued to the sheet music in front of him as though he'd never learned the simple words. When the strains died away, he looked up and saw the newcomers with Josette. The color drained from his face.

"We went to see them," Josette said quickly. The anticipation was gone from her manner, replaced by trepidation.

Emeri shot her an angry glance. "You shouldn't have interfered."

"They wanted to see you."

"It's none of your business!"

"I care about you!" Josette's voice wobbled, but she held her chin high, her eyes flashing with a hint of her own anger. She swallowed hard, then added more calmly, "Pauline left André their address."

"Son," said Emeri's father.

Emeri's attention snapped away from Josette. He stood up slowly, not taking his eyes off the couple in the doorway. Ariana felt her heart go out to him. The fake smile he usually wore had faded to no expression at all. Only his watery eyes showed how much the outcome of the next few minutes meant to him.

"Why are you here?" he asked.

"We've missed you, Emeri," said his mother.

His father took a step into the room. "Can we talk?"

"These are my friends," Emeri said. "We can talk here."

Monsieur Fauré hesitated. "We'd like you to come home."

"You didn't want me before."

"Yes, we did," his father said. "There was more to it than that."

Emeri's voice became faint. "You didn't come for me."

Madame Fauré took a step forward, her hand outstretched. "I wanted to. God in heaven only knows how much. Only He heard my prayers. I looked for you, but I couldn't find you. Not anywhere. I thought you didn't want to be found. Dear, dear Emeri—my boy." Her voice broke and tears ran down her cheeks. "If you ever cared even a little, please give our family a second chance."

Emeri tore his gaze away from them and stared at the carpet. In the abrupt silence, the grandfather clock in the corner chimed nine-thirty. Ariana wished she could put her arms around Emeri, but she knew she shouldn't interfere—not yet.

"I love you," Emeri's mother offered.

Emeri glanced at his father, whose face wrinkled with worry. "I love you, too." The words were obviously difficult for Monsieur Fauré.

"I'm sick," Emeri said.

"We know."

Emeri's expression again showed no emotion. "You still want me to come home?" There was a slight catch in his voice that his immobile face couldn't hide.

His mother was across the room in an instant, gathering him into her arms. Monsieur Fauré was only a step behind. Emeri's broken sobs filled the room. "We're going to be here for you—whatever it takes," his mother said.

The tension in the room dissolved, and everyone relaxed, gazing at the Fauré family with open curiosity. Louis-Géralde resumed his survey of the presents under the tree, his interest in Emeri's parents vanishing completely.

Ariana stood and put her hand on Emeri's arm. "We'd like your parents to stay, if they will. I know you have a lot to talk about, but perhaps it could wait a little while? Remember there's still dinner, and you have presents to open after." She wasn't sure if she was overstepping her bounds, but something told her this reunited family needed to be in a non-threatening atmosphere while they adjusted to each other again.

Emeri smiled—a normal smile this time. "Thank you." She'd never heard his voice so sincere.

"We don't want to intrude," said Emeri's father.

"You won't be. We planned on your coming." Ariana gave Emeri's arm a final squeeze and returned to the couch. Jean-Marc had brought in a couple of kitchen chairs for the visitors, squeezing them between the tree and the couch, and soon they blended into the rest of the family.

They sang songs, gradually working from the fun ones to the ones with a deeper, more spiritual meaning. After all the singing, Marc presented the true story of Christmas. He told of the Savior's birth with feeling, and Ariana was amazed to see the spiritual growth he'd made on his mission. Was this the same boy who had teased his sisters so mercilessly? Too bad Josette couldn't make the same progression. But then she, too, seemed different now— not as changed as Marc, perhaps, but on the right road. It was a beginning.

The Faurés were very touched with this special family evening. "I never knew Christmas could be like this," Emeri's mother murmured to Ariana as they left for the kitchen and the dinner, kept hot in the oven. "Thank you so much for everything— especially for . . . for loving my son."

"I only wish I would have met him sooner. He and my daughter were in love, did you know that?"

"Your children told me, but I have so many questions."

"Ask Emeri," Ariana said. "I'm so glad you came tonight. He needs you. As much as we care for him, no one can replace his parents."

Madame Fauré looked fearful. "What can I do? How can I have him back, only to lose him again?"

Ariana understood exactly what Emeri's mother was asking. Hadn't she asked the same question of herself before she accepted responsibility for Pauline? "That I can't tell you," she said. "But I do know that it will be worth every second."

"Looking at you and being with your family here tonight, I believe that's true."

Ariana smiled and led her guest into the kitchen that welcomed them with laughter and love. Everyone helped move the food to the table, and in the confusion Ariana made sure Louis-Géralde didn't see his father sneak from the room to help Father Christmas lay out additional presents and Christmas goodies. Other years they'd opened presents before eating; but always when the children had been young enough to believe in Father Christmas, they'd done it this way. The idea was to build anticipation during dinner, and it was certainly doing that, at least for Louis-Géralde. "I'm so excited," he kept saying.

Emeri looked happier than Ariana had ever seen him. She saw him whisper into Josette's ear and noticed her daughter's quick return smile.

Ariana hardly had time to miss Pauline until much later, when Emeri opened the present Pauline had left. Inside the flat box was a set of scriptures she'd sent out to be newly bound in a raised leather cover. A card said in bold letters: *To Emeri—I love you with all my heart—forever.* Taped onto this was a thick gold band that Ariana had been looking for earlier in Pauline's room.

There was silence in the room as Emeri stared at the ring.

"It belonged to Pauline's birth father," Ariana said. Silently, she berated herself for not opening the present to save Emeri the pain the gift must cause him.

Emeri's laugh startled her with its unexpectedness. "Pauline was right about a lot of things," he said in an odd voice. "Who knows? Maybe she was right about this." He slipped the ring onto his finger.

From behind the couch, Emeri retrieved another present Ariana hadn't seen before. She and Jean-Marc had bought Emeri as many gifts as they had for the other children, but she hadn't expected anything in return. "I bought it for Pauline," he explained.

Ariana unwrapped the merry-go-round with an exclamation of delight. "It's beautiful. She would have loved it. *I* love it." She set the unicorns in motion and the tinkling music filled the air, sounding curiously like Pauline's laughter.

Somehow, everything was all right.

Chapter Thirty-eight

The day after Christmas, Josette took Marc to the airport. "I'm going to miss you." She hugged him as tightly as she could.

"I'll be back at the end of April, Jose," Marc said. "That's only four months away. Then we'll be together again."

Josette didn't reply. She didn't think she'd be at home when he returned, but she wasn't sure enough to tell him.

Marc carried his scriptures in his hands. They had deep puncture marks in the lower corner. "What did you do to the scriptures I gave you?" Josette asked, glad to change the subject.

He lifted them. "What? You haven't heard that story? Where have you been? I must have told it a hundred times in the past week."

"Sorry, I've been preoccupied."

"Well, these saved my life. You can't know how precious they are to me."

Josette suddenly felt like crying. "I'll write you," she promised.

"You've said that before. You should take lessons from your friend, Brionney. She writes her brother every week."

"Maybe he's nicer to his sister."

"What? I'm the nicest brother you've got."

"No, Louis-Géralde is the nicest brother I've got. He shares all his sticky suckers with me. Besides, maybe if you were as good-looking as Elder Fields, I'd write you every week."

Marc slapped his open palm on his forehead. "Oh, no! Not you, too."

There was an edge to Marc's voice that Josette hadn't noticed before. "What do you mean?"

"Nothing. Just get him out of your head. He's not your type, okay? Besides, he's a year younger than us."

"What makes you think I'd even be interested in him? I'm through with men."

Marc took a staggering step backward. "What! You?" He laughed so hard that he began to choke. "That's like bread without butter, Christmas without presents, songs without music . . ."

"Get on your plane."

". . . dogs without cats, babies without pacifiers . . ."

"Good-bye!" Josette started to leave.

". . . cheese without mold, banks without money . . ." He hesitated.

"What about missionaries without missions?"

"That, too." Marc cast her a cheerful grin, picked up his carry-on, and was gone.

Josette laughed softly. Marc always knew how to cheer her up. The bleakness of facing the next months without him was swallowed up in her twin's undeniable love.

Chapter Thirty-nine

Emeri and his parents drove home from the Perraults' early Christmas morning, and in the silence of the car, the euphoria and peace Emeri had felt with Pauline's family vanished. *What will happen now?* he worried. How could he and his parents make up for the past?

Yet when they arrived home, he found Christmas waiting all over again: presents stacked around the tree, his room cleaned, the bed freshly made.

Emeri stood in the hallway between his room and the living room, astonished. "But you didn't know I would come."

His father shook his head. "No, but we hoped."

Emeri swallowed hard. He remembered his father's face the way it had been two years earlier, how his finger had pointed out the door. "Why?"

"Because we want to help you."

Bitterness filled Emeri's throat. They only wanted him now because he was going to die. They wouldn't have to deal with his shady friends or bad habits because there wasn't strength left in his body for rebellion. Besides, it was certainly the proper thing to do. The old familiar ache began in his chest. Why couldn't they want him for himself? Emeri wanted to run into the night and scream out his anguish, but his father's next words halted his flight.

"I was wrong to send you away. I wish we could have talked more. I wish . . ." His worn face crumpled. "Oh, son, I wish we had more time! I'm so sorry. Can you ever forgive me?"

Tears flooded Emeri's vision. "It was my fault." He'd known that all along, just as he knew he deserved to contract AIDS.

His father snorted. "You were only a child. I shouldn't have been so hard on you. I should have let you know that I still loved you, and that you were welcome to come back once you were ready. I will regret that moment to the end of my life. But I promise you I will do everything I can to make it up to you now. Will you let me?"

Emeri nodded, fighting tears as he accepted his father's embrace.

Thank you, he said silently. Then he wondered to whom he spoke. Pauline? Himself? His parents? Certainly it wasn't to God . . . or was it?

His mother began shoving presents at him then, and he was caught up in the excitement, despite the early hour and his exhaustion. He felt like a small child again and found it impossible to maintain his emotions as he normally did. "I'm sorry," he said, "I don't have anything for you."

His mother rubbed her hand on his back. "You're here."

In her eyes he saw happiness, and warmth filled his heart until it almost hurt. He'd never expected to find a reason to live after Pauline died, but maybe for that look on his mother's face and the comfort of his father's hugs—maybe those would be enough to give him the courage to live a few more days.

The two long breads in the cloth bag were warm under Emeri's arm and side where he carried them, fresh from the small neighborhood bakery. Their smell tantalized him, and he reached in and tore off a piece as he'd always done as a child. His mother had never minded the missing piece, and it tasted so much better hot and flaky like this.

Pauline's ring flashed in the weak December light. The band on his finger was a constant reminder of Pauline and her love. In fact, all the good changes in his life also were evidences of her love. Having his parents back made up for the long months of suffering alone before meeting Pauline. He wished his parents could have met her.

As he approached the house with his warm bundle, his mother opened the front door. He handed her the bread. "Here you are."

She must have been watching for him out the window, as she had when he had gone at five years old to fetch the bread alone for the first time. He'd felt so proud that day, clutching the francs in his clammy hand and marching to the corner store like one of the big kids. Close on the heels of that memory came others: of him sullenly refusing to do the simple errand, of his choice to leave with his friends rather than taking time to help his mother.

Shame washed over him, and he kissed his mother's cheeks tenderly. How could he have been so blind to the importance of his family? Those so-called friends were gone now, replaced by others who had come and gone over the years, but he was learning that families were special. Hadn't Pauline said that to him a hundred times?

"Thank you, Emeri." His mother peeked inside the cloth bag and laughed. "Some things never change. Will you even be hungry for dinner? It'll be ready in an hour."

"For your cooking, I'll always be hungry," he lied. It wasn't that his mother's cooking was bad, he simply didn't have much of an appetite due to his illness. But for her, he would pretend. "Besides, when you say an hour, I know that means at least two."

She laughed. "Oh, well, but it'll be good." She put her arm around his waist and squeezed briefly before turning into the kitchen. Emeri heard her humming, a sure sign of contentment.

It was still hard to believe his mother loved him after the

horrible things he'd put her through in his rebellious years. He vowed to make it up to her by being the son she deserved.

Before this last thought was complete, panic filled his heart. What if there wasn't much time? How could he bear to leave them? Now that his parents were beginning to trust in his love, how would they face life without him? How long would his parents mourn his death? For the first time, Emeri understood how Pauline had felt about her family.

He walked into the room he'd used since childhood, fighting the torment. How had Pauline faced this fear?

With her faith. It was that simple.

Before he realized what he was doing, Emeri fell to his knees on the throw rug covering the wood floor. "I don't know if you exist, God," he said. "But I want you to. Oh, how I want you to! I can't bear thinking of the pain my parents will have to go through again when I die. Haven't I hurt them enough? Oh, God, please!"

Tears overcame him and he could no longer voice his thoughts. *I miss Pauline so much. Will I see her again? I love her still. I will always love her. This feeling is so strong—how could it simply end? Do you exist?* He paused, focusing all his attention out to the universe beyond. *Oh, God, if you do exist, do you love me as Pauline said? Is there a plan?* The words came from the depths of his soul, releasing the yearnings he'd felt perhaps all of his life. *There has to be more than what I see.*

He knelt in the middle of the room until his knees ached and the cold in the unheated room crept into his body. His face lifted earnestly toward the heavens in silent pleading. Just when he thought he could stand no more, the answer flooded warmth into his body, penetrating each vessel and deep into the part of him that was his soul.

The next thing he knew, his mother was holding him, her cheek pressed tightly against his. "Wake up, Emeri," she was saying frantically. "Are you all right? Do I need to call the doctor? Emeri, please!" He felt her tears on his cheeks.

He opened his eyes and saw the face that was so dear to him, etched with worry. "Oh, Mother," he said. "I'm all right. I've never been better than today. I know that God lives."

The Sunday after Marc returned to the mission field, Josette met with the bishop privately in his office at the church house. "What can I help you with?" he asked. His warm smile and sincere manner told Josette he cared, and she felt all her reserves dissipate. They talked for a long time, and Josette poured out her heart to him as she never had before. The little sins she'd committed, things she'd never thought twice about before, came bubbling to the surface like sour blotches on her conscience. Some were embarrassing, but she was determined to free her soul from even the smallest thing that might keep her from being one hundred percent pure—or at least as close as she could come.

"We are a people of obedience," the bishop said. "And that means not stepping on the lines the Lord has drawn. I think you've done that quite regularly, but I can also see that you are repentant. I know it's not easy coming to me like this, but be grateful you've seen the seriousness of your path before it led you to some real heartache."

Josette was beginning to understand that her actions had caused a great deal of her inner loneliness and pain. The way she behaved had attracted a certain kind of boy—completely opposite from Mathieu and others like him. Even Grady's attack might never have happened if she'd been more careful in her choice of dates or more mindful of her own priorities.

"I guess it's been a game with me to see if I can get all the guys to like me," she said, her face flaming.

The bishop smiled. "That in and of itself is not such a terrible thing, but you need to always keep your standards very high. However, I want to make it very clear that in the situation with

Grady, he was definitely in the wrong. While you might have prevented the attack, you weren't responsible for it. There is no excuse for what he did."

Josette knew that, but she was glad he told her all the same. "I'm through with men," she said in a low voice.

"Well, that's all right, for now, but someday your feelings will change. Until then, you need to make something of your life. Make yourself a worthwhile contributor to those you love and to the Lord's cause. Then you will have something to offer a spouse."

Josette didn't think she'd ever want to have another relationship, much less get married. How could she know if he would be another Grady? Or reject her like Mathieu?—that still stung more than Josette cared to admit. But making something of herself wasn't a bad idea. *I want to be proud of me,* she thought. *I want my mom to be proud of me.*

She looked over at the bishop, sitting easily across from her. "How do I begin?"

"Well, I have an idea." He turned his laptop in her direction. "Do you recognize this site?"

"Yes," she said. "In fact, I think that's why I'm here."

When Josette arrived home later that afternoon, she found her family waiting anxiously for her. "Emeri's in the sitting room," André said with a wide grin.

"Go on, talk to him," her mother urged.

Josette hurried into the sitting room where Emeri stood by the Christmas tree, toying with one of the ornaments. Immediately, she saw that he was different. The hard look in his eyes had softened, and he held himself with a confidence that was real, not faked like before.

"How are you?" she asked. She'd talked to him several times

on the phone in the four days since Christmas, but he'd been too involved with his parents for any more of her awkward lessons.

He turned toward her, smiling. "Thank you for not giving up on me."

"I care about you."

"See?" he said. "That's part of it. Like with Pauline, when I first saw her walk into that room at the clinic. It was like I knew her already. I knew I would love her and that I would never find anyone who would love me more than she did. She felt it too. It was . . . indescribable. I had some of the same feeling when I met your family. I think you all must have promised both Pauline and me up in heaven that you'd help me find the truth when the time came."

Josette felt tears on her cheeks, but she almost laughed. "And did you?"

"I prayed about it." He shook his head. "It seems so stupid, but I got to thinking about how my parents still loved me, and how I felt when I first saw Pauline. That was meant to last. There was only one way that could happen: it must be true."

"It is!" Josette said fervently.

"I know." He hugged her. "I asked André if he'd baptize me next Sunday. My parents have agreed."

The whole family came in then, spilling through the entrance to the sitting room in a way that told her they'd all been listening at the door. For a long while Josette just watched them, feeling the love in her heart. She would miss them all.

"We've finally set a wedding date." Marie-Thérèse held onto Mathieu's hand as she always did. Mathieu had begun a new job, but on his days off and every other spare moment, he'd become a permanent fixture in their home. Part of Josette would be glad when she didn't have to look at him anymore and remember what had happened between them. She envied his love for Marie-Thérèse. Was there anyone out there so wonderful for her? She seriously doubted it.

"Good, then you two can stop mooning over each other in front of us," Josette said, forcing her voice to be light.

Marie-Thérèse grinned. "Well, it's not until May, right after Marc comes home. We'd wanted to get married sooner, but this way we can all—"

"If you wait until May I won't be there," Josette said.

Her sister dropped Mathieu's hand. "You're not still mad about . . ." She trailed off, obviously not wanting to bring up the past in front of their parents.

"No, no. It's not that. I just have plans."

"Are you going back to BYU?" her mother asked. "The semester ends in April, doesn't it? That shouldn't be a problem."

Josette laughed, enjoying their puzzlement. This wasn't the way she'd envisioned telling her parents of her decision, but since everyone else seemed to have a life-changing announcement, who was she to fight fate? She jumped up onto the couch, trumpeting through a make-believe instrument she made with her hands.

"Hear ye, hear ye! Take your seats or grab something to hold on to, because you are all not going to believe this. I'm going on a mission."

Chapter Forty

"Are you sure you want to do this?" Emeri's mother asked him as they arrived at the church.

Emeri smiled gently at her worried expression. "Yes, Mom. I have never been so sure about anything as I am about this."

His father cleared his throat, a sure sign he wanted to say something. Emeri waited. "I think," his father began finally, "that you're really vulnerable right now, with your girlfriend dying and your own illness. We just don't want to see you hurt, that's all."

"This isn't a whim brought on by my illness," Emeri replied. "I've been dealing with my sickness for two long years. I've grown resigned to it. But now I know there's hope. And do you know what I want more than anything in the world?" His parents shook their heads. "I want you to know as I do that God lives so we can be a family forever."

His father shook his head sadly. "I don't know, son. I just don't know. I believe God lives, but I don't know about the rest. It all seems so . . . so different from what I believe."

"All I ask is that you try," Emeri said earnestly. "I pray the Lord will let me live long enough to help you understand the truth."

His mother was crying again. She seemed to spend all of her

time since his return either being incredibly happy or mired in despair. Emeri jumped from the car and helped her out, putting his arms around her. "I love you, Mom."

"You are so changed," she said. "How can it be that your terrible experiences have led you to this happiness? How can bad lead to good?"

"It isn't bad leading to good so much as it is submitting to the Lord's will and becoming strong through the challenges. I think—I had a lot of time to think—and I've decided that maybe I needed all of this to change, to believe. To be humbled. Maybe it was the only way for me to recognize the truth."

"That makes a person worried to pray," his father said. "For fear of what God might send. We prayed for you to come back, but if it could have spared you this horrible disease, perhaps it would have been better for you not to return to us."

Emeri smiled, recognizing a beginning of faith in his father's words. Prayers that brought trials were still prayers being answered. "I contracted AIDS before I left home," he said. "And I know it might sound pretty stupid, but I wouldn't change knowing Pauline and the gospel for all the health in the world."

"She must have been very special."

"She is. And one of these days you'll know just how special."

His parents nodded and followed him into the chapel.

During the baptismal service, Emeri felt the Spirit strongly. From the reverent expressions on his parents' faces, he knew they felt it too. Gratefully, he noted that Ariana and Josette sat next to them on the front row and appeared to be answering their questions.

When he arose from the water, feeling curiously refreshed and stronger than he had in months, he saw Pauline grinning at him from one of the chairs in a front row of the baptismal font. Happiness radiated from her being, like light from the sun. He waved and blinked the water from his eyes, and Josette replaced the vision of Pauline. She lifted her hand in answer to his wave.

Emeri wasn't sad. Maybe he hadn't really seen Pauline as whole and beautiful as she was in heaven, waiting for him, but he believed she was up there all the same. An angel—his angel.

His parents met him as he came from the dressing room. Ariana and Jean-Marc stood near them. "I'm so proud of you," Ariana said, hugging him.

Josette came out of the room where they would hold the confirmations. "They're about ready to begin." She put her hand on Emeri's father's arm. "And I talked with the missionaries like you asked. They said they were looking forward to teaching you."

"Thank you."

To Emeri, his father appeared confused. Could it be that Josette was forcing the discussions upon them, the way she'd tried to force Emeri? As they entered the room, his father leaned over and whispered to Emeri, "I know this sounds strange, son, but I could have sworn that girl wasn't the one sitting next to me during the baptism. She looked younger. I guess my memory's getting soft in my old age."

Emeri relaxed. He slapped his father on the back. "I guess it is." Then he added silently, *Or maybe you saw Pauline.*

Chapter Forty-one

Portugal? There must be some mistake! The words stayed with Josette for a long time. When the shock faded, she busied herself with preparations. She was to leave for the Missionary Training Center in Provo in early February, shortly before her twenty-first birthday.

"What I don't understand is why you have to go there for training," Emeri said. "And then back to Europe to serve."

"We'll that's not usually how they do it. There is an MTC in England where—"

"Then why don't you go there?"

"They don't teach Portuguese. Spanish, yes, and another language, I think. But no Portuguese."

Her friend's head wagged back and forth like the pendulum on her parent's grandfather clock. "Weird, you going to Portugal."

"I know. It does happen, though."

"Must be a reason."

Josette moaned. "Yeah, to torture me with another language. But maybe once I get to the MTC, they'll change it on me, and I'll stay in the States to serve. That's happens sometimes, too."

"At least you'll be able to attend my parents' baptisms before you go," he said. "Funny, them accepting so quickly when it took me so long."

"Some people are simply prepared," Josette said.

Emeri grinned. "So I'm stubborn?"

Josette put an arm around him. "You are. But I wouldn't have you any other way."

The days flew by quickly. Marie-Thérèse opted to move her wedding to the week before Josette left France, and Josette had the opportunity to receive her endowments in the German temple before seeing her sister sealed. Both were touching experiences, but Josette almost cried when she saw how much Mathieu loved Marie-Thérèse. *Why couldn't someone love me like that?* she thought.

She put the thought aside and threw herself into last-minute mission plans. The day before her flight to Provo, she received a package in the mail from Marc. She laughed when she recognized the scriptures she'd bought him before his mission—the ones with the deep bite marks. "These'll keep you safe," Marc wrote, "since I won't be there to do it."

The other thing she did before leaving France was to have her long hair cut to shoulder length. There would be no time to take care of it on her mission, and though she missed the feel of it against her back, it felt good to be free of the weight. Her neck no longer ached from the tight, heavy braid, and her frequent headaches disappeared.

Brionney picked her up at the Salt Lake airport. "I missed you. Dang it! I wish I could go with you on your mission." Everything she said, except for the "dang it," was in passable French.

"Wow, your French is getting better. You must have been practicing."

"Not much else to do," Brionney admitted.

"That's a relief, because I haven't practiced English at all. If you don't mind, I'd like to continue in French."

Brionney appeared pleased. "Okay." She hefted one of Josette's suitcases. "I can't wait to tell my brother you're going on a mission."

The thought of Brionney discussing her life with Elder Fields bothered Josette. She didn't want anything to do with men, and that included him. Besides, from what Brionney had told her, Zachary Fields was a lot like Mathieu, "except he jokes around a lot more." What would he say about her?

"Don't tell him about me, Brionney. Please."

Brionney looked surprised. "He likes it when I write about you. When you lived here, he asked all the time about how you were doing."

"Probably because I'm Marc's twin," Josette said. "But please, don't say anything to him. Or to anyone we know. I want to go on a mission without everyone talking about it."

Brionney shrugged. "All right, I guess. But Zack is hardly just anyone. He's my brother."

Josette put her arm around Brionney. "I'm sorry. I don't mean anything bad by it—I guess I'm just not quite ready to face what I'm about to do."

Brionney giggled. "I remember you once saying that the only sisters who went on missions were ones who couldn't catch a man. I never thought you'd be in that category."

Josette hid a grimace. She was *not* running away. "I want to go on a mission," she said a little too fiercely. "You should have seen it when Emeri was baptized last month. I want to see that joy again, Brionney. It was incredible!"

"Do you think he and Pauline will get together in the next life?"

Josette was only too glad to change the topic. "Oh, yes!" That strong feeling was something she would hold on to for the rest of her life.

At the MTC, Josette plunged into learning the language and the discussions. She had little time to miss her family. The busy, reclusive life of the MTC was exactly what she needed to keep her mind away from her personal insecurities. As the weeks passed, only the language remained a problem. The sisters were friendly, and the elders reminded her of her little brother, André, so at least there were no problems with romantic attachments. While many were admiring, they were too young to be taken seriously. Josette simply wasn't interested.

"Will you write to me?" asked an elder in her district. He was going to Brazil, so it wouldn't be against the rules to keep in touch.

"Maybe," she said, not wanting to hurt his feelings. He was the second elder who'd asked. Should she tell him them she simply wasn't interested? "I have problems writing my own brother," she added. The missionary looked disappointed, but Josette felt sure he should be concentrating on his missionary commitment instead of paving the way for future romance.

When she wrote Brionney about it, her friend replied in her next letter, "I'm glad you were nice. Once you would have laughed them out of the room."

The information shocked Josette. *Could I have been so cruel?* She vowed to be more careful in the future.

For the first two months, Josette hated everything about Portugal. While the people were kind, there were many cultural differences—much greater than she'd noticed in the States. Three things bothered her in particular. There was visible poverty in the country—a life that before had only been real on the TV or in books. Not that poverty didn't exist in France or America; it simply hadn't been a substantial part of her world.

She later found that many places in Portugal were similar to her homeland, but her first few months in Portugal were spent in Chelas, which included large stretches of cement or wooden shacks. The people who lived in these hovels were very poor, though perfectly willing to share anything they had with the missionaries. Many had no running water, but used a communal water spigot in the center of the dwellings. These poor people readily accepted the gospel, though many did not have the stamina to stay active after the missionaries moved on.

"They don't have the membership here yet to fellowship them," said Sister Jackson, her American trainer. "But one day they will come back. I just know it."

The first few times they taught these impoverished souls, Josette tried to give part of the discussion in her meager Portuguese, but faltered as she saw fleas hopping onto her body. A few hours later her skin was raw with the bites.

Nothing in these poor houses was very clean, and she shuddered to think what some of the children ate before they went to bed. Her companion often rolled up her sleeves and cleaned with the mother, while Josette tried to entertain the grubby children. It was a part of life she would have preferred not to see.

Even worse for Josette was the language barrier. Accustomed to being the center of attention, she was abruptly plunged into silence. The language they spoke didn't seem to be the same one she'd learned in the MTC. It was all "sh" sounds and endless empty vocabulary. At least the nasal vowels came easily because of her French.

The third thing Josette had difficulty getting used to was the incessant walking. In France she'd walked a great deal, but it was nothing compared to her mission. They walked nearly everywhere they went because using the bus wasn't usually practical. Many of their investigators lived on opposite sides of the city, and a few of the tallest apartment buildings didn't have working elevators. The backs of her calves burned with the effort of reaching them, and even when that faded, a constant physical weariness ate at her. She felt as though her companion was determined to single-handedly teach each of the twelve thousand people in their area before she was released.

"I love Portugal," Sister Jackson said when Josette had been in the country less than a month. "I don't want to go home—ever."

Josette hid a grimace. Sister Jackson had only three months before she left; Josette had five times that.

To make matters worse, the room they rented in the unheated apartment of an inactive sister had broken glass in the window, and the green carpet was so dirty that it made her shudder to walk on it without her shoes.

"Think of it as camping," Sister Jackson said brightly. "That's what I do. I've never cooked on a gas stove before."

Josette groaned. "The stove's not the problem. I use the same kind at home—well, ours lights automatically. It's the carpet I'm worried about. We could grow beans in it."

"At least we wouldn't starve."

"No, but we might freeze to death." Josette knew she was whining, but she couldn't help herself. "If I have to take one more cold shower, I'll die!"

"Fernanda bought a bottle of natural gas today," said Sister Jackson. "I saw her hooking it up." Their landlady had no husband, but lived with her young son, a child with a vision impairment, and she used the money they paid in rent to subsist each month.

That night Josette huddled in her bed, feeling the bitter breeze from the broken window. She wore flannel pajamas, and on top of the blankets Fernanda had given them, she'd thrown her heavy coat.

Camping, she thought bitterly. She was beginning to have second thoughts about serving a mission. Why was she so impulsive? She could be at home right now in her own warm bed. What she would give for a week of uninterrupted sleep!

I'll just do my time and never look back, she thought. *I'll never be sorry to leave this miserable country.*

Two months later found Sister Jackson in bed with a severe cough and fever, and there was no way she could work in the April rain. "You don't have to worry about anything," she said to Paula Muxana, the young member girl who'd be going on a division with Josette. "My companion will do all the talking."

"But we have five lessons scheduled for today." Josette felt overwhelmed, knowing they'd planned to invite all of their investigators to be baptized.

"You can do it," Sister Jackson said. She coughed violently for a few minutes before adding, "It's not like you have a problem with the language anymore. I could never have done it with only a few months in the country."

"You do speak well," said Paula. "Much better than I speak French, and I've been learning it in school for years. It must come easy for you since the verbs are similar."

"Not to mention the backward way you Europeans arrange your sentences." Sister Jackson heaved a sigh. "It's enough to drive me nuts."

Josette thought about what they were saying and found it was true. After all that study and prayer, the language had stopped being a problem. It was certainly a lot easier than English. She closed her mouth, unable to complain again about the lessons she would have to give all alone. The Lord had blessed her.

She still didn't understand why she'd been sent to Portugal. Would she break all the baptizing records in the mission? Become a media figure and bring millions to the truth? What could it be? Something great, she supposed. Maybe she'd find out soon. Maybe even today.

Chapter Forty-two

"You left your towel on the bathroom floor again this morning," Marie-Thérèse said as Mathieu kissed her lightly on the mouth.

"What, are you a member of the towel police?" He lifted her head from the armrest of the sofa and sat on the couch, cuddling her head on his lap. The sofa, coffee table, and floor lamp were the only pieces of new furniture they'd been able to afford for their rented apartment, and they were still paying on those.

"No, it's just that I seem to spend a lot of time there now." She lifted her arms and let them slide to the back of his neck, but she didn't repeat their kiss for fear of losing her last snack.

The six months since she married Mathieu had been the most amazing of her life. Oh, there had been disagreements, especially about money, but nothing overly serious. As for day-to-day living, Mathieu was as easy to live with as he was to love.

Except that now she couldn't seem to get off the couch unless she crawled, brush her teeth without gagging, or even give her husband more than a peck for a kiss. She'd much rather be tracting with Josette.

"What's for dinner?" Mathieu asked.

Marie-Thérèse groaned. "I was afraid you'd ask that."

He laughed, but it sounded sympathetic. "I'm kidding. I stopped for something on the way home." He smoothed her forehead.

"Good, I'm getting hungry—and you know what that means." Mathieu had already cleaned up after her several times when she hadn't made it to the bathroom.

He planted a hasty kiss on her forehead. "I'll be right back then."

She held onto his hand a while longer. "Are you sure we have money to keep getting take-out like this? If only I weren't so sick."

"They say it eases up after three or four months." He said the words often, as if trying to convince both of them. The thought gave her some comfort in a world where all her days blended together with the soggy, rolling feeling that encompassed her every waking moment.

"Must be a boy," she said, remembering what Pauline had said before she died.

"Or a girl with attitude like Josette."

He had a point.

"I'll never forget her face when she got her call," Mathieu said.

"Neither will I."

"Portugal?" Mathieu mimicked in a high, disdainful voice. "That small country? I can't believe it! Why, practically nobody outside of Europe even knows where it is."

Marie-Thérèse giggled, regretting it almost immediately as a wave of nausea hit her. "Mom was excited because she has friends there, but Josette isn't even serving in their mission."

"I hope serving is what she's doing, instead of sitting around complaining."

"She wasn't excited to learn the language, that's all," Marie-Thérèse said in her sister's defense. "You know how she struggled with English. The call to Portugal took her totally by surprise. Hardly anyone I know here has been called out of France."

"I knew two guys who went to England, and one to Germany."

"Well, there has to be a reason for it. I wonder what?"

"Maybe so she'd be humbled?" Mathieu suggested. "There's nothing like being plopped in a foreign country all by yourself without knowing much of the language. That took me down a peg or two, I tell you. When I first went to BYU, I mean."

"That could be part of it." Marie-Thérèse was the first to admit that Josette had always been a little arrogant. Maybe this mission would be more for her own good than for anyone else's.

With that, Mathieu left to heat up the dinner in the microwave they'd received as a wedding present. It was quickly becoming her best friend.

A crinkling sound reminded her that she'd been reading Josette's latest letter before Mathieu came in. She lifted her back and fished it out from where it had fallen. When the queasiness had passed, she began to read.

Chapter Forty-three

She was transferred to Campo Grande after three long months in her first area. The president had pulled out the two elders in the area and sent Josette and another sister in their place. Finally, she was the senior companion and would direct the work. Maybe now she'd discover why she'd been sent to this small country.

Her new companion was a native greenie, Sister Carvalho, who had wiry black hair and a pale complexion. She was generally cheerful and willing to give her best effort.

"Oh, I'm so tired!" Sister Carvalho complained at the end of their first week, collapsing on her bed. "If I walk another step, I'll die!"

"At least you don't have to worry about the language," Josette said sympathetically.

"You don't seem to have a problem."

Josette laughed. "I think I got some help from—how do the Americans say it?—the man upstairs. I was horrible when I first got here."

"I don't believe it." Sister Carvalho began to scratch her arm.

"It's true. I used to lie in bed at night and wish to be transferred to France. But I got used to it. There wasn't much choice."

Her companion moaned. "Dang these fleas! Ever since I got here, they won't leave me alone!"

"That's another thing you won't have to worry about. On P-Day, we'll scrub this whole place down and get rid of them once and for all."

"How'd they get here? This is a clean place."

Josette looked around. This tiny one bedroom apartment was vastly different from the apartment in her first area. Not only was it immaculately clean, but they lived there alone. The widow member who rented it to them had gone to live with her grown daughter, and now she came a few times each week to clean and pick up their laundry, which, like the elders before them, they would pay her to wash.

"The missionaries here before us must have been working in the shacks," Josette said.

Sister Carvalho stopped scratching at the tone of Josette's voice. "Is there something wrong with that?"

"No, not really. I've met some really wonderful people there." She hesitated. "They have a tendency to accept the gospel, but they don't stay active."

Sister Carvalho pushed herself up on her elbow. "That's not what we need here, is it?"

Josette shook her head. "Someday, I hope the members in your country can reach out better to the poor." The truth was that many people here worked hard to eke out an existence and had little to share. Those who did were often overburdened because of their generosity.

"Don't worry," Josette said, removing her shoes. "We won't tract in those areas. We have plenty of contacts in this city. And members, too. Let's use them. The fleas will be gone soon."

Campo Grande, for the most part, was similar to the large cities near Paris. Half of the area consisted of older buildings, but on the far north side, expensive new apartment buildings stretched far into sky. On each floor there were eight large apartments. For part of every morning, they knocked doors at these new buildings. First they had to convince someone to let them in the outside door, as the new doors were never broken or left open. Then they would ride the elevator up to the top and start knocking until they reached the bottom. Occasionally people let them in, but most refused to have anything to do with them or their message.

"Is tracting always so fun?" asked Sister Carvalho after three weeks in the area with no success. There was no missing the sarcasm in her voice.

Josette laughed. "It's all in the attitude. You get used to being rejected." But it was getting to her as well. In three weeks they'd had no baptisms—something that had rarely happened to her before. She knew that soon the president would want to know which commandment they were breaking.

Having baptisms each week was common in Portugal, especially among the sister missionaries. If the missionaries worked hard, were obedient to the mission rules, and prayed, baptisms would literally follow their path. It was the one thing Marc envied about her call to serve in Portugal. Thoughts of her brother brought a wave of homesickness, a feeling she usually managed to keep at bay. He'd gone home from his mission in late April, and was probably immersed in his studies by now. André had turned eighteen and was serving his mandatory time in the French army. Before she returned, he'd be on his own mission. Marie-Thérèse would also have her baby before Josette left Portugal. Life at home, it seemed, had continued on without her.

On the way home for lunch, they sang hymns to cheer themselves. "It's beautiful here," her companion said.

Josette lifted her face to the warm sun. It would be a normal August day—hot and sweaty—but for now there was a fresh breeze in the air. On the other side of the street lay a large strip of undeveloped land where trees, bushes, and grasses made up a small forest. She felt her feet nearly skip on the new cement sidewalk, so like those in America instead of the more common cobblestones.

"It is," she said. "Thanks for reminding me." Sometimes she became so involved in finding people to baptize that she didn't take time to notice the world around her. "Your country has some great beauty—and the people are nice."

Only yesterday they'd asked directions, and a man had insisted on personally showing them to their destination. He refused to give them his own address, but Josette was sure he'd have given her his shirt, shoes, or even money had she asked for it.

They passed a large area where wooden shacks crowded in upon each other, most covered with peeling paint—if they had any at all. Toward the edge of the settlement, a woman in a long black skirt collected water in a basin at the communal water spigot. Aside from an occasional weed, there was no grass or greenery anywhere in the little settlement—only dusty earth.

The wind died and the sun beat down on them relentlessly. Before long, the heat would make walking outside almost unbearable. "Let's cut through the woods," Josette said impulsively. "It should be shady there. We can get the bus for home on the other side."

Her companion agreed, and Josette's body relaxed as the shade chased away the heat. Green spread out in every direction before them. Birds called, and unseen things moved in the brush. Her companion plucked a stem of long grass from the ground and chewed on its sweetness.

All at once, Josette's smile left faster than it had come. To their left, deeper in the woods, she could see another settlement of shacks, much smaller and poorer than the others. They were made of cast-off wood of varying lengths; a few had rough shelters big enough to protect the blanket mounds they called beds. Josette counted at least three hovels that were simply two pieces of wood propped together in a short A-frame. A couple of children played in front of one of these, and Josette's heart went out to them. But what could she do? She had nothing to give except her own food money, and she didn't carry it with her.

In silence, they made their way to the bus stop at the edge of the forest. Not for the first time, Josette felt inadequate to carry the burden placed upon her as a missionary. *I want to do my best,* she prayed. *Please give me help and direction.*

Next to the bus stop, a man dressed in a dark suit and carrying a black briefcase waited at the front of the short line. Sweat beaded on his forehead, and Josette felt sorry for him. At least he wore no tie, which was odd to Josette, who was used to seeing the elders and other suited men at church.

Some space behind the man, two women carrying empty wicker shopping baskets talked animatedly. One wore a black dress, signalling mourning, while the other's dress was a simple plaid, and she had a matching scarf tied around her hair.

Josette and Sister Carvalho came up behind the women. They looked at each other, knowing they should use this time to make contacts, but after all the rejections of the morning, their confidence level wasn't very high.

Josette sighed and waited for an opportunity to approach the women without interrupting their conversation. It wouldn't be too hard; already the women were eyeing their black name tags. But when Josette moved toward them, the women promptly turned their backs and began talking again rapidly to each other.

More people came up behind the sister missionaries—two more women, both short, stout, and poorly dressed. They had four children with them, including a babe in arms. Curious brown eyes gawked at the missionaries from the depths of dirty faces.

"What's them tags for?" asked a young boy, obviously the oldest of the children. Josette judged his age to be older than Louis-Géralde, probably eight or nine. His hair was dull with dirt, but he wasn't overly thin. At least he was getting sufficient food.

"We're missionaries," Josette explained. "We go around teaching people about our church. And who are you?"

"I'm Valter. This is my brother, Jorge, and my mom and my aunt. That's my aunt's baby. And the one behind her is my cousin, Zezinha."

"Nice to meet you." Josette said.

"What's your name?" Valter's mom asked. She had her hair pulled back in a ponytail at the nape of her neck, making her worn face seem even rounder than it was. She ducked her head and giggled like a young girl, a shy smile on her face. Josette shifted her feet uneasily. Was this woman as young as she sounded or as old as she looked? Had her life been so hard?

"I'm Sister Perrault, and this is my companion, Sister Carvalho." When she saw their blank stares, Josette added, "Sister is a title we use while on our missions."

"You say you teach people," Valter said. "Why don't you teach us?"

"Sure," Josette said. "If that's okay with your mom."

The woman nodded agreeably. "We live in the shacks on the other side of the forest. In number ten. It's not hard to find."

Josette's suspicions had been correct. These people came from one of the very places she'd planned to avoid. She bit her lip and glanced at her companion, who was crouched in the hard-packed dirt, talking animatedly to the little girl with the tangled brown hair. She sighed inwardly and wrote down the name Valter's mother gave her: Elsa Sousa. "And what's your name?" she asked the woman with the baby.

"I'm Claudia Monteiro." She transferred her baby daughter to the other hip.

"And your address?"

"Number fourteen. But I don't want you to go there. My husband don't like it. I'd have to ask him first, I mean."

"My sister can come to my place and hear you," Elsa said. "I'll send one of the kids to go get her when you come."

"How about tomorrow at two?"

Elsa's face crinkled in a warm smile, as though Josette were her new best friend. "We'll be waitin'. Thank you so much. We'll love hearin' you."

Josette and her companion boarded the orange and white

bus that pulled up at the stop, showing their monthly passes to the driver. Elsa and Claudia and their children piled on after, handing the driver their tickets. They sat near the end of the bus, waving periodically at the missionaries. In a world where children grow up using the public transports, these youngsters were openly excited at the bus ride. Josette knew this must be a special treat for them.

The next day, her heart felt heavy as they made their way through the cool forest and across the road to the shacks. With her greenie's spirit, Sister Carvalho was excited to teach the family, but Josette fought to keep her aversion hidden. They quickly found number ten, where Valter and Jorge ushered them inside a fenced area in front of their shack. The small expanse was littered with dirty straw, and along one edge stood a row of rabbit cages. The smell was unlike anything Josette had ever experienced, and she had to force herself not to pinch her nose.

The blanket covering the doorway moved, and Elsa emerged with a big grin. Behind her a girl of four or five peered out curiously. She was much thinner than Valter. "Go, quick, and get your aunt," Elsa said to Valter. He disappeared at a run.

"How many children do you have?" Sister Carvalho asked.

"Three," Elsa said. "Claudia has two. She's older than me but I started havin' babies first."

Valter came back, breathing heavily. "She'll be here in a minute. She says to wait."

"Is there anything we can sit on?" Josette asked. Evidently, they were to give their lesson here in this odorous play yard. She was only too happy to oblige, having glimpsed the dark interior of the shack when the blanket was lifted. They probably didn't have proper windows or lights.

Elsa and Valter found old wooden crates that, once propped up on end, made usable seats. The children settled around them on the dirt and straw, giggling in anticipation.

Claudia finally arrived with her two daughters, who settled

themselves with the other three. The women folded their arms and waited.

"Do any of you know how to pray?" Josette asked. The children shook their heads.

Something bit Josette's shin, and she leaned over to see a tiny black flea jump from her leg. *So much for getting rid of the fleas,* she thought.

She explained the steps of prayer, using examples of things they might say, and Valter readily volunteered to try it out. Usually Josette or her companion would offer the opening prayer to show them how, but they would never turn down a willing volunteer.

Valter squeezed his eyes shut, his arms folded snug against his body and his round cheeks sticking out like apples. Everyone bowed their head except for the baby, who watched with wide eyes.

"Heavenly Father," Valter began. "Thanks for sendin' these sisters to teach us stuff. Bless us to understand. In the name of Jesus, amen."

Josette opened her mouth to begin, but she hesitated, staring down into the dirty but eager faces of the children. She glanced at the hovering mothers and saw that they appeared equally enthusiastic. At once, the smell of the yard, the stark conditions, the fleas—all of it—meant nothing. These simple people and their faith were enough to invoke the Spirit's presence.

I've been so wrong, she thought. *They need to learn the gospel now.*

The truth had been staring her in the face all along. These humble people had come up to her and had asked to be taught, unlike those of better means who continually turned the missionaries aside. Elsa, Claudia, and their children had a great love inside them that hadn't been dulled by material possessions. Josette knew that Jesus would not have neglected them because they were poor. She couldn't change their circumstances, but she could give them the greatest gift she had: the true gospel. Even if she only soothed their suffering for a short time by helping them understand the Lord's love, it was worth every flea bite and other discomfort she would have to endure. She hadn't been sent to Portugal to break baptizing records or to become a media figure, but to teach the least of her fellow man. These families were why she'd come.

Would they be baptized only to become inactive?

Josette didn't know, and she decided it wasn't hers to judge. She would teach them with the Spirit and help them gain a testimony; the rest would be up to them and the Lord.

Please watch over them, she prayed.

The baby stood up by the crate, balancing precariously on her unsteady feet. Josette lifted her onto her lap. The other children crowded closer, as if sensing her acceptance.

Josette opened her mouth and began teaching them about Jesus. She had never felt the Spirit so strongly.

Chapter Forty-four

The rest of her pregnancy had gone by quickly for Marie-Thérèse—except for the last month. She and Mathieu had celebrated their first wedding anniversary four weeks ago and since then, depression had been her constant companion. Had any woman on the entire planet ever been as fat and uncomfortable as she was? She no longer recognized her own ankles—when she managed to catch a glimpse of them at all. Every time she stood, Mathieu had to help her from her chair.

She fingered the letter from Josette that Mathieu had brought up from the locked mailbox in the lobby. She couldn't wait to read the latest news.

> *It's raining here, even as I write. Sometimes the whole sky just opens up and dumps its contents onto the ground. The roads become shallow rivers. I've never seen such a thing—or maybe I've never walked around in the streets long enough to notice. I guess that's what comes of having led such a sheltered life.*
>
> *Here in Campo Grande, I've been teaching several poor families. All of the woman and children have accepted the*

gospel as though they've been waiting for it all their lives. I feel grateful to be a part of sharing it with them.

Often when we teach, all the neighborhood children living in the shacks will come to hear our stories of Jesus. They are all so incredibly precious, but two have particularly caught my attention. They are a brother and sister, Sara and Miguel. They live in a poor hovel with a miserable-looking lady. I don't know if she's any relation to them or not, but they call her by her first name. I know she drinks, and at first I thought she hated the children, but lately I've seen a different side of her. I think she loves Miguel and Sara, but the alcohol prevents her from taking proper care of them. What problems drove her to start drinking? I can only guess.

Sara is the most beautiful, trusting child I've ever seen. She has dark hair streaked with thin bands of a lighter color—all natural, of course—and her huge brown eyes have flecks of gold in them. She sings the hymns perfectly after hearing them only once. I wouldn't believe it if I hadn't seen it myself. Her brother, Miguel, is equally amazing. He's tough-looking and insolent at times, but he is very careful of his little sister and treats her with a tenderness he doesn't show toward anyone else. His eyes burn with intelligence, and I think it's so sad no one has taught him to read (though he won't admit he can't to anyone but me). I worry that he and Sara aren't getting enough good food, and I always try to bring a little something for them. Besides telling him about Jesus, I've made it a point to teach Miguel about nutrition. Can you believe me teaching someone what to eat? He soaks up my words, and his occasional questions show that he understands exactly what I'm saying. I wish everyone could understand equally well. He's too young for baptism, even if the old lady would allow it. Lately, she has threatened to not let them even listen to our stories at all.

My heart aches for Miguel and Sara, and I wish I could take them home. But I have to remember my purpose here and trust that the Lord will take care of them. As He is aware of the tiny sparrow, so is He aware of these precious children's needs . . .

Marie-Thérèse stopped reading, her eyes overflowing with tears. Josette's letters no longer showed her distaste for working with the poor, or mentioned anything negative at all about the rigors of missionary work, though Marie-Thérèse could sense that it wasn't easy for her, either physically or emotionally. A serenity came through in her communication now—and a searing joy.

It isn't fair! The thought came before Marie-Thérèse could stop it. *It should be me out there tracting and meeting those people whose lives are empty without the Lord. It should be me holding their children on my lap and teaching them the gospel. I should be washing the poor children's heads in the communal water spigot before taking them to church. I should be filling out those baptismal forms and posing for the baptismal pictures. I would have worked hard. I wouldn't have minded.*

Mathieu came in from the kitchen where he'd taken their dinner dishes, the daily newspaper under his arm. "What's wrong?" he asked when he saw her face.

Marie-Thérèse wiped impatiently at a stray tear. "I'm just pregnant, that's all."

He sat beside her and pulled her close. She closed her eyes and sighed.

Trade Mathieu for a mission? The idea was ludicrous. She loved him even more than she had when they married. Losing him would have been the biggest mistake of her life.

Yet . . . would he have waited for her? Could she have had both?

Maybe. The thought bothered her. While her love and appreciation for Mathieu had increased over the last year, the urgency of their love had faded. Before their marriage, waiting to be sealed had been such a torturous thing that she could hardly bear to be separated from him at all. Now their months together had dimmed that intensity. In the face of an eternity as man and wife, eighteen months didn't seem like a long time to wait. Maybe she should have gone on a mission after all.

The baby inside her kicked. "I felt that." Mathieu poked her belly where the kick had come from, and the baby kicked again.

Despite herself, Marie-Thérèse laughed.

Mathieu grinned, his eyes meeting hers. "Everything's going to be all right."

She nodded. If only she could rid herself of the what-might-have-beens. Josette was doing well on her mission, converting enough for the both of them. Marie-Thérèse silently prayed for acceptance and understanding.

"I thought we might buy a second car," Mathieu said without warning. "For you."

Her thoughts scattered. "What? I don't need a car. I don't like to drive in this city. It's too busy, the traffic's too fast. Besides, I can use the metro if I need to go somewhere while you're at work."

"But it wouldn't be fun hauling the baby."

"I won't mind. It'd make me feel better to know we're less in debt. This isn't Provo, and we're not Americans. We don't need to spend like them."

Mathieu looked wounded. "I make a good living, and it's only a matter of time before I'm promoted."

"Then can't we wait until that happens? I'm still worried about all that baby furniture you charged. The baby could have slept with us for a time. Or my mom still has Louis-Géralde's old crib."

A sheepish look appeared on Mathieu's face. "I got carried away," he admitted. "It was cute, and the clerk was very persuasive."

Marie-Thérèse sighed. "She probably got a big commission."

"I want everything to be perfect for our baby," Mathieu said, stroking her arm.

"I know you mean well." She still felt irritated—at everything—but a sudden sharp pain shot through her midriff with amazing intensity, pushing away all her unhappy thoughts. It was similar to the false contractions she'd been experiencing for weeks, but this time it hurt so much that she could hardly breathe.

"Marie-Thérèse!" Mathieu's voice showed his concern.

"I . . . think . . . the baby . . . is coming," she said between gasps.

A silly smile appeared on his face. "Oh."

The drive to the hospital was difficult because of the late-night traffic. When they arrived, her parents were already there waiting for them.

"I can't believe we're going to be grandparents!" Jean-Marc said.

Tears wet Marie-Thérèse's cheeks, her feelings vacillating between apprehension and inexpressible joy.

The labor was short but intense. There was no time for the drugs to take their full effect, and Marie-Thérèse was forced to bear the brunt of the labor. The rending pain almost made her wish she were dead, but when they laid the tiny, wrinkled bundle in her arms, it was abruptly worth every agonizing second.

"Hello there," she cooed at her daughter.

The baby opened her dark eyes, and Marie-Thérèse saw her answer in them. A mission was important, but it could never equal the great significance of being a mother. God had entrusted her with this baby and knew that she was prepared to take on the responsibility—unlike Josette who needed to grow spiritually and put her priorities straight.

The baby yawned, but she didn't close her wise eyes. Marie-Thérèse was in awe at the incredible miracle.

This child's whole future is in my care, she thought. Gratitude to her Father in Heaven flooded all her senses. She wouldn't look back again.

"So what are we going to name her?" Mathieu asked. "We don't have any girl names picked out. You were so sure she was going to be a boy."

"Well, Pauline said that my little boy would be all right, so I just assumed the baby would be a boy." She grinned up at him. "Guess we should have found out before when they did the ultrasound, but wasn't it better as a surprise?"

Mathieu put his cheek next to hers. "I don't care what sex the baby is, just so she's healthy and you're safe. I love you so much."

Marie-Thérèse saw the sheen of tears in his eyes, and it touched her deeply. "I love you too."

"Are you happy?"

Knowing him so well, Marie-Thérèse understood what he asked. "There's no place I'd rather be than here with you," she told him. "No place."

The expression on Mathieu's face was worth more than anything he could have said. His eyes slid down to the baby. "Shall we name her after your mother and your sister, Pauline?"

Marie-Thérèse thought for a long time. "I love them," she said, "but I think it's time for something else. I want our baby to start a new legacy—something removed from AIDS and the death."

"How about Juliette?" Mathieu asked, his eyes dancing.

Marie-Thérèse groaned. "That's even worse. I want something unconnected to tragedy. Something like . . . Larissa. I read it once in a book when I was at BYU. I looked it up. It means 'cheerful one.' "

"I like that."

Larissa's eyes drooped, as if to signal the discussion closed.

Marie-Thérèse cuddled her baby, and Mathieu put his arm around her. She knew she was right where she belonged.

The next day, Mathieu came to take her home from the hospital. He carried a large basket filled with a variety of different potted plants. Wound among the green and variegated leaves was a thick gold necklace. Marie-Thérèse stared at it for a full minute without speaking, her exclamation over the plants dying on her lips.

"Don't you like it?" Mathieu asked. "It matches the

herringbone bracelet I gave you for your birthday when we were in Provo. Every time I see you wear it, I remember about buying it for you. I had a buddy get it at the same store in Provo and send it to me."

"We can't afford this." A tight feeling was growing in her chest. It seemed that each week they sank further into the bog of debt.

"But you should have something to celebrate our baby's birth. It's one of the great days of our lives. Now put it on, love. I want to take a picture. Here, let me help you."

Marie-Thérèse's heart sank further, but in the face of Mathieu's joy she couldn't refuse. What wife would complain because her husband bought her a gift to celebrate the birth of their baby? Was she making a big deal out of nothing? Or did Mathieu actually have a problem with spending?

She longed to tell her husband exactly how she felt, but she knew from experience that this particular complaint would fall on deaf ears.

Chapter Forty-five

Zack had finished giving the couple's son a blessing when the recognition came. He snapped his fingers. "I know who you are!"

Jacques de Cotte looked at him blankly. "We've never met." He glanced at his wife, Charlotte, who shook her head, sending her shoulder-length blonde hair swinging. She tucked the quilt around her sleeping child, checking his fever again.

Zack lowered his voice. "I had a companion, Marc Perrault. He told me your name and that the last he heard you lived in this area. He said he has a piece of you."

Jacques and Charlotte exchanged glances as smiles spread across their faces. Charlotte motioned them outside the room.

"Yeah, he has a piece of me, all right," Jacques said once they were back in the sitting room. "My kidney. Would you elders like to see the scar?" He started to untuck his shirt.

"No thanks, Brother de Cotte," Zack said hastily, answering for both himself and his new American companion, who'd only been in the country for a week. "I've see Marc's."

"Oh." Jacques seemed disappointed. He sat on the couch,

waving them to be seated opposite him on the loveseat. "He's a good boy, Marc. I'm glad he was able to go on a mission."

"He was a great missionary," Zack said.

"Like his father." There was a curious note in Jacques' voice, and though Zack couldn't be sure, he thought it sounded like respect. "His mother was also a good missionary."

He glanced at Charlotte, who squeezed his hand. There was no doubting the love they shared, but Zack felt it hadn't come easily.

"How is the Perrault family?" Charlotte asked. "I meant to keep in touch, but with a three-year-old and another on the way . . ." She patted her gently swelling stomach.

Zack felt his smile leave. "Marc's younger sister died."

Jacques' dark-blond head jerked toward him. "Pauline."

"I saw Marc a few times at zone conferences," Zack continued. "He took it well. I don't know what I would do if my little sister died."

"They had time to prepare," Jacques said. "That helps." He had a faraway expression, but Charlotte cuddled closer to him on the couch and the look disappeared.

A tiny whine came from the hall, forcing Charlotte to her feet. "I'm going to check the baby again."

Zack cleared his throat. "Marie-Thérèse got married and had a baby girl, or so my sister tells me." This was their first visit to the de Cottes' apartment, and though Zack was grateful it had coincided with their little boy's need for a blessing, there hadn't yet been time to discuss the possibility of teaching their nonmember friends. He'd heard that Brother de Cotte was the president of a large carpet company, so he should be a great source for finding responsible investigators. Since the Leandro family's baptisms, the only investigators Zack had helped joined the Church were Madame Legrand and her daughters, and that had been in his last area. In this new city, he had decided to try more effective ways to find people to teach, and working with members was at the top of his list. But he and his companion had another appointment soon and needed to get going. They would have to revisit the de Cottes at a later date. He shifted his weight to the edge of the loveseat.

"Marie-Thérèse married a member, I'll bet," Jacques said.

"I think so. Marc doesn't write much, but I remember my sister saying the man was a friend of the family that Marie-Thérèse met again at BYU. They got married last year or something."

"And Josette?" asked Jacques. "She was always the beautiful one. And such fire! Just like her mother."

Zack recalled only then that this man had been Marc's mother's first husband, and despite the love he had for his current wife, he obviously still had tender feelings toward Ariana.

"She is beautiful," Zack said.

Jacques looked at him sharply. "You've got it bad, haven't you? Well, you should know that loving a woman like that won't come easily, but it will be worth it."

"I haven't even met her," Zack protested. "Besides, I'm a missionary. I don't have time for those thoughts."

Jacques laughed. "One look is all it takes. From across a crowded room or at a picture, it's all the same."

The real truth was that Zack had only one month left before he returned to the real world. For the most part, sadness filled him when he thought about leaving France and the people who'd become so much a part of his soul, but he couldn't deny that another part felt quite differently. That renegade part anticipated the moment he'd meet Marc's sister. As much as he loved his old companion, he admitted—if only to himself—that the girl in the picture was the real reason he planned to visit Marc before returning to America. He had to know why he felt so powerfully drawn to her, why he dreamed of her, felt warnings for her.

This last thought reminded him of the attack on Josette and the anger and frustration he'd felt hearing about it after the fact.

Zack jumped to his feet. "We'd better be going. We have another appointment."

"Leaving so soon, elders?" Charlotte moved into sight from the dark hallway. "But you haven't told us why you wanted to meet with us."

"They want us to give references," Jacques said with a grin. "Isn't that right?"

Zack nodded. "You got it."

"Come back on Monday night then. We'll have a special family night and invite our neighbors."

"But go gently on them," Charlotte said.

Now it was Zack's turn to grin. "Don't worry, we're trying to save them, not scare them to death."

Jacques chuckled, and Charlotte joined him hesitantly.

Zack whistled as they emerged on the street below the de Cottes' apartment. They would be slightly late for the next appointment, but it had been worth a first contact. The night was going better than expected.

He reached into his shirt pocket to check the address of where they were headed, but instead his hand closed over a snapshot of Brionney. Laughing at her side was Josette. She sat on a couch with her knees pulled up to her chest. The long, straight locks fanned out around her shoulders and knees like a shiny dark coat. Her brown eyes seemed to speak directly to him.

What would he say to her at the instant they met? He hadn't decided—perhaps he wouldn't until that crucial moment. Whatever it was, he would be true to the feelings in his heart.

He could only hope that her real self matched the woman he dreamed she was—spiritual, caring, and intelligent.

With effort, Zack put these thoughts aside and locked them in the most tender part of his mind. *I am yours, Lord,* he prayed silently. *Please, lead us to those who are ready. For this month, at least, my whole heart is dedicated to this mission.*

And then . . . his heart said, but his mind was too bent on the work at hand to answer.

Chapter Forty-six

The words of the letter in Marc's hand blurred before his eyes. Had a whole year passed since he'd finished his mission? Where had the time gone? Josette would be home in another three and a half months, and Marie-Thérèse and Mathieu already had a six-week-old daughter. Now Elder Fields was finishing his mission and coming to Paris for a visit before leaving France.

Marc had written Zack once after Pauline had died and at Christmas last year, but he'd been too involved in his engineering studies to write much. He managed to write to Josette each week, remembering how much he'd craved hearing from her on his own mission, and to his surprise, she answered him. Most of the letters had been lighthearted and typical of his sister, but during the last six months there'd been a notable change. Josette seemed to be more thoughtful about things, and she hadn't complained at all in the last half dozen or so letters. It was odd, but not unwelcome.

He checked the dates in Zack's letter and went to find his mother, who was reading a novel in the television room. "We're going to have company, if that's all right," he said, showing her the letter.

Ariana looked pleased. "Of course it's all right. I've been looking forward to meeting the Fields after all they did for the girls while they were in Provo. Is it just them and your companion?"

"They don't mention anyone else, so I guess that's all."

"Well, we've enough room, with the girls gone."

"What's up?" André clomped into the room wearing the boots he'd been given during his army service.

"One of my old companions is coming to visit," Marc said as his brother sat beside their mother on the couch, placing an arm around her shoulder.

"Yes, war stories!" André exclaimed. Next month he would leave on his own mission, and he loved any opportunity to hear about mission experiences.

"He can stay with me in my room," Marc said, "now that André and I don't share anymore."

Their mother nodded. "His parents can sleep in Josette's room. I hope they don't mind two single beds."

"They won't care."

"Let's have a big dinner to welcome them," Ariana suggested. "Do you think we should invite Emeri and his parents?"

Marc laughed. "Good idea. Let's have a big party."

Their father entered the room with Louis-Géralde hopping at his side. "Look what we got, look what we got!" the little boy sang. In his arms he carried a small package from Josette. "Can I have the stamps, Mom?"

Ariana smiled. "Of course. I'm sure she picked them out just for your collection."

"The package is addressed to André," Marc said, peering closer.

Louis-Géralde handed André the box. "Be careful of the stamps."

André ripped off the brown paper and opened the box. Nestled inside were a set of scriptures with bite marks and a note that read: "These have already kept two Perrault missionaries safe. Since I'm nearly finished, I thought it was your turn to have them."

"Cool," André said.

Marc laughed. "That's Josette for you. Always trying to take care of us." Or at least she had when she was younger, before she'd become so self-centered. Had she actually changed? A mission would do it, if anything could. Marc hoped she had changed because more than anything, he wanted her to be happy.

The next week, Marc opened the door to Elder Fields and his parents. His old companion was as tall, blonde, and blue-eyed as always.

"Look at you!" Elder Fields said, giving Marc a bear hug. "You've lost weight."

"A bit," Marc admitted. "Weight I needed to lose, I might add. My mom doesn't feed me as well as the members did on my mission."

"Force-feed you, you mean. Boy, it's good to see you."

"You, too." And it was. Marc had several companions he'd enjoyed working with, but he decided that Elder Fields had been the best.

Marc's family, including Marie-Thérèse and Mathieu, gathered around for introductions. "And these are our friends, the Faurés," Marc said, introducing Emeri and his parents. He hoped he'd already written to Elder Fields about what Emeri had meant to Pauline and about his illness because he couldn't exactly explain it at the moment.

"Nice to meet you all." Elder Fields presented his parents and began translating for them, but when he learned that Marie-Thérèse could translate, he left her to help his parents and pulled Marc aside. "Where's your other sister?" he asked.

"Josette?" Marc blinked in surprise. "I thought you knew. She's on a mission. She's in Portugal, if you can believe it."

The light went out of those blue, blue eyes. Elder Fields swallowed hard. "You didn't mention that in either of your letters."

Marc knew he'd purposely avoided mention of Josette; protecting his twin came naturally to him. "I didn't think it would make a difference," he said. Maybe he'd been wrong about Josette and Elder Fields. Maybe he didn't need to protect her. "Besides," he added, "didn't your sister tell you? I know she writes to Josette."

Zack frowned, then licked his lips as if tasting something sour. "She didn't say." He paused for a moment, his gaze resting on a large family photograph in the hall. It was an old one, taken before Marc's mission when Pauline was still alive; Marc supposed his mother would always keep it there.

"Guess it wasn't meant to be." Elder Fields made a rolling movement with his shoulders that approximated a shrug. "I just don't understand why I felt—" His words broke off. "So are you going to show me the Eiffel Tower, or am I going to have to find my own way there?"

Marc clapped his friend on the back. "We'll probably have to eat first—you know how mothers are. But don't worry because I have a whole list of places to take you and your parents. Be prepared to see the Paris you've always imagined and more!"

Chapter Forty-seven

"I can't believe you didn't tell me that Marc's sister was serving a mission," Zack said to Brionney. He sat next to her in the back seat, while their parents talked quietly in the front. Outside the car, the landscape along I-15 streamed by.

"What! You're back in Utah less than fifteen minutes, and that's all you have to say to me?" She shook her head and rolled her eyes.

He put his arm around her. "I'm glad to see you, Bri, I really am. You're so grown-up, though."

"I'll be a senior in the fall."

"You think I don't know that? Man, you make me feel old."

"So why did you want to know about Josette?"

Zack shrugged, feeling suddenly very idiotic. "I don't know. I just think it's odd that you didn't tell me. Or that Elder Perrault didn't—Marc, I mean. He sure doesn't like the idea of . . ." Brionney stared eagerly at him, but Zack didn't feel like finishing the statement.

"Josette didn't want me to tell you," she said.

He felt as though she had punched him in the stomach. "Why?"

"Don't take it personally. She didn't want anyone to know. I think she was a little embarrassed to be going at all."

Zack didn't understand why, but the way his sister said the words made it obvious that he should understand. He opted not to say anything and reveal his ignorance. If he listened closely, he might figure it out without embarrassing himself further.

"Anyway, she's pretty sour on guys," Brionney continued blithely. "Ever since the attack. It's a sad thing, too. Guys would always line up at the door to take her out." Her words were admiring, with a trace of envy.

This new idea of Josette being afraid to care for a man made Zack hopeful. But on the heels of hope came the stark realization of how impossible his fantasy of meeting her really was. They were separated by an immense ocean, and she didn't even know he cared. Would it even matter if she knew? Could Marc be right when he said Zack wasn't good enough for her?

"In fact, the only guy she writes me about at all is someone named Emeri. He's a friend of the family, and he and Josette are close. They write all the time."

"I met him," Zack said shortly. In his opinion, Emeri was a great young man and it was plausible for Josette to be interested in him. Now that Zack thought about it, Emeri did have an air of intenseness and tragedy about him, despite the happy smile and apparent good health he'd showed in their brief meeting. Maybe he had that certain something that attracted beautiful women. Zack gave a long sigh.

"What's wrong?" Brionney asked him. Something about the way she said it made Zack stare. Then he realized she was speaking in French.

"It's nothing," he replied in the same language. He and Brionney had always been close, but he wasn't about to expose his irrational feelings about a girl he had never met. What he needed was to forget about Josette and go on with his life.

There was instant hurt in Brionney's eyes, and Zack felt terrible for being the cause. He searched for some way to change the subject. "Your necklace," he said, noticing for the first time.

"Where's your half of the charm?" Loosening his tie, he brought out the jagged half of the heart he'd kept tucked inside his shirt during his entire mission.

Brionney flushed. "Oh, that. Well, you see, it's like this. Josette and I got to be good friends, and she gave me a pin. It's really beautiful. It's gold and has sparkly diamond dust all over it. And then I wanted her to have something to remember me by, and all I had was that charm. I meant to go and buy another set before you got back, but I didn't have the money. You're not mad, are you? I just wanted two of the people I love most to have something from me."

Zack tucked the necklace back inside his shirt. "Of course I'm not mad. That was very unselfish of you." Though he wasn't going to admit it to anyone, the idea of Josette having the other half appealed to his romantic side.

"I thought you'd say that. Besides, it's not like you'll be using it anymore, now that we're back together. I mean, most guys at church don't wear necklaces."

Zack understood what she meant. When Brionney had first given it to him, he'd only agreed to wear it because he'd seen how much it meant to her. However, in France, his views had changed considerably about men and jewelry, and now that he'd learned who had the other half, he wasn't about to give it up. Not yet, anyway.

"Why don't you write to her?" Brionney said, breaking his concentration. "I mean, if you want to." She smiled at him to show she was teasing, but Zack didn't take the bait.

"That," he said, "is exactly what I'm going to do."

Chapter Forty-eight

During the last two months of her mission, Josette served in Benfica, where the city was divided between the sisters and the elders. The sisters' half of the city was mostly solid buildings with few open areas except for the large city zoo. There were no makeshift shacks or poor cement houses that Josette ever found.

Despite the tender experiences she'd shared with the poor in other areas, she felt grateful not to confront the emotions that churned inside her when she thought about how little she could do to better their physical circumstances. At first, she had trouble sleeping at night in the new area, spending many hours worrying about the fragile, impoverished converts she'd left in her previous area. Finally, she begged the Lord to take care of them and relinquished them to His care.

Unlike her districts in other areas, her new district didn't hold street meetings, and though the church congregation in the area was exceptionally supportive, most of the members lived in the elders' side of the city. This meant Josette and her companion spent nearly all their time tracting. Josette no longer felt even a twinge of fear when she knocked on strangers' doors. When they were lucky enough to get someone to open up, she always found a way to keep them talking to her, and rarely was anyone rude.

"You make me laugh," said Sister Nabb, her new American companion. "Three months in the mission field, and I never knew knocking doors could be so fun."

Josette laughed, flattered, but her body sagged with weariness. She felt as though she could go to bed and sleep for days without awakening.

"It's time we headed home," she said. Once again they rented a room from a family, but this was the first time she'd lived with non-members. Josette wanted to pave the way to teaching them someday, though they didn't yet show an interest.

"They're very good people," Sister Nabb said, as if reading her mind. The Tiza family were devout Catholics and the mother, Graziela, spent a portion of each day doing some kind of charity work. After three weeks in the area, Josette had grown quite attached to them.

When they arrived home, the whole family awaited them: Senhor and Senhora Tiza, their teenage daughter Tininha, and Roc, the red Labrador who was treated like another member of the family.

"Oh, Sister Perrault," Senhora Tiza said the minute they walked in the door. "Mail came for you. The elders dropped it by."

"Great. Where is it?" When the elders had mentioned they were going into the mission office for supplies, she'd asked them to check for any forwarded mail. She'd begun receiving mail from her family again, but since her parents and Marc wrote her faithfully every week, she knew a few of the letters sent to the previous address were still missing.

Thin Graziela wrung her long hands with a nervous laugh. "There were six letters. I put them on the table, and when I came back Roc had them. He chewed half of them, and one is missing completely." She grimaced. "I'm really sorry."

No one said anything for several long seconds, and then Sister Nabb doubled up with laughter. "The dog ate the letter! If that isn't a first!" She laughed so hard that tears came to her eyes. Josette saw the absurdity and joined in.

"In school," Sister Nabb said, gasping for breath, "I always tried to get my teacher to believe my dog ate my homework, but she'd never believe me. 'Dogs don't eat paper!' she'd say. Well, I guess good old Roc proved her wrong."

The Tiza family laughed with them. "I'm really sorry," Graziela repeated when the laughter died down.

Josette wiped her eyes and took the letters. "That's all right." Five letters in one day was still a good thing.

The two mauled letters were from Marc, and by piecing the shreds together she could read them. He mentioned Zachary Fields' visit, and for a moment Josette wished she'd been there to meet him. But would he have been interested in her? If he had been, would his interest stem from her beauty or who she was inside? Better not to know.

Two of the other letters were from her parents, and there was also a thick one from Brionney. So who had written the sixth— and by now partially digested—letter? Perhaps Marie-Thérèse had written to recount her daughter's latest abilities or her husband's virtues. Josette sighed. As envious as she was, she would have enjoyed reading the details. Or maybe André was writing to tell her about his own mission.

Shrugging, Josette opened Brionney's letter. She'd written in her usual mixture of French and English, which Josette had come to understand perfectly.

Dear Josette,

I hope this letter gets to you, what with your being transferred and all. I can't believe you're almost done with your mission. Are you sure you won't come back to BYU? I miss you like crazy. Maybe I'll come to France to visit you—if I can get my parents to pay for it. I was going to go when Mom and Dad went to pick up Zack, but I really couldn't miss two weeks of school since we were nearing finals. My good grades are about all the enjoyment I have in life. Anyway, you wouldn't have been there, so what was the point? Maybe I'll come after you get back. Then it'll be just you and me roaming the streets of romantic Paris.

Zack is different since he came home. He still teases me, but he's more spiritual—or something. I don't know. I'm glad he's back. We do stuff all the time now. I tease him that he'll never find a wife this way, but he just laughs.

That reminds me. Boy, was Zack ever irritated that I didn't tell him about you being on a mission. He didn't yell or anything, but I could tell. He wouldn't say why. I bet he has a crush on you (like practically every other guy in the world). I told him he didn't stand a chance since you didn't like men anymore. And besides, with all those romantic French hunks, you don't need a boring American. Ha! Ha! He didn't like that. But don't worry, he has a date this weekend with a girl in one of his summer classes at the Y. I'll try and get him safely married so you can come and visit me with no worries of being hounded.

Josette stopped reading, and thumbed through the photographs Brionney had sent. There were many of her and Zack, but looking at them made Josette strangely depressed. She threw them into a deep corner of her suitcase and didn't look at them again.

All at once, she wished she could talk with Pauline. She needed one of her special hugs now.

Later that night Josette prayed harder than she'd ever prayed. The veil seemed very thin, and Josette felt comforted.

"You know, it's funny how things work out," Josette said to Sister Nabb. "When Grady attacked me, I thought my world had ended. But it made me think about what I really wanted in life.

Then they told me about my sister, and I wanted to die, but when I saw her and hugged her, and she seemed so peaceful, it was okay. Then there was Emeri, and I had to help him join the Church for Pauline, and that led me here. It's strange to say, but if the bad things hadn't happened, I wouldn't be here, and I couldn't have helped any of the people I've met."

With regard to her missionary service, Josette's joy knew no bounds. She looked backward on her life and mission and saw a chain of connected events, some horrible, some pleasant, but each making up a vital part in the intricate tapestry of her life.

She cried when it was time for her to leave Portugal. How could she have ever thought she would serve her time and never look back? In her heart, she felt a mixture of satisfaction at a job well done and sadness at leaving it behind. The country would be a part of her forever.

Before the plane landed in France, she forced herself to wipe the tears from her face and look forward. But aside from the joy of being reunited with her family, her future didn't seem very exciting. What could equal working single-mindedly for the Lord and feeling His Spirit so strongly each day? It would be a hard act to follow.

The entire Perrault clan waited for Josette at the airport in Paris. Marie-Thérèse carried the newest addition, five-month-old Larissa, in her arms. At her side was Mathieu. He looked much the same, but the attraction Josette had felt for him was completely gone. Had she ever really loved him? Compared to the feelings she had for those she'd baptized in Portugal, her romantic feelings for him meant absolutely nothing.

"Your daughter is beautiful," Josette said as she hugged Marie-Thérèse. "Look at those cheeks! Hello, little one, I'm your Aunt Josette." The title sounded odd to her, but no one else seemed to notice. The baby reached out and grabbed a lock of Josette's hair that had grown back almost as long as before her mission. She'd been meaning to get it cut again but had never found the opportunity.

"It's so good to see you," Marie-Thérèse said as she untangled her daughter's hand.

Josette laughed. She didn't know until seeing her family how much she'd missed them, especially Marie-Thérèse and Marc.

"Hey, Josette, what about me?"

Josette faced the voice she recognized, but was startled at the change in Emeri. He was much thinner than he'd been when she'd left on her mission, and he wore a hat to hide the loss of his hair. She knew that meant his cancer had returned. Why hadn't he mentioned it in his letters? She held out her arms to hug him. "Oh, Emeri, it's so good to see you! I sure loved your letters."

"I'm an elder now," he said. "Just last week. And I've been doing some splits with the missionaries. It's pretty fun."

Josette laughed. "I'll bet you're a great missionary. Look how fast you converted your parents."

"It wasn't me," Emeri said. "It was the Spirit. You know that."

"Yeah, I guess I do."

Marc put an arm around her. "Come on, Jose. You look like you could use a soft bed."

"A bed? I could sleep for a week!"

She nearly did. But at the end of that week, she got out of bed and went to her mother. "Did you take care of it?" she asked.

"Yes. But are you sure about this, honey?" There was concern in Ariana's eyes, and more than a little reluctance.

"I've got another three weeks before I need to leave," Josette replied. "And it's not like it's forever. I may not even finish my schooling at BYU." She hesitated. "I have to go there for a least a semester. It's like I said in my letter—I just have to face it. You know, what happened with Grady and all. I need to be there again as the person I am now." There was more to it that she didn't expect her mother to understand. How could she, when Josette didn't understand it completely herself? She only knew it had something to do with proving to herself that her life was actually as changed as she felt it was. At BYU she could face her demons, both real and imagined.

Ariana dug something out of the cedar chest at the base of her bed. "Here are your school papers and the address of the apartment we rented for you. You'll have your own room, but there are four other girls in the apartment."

"You didn't tell Brionney's family, did you?" Josette hadn't told anyone except her family about the decision to return to BYU. After she resolved whatever it was that pulled her to Provo, then she'd call Brionney and surprise her.

"No, the missionary who baptized me helped," Ariana said. "He still works at the university."

"Good." Josette smoothed the gentle creases in her mother's cheeks. "Oh, Mom, don't worry. I'm following the Spirit."

Ariana hugged her. "I guess you've learned to do that well enough in these past eighteen months. I'm so proud of you. Do you know that?"

Josette's heart filled with exhilaration. It meant everything to have her mother say those words, especially because she knew they hadn't always been true. She wished she didn't have to leave again at all.

Three weeks later at the airport in Paris, Josette said good-bye to Marc and Emeri. "You've got to give up this man-hating thing," Emeri told her. "Just because one guy turns out to be a creep doesn't mean that all guys are. Take me, for instance. Underneath my creepy exterior was this incredibly sweet guy."

Josette laughed. "Right, Emeri. But alas, you're taken. Pauline would kill me if I made any moves on you."

Emeri's return laughter ended in a bout of coughing. Josette peered at him worriedly. "Maybe I shouldn't go."

He held up his hands. "Oh, no. Don't stay to fuss over me. I've got my parents for that. That's all I need is another weepy woman. I've got my dear mother for that, thank you very much." His kissed her good-bye. "Now, behave yourself." He looked at Marc. "I'll leave you to say goodbye. I'll be waiting in the car."

Marc walked with Josette to the security gate entrance, where he hugged her and kissed both cheeks. "I wish I could go with you," he said. "I don't like the thought of you going by yourself."

Josette laughed. "You just don't want me to go at all. But don't worry, I'll be all right. And I'll be back soon, I promise." She touched his face briefly. "I'll always come back to you, brother. You're my other half."

"Just so you remember who's the younger half. The older sibling always has to look out for the younger, you know."

"I'll be back to do my duty," Josette said, rolling her eyes. "Though why five and a half minutes makes a difference, I'll never understand. Now can I go already? The plane's about to leave."

"Just one thing." Marc hesitated, as if considering an important decision. "I'd like you to look up Zack for me, if you will. Tell him I sent you. He'll understand."

"I'm through with men. I told you that."

"Zack's not a man. I mean . . . well, he's more than a man. He's my friend. Come on, you'll be seeing his sister anyway."

Josette didn't have time to argue. "Okay." Blowing him a kiss, she turned and made her way to the security gate.

Chapter Forty-nine

The mid-September morning carried a brisk breeze, unexpected after the heat of summer. Zack's T-shirt let in the cold, but he knew that later in the morning the sun would burn away the clouds and heat the world again. He opened his car door and let Brionney inside.

"How's Suzy?" Brionney asked as he settled in the driver's seat and started the engine.

Zack shrugged. "I don't know. I haven't called her."

"I thought you liked her."

"We were just friends. I think she's going out with a football player now."

She checked her makeup in the passenger-side mirror. "You could fight for her."

"Have you seen those BYU football players lately? Boy, one would think you don't want a brother at all."

Brionney laughed. "You're nuts. If you don't start dating those girls who are always calling the house, you're going to end up an old bachelor."

He knew he should make a better effort to find a spouse, but his heart simply wasn't in it. There was only one girl he wanted to date, and she hadn't even answered his letter. "I've only been off my mission four and a half months. It's not like I'm old yet. Give me a little time."

"No way. I'm your sister. I'm supposed to bug you." She waved as she got out of the car at Provo High School. "Thanks for the ride."

Zack put the car into gear and drove on to BYU.

Josette had never answered his letter, and now he was embarrassed to have sent it at all. What had he been thinking, writing to a girl he had never met? He couldn't really blame her for not answering, could he? What had he written anyway? He'd tried to come across suave and debonair, but maybe he'd been sappy and awkward. One thing for certain, he'd bled all over the page, laying bare his heart and soul. What had she thought when she'd read it? He would give a lot to know.

Since he'd received no response, he'd put aside all ideas of returning to France to meet her. He still thought about her in his spare time, and she even appeared in his dreams. Not that he had much free time to dream. He worked full time at his father's real estate office, and also had three college classes. Maybe next semester he would cut down and go out on more dates.

Soft drops of rain left splotches on the cement, and Zack took a moment in the parked car to breathe in the smell. From childhood, he'd loved the pungent aroma of rain on the pavement. Tucking his head against the pelting drops, he hurried toward his first class. The rain came increasingly faster, and he wished he'd thought to bring a jacket.

He looked up as a girl sprinted toward him on the wide cement pathway, her dark head bent against the rain. Before he could slow his own momentum, they collided and the backpack on her shoulder tumbled to the ground. She scrambled after it in a mess of incredibly long, damp hair, and Zack went down with her, trying to help.

"I'm sorry," she muttered in accented English. Her voice was low and attractive. A gold necklace around her graceful neck glinted dully in the subdued light. "I didn't see you."

"That's all right. The rain—" His words broke off as they arose together and he saw her clearly for the first time. His pulse raced, and for a moment he couldn't make his mouth work. She stared back at him, her dark eyes wide and full of emotion.

Students streamed past them, but it was as if they were in a world alone. For so long Zack had been waiting for this moment, so long that he'd almost let go of the hope that it might ever happen. Now here she was, and between them flowed a recognition that went far beyond a few pictures and shared friends. Zack imagined he knew her, clear to the deepest part of her soul, and he felt she knew him as well. There was only one thing left to say.

"Vous voulez me marier?" Will you marry me?

"Oui," she answered.

Zack leaned down and kissed her. Nothing had ever tasted so sweet.

Chapter Fifty

The first thing Josette noticed when the man drew back and she finally managed to open her eyes was the black mole on the lower part of his left check. The extraordinary blue eyes, the white-blond hair, the handsome angular face, were as she remembered from pictures, but that little mole was something she'd never noticed before.

She marveled at the emotion she felt. How could she love a man at first sight? That was ridiculous, wasn't it? But she felt as though she had known him somewhere before.

Elder Fields—no, Zack, she had to remind herself—bent to kiss her again. He was taller than she imagined he would be, but with a little bending and stretching, they fit together perfectly.

The cold breeze, the falling rain, the jostling students, nothing penetrated their world. Then, as if even the heavens were seared by the passion in their hearts, the rain stopped and the clouds parted.

Zack chuckled. "Amen," he said, looking up into the warm face of the sun.

Josette smiled, and Zack did too. He watched her with an odd expression on his face, one Josette had never seen before—except perhaps on her father's face when he stared at her mother.

"What are you thinking?" he asked in French.

"I'm wondering if you can see how fast my heart is beating." Even as she said it, she recognized that once she would never have confessed such a thing.

He chuckled. "Like a freight train going down a hill without brakes? Oh, I know the feeling."

Josette laughed, experiencing an astonishing joy, rivalled only by the times when those she loved had accepted the gospel. This feeling was a hundred times stronger.

The path was clearing of students, and Josette knew she'd be late for her first class. She pictured what she might say to the teacher. "Excuse me for being late, but a man I've never met before just asked me to marry him."

And she had said yes!

Oh, dear.

Josette stared at the ground.

Zack bent down, twisting his head around to see her face. "I'm holding you to it," he said softly. "Don't worry, I'll prove myself to you."

He kissed her again, but it was too quick for real enjoyment. "You're going to be late to class, aren't you? So am I. We'll have to talk later."

"But . . ."

He withdrew a necklace from his shirt. "See," he said, pointing to the half-charm on her chain as if that explained everything. Then he left, whistling cheerfully.

Josette felt relieved to be alone to sort out her feelings. Love? Was this love? It all seemed like a dream, and by the end of her first class, she'd convinced herself that she had imagined the whole incident. Or at least the crazy feelings. Yes, she'd run into Zack Fields, but the rest had been her overactive imagination.

That afternoon when she arrived at her apartment, Zack was already in her front room with a bouquet of flowers. Her roommates giggled and made themselves scarce.

"How did you find me?" she asked with sudden shyness.

He handed her the flowers. "I have my ways."

"I bet you called campus information."

"Maybe."

"How did you know I don't like roses?" The bouquet he had brought her had just about every flower she was familiar with except roses. Roses. The flower most men had brought her.

"You're too beautiful for only one type of flower. Now, I have to go back to work for a while, but what I came for was to ask if you'll come to dinner tonight . . . at my parents' house."

"I haven't even told Brionney I'm back."

"She'll understand, especially when we tell them we're getting married."

Josette held her breath. She really hadn't been dreaming earlier! "But . . ."

"Yes?" He stared at her, as if daring her to go back on her word. What could she say, that he was crazy? That they were both crazy?

"You're not really going to tell your parents."

"Why not? Maybe we should call your parents, too. And your brother. I'd like to hear his reaction when you tell him."

"He told me to look you up," Josette said, remembering. "He said you'd understand. Do you?"

Zack laughed until his face turned red. "Old Marc's finally come to his senses, that's all. I don't know how or why, but I'm grateful. It'll make things easier."

Josette didn't know what to say.

"That's funny," Zack said. "I'd never figured you for the speechless type, especially after knowing Marc. Man, that guy never shut up. But that's okay. I guess there'll be time to get to know each other before the wedding. Which temple do you prefer?" He glanced at his watch. "Oh, dang! I've got an appointment to show someone a house. I'll be back at six-thirty." He leaned forward and planted a soft kiss on her cheek before running out the door. Josette heard his voice float back to her as he plunged down the stairs, "If you can, leave Saturday open, so we can look for a ring."

Josette sat down on the couch and stared at the flowers. "Oh, boy," she whispered. It would only take one of them to call the other's bluff, but it wouldn't be her. She wanted to see where this brakeless train was heading.

After a while, she picked up the phone and dialed home. She waited the few seconds for the call to go through and start ringing. To her relief, Marc picked up at the other end. "Hi, Jose," he said brightly. "Had enough? Are you coming home?"

"Zack asked me to marry him," she said.

"What? You've only been there a couple weeks! Don't you think that's a little soon?"

Two long and lonely weeks, Josette corrected silently. Weeks that she'd been walking around feeling empty, wondering if returning to BYU had been a good idea at all.

"I only met him today."

"You *what?*" her brother sputtered.

"We just met this morning, and he asked me."

"Is he rushing you?" Marc sounded angry.

"I said yes."

"Oh. Well, then congratulations . . . I think. He's been waiting a long time to meet you but I didn't know you even knew about him."

"Are you kidding? He's all Brionney ever talked about."

"He's a good guy. I couldn't recommend better. He was one of the most spiritual elders I know.

"Then why didn't you try to set us up?"

"I didn't think it'd work, that's all."

Josette was close enough to her twin to know when he lied. "You didn't think I was good enough for him, did you?" she asked slowly.

Marc's reply came even more slowly. "I just didn't want him to hurt you. But for what it's worth, I think you and he would make a great couple—if you're really serious about this. Don't let him rush you into anything. You're entitled to your own revelation."

"I know that."

"You could always tell him to get lost, or I will for you, if you want."

Josette laughed. "I'll keep that in mind. I may still take you up on that."

"Isn't it funny?" Marc said. "Sometimes true love can be just under your nose, and you don't see it."

"Zack wasn't under my nose, thanks to you."

"Well, you know what I mean."

They talked for a long time before hanging up. Marc agreed to keep her news a secret until she was ready to make an announcement in a few weeks—if she still felt right about it then.

As promised, Zack picked her up later that evening and took her to his parents' house. Terrell and Irene were just as Josette remembered them, and the smiles on their faces as they welcomed her were genuine.

"I can't believe you didn't tell me you were coming!" Brionney said, flinging herself into Josette's arms. She was still short and plump but had grown out of some of her awkwardness. Josette knew she would soon be eighteen. "When Zack called and said he'd found you and was bringing you home, I couldn't believe it. Why didn't you tell me?"

"I wanted to surprise you . . . after I got settled. And I've been trying to find a job."

"A job! You're kidding. Well, no matter. I bet Zack and Dad can use you at the agency, can't you?" Brionney looked at them expectantly.

"That's a good idea," Zack said. "Keep it in the family."

Everyone fell silent. "What?" Brionney finally asked.

Josette stared at the ground, wishing Zack would have waited a few weeks. Could he really be that sure?

"We're getting married," Zack said. "That's why I wanted

Josette to come to dinner tonight. We wanted to make the announcement."

There's no going back now, Josette thought, panicking. *Is that why he's rushing to tell them?*

"Oh, now I know why you haven't contacted me," Brionney said with a smirk. "You've been too busy going out with Zack. You must have gotten his letter." She glanced at her brother. "Oh, I know you sent one, but when Josette didn't say anything, I didn't want to pry."

"What letter?" asked Josette, looking at Zack. "I never got a letter. Did you write one?"

Zack grinned. "You didn't get it? Oh, that explains everything!"

"It was about the time you were transferred to your last area," Brionney added.

"Strange," Josette said. "There was only one time that . . . . Oh, the dog ate it!"

"Now that's a new excuse," Zack drawled. He put his arm around her shoulders.

"It's true." Josette tried to explain, but her heart had begun that curious, rapid beating, and the English words fled from her brain. She held her hand to her heart.

"Is something wrong?" Zack asked.

She gave a short laugh. "No, it's just the freight train again," she said in French. He pulled her closer and planted a kiss on her temple.

During the whole announcement and ensuing discussion, Irene and Terrell Fields had remained silent, and Josette hadn't dared meet their eyes. What would they say if they knew that today was the first time she and Zack had ever met?

Irene touched her shoulder. "Welcome to the family." She sounded happy, excited even, and Josette looked at her in relief.

Behind Irene, Terrell smiled. "We'd just about given up hope on old Zack finding a girlfriend," he said. "But now we know he was holding out for the best-looking girl in France."

Josette felt an emotion in her breast that she couldn't name. This wonderful family accepted her. Better yet, a good and worthy man, not someone just out for a good time, believed he was supposed to marry her.

"Come on into the kitchen for dinner," Irene said.

Zack let his arm fall from Josette's shoulders and gripped her hand instead. On the other side, Brionney hooked her arm through Josette's. "Tell me, if it wasn't for the letter, then how did you meet, Zack?"

"In our dreams," he said.

Josette didn't know him well enough to tell if he was joking.

Brionney snorted. "Well, that's okay—don't tell me. I don't need to know. But thank heavens you chose each other. I didn't like the idea of my brother marrying just anyone." She snapped her fingers. "Good thing I never bought another heart charm. I guess I knew you belonged together."

Zack laughed. "Okay, sis, I guess I'll let you off the hook."

"So when is this wedding anyway?" Brionney asked.

"Next week," Zack said.

Josette stared at him in horror. "Are you crazy?" she asked in French, not caring that Brionney would understand.

"I'm kidding." He squeezed her hand. "We'll take it slowly— for now."

Chapter Fifty-one

Everything went perfectly during the dinner, and Zack felt happier than he'd felt in a long time. From the way his parents acted, they liked Josette. Of course Brionney was crazy about her, and his three married sisters would also love her when they met her at the customary family dinner, held twice a month. How could they not? She was so beautiful.

Only one thing about the evening disturbed Zack. Josette wasn't as outspoken as he'd imagined she'd be after hearing about her from Marc. Was this the same girl at all? Was something wrong?

Maybe he was pushing too fast. Every time anyone mentioned their coming wedding, she paled and fell silent.

Maybe she's overwhelmed, Zack thought. *Heck, I'm overwhelmed.*

To him, it didn't matter if she was outspoken. They were together, and that was what counted. Still, he wondered if her aloofness meant that she was unsure about them. He would have to work harder at showing her how right they were for each other.

That night he kissed her chastely, fighting his desire to wrap his arms around her and never let go. "You're so beautiful," he whispered. "I love you."

A hesitant smile played on her lips, but she didn't meet his eyes. "I had a nice time, Zack. Thank you."

He hugged her then, and it was all he could do to let her go. "See you tomorrow night."

"Tomorrow?"

"Do you already have plans?" How dumb of him to assume that a girl as desirable as Josette wouldn't have plans on a Friday night.

"No, I'm free, but we hadn't talked about doing anything together. What do you have in mind?"

"I'll surprise you. Dress casual—jeans or something. Okay?"

To his delight, she gave a low laugh. "Okay, Zack." He loved the way she said his name.

The next evening Zack was at her door at six-thirty. He'd wracked his brains for something original—something that would not only relax them both, but make her happy.

"Hi," she said when she opened the door. She wore jeans that were exactly the right fit for her slender curves, and a simple white cotton blouse with tiny buttons down the front. Her long hair swung down her back in a thick braid, showing the fine planes of her face. Her eyes traveled to the two pair of in-line skates he held in his hands. She laughed, and her whole face shone with pleasure.

"Here," he said handing her the smaller ones. "This is my old pair from junior high. I would have borrowed Brionney's, but she's got such tiny feet. I mean, I thought these would be more comfortable for you."

"That's the first time anyone's ever said I have big feet."

"That's not what I meant—" Then he saw she was teasing.

"Marc and I always used to go blading," she said as she laced the skates.

"He told me. That's practically all he ever talked about. You and those skates."

She stopped. "He didn't tell me much about you. Of course, in the last three and a half years, we haven't been together more than a few weeks."

"I bet you miss him."

Her eyes became luminous. "I do. We've always been really close. Have you ever felt like a part of you was missing?"

He had to clear his throat before he could say, "I think I felt that way every day until I met you."

Her hand took his, and she didn't have to say anything because Zack knew she understood.

"Where are we going?" she asked after a few moments.

"You'll see. But bring a sweater. It might get cold before we get back." He wore his own denim jacket.

At first he led the way over the sidewalk, but Josette soon skated ahead, her red sweater tied around her waist. "Race you," she called.

She was better than he was, and he had to use all his strength to catch up. "It's all those stairs on my mission," she said with a laugh. She glanced at a group of passersby who watched them with indulgent smiles. "I've never felt so conspicuous," she said.

They slowed and skated hand-in-hand. At each street corner, Zack indicated which way to turn. Soon their destination was in sight.

"The temple," she said.

He took her to the grassy hill on the east side of the temple, where they sat for a long time without speaking.

"I'd like to get married in this temple," he said finally, trying to sound matter-of-fact.

She bit her lip. "I don't even know what you're majoring in."

"Business management. But I'm already working full time as a real estate agent with my dad. And you?" For all of the times Marc had talked about his twin, he'd never said what she was studying at BYU.

"Interior design." She flushed and plucked at the grass. "I know, it sounds kind of stupid. Unimportant. I mean, what eternal significance will that have on anyone's eternity? I've been thinking about changing, but I really enjoy it. I don't know what else I should do."

Zack stretched out on the grass. "I think it's perfect. Picture this. Besides selling houses, I'd like to invest in a few old ones and restore them. You know, fix what's wrong and decorate. You could help me, if you wanted. We'd make a great team."

"That sounds fun." She leaned over to hug him, but pulled back after a brief embrace.

"What is it?"

A frown covered her face. "I think . . . well, it's been a long time since I dated."

"Don't do that." He gently touched the corner of her mouth. You're so beautiful when you smile." The truth was, she was beautiful no matter what she did, but he wanted to see her happy.

She looked away, and Zack wondered what he'd said wrong. Instinct warned him not to push.

They talked for a long time and were surprised when the outside lights of the temple began to show in the twilight. He took her hand, and it felt soft and warm.

"Tomorrow," he said, "we should find a ring."

Josette must have tried on a million rings before both agreed they'd found the perfect one. During the search, they giggled like small children and held hands at every opportunity. When one of the sales clerks tried to convince them to settle for a ring they weren't sure about, Josette firmly refused. Zack was glad to see that no one could push her around. Maybe it eased his conscience.

Fortunately, the third store they visited had the ring for them. To his surprise, Josette wasn't interested in a big diamond, and he had to encourage her to get one that was a little larger. "Wouldn't you like it?" he asked.

"Oh, yes. But I don't want to be too showy." Then she added in an undertone, "I can't believe I just said that."

He threw back his head and laughed. "Well, I don't want to be called a cheapskate. I have four sisters, you know, who'll never let me forget it. Besides, what would your parents say?"

"They wouldn't care. At least my mom wouldn't. She doesn't go in much for jewelry. Besides her wedding ring, the only jewelry she wears is a rose pin my dad gave her."

"Even so . . ." Zack looked at the sales clerk. "Put in this larger stone," he said, pointing out the size.

"That's a good choice," the clerk said. "We can have it ready for you by next week."

After grabbing a warm pretzel to munch on, they took a drive in the mountains, and Josette made him stop the car so she could gather an armload of colored leaves. Without warning, she tossed them onto his head and ran up the trail. He caught up to her and dumped a handful over her. The stems and pieces stuck in her braid.

"Oh yeah?" She put her foot behind his feet and pushed, tripping him backwards onto the ground and piling more leaves on top of him. Zack fought back, and both of them began giggling uncontrollably.

"Enough!" Josette cried after a while.

Exhausted, they fell back onto the leaves, still laughing. Josette tried to brush the leaves out of her hair.

"You'll have to take out the elastic." Sitting up, Zack pulled out the elastic and began to undo the braid. "Besides, I love your hair loose—like that day in the rain." Had it only been two days ago?

It seemed he'd known her forever. "You should always wear your hair like this," he added, his fingers combing through the long strands. "Did I tell you you're beautiful?"

Her smile faded. "Yes."

He released her hair, and the ends fell to mix in with the leaves on the ground. "Why do you look away when I say it? Am I making you uncomfortable? Or don't you believe me?"

For a moment, he thought she would answer, but instead she laughed. Not a real laugh—a force one with out real mirth. "Of course I believe you."

"Is there anything wrong?" he asked, feeling there was something he was missing.

"No, silly." She picked up the ends of her hair and swatted him playfully.

He hugged her then, and everything returned to normal, but the incident worried Zack. He hoped that in time she would learn to trust him.

Chapter Fifty-two

Business was slow as Josette waited for Zack to come back to the office with the couple he'd taken to show a house. Josette had finished her work at the reception desk, but she wanted to see Zack before she went home. They would probably end up doing something together as they had every night for the last two weeks.

The new engagement ring on her finger still felt awkward. It was beautiful and she was glad Zack had insisted on a larger stone, though she'd been reluctant to admit it was what she'd always wanted. Did a large diamond really matter in the eternal scheme of things? No, she had to admit. Jewelry was no substitute for the real love she felt for Zack.

Her cheeks burned at the thought. Love. It really was love. Was it too good to be true?

Her head ached from the weight of her single braid. Zack liked her hair free, and it certainly felt better that way. During school and work hours, she kept it pulled back, but now she undid the elastic and shook out the braid. Already, her scalp felt relief from the pressure.

She gave a short laugh and refocused on the stationery before her. Last week she'd received a letter from Emeri, urging her to return to France and the people who loved her. He and his parents had recently attended the temple, where they'd been sealed as a family. Josette wished she could have been with him, but she knew her place right now was with Zack. The urge to come to BYU had been too strong for her to deny. She wanted to tell Emeri about Zack, knowing he would be happy for her, but so far, she was still holding back.

Josette's attention was pulled away from Emeri when Zack came into the office, accompanied by a young couple. He gave a thumbs-up signal behind their backs. That meant they liked the house he'd shown them and would make an offer. Now he'd have to fill out the earnest agreement with them and afterward present it to the owners. For him that meant working late, but the commission would be worth it. Maybe she'd tag along with him. It'd be better than facing her apartment alone.

She scribbled a few more words to Emeri, then gave it up. *I'll just call him tomorrow,* she thought.

Josette felt as though the past sixteen days with Zack had been better than any dream she'd come up with in her childhood. Why did she feel as though she'd never been out with a boy before? Or ever kissed a boy? Until Zack.

She still worried that she wasn't good enough for him, but the feeling that their relationship was moving too fast had subsided to a faint memory. At the moment, to be with Zack was her one great desire. She didn't want to think about life without him.

Only one thing made her nervous. What if he woke up one day and didn't love her? What if he grew tired of her beautiful face? She understood that beauty alone could never hold a man for more than a few years, and certainly not for eternity.

Zack emerged from his office with the couple. "I'll let you know as soon as I have their answer," he said to them. "If it's yes, or just a little different, I'll swing by your house and get it taken care of tonight."

"We'll be waiting." The man shook Zack's hand, and the wife gave a happy nod.

When they were gone, Zack flipped the "closed" sign on the glass door and sauntered to her desk. He pulled her out of the chair and into his arms. "I missed you," he said, burying his face in her hair.

She clung to him. "I missed you, too."

"Will you come with me to get this signed?"

"Sure." She bent down to scoop up her book bag.

"I like your hair like that."

His words made her flush. "I know."

They drove to the house the couple wanted to buy. It was the largest house Josette had ever seen. "Why does that couple need something so big?" she asked.

"They have six children."

"They didn't look that old."

Zack laughed. "The children are still small, and besides, they had to use fertility drugs. They got triplets the last time."

The owners of the mansion accepted the offer, and Zack whistled as he drove the car to another section of town. Josette assumed they were going to tell the couple and their six children that the mansion was theirs, but Zack stopped at another house instead. Dark windows signalled its vacancy. "I want to show you something," he said with a mysterious smile.

He led her up the cement walk to the house, where he pulled out a key and opened the front door. "It's a repo," he said. "The people couldn't pay the bank, so the bank repossessed. It needs a little work, but for the price, it's an excellent deal. Look at this wood floor and the tile in the kitchen. That's expensive stuff, and it won't have to be redone."

"I like that bay window," Josette said. "And this entryway. It's small, but I like the idea of not having to walk into the front room when you want to go to the kitchen."

"It reminds me of France," Zack said.

Josette wondered why he'd brought her here. Was this a new house he'd been commissioned to sell? No, it was a repo. Exactly why were they here?

Zack took her into the empty front room. "This rug needs replacement," he said, poking the large area rug with his shoe, "but underneath the wood is better than in the entryway. "Do you like it?"

"Yes, but—"

He looked at her earnestly. "It can be ours, if you want. We'll need a place, and this is too good to pass up. Even if we decide we don't want it later on, we could sell. What do you think?"

Contrasting emotions bubbled up inside Josette. One part of her wanted to sing out with happiness and run wildly through the house, making plans for renovation. To think—a whole house for only the two of them! With plenty of yard space for plants. To a woman who'd been raised in a city apartment, the large plot of earth was the greatest pull. Her children could play on swings in the backyard. She could plant a garden, though she didn't know where to begin, and they could paint and wallpaper until everything was exactly the way she wanted.

The other emotions were every bit as strong. Buying this house meant they would be making their home in America. It was the one subject they hadn't discussed. How could she give up her native land and everything she held dear?

Images of her family flashed before her. Several stood out in her mind, but strangely she remembered most the look on Emeri's face when he finally understood how much his parents loved him. How much time did he have left on earth? The separation from her family during her mission and for school had been different because it was only temporary, but this was for much longer. How could she live without her family, especially her twin, her other half?

But there was also no life for her without Zack. While she had insecurities regarding their relationship, the circumstances leading to their meeting left no doubt in her heart that he was her soul mate. As heartbreaking as it would be for her to give up her family, for him she would do it.

"You look so sad," Zack said, touching her cheek tentatively. "Don't you want to marry me?"

"Oh, yes, I do." Josette pushed her homesickness out of her mind, letting her love for Zack fill the emptiness. "I love you, and I love this house."

He picked her up and whirled her around. "Then hurry outside. We've got to do this right."

Puzzled, Josette followed him to the front step.

"We'll build a porch here," he said. Before she could reply, he scooped her up and carried her over the threshold. "I don't know if they do this in France, but it's an American tradition," he told her. "The groom always has to carry his bride into the house."

"Why?" She nearly choked on her laughter.

"I don't know. They just do it."

She struggled in his arms. "Well, we're not married yet. Put me down!"

"Hey, I'm practicing. I want to get it right that day. You don't want me to accidentally drop you or something, do you?" Zack set her down, his eyes dancing.

They examined the rest of the house, and Josette let her imagination free reign. "This is so fun!" she said, as she described the curtains she wanted to design for the living room.

"I know. But we can't live here until we're married. Maybe we ought to set the date." His words were gentle but probing.

"I haven't told my parents, yet," she protested. Why was she stalling? The past weeks had been the most wonderful of her life, and she believed she loved Zack. The problem was the look in his eyes when he told her how beautiful she was. Why should that bother her so much?

"Well, we could call tonight," Zack suggested. "If you want." He looked so hopeful that Josette didn't have the heart to object.

"Okay," she agreed.

Zack whooped and nearly knocked her over with his exuberant hug. "Let's go finish this business with that house, and then we'll call."

"It'll be too early there," she reminded him. "We should wait until at least eleven. We can watch a video first and then call. My roommates don't have plans for the TV—they're going dancing tonight."

Less than forty-five minutes later, they arrived at Josette's apartment. "You know, I did tell Marc about us that first day we met," she told Zack, as he popped in the video they'd rented on the way home.

"Then maybe your parents already know."

"Marc would never give away my secret."

"Maybe he's hoping you'll change your mind." Zack's voice sounded serious.

She punched his arm. "Let me handle Marc."

After the video, Josette dialed her parents' number and listened to the beeps that signalled the different paths making up the overseas connection. Finally, it began to ring. Her mother picked up the phone.

"Hi, Mom," she said a bit breathlessly. "It's me, Josette."

"Oh, honey, I'm so glad you called. Something's happened." From her tone, Josette knew it wasn't good news.

Chapter Fifty-three

Zack watched as Josette's face drain of color beneath the remnants of her summer tan. She made a desperate noise in her throat. "No," she said faintly.

She was quiet while her mother continued to speak. Zack could hear the soft, melodic voice coming from the phone, but Josette didn't appear to be paying attention. The receiver slipped from her ear, and only Zack's quick catch stopped it from hitting the linoleum floor.

Josette walked out of the kitchen, moving like someone in a trance. Zack put the phone to his ear. "Hello?" he said in French.

"Who's this?"

"Zack Fields."

"Oh, yes, I remember you. Marc's old companion. Is Josette all right?"

"I think so. I'll take care of her."

"I appreciate it. She and Emeri were close. She didn't expect him to die before she came home. None of us did, really. He'd actually started to improve."

Zack stopped hearing her words. Emeri was dead! No wonder Josette was so upset. He knew how much Emeri meant to her. He'd even felt jealous of Emeri before meeting her, and still suspected that Emeri was the reason for her reluctance to set a wedding date.

Hadn't he seen a letter addressed to him on her desk earlier? What had she been writing?

"When did it happen?" he asked, forcing his thoughts back to Ariana, and to the questions he knew Josette would think to ask once the shock wore off.

"During the night. He died peacefully in his sleep. He'd been in a little bit of pain since he and his parents returned from the Switzerland temple a few weeks ago, and he'd been on some pretty strong medication. He wasn't aware of much after that."

"How is his family taking it?"

"Remarkably well. Emeri helped prepare them, and we're all here to give them support. I think they'll be all right. They're wonderful people and have great faith. They actually have plans to adopt a young orphan boy who also has AIDS. He's one of Emeri's friends."

Zack felt amazed at their willingness to mourn another son. "I'll talk to Josette and we'll call you back," he said.

"I'm so glad she's with your family. Maybe your mother can—"

"We're not with my family. We're at Josette's apartment."

There was a long pause and then, "Tell me." The comment showed Ariana's perceptiveness. It wasn't easy to reach across the thousands of miles separating them, but she did it easily.

"I love her," Zack said, "and I'm going to marry her."

He expected to hear outrage at the uncompromising way he'd made the statement, but Ariana laughed. "I'm glad you're there, then. Have her call us later."

Zack hung up and went to find Josette. She was in her room, lying stomach-down on the bed with her hands pulled under her chest and her face turned to the wall, covered by the disarray of her dark hair.

He'd never been in her room before. Besides the single bed there was a small desk and chair, a dresser, and a closet. Clothes were piled on the chair, giving him the impression that Josette wasn't quite as organized as he liked to be. He didn't care. On her dresser was a picture of her family, a jewelry box, a small stack of opened letters, and a bottle of perfume knocked on its side.

"Josette." He sat on the bed, and when she made no move to turn to him, he smoothed the hair from her face. His hand came away wet from her tears. Frowning, he let the hand fall to caress her back. "I'm so sorry."

She turned toward him, curling her body around his, and he saw that in her hands she clutched a brass-framed photograph of two laughing young men. Marc and Emeri.

"I was writing him a letter," Josette said. "I've meant to do it for weeks now, but I kept putting it off. He's written me three times already in the month I've been here. I only sent him a postcard."

"You couldn't have known."

"Why now?" She started to sob.

Zack gathered her in his arms, feeling close to tears himself. He rubbed her back awkwardly as she clung to him.

When her tears subsided, she pulled back slightly. "Thanks for being here."

"Where else would I be? I love you. We're supposed to be here for each other."

Her face crumpled, and tears once more slid down her face. Strands of hair caught in the moistness and stuck to her left cheek.

"You loved him," Zack said. "Is he why you didn't want to set the date?"

She shook her head. "Oh, no. Emeri is Pauline's."

"Then shouldn't you be just a little happy for them? They're together now."

Josette blinked twice. "You're right. I do know that—with my mind—but my heart feels like I'm losing so much."

"What do you mean?" he asked. "You've got me."

She watched him for a full minute before replying. "I know. I'm so lucky to have you."

"I'm the lucky one," he said, brushing the hair from her cheek. "You're so beautiful."

"Don't say that," she said, looking away.

"Why shouldn't I?" He couldn't keep the annoyance from his voice completely. "You are, you know."

She didn't meet his gaze. "What if I'm not always beautiful? What if I got in an accident or something? Or when I get old and wrinkled?"

"I'll still love you."

"Not if that's what makes you love me." Her eyes met his now, a pool of watery brown. "Oh, Zack, I know you mean well, but a lot of men have told me how beautiful I am, and it really didn't mean anything. I want you to love me for *me.*" She tapped her chest. "For what I am inside."

Now Zack understood. He moved his head into her line of sight. "What if I looked different? Would that change how you feel for me?" She shook her head reluctantly. "Well, neither would it for me. When I say you're beautiful, I don't mean just physically. I mean what I see inside. I love you because when I'm with you I'm happy, because when you look at me I know I can do anything." He took her hands in his. "Josette, I fell in love with you before we met, but it wasn't only because of your picture. It was because of what I learned about you from Marc and Brionney, and from the Spirit. I know we're meant to be together. No matter what you look like on the outside, you'll always have all of my heart."

She hugged him then, fiercely. "For that I'll marry you tomorrow, Zack Fields."

He laughed. "I don't know if we can get the house ready that soon."

She kissed him, and he tasted the salt from her drying tears. "We'd better get started then."

"Uh, we have to call your mom back first. She's worried about you. Besides, I told her I was going to marry you, and I think she wants an explanation."

Josette's jaw dropped. "You told her?"

He grinned. "Sometimes if you want something done, you have

to do it yourself." He paused, fingering the folds of the blanket. "Actually," he said, hating the catch in his voice, "your mother sounded worried. I wanted her to know that someone who loves you is here to help."

"That just moved the wedding up again," Josette said. "How does tonight sound?"

He hugged her. "Just about right."

They called France and had a long conversation with the Perrault family. Everyone, including Marc, acted pleased with their impending nuptials.

"Boy, you never give up, do you?" Marc teased Zack when it was his turn to talk.

"The best is worth fighting for," Zack said. "But between you and me, I don't think she remembers I'm a year younger than you guys. Don't remind her, okay?"

When he said good-bye, he found Josette in her room again, reading a letter. He sat next to her on the bed. "It's the last one Emeri wrote," she said. "Listen. 'I can't imagine where I'd be if I hadn't met Pauline and learned about the gospel. I was lost and she found me. It was nothing short of a miracle. There are no words to thank you for helping me recognize the truth. God loves me, there is a plan, and I'm no longer afraid.'"

"He sounds like a great guy," Zack said. "I wish I could have known him."

Josette leaned against him. "One day you will."

Chapter Fifty-four

Marie-Thérèse finished the last of Madame Cerro's ironing as she heard Larissa calling from her room. She put the iron to cool on the counter, making sure the cord was out of reach from curious hands.

Larissa waited in her crib with arms outstretched, looking like a chubby angel in her fluffy pajamas.

"Good afternoon, baby. Did you sleep well?"

Larissa grinned and babbled something Marie-Thérèse didn't understand. She picked the baby up and kissed her.

"Dolly blahda fahma," Larissa said, pointing to a doll on her shelf next to the window.

Marie-Thérèse walked to the shelf and picked up the rag doll that had belonged to Pauline. She hadn't let the nine-month-old Larissa hold Dolly more than a few times because she wanted to keep it nice for her when she was older and could understand how special it was.

Larissa hugged the doll and kissed it before trying to peel off the embroidered eyes. "They don't come off, Larissa," Marie-Thérèse said. "But her clothes do. Want to see?"

The door buzzer interrupted their play. Marie-Thérèse left Larissa with Dolly and went to the door.

"Oh, hello, Madame Cerro. I'm finished with your ironing." Marie-Thérèse stepped back to let the bulky woman through the door. "Larissa just woke up from her nap, and I was going to bring it over."

"Goodness, it's cold in here," the woman observed. "Don't you have the heat on?"

Marie-Thérèse didn't want to admit that she kept it down on purpose to avoid the high bills. Every bit of money she could save was more she wouldn't owe later. She was accustomed to the cold now, and she dressed Larissa warmly so the baby wouldn't suffer. Besides, Marie-Thérèse kept busy, and it wasn't often she had time to think about it. "I like it this way," she said. "When I do the ironing, I get hot."

"Well, I suppose," Madame Cerro said doubtfully.

Marie-Thérèse led the way to the kitchen, where she had installed a bar to hold the rows of shirts and dresses she ironed. When Ariana had announced Josette's impending marriage in America, Marie-Thérèse had been determined to attend the wedding. But because of Mathieu's impulsive spending habits, she was already having trouble making his wage stretch to cover their bills. The only alternative was to earn the money herself by doing something at home. Taking in ironing seemed the perfect solution. Their landlady, Madame Cerro, who lived in the same building, had been one of the first to take her up on the offer.

Madame Cerro bent her graying head and examined the clothes. "You do a good job," she said grudgingly.

"I really try." Marie-Thérèse refrained from mentioning that Madame Cerro's dresses contained twice the material of most women, and the fabric was one of the most difficult to pleat.

The older lady gathered her clothes, careful to hold them by the hangers. "Well, thank you. I'll bring you more when I have some." She turned to leave.

"Uh, Madame Cerro. What about . . . I mean, the payment." Marie-Thérèse was embarrassed to remind her, and wouldn't have if she hadn't been counting on the money to help pay her way to America.

Madame Cerro was shorter than she was, but the woman did an excellent job of looking down her long nose at Marie-Thérèse. "Well," she said. "I thought you knew. Yesterday when your husband came by with the rent—two weeks late, I might add—I didn't charge him the late fee because I knew you were doing the ironing." She looked down at her burden. "This makes us about even, don't you think?"

Marie-Thérèse tried not to grimace. "But you said you understood. It was first time we were late."

"I do understand. That's why I allowed you to do ironing. I know things are tight when you are first getting started. Regardless, a contract is a contract." She gave Marie-Thérèse a patronizing smile. "Don't worry, dear. I'm sure I'll be bringing a lot more ironing. And don't bother about seeing me out. I know the way."

Marie-Thérèse sat down on a kitchen chair. It was part of a nice set Mathieu had bought her for her birthday last week. She had wanted to continue to use their hand-me-down table, but his boyish enthusiasm had made her relent. Now the purchase meant one more monthly payment.

Marie-Thérèse opened a drawer, took out an envelope, and counted the money she had saved. It wasn't enough to get one person to Utah, much less a couple and a baby.

Frustration welled up inside Marie-Thérèse. *Things have to change.* She had thought it before but hadn't the will to carry through. *Tonight I'll talk with Mathieu. We can work it out.* Mathieu earned good money, and she knew if they could live frugally for a few years, they could get out of debt—perhaps even buy a house like Zack and Josette were doing in Provo.

Larissa crawled into the room, her large eyes bright and happy. In one chubby fist she gripped Dolly's hair, dragging her rag body across the tiled floor. She pulled herself to her feet next to the chair and laid her head on Marie-Thérèse's knee. After studying her mother quietly, she offered the doll and a coaxing grin.

Marie-Thérèse smiled. "Thank you, sweetie."

The baby wandered away on hands and knees while Marie-Thérèse stared at the doll. Without warning, emotion boiled up inside her, a pounding wave of longing that crashed into her being, reaching deep into a part of her that she hadn't felt for a long time. *My sister is gone!* her heart cried. Tears coursed unbidden down her cheeks.

Why did it hurt so much? Why now? In three weeks it would be two years since Pauline's death. Two long years since she'd seen that sunny smile.

Frantically, Marie-Thérèse seized Dolly to her chest as she remembered how Emeri had held Pauline that last day. She closed her eyes against the assault of her emotions. What was Pauline doing now? Did she ever think of Marie-Thérèse? Was she happy?

Of course, Marie-Thérèse thought. *She's with Emeri and our parents . . . and with Jesus.* This time the assurance didn't ease the hurt. She remembered how Pauline had made her smile, her positive attitude in the face of suffering and trials, and her trusting, all-encompassing love. Marie-Thérèse missed her dreadfully.

Gradually her tears seeped away, and when Larissa came to sit in her lap, love for her daughter eased the terrible grief. Marie-Thérèse took several deep breaths. "I must remember the greatest lesson Pauline taught," she told Larissa. "Endurance."

Larissa giggled, and Marie-Thérèse managed a soggy smile.

When she'd calmed down, Marie-Thérèse went to see her parents. The walk in the brisk air and the brief ride on the metro helped clear her head.

Her mother opened the door with a smile. "I was just going to call you," she said, holding out her arms for Larissa. "Well, hello there, beautiful. Give Ga-ma Ariana a kiss."

Obediently Larissa gave one of her famous open-mouthed kisses.

Ariana laughed. "Come in and sit down a while," she invited.

"I still don't have the money for the tickets," Marie-Thérèse blurted as she followed her mother to the sitting room. "Maybe you should buy yours without us. I don't want you to miss finding space on a plane."

Ariana waved the words away and sat down on the couch. "Don't worry about it. Your father had to pay for the tickets yesterday, so it's all taken care of. I was just going to call you. We want you accept them as our gift."

"I can't do that, Mom. You've done too much for us already. Mathieu and I will pay you back." Marie-Thérèse wished she had the courage to tell her mother about their financial situation, but she felt doing so would somehow betray Mathieu.

Ariana looked at her with concern. "What's wrong? There's something you're not telling me."

"I'm fine, really, Mom. I just . . ." Marie-Thérèse stared after Larissa, who had decided to investigate behind the couch.

"It's Pauline, isn't it?" Ariana said softly.

Marie-Thérèse nodded and bit her lip. "It's like I only now felt her gone." Her voice wavered, and the tears she had thought were all cried out threatened to return.

Ariana slid closer and put her arms around Marie-Thérèse. "I've been worried it might affect you like this. I was grateful at the time that you had your new relationship with Mathieu to help you cope, but it's rather hard to mourn properly when you're so much in love."

"I never really mourned her." Marie-Thérèse felt a keen sense of guilt at the words. She remembered feeling numb when Pauline had died, which she knew was often the first step in grieving, but Mathieu had been so comforting, and her sorrow had been consumed in the joy of their love.

"You've had so much going on in the past years—a husband, a pregnancy, a new baby," her mother continued. "You've had a lot to keep you busy. It's no wonder it only hit you now. It does that sometimes with me, and I went through the whole grieving process. It's pretty overwhelming."

Grief. Now Marie-Thérèse recognized her emotions for what they were. She knew the feelings well. For several years after her parents' deaths she'd seen a counselor to help her understand that her varied feelings were not only valid, but common to those who'd lost a close loved one. After Pauline's more recent passing, Marie-Thérèse had congratulated herself several times on how well she'd dealt with losing her beloved sister and only blood sibling, but at this moment of glaring revelation, she felt as though she might never be all right again.

Why now? Marie-Thérèse searched herself for the answer, examining her feelings as though they came from someone else. Once she'd been protected by the walls of newfound love, but her anger at Madame Cerro for her uncaring attitude and at Mathieu for his spending habits had left her with no safe barrier. That must be why she was able to feel the freshness of Pauline's death as she hadn't years ago. *My dear little sister, how I wish I could hold you!* A part of Marie-Thérèse relished the pain. It was almost better than thinking of facing Mathieu.

Why can't he live within his means? Marie-Thérèse knew he'd experienced a humble upbringing by his widowed mother. So where had he learned to spend without apparent restraint?

Ariana held her and rubbed her back, and despite Marie-Thérèse's unwillingness to release the hurt, she felt comforted. For that moment, Pauline wasn't far away, and now that she knew why she was feeling the way she did, perhaps she could better deal with the emotions.

Later, when she and Larissa were making their way home, Marie-Thérèse felt much better. "I love your daddy," she told Larissa. "I just have to make him see. I only wish he wouldn't get so defensive every time I bring it up. Maybe I'll wait until after Christmas." Larissa nodded her head as though she understood.

Marie-Thérèse kissed her daughter's dark hair, feeling love for her blot out every other emotion. "And I'll earn our way to Josette's wedding—even if I have to iron every shirt in the entire neighborhood!"

Chapter Fifty-five

Brilliant white blanketed the earth. It was two weeks before Christmas, and colder than Josette ever remembered any day being—in Utah or France. But Zack's smile as he picked her up at her apartment warmed her. In seven days they would be married in the Provo Temple. Her family would arrive today from France to join in the last-minute preparations. After Christmas another celebration would be held in France, where they planned to spend their honeymoon.

"I hope their plane isn't delayed because of the snow," she said as they plodded through the mounds of white on their way to the van Zack had borrowed from one of his married sisters.

"It's stopped now. There's not a cloud in the sky. Look at all that blue."

Josette slipped her gloved hand in his and scanned the sky. Sure enough, it was clear, and the biting cold indicated that new snow wouldn't be falling any time soon.

"We'll have plenty of time to do some Christmas shopping and check out the lights at Temple Square before we go to the airport," Zack continued. "The roads ought to be fairly clear."

Catching a glimpse of a snow-laden tree near the walk, Josette purposely steered him under it and tugged on the branch. A flurry of dry, powdery snow rained on Zack, carrying with it a few crustier pieces that hadn't come with the snowfall the night before.

"Why, you . . ." Zack lunged toward her. Josette gave a short cry of alarm before they both fell into the snow. He scooped up a handful and hurled it toward her. Most of the powder fell short, but enough hit Josette in the face to make her eyes sting. She pushed more snow back at Zack.

"This stuff's no good for snowballs," Zack said, scooping up a huge armful and dropping it on top of her.

The snow fight went on until they were both too cold to move. Zack tried to kiss her, but Josette shook her head. "Are you kidding? Our lips will freeze together."

"Let's run to the van. We can dry out on the way to Salt Lake." Zack brushed the snow from her hair and coat as he talked.

Josette darted away, but she was no match for Zack's long legs. He had the van door open for her by the time she reached it. She was glad to slip into the warmer interior.

They fell into an easy silence. Josette watched Zack out of the corner of her eye. In seven days they would be married! She could hardly believe it was true.

Because of school and her parents' schedules, they'd agreed to wait until the Christmas break. The two months had appeared much longer at the outset, but now it seemed the time had gone by quickly.

She was anxious to see her family again. Everyone was coming except André, who was still on his mission, and Grandma Louise, who wasn't able to make the long trip. At least she would be able to see Grandma Louise when she and Zack arrived in Paris. Josette could thank her parents for that; if they hadn't offered the plane tickets as part of their wedding gift, she and Zack would have spent their honeymoon in their own home.

Everything wasn't as perfect as Josette would like to pretend. Marc wasn't happy about her staying in Utah, and neither was her mother. Josette had never mentioned the objections to Zack and felt relief when her family had finally become resigned to her decision. As had she. She tried not to worry about the future.

At the airport, Josette hugged and kissed her family. Everyone looked the same except Marie-Thérèse's daughter, who was nearly walking. Marie-Thérèse herself looked rather thinner than normal, but she assured Josette that she was fine.

"Snow! I want to play in the snow!" Louis-Géralde said, dancing from one foot to the other.

Josette laughed and ruffled his hair. "Tomorrow morning will be soon enough for you. I even bought you some snow boots."

"Where are we going to sleep?"

"At the new house Zack and I bought. It's not big, but it's got a huge yard. Tomorrow you can come to my apartment and help me move in the rest of my things."

"Will you be able to build a snowman with me?"

"Well, the snow we have right now isn't much good for packing, but it'll probably snow again before you leave."

Louis-Géralde's face grew solemn in thought. "I didn't know there was different kinds of snow!"

"Well, there are. Besides, I still have classes tomorrow. But I promise I'll spend the rest of the day with you. I took the time off work to be with all of you."

Marc put his arm around her. "So this is America." He grinned pointedly at Zack. "I hope you have some sights to see. I don't want to spend the whole week I'm here watching you two make eyes at each other."

"You think we don't have anything to compare with the Eiffel Tower?" asked Zack. "Well, you've got another *think* coming. I'm going to show you the building that houses the prophet of God. That's certainly something you don't have."

"I'm hungry," Louis-Géralde put in. "You have a McDonalds, don't you? Or haven't you got them yet?"

"Of course we have," Zack said. "We're the ones who started that restaurant chain."

The boy blinked at him. "I thought you and your dad sold houses."

Zack faced the laughter with a good-natured grin, giving up the explanation altogether. With one arm encircling her twin and the other her fiancé, Josette was happy.

A week later, Josette married Zack for time and all eternity in the Provo Temple. During the ceremony, as they knelt across from each other at the altar, the elderly gentleman officiating fell into an abrupt silence. The room was utterly quiet as he stared into the distance without completing the words of the ceremony, his head bobbing slightly as if he couldn't keep it still. Josette wondered if he was too old to remember the words. Or was he falling asleep? Her worry must have shown in her face because Zack's fingers tightened on hers, giving much-needed reassurance.

With a sharp movement, the sealer moved his eyes back to Josette and Zack. His mouth opened, but he didn't pick up where he had left off. "It has just been given to me to know," he said, "that you two made a promise in the premortal world to find and marry each other." He paused and stared, his gaze moving back and forth between them. "It is very rare for individuals to have made such promises; and of the ones who do, most do not find each other and end up marrying someone else. I thought you would like to know."

Reeling with surprise, Josette met Zack's eyes and saw eternity in their blue depths.

Everything in my life prepared me for this moment, she thought. She and Zack had found each other despite the distance between them and their different circumstances. How grateful she was for parents who had raised her in the Church. How grateful for gospel principles that had kept her feet from treading too far from the straight and narrow way. No longer did she worry about Zack falling out of love with her, or about her own unworthiness. The past was gone, the future yet unwritten.

Only one thing marred the day: the look on Marc's face when she and Zack left the reception held at the church house. "I'm going miss you," he said in her ear. "It's not the same at home without you."

"I know," she whispered back, her own heart torn in two, "but you'll find someone yourself one day, and then it'll be okay."

Chapter Fifty-six

Zack couldn't believe two months had gone by since his wedding. Zack knew Josette missed her home and her country, but she seemed content enough with his family as a substitute. Both he and Josette worked and attended school, so they didn't have a lot of free time, and he was glad she had no friends besides Brionney to interfere with the time they spent together. As it was, Zack often had to hint for his sister to leave so he could be alone with his wife.

Josette hadn't been to work for two days, and he missed her more than he'd expected.

"I think I'm coming down with something," she said. "I keep falling asleep in class. And I feel kind of sad. I don't know why. It doesn't make sense."

"Are you sure it's not because you miss your brother?" A week earlier she'd celebrated her twenty-third birthday, and Zack knew that except for their missionary service, it had been the only time in their lives that the twins hadn't been together on that day.

"No. It's not that."

Maybe she's working too hard, Zack thought. Josette studied almost constantly, and the office had never functioned so smoothly. Even his father had noticed the change and had mentioned the additional business she'd brought to the firm. Today they'd discussed hiring an assistant for her, and Zack planned to tell her about it tonight.

Darkness still came early in February, and Zack found himself longing for summer. He'd take Josette camping and show her all of his favorite spots—just the two of them, with no interruptions. Life was good.

The smell of roasting meat came to him before he opened the door to their home. *Good, that means Josette's feeling better.*

"You're home!" Not waiting for him to close the door, she raced toward him and threw herself into his arms. Her exuberance, her love of life, was one of the things he adored most about her, but today there was an added excitement.

"I see you're feeling better," he said.

"Of course. It's night."

"What does that mean? Do you need to sleep?"

She grinned at his confusion. "No, but tomorrow morning, I'm going to feel bad again."

Zack's heart pounded and his mouth moved without utterance.

"We're having a baby!" Josette said. "I should have thought of it before, but today I went and got one of those tests. Come on, I'll show you." She led the way to the bathroom, where the proof was sitting on the counter top.

Zack felt like dancing and shouting the news to the world. He was going to be a father! "Who have you told?"

"Just you, silly. Isn't the father supposed to know before everyone else?"

Zack waltzed her around the room. "I'm so happy." Then he stopped dancing. "But are you? I mean, I know we agreed to let the Lord decide whether or not we were ready to have children, but you hoped to finish school first . . ."

"I'm glad. I think a baby will make this place more like home."

Her solemn words reiterated the loneliness he knew she felt. Home to her was still France, not America or even this house they'd worked on so hard together. A baby would help with that, wouldn't it?

Before he could say anything, she drew away from him with a groan. "Oh no, the meat." She rushed to the stove and threw it open, her nose wrinkling at the smell. "It's a little overcooked," she said with a self-derogatory laugh. "I guess I got carried away dreaming."

Zack grinned. Neither he nor Josette had much luck at cooking, although they were better now than in the beginning. "I like my meat well done."

"Nobody likes it *this* well done. No humans, anyway. We might want to think about getting a dog." She flipped off the stove. "I guess it's cold cereal for us. Or maybe pizza—I'm hungry enough to even endure that. Or maybe your mother has extra. We could go by just to tell them the news, and . . ." she let the sentence dangle, already heading for the hall closet and her coat. Zack felt so full of happiness he wondered if his heart would burst.

I'm going to make you as happy as you've made me, he vowed silently. *Just you wait and see.*

Chapter Fifty-seven

It was Saturday, and finals were over at last. Josette was looking forward to a long vacation from school. She knew she should take at least a few summer classes, but she couldn't bring herself to do it. More than anything, she wanted to rest.

She wandered into one of the two spare bedrooms. She'd set this one up as an office, with Zack's desk, her father's old laptop, and two large easy chairs bought second-hand from an ad in the *Daily Herald*. They'd spent many late-night hours here studying since their marriage, but it was also where Josette came to write letters and to dream. The room was on the east side of the house, and the morning sun made it cozy.

"Honey, I'm going out to till the garden." Zack was dressed in his oldest jeans and a faded flannel shirt. "It's a beautiful day outside." He leaned over and put his mouth next to her stomach. "In a few months, we'll go camping," he said to the baby. "I know you won't be able to see the mountains from in there, but I'll tell you all about them." He straightened and grinned at her, making her laugh. If possible, Zack was more excited about this baby than she was.

"Are you going to come out?" he asked.

"In a while. I want to finish Marc's letter before the mailman comes."

"If you're not out by the time I finish tilling those rows, I'll come back inside. I need your opinion on what we should plant."

He blew her a kiss as he left, and Josette grabbed it in mid-air and slapped it to her cheek as her father had always done with her blown kisses as a little girl. Homesickness came in a drowning wave, and for a moment she shut her eyes and let it wash over her.

When she opened them, she could see Zack out the window, breaking the earth with his parents' tiller. The two rows of peas they'd planted last month had already sent sturdy tendrils from the earth. She knew she should go out and help, but bending over made her worry about hurting the baby, even for all of Irene's assurances.

During the past three months, her body had changed with the pregnancy. Her emotions had changed too, and that left her sometimes feeling desperate. Like now.

She left the window and sat at the desk, pulling her feet under her. Still on the desk was the letter she'd begun to Marc the night before. She hadn't written him since they'd talked on the phone on their birthday in February. Somehow letters didn't fill the void, nor did anything else she tried. What was wrong with her? She had the most wonderful husband in the world, a comfortable home, and was expecting a baby—all her childhood dreams were at last in place. Why wouldn't the sadness leave? She couldn't remember feeling so unhappy since Pauline's death.

Had it been almost two and a half years since she'd said good-bye to her sister? Memories came filtering through the months that separated her from the actual occurrences, like sunlight through a shuttered window. Josette threw open those shutters and let the memories envelop her: the family pulling together, their mourning tempered by the assurance of eternal life, Marc's loving arms around her and his ready smile, André's steadiness, Marie-Thérèse and her unwavering love, Louis-Géralde with his innocence, her parents' warm laughter.

Homesickness worse than she'd ever experience assaulted her. More than anything, she wished she could have a few hours alone with her mother. She longed to discuss the baby, her marriage, and life as she never had before. Why hadn't she appreciated Ariana before? *I wish I could tell her.*

And Marc. Josette felt her heart breaking. She longed to go skating with her brother, to walk along the Seine, to see the familiar skyline of Paris, to eat warm chestnuts from the vendor's cart at Christmastime. All that was now lost to her. Tears fell from her eyes before she could stop them. She laid her head on the desk and sobbed quietly, smearing the words she'd written on the page.

"What's wrong?" Zack's voice came from the doorway, followed almost immediately by his warm hands on her shoulders, kneading, caressing. As always when they were alone, he spoke French, which was still considerably better than her English. The concern in his voice brought her a sense of guilt.

"Nothing." She sobbed harder. "I'm just emotional, that's all. The pregnancy—"

"I know you well enough to know it's not only the pregnancy," he said, pulling her up from the chair and into his arms.

As their bodies touched, Josette was conscious of the growing life in her stomach, though she couldn't yet feel the baby's movements. Again the thought came: she had Zack and her baby, so why couldn't she be happy?

"Tell me," Zack said.

"I was writing a letter to my brother, that's all." She wiped at her face with her hands. If she could just stop the tears, her contentment with Zack would make everything all right.

"You miss him."

Josette sniffed.

"Josette, tell me," he urged again.

Her resolve broke. "It's like a part of me is gone. I'm so lonely— even when I'm working or whatever." There was pain in Zack's eyes, and Josette faltered. "I love you so much, and I want to be here with you, but I wish I could see my family more, that's all," she finished lamely, feeling selfish and mean. Why couldn't she stop herself from hurting Zack?

"Do you want to go home?" he asked, holding her back to see her better. "Do they mean that much?"

"Not more than you. I love you more than anything."

"But that doesn't stop you from missing them."

Josette replied softly, "No."

There was a silence between them, though their love flowed through their joined hands.

"I've been thinking about us moving there," Zack said finally.

"But your job, your future, is here." Even so, his words brought a leap of hope to her heart.

"My future," he said slowly, holding her gaze, "isn't in a country, but with you. Wherever you are, is where I want to be. If you're not happy here, then why can't I take you to where you will be happy?"

"What would you do there?"

"That's the one thing about real estate. Everybody's got to have it, even in France."

Josette looked out the window, feeling the warm sun on her face. Was this too good to be true? "What about your family? If we move to France, won't it be hard for you?" She held her breath, waiting for the answer.

"I don't know. But I have to try."

"Do you really mean it?"

He hugged her tighter and laughed. "Yes, I do."

"When?" It was all she could do not to run into their bedroom and start throwing things into her battered suitcase.

"Well, my passport is still valid, so there's no problem there, though I'll have to apply for residency and a work permit there. But there's the house . . ." He released her hands.

"Where are you going?"

"To my parents' house to talk to them, and then we'll place a newspaper ad on the house. No use finishing the garden, since we won't be here to take care of it. It's better that we start making plans to move. I'll need to give Dad notice at work. There are a few accounts I'll have to finish up."

"Can you wait until I grab a snack? I'm feeling a little nauseated."

He pushed one of the easy chairs into the sunlight. "Why don't you sit right here and eat? I'll talk to my parents and come right back."

Josette sighed with relief. She knew that Irene and Terrell would be as happy about their son moving to France as her parents had been with the idea of her staying in America, and though they'd be gracious, she'd rather not face them just yet.

As Zack left the house, Josette cuddled into the easy chair with a hunk of french bread heated up in the microwave. The crust was chewy and a poor substitute for the real thing, but it didn't matter now. Soon she'd have all the real french bread she could ever want.

I won't finish the letter to Marc at all, she decided. *I'll surprise him. Imagine his face when I arrive home.*

The heavy shroud of despair vanished, leaving her heart as light and warm as the sun streaming through the window. She tried not to think about what Zack was giving up for her. He would be happy in France. He had to be.

Zack should have known that loving an exceptional girl like Josette would exact a large sacrifice, in this case his country and his family.

"It's no more than she was willing to give for me," he said aloud.

In truth, Josette's sacrifice was greater because unlike her, he not only had an excellent command of French, but also a deeply ingrained missionary's love for the country and her people.

However, he knew his parents wouldn't be happy about his decision. His three married sisters had stayed close, and everyone had assumed that he and Brionney would do the same. But this was the only choice he could make for his wife. He smiled wryly. Love certainly changed a man's priorities.

He hoped his parents would understand. Didn't the scriptures say that when a man married he should leave his parents and cleave unto his wife? That was what he planned to do.

Even if it meant in another country.

His parents were in the kitchen, eating a late breakfast. Brionney was nowhere to be seen.

"Have a seat," his mother invited.

Zack took the proffered chair. "I have to talk with you."

His mother paused at the dish cupboard. She held very still, as if knowing her life was about to change.

"Josette's not happy here," he began. "In America, I mean."

Irene set the dish in her hand carefully on the counter top. "I've seen it in her eyes. But we've tried to make her feel welcome. We love her like we do you and the girls."

"That's not the problem. She adores you guys. But she still misses her family, especially Marc, even though she tries to hide it from me. I thought the baby might change things, but it's not getting better. I've been praying about what to do, and I've been feeling we should move to France and try it there for a while."

Resignation filled Irene's eyes. "I think I always knew it would come to this."

His father placed his fork, prongs down, on his half-eaten pancake. "We all knew it would be hard on you and Josette. Not so much because of the merging of cultures as because of the distance separating the two countries. It's nice to be on your own, but that's a little too far."

"Especially without enough money to visit," Zack agreed.

"Your mother and I talked about this when you got engaged," his father continued. "We worried about what it might mean for you in the future. Leaving your country is not the same for a man as it is for a woman, especially if she plans to stay home with her children, like Josette. In France, you'd have your job and business associates, but once she finishes school, Josette will have none of that. I imagine it will get lonely with the language barrier."

His mother nodded. "Having your first baby is wonderful, but it can also be very scary. She probably needs her mother. I've tried to be there for her, but I can't take Ariana's place. They're very close." Her words sounded calm, but tears gathered in her eyes.

Zack's own eyes felt moist. "I'm not saying it's forever, Mom. It's just for now. Who knows? Maybe after we have a few children and Marc's married, things will change. I mean, you live far away from your parents."

"We still see them every few months," Irene said. "Montana's not that far away. At least not compared to France."

Terrell slapped Zack lightly on the shoulder. "For what it's worth, I think you're doing the right thing, son. But it's going to take us some getting used to."

"We still have to sell the house. With the restoration we've done, we'll make a good enough profit. Enough to start out with in France." Zack grinned at his mother. "You always said I had it in me to make a million. I guess now we'll have an added incentive—so we can visit more."

Irene gave him a watery smile. "Just promise me one thing. Teach your kids English, too. I'm too old to learn French."

Zack left them, feeling more determined than happy. What if this change didn't work? He heaved a long sigh. The Spirit had confirmed beyond any doubt that Josette and he were meant to be together. He just hadn't understood how difficult securing that happiness would prove to be.

"But now *I'm* losing *my* brother!" Brionney wailed as she saw the plane tickets.

Josette hugged her, understanding exactly how the younger girl felt. "I know, and I'm sorry. But there is good news." She fanned out the tickets. "Remember how you said you were going to visit me in France? Well, you are. Look! Three of them. You're going to stay with us for the whole summer. We leave the last week of May, so you need to make sure your tests are all over by then."

Brionney grabbed the tickets. "Yay!" She jumped to her feet. "Now you're talking."

"Maybe you'll meet one of those handsome French guys you're always dreaming about."

"Yes," Brionney said dreamily. "He'll be a multi-millionaire, so we can have two houses—one here and one there."

"I guess that lets my brother out," Josette said. "He hasn't made a million yet."

"He's cute, but I don't know if he likes plump girls, much less ones who are nearly five years younger than him."

"How do you know? When he was here for the wedding, you didn't even see him long enough to say two words to him."

"My French is so bad. I didn't want to be embarrassed."

Poor Brionney. Josette felt embarrassed by her English, but it had never stopped her from meeting men. She could relate to the fat thing, though. In the past weeks while searching for a buyer for their house, her stomach had grown tremendously. She'd taken to watching pregnant women and wondering how much longer until she began to waddle.

She heard the car outside. "Zack's home."

"Did you make dinner?"

"I just got home myself, right before you came. We'll have to cook a frozen pizza. You know, I think I'm actually going to miss that junk."

Brionney grinned wickedly. "If it'll make you feel better, I'll go out and see if I can find any snails in the bushes."

"Would you?"

Both burst into laughter as Zack came through the door. "Did I do something funny?" he asked.

"I was just telling Brionney how I was going to take you both out for escargot when we get to Paris."

Zack's face twisted in a slight grimace. "You and Brionney can go. I think I'll be too busy."

"Coward." Brionney punched his shoulder.

"Hey, I've tried those slimy little gray things before, and I still have nightmares of being trapped in a room full of them." He put an arm around Josette. "I vowed to love you for eternity, but I don't remember any mention of having to eat snails."

"I guess you're off the hook, then."

"That's a relief." Zack's voice took on a note of suppressed excitement. "But guess what? I found a buyer for the house. It's a good offer, too. Looks like we're on our way."

Chapter Fifty-eight

Josette's father picked them up at the airport in Paris on Friday shortly before noon. Only he and Ariana knew they were coming, but they had gathered the family at the apartment under the pretense of a special announcement.

"Rumor has it I'm receiving a new church calling," Jean-Marc joked. "It's kind of funny, really. You see, the stake president is going to be released, and now they're looking for a replacement. People think our bishop will be the new stake president, and the children tease that I'll take the bishop's place. Imagine me as a bishop! I don't think so. Serving as a counselor is as close as I ever want to get. Anyway, the kids think we've called them in for that kind of announcement. They have no idea you're here."

Josette and Zack laughed with him, but Brionney stared blankly. Josette repeated the conversation slowly so she could understand. They had agreed to speak only French so Brionney could gain more fluency during her stay.

"Marie-Thérèse wasn't there when I left," Jean-Marc added. "I hope she and Mathieu get there on time. Their car's in the shop, and they'll probably use the metro."

Brionney said little during the drive, her face showing the

wonder of being in the famous City of Love. Josette also fell silent, her heart singing with joy at being back in her beloved France. She clung to Zack's hand while he and her father discussed the steps Zack would have to complete before being allowed to sell real estate in the country. Since her father was so widely known and respected, he was going to be a great help in making the transition, but the bottom line, of course, would be work.

When they arrived at the apartment, Ariana let them in. "Everyone's in the living room," she whispered after hugging Josette and exclaiming softly over her growing stomach.

The room burst into a cacophony of questions as they entered. Before anyone else could move toward her, Marc jumped up from the couch and enveloped her in a bear hug. "You didn't write," he said. "I was just about ready to go to America and kidnap you!" He pumped Zack's hand before pulling him into a hug. "How long are you staying?"

"We're moving here," Josette said.

Marc's jaw dropped, and his eyes went to Zack's for confirmation.

"I knew how much you missed me," Zack quipped. "I thought with you and André going into engineering, we could work together. You build 'em and I'll sell 'em."

"Well, I don't know anyone who'll buy a bridge or a road," Marc said. "Except a city. But maybe I can work on an apartment complex or two."

Zack grinned. "That's a guy."

There was a silence, and then Marc added in a choked voice, "Thanks for bringing my sister back."

"Well, I won't be going skating anytime soon," Josette said, touching her belly.

Marc shrugged. "I haven't been since you left anyway."

"Look who else is here." Josette propelled Brionney forward. The girl immediately turned a bright shade of red.

"Hello," she said timidly.

Marc grinned at her and then at Zack. "Your sister is very pretty."

"I remember saying something similar about yours."

"Exactly." Marc moved closer to Brionney. "Consider me your official tour guide while you're here. That is, when I'm not in school. I'm going to be a civil engineer, you know."

Brionney stared at him blankly.

"You're speaking too fast," Josette said. "She speaks and understands well, but isn't quite fluent yet."

Marc shot a teasing glance at Zack. "That's okay. There's one language that doesn't need translating—the language of love."

Brionney did get that, but instead of turning a darker shade of red, she giggled. "You are exactly like Zack. I know how to take care of you." She punched him in the shoulder hard enough to make Marc rub it with his hand.

Josette extracted herself and went to talk with her grandparents. Her mother's parents, Géralde and Josephine, were as she remembered, but Louise, her father's mother, seemed older. It struck her that had she stayed in America, she might never have seen Louise again. Behind Grandma Louise, Aunt Lu-Lu and her two young children awaited their turn to greet her, but Marie-Thérèse and Mathieu were nowhere in sight.

Josette excused herself a short time later to go lie down in her old room where she and Zack would be staying until they found an apartment of their own. On her way, she had to pass through the kitchen, where she lingered for a moment with her mother.

Ariana was on the phone, but she hung up when she saw Josette. "I was calling Marie-Thérèse's, but she's not there so she must have already left. It's not like her to be so late."

"When she gets here, tell her I'm in my room. I need to lie down for a while."

"Are you feeling all right?" Ariana asked.

"Yes. I'm just tired from the trip, and the time difference. For us it's the middle of the night. But I'm so glad to be home."

Ariana inclined her head, a warm smile on her lips. "I'm happy you're here, too. I've missed you."

Josette hesitated before saying, "It may not be forever."

"We'll take each day as it comes."

They fell into silence, and Josette wished her mother could see into her heart instead of her having to piece the words together. How could simple words convey her depth of feeling? "Mom, I've been wanting to tell you how much I love you," she said hurriedly. "Appreciate you, I mean. I don't think I've ever told you before."

Her mother seemed to understand what she was saying, though the words were dreadfully inadequate. "I remember feeling the same way about my mother after I had you and Marc. Becoming a mother changes everything, doesn't it?" She smoothed Josette's hair. "Thanks for telling me."

Happiness filled Josette's heart as she made her way to her room, where already her father had put their suitcases near the bed. Nearly everything they owned were in those four suitcases and two flight bags, but Josette felt rich. She was back where she belonged.

Chapter Fifty-nine

The lights in the underground train had been off for ten minutes, and there was still no word from the engineer. Baby Larissa had tried constantly to escape her mother's arms, and Marie-Thérèse had finally let the fifteen-month-old down to toddle near the seats. The other passengers smiled and waved at the baby as she approached.

"Don't let her go too far," she warned Mathieu.

He grabbed the baby as she passed him and pulled out a pen to entice her to stay on his lap. Larissa pushed it away and struggled to get down again. "We wouldn't be here if we had a second car," he said.

Marie-Thérèse sighed. He was right, but that didn't mean they should buy one. How could they possibly afford one more bill? "We have to live within our means."

No matter how nicely or thoroughly she explained it, he didn't seem to have a grasp on their circumstances. The money he earned simply wasn't stretching to cover the never-ending pile of bills. Sometimes she thought if she had to iron one more shirt from someone else's wardrobe, she would go crazy.

The overhead lights flickered and a weak cheer went up from

the crowd. The train lurched a few times before beginning its smooth humming. Larissa stopped struggling and stared out the window, laughing at the occasional light in the dark tunnel.

"We're going to be late," Marie-Thérèse said.

Mathieu shrugged. "They'll understand. It couldn't be helped."

Marie-Thérèse felt his words as an accusation, but this time she would not relent. As much as she loved Mathieu, things had to change. With his impulsive spending, she couldn't plan for anything in the future. Nothing was assured. She might have tried to save for a new set of dishes or cutlery, but any extra money was immediately gone for bills or for whatever Mathieu thought appealing. Both she and Mathieu recognized there was something wrong between them, but neither could agree on what it was or how to fix it.

Mathieu leaned close to her and put his arm over the top of her shoulder. His physical gesture told her he wasn't upset, but Marie-Thérèse couldn't relax. She could only identify the emotion in her heart as a looming fear. What was coming next?

She didn't have long to wait. At the base of the stairs leading out of the metro, an old woman dressed in black sat on a dingy gray blanket with a chipped coffee mug in her frail, thick-veined hands. She was only one of the hundreds Marie-Thérèse had encountered in the subway over the last few years.

The old lady pushed her mug toward them in silent pleading. Marie-Thérèse fished in her pocket for some change, but Mathieu reached into his wallet and pulled out several bills. "Here, old woman," he said kindly.

Marie-Thérèse couldn't believe her eyes. One part of her commended the unselfish gesture, but with that money she could have made a payment on one of their credit cards or bought food for three days. How could he give away so much money when she couldn't sleep at night for worry? The possibility that the old woman might use the gift for drink, or give it to a family member to buy alcohol, made Marie-Thérèse even more upset.

She clutched Larissa to her chest and bounded up the metro stairs ahead of Mathieu. He caught up to her, talking blithely about the possible reasons her father had asked them to the house. "Maybe he got a new calling," he guessed. "Or maybe he's planning a surprise party for someone."

Marie-Thérèse walked stiffly, her teeth clenched in hostile silence. It took a long while before Mathieu perceived her anger. "What's wrong?"

She turned on him, letting her anger take control. "The bills aren't paid, I need grocery money, but you're more concerned about a beggar than your own wife and daughter." Even as she said the words, she felt stingy. For all she knew, that old woman did need the money more than she did.

Mathieu stopped. "We're supposed to help people."

"We're supposed to get out of debt so that we can be in a position to help people. We're not supposed to live beyond our means."

"We're not. I make enough to pay the bills."

"To pay the interest on the bills, you mean."

"But I'll be getting a raise soon—"

"And you'll get a new bill to use the money."

"Marie-Thérèse, that's not fair."

"Isn't it? You know we need to pay off bills, but what did you do when you got that bonus? You bought that crocheted bedspread from Sister Gill. Never mind that I know perfectly well how to crochet and would like to have money to buy the thread to do one myself."

"But now you won't have to do it."

"I *want* to do it. I like crocheting, and I want to have something to pass on to Larissa. She's not going to give a hill of beans for a stupid bedspread that someone else made. It's not going to be a family heirloom."

Mathieu's eyebrows drew together and he stared hard at her. "You know Sister Gill needed the money to support her son on his mission."

This was the point in their argument where she would normally break down and admit that he was being the better Christian, but not today. Something in what he said didn't agree with what was in her heart. Either her feelings were wrong, or he was. There was no compromise.

"She doesn't need it any more than we do," she insisted. "If she can't pay, the church will help. Why do you think we donate money to the missionary fund each month?"

In her arms Larissa whimpered, and Marie-Thérèse knew her daughter was reacting to their argument.

Mathieu glanced at Larissa and the tenseness in his voice relaxed. "I don't see the problem."

Marie-Thérèse grimaced. "That's the biggest part of the *problem,*" she said scathingly. "If you could admit you have trouble managing money, we could talk about it and work something out, but you don't see anything."

The fact that he didn't lash out at the ugly tone of her voice showed what kind of a man he was, but Marie-Thérèse didn't want to count his good qualities. The money situation threatened to drive her to a nervous breakdown, and it all but consumed her.

She started walking again, rapidly, with Larissa still whimpering in her arms. "Shush, honey," she mumbled, patting her back. "I'm sorry. It's over now." Marie-Thérèse knew it was a lie, but saying it made them both feel better.

When they arrived at her parents' apartment, Louis-Géralde let them in. "Finally! We've been waiting for you." He smiled, bursting with a secret. "Josette's here, and she came to live with us. She's staying forever. Well, in France anyway."

Marie-Thérèse's mood lightened. Josette back in France! This was just what she needed. "Where is she?"

"She's in her room. I think she's tired. She's got a baby inside her, you know."

Larissa kicked to get down and Marie-Thérèse let her toddle off with Louis-Géralde, knowing he'd watch her closely. Without a word to Mathieu, or even glancing in his direction, Marie-Thérèse went into the kitchen and down the hall. She felt relieved that she wouldn't have to face all the relatives while she was still so angry. By the time she returned, maybe she'd be able to put the fight behind her.

Until the next time.

Marie-Thérèse sighed heavily. Then she forced her mouth into the semblance of a smile and rapped on the door to the bedroom she and Josette had shared while growing up.

"Come in," said a tired voice.

Marie-Thérèse pushed open the door. "Are you sleeping? I can come back later."

"No! I'm so glad to see you." Josette eased off one of the beds and hugged Marie-Thérèse.

"You look great. I mean, you barely look pregnant. How far along are you—four months?

"Yes, but I feel like I weigh a ton already."

Marie-Thérèse wrinkled her brow sympathetically. "I remember that." They sat together on the bed. "So what made you decide to come home?"

Josette's face softened and her eyes began to water. "It was Zack's idea. He thought I'd be happier here. I've been so lonely, especially without you and Marc, and with the baby coming and all, I . . ."

Marie-Thérèse squeezed her sister's arm. "You don't have to explain. I understand. Everything's suddenly different when you have a baby."

"That's what Mom said. I thought that if anyone was independent, it was me, but I've been fooling myself. I need my family."

"What about Zack? Do you think he'll be happy here?"

Josette's lips turned slightly downward, not quite a frown, but almost. "We'll just have to wait and see. I couldn't bear for him not to be happy."

Marie-Thérèse thought Josette's words showed how much she had changed over the past few years. She was no longer the self-centered, greedy young woman of the past.

Josette's fingernails slid lightly over Marie-Thérèse's arm. "Why are you so sad?"

Marie-Thérèse blinked rapidly to keep her tears from falling. Lately it seemed she was always crying. "Since when did you get to be so perceptive?"

Josette's smile flashed and was gone. "I think it was the mission. You have to listen to what people aren't saying. Tell me."

Marie-Thérèse opened her mouth to say it was nothing, but to her surprise the problem flooded out before she could stop it. Instead of laughing it off or making a negative comment about Mathieu, Josette listened without interruption.

"Have you told anyone about this?" she asked when Marie Thérèse finished.

"I've been too embarrassed. I mean, everybody loves Mathieu so much, and I don't want them to think badly of him. Besides, it kind of makes me sound selfish, doesn't it?"

"Not to me. It sounds like you want some security."

"That's it exactly. I don't want presents, a second car, or even furniture. I just want security. And freedom, I think. I want to be free to do a few things without worrying about paying on them for the rest of our lives."

"I think you should counsel with the bishop," Josette said. "I'll bet he'd have some suggestions or know someone who does."

"I'd be embarrassed to tell anyone."

"You told me."

Marie-Thérèse had to admit she felt better with someone knowing how she felt. "But we're getting a new bishop."

"Oh, that's right. Well, that's as good a time as any, isn't it? I'm sure it'll be someone experienced. What about Mathieu? Would he go?"

"I think he will, if only for the bishop to straighten me out. He doesn't see that we have a problem. He thinks it's something else entirely, but he doesn't know what. My uptightness, probably."

They fell into silence, but Marie-Thérèse's heart was lighter now. Josette giggled.

"What's so funny?"

Josette made a face. "Oh, I'm sorry, Marie-Thérèse. I was just thinking what would have happened if it had been me who had married Mathieu before my mission. Can you imagine it? We would have been so far in debt, they'd have to dig us out with one of those huge machines. You know, one with those big claws on the end. They'd keep digging and find me at the bottom with a stack of worn-out credit cards."

Marie-Thérèse couldn't help joining in her sister's laughter. "That's for sure."

"Zack tears up any card offers we get. I told him about my weakness."

"That's good." Marie-Thérèse sighed before adding thoughtfully, "I wish I'd known about Mathieu's problems with money before we married."

"Wouldn't you have married him?"

"Of course I would have. But maybe we could have talked about it beforehand. I mean, now that I look back, there were signs, but I didn't really notice then. Remember how he always took us out and paid for it with his credit card?"

"Yeah, I remember."

"Well, we're still paying for those meals." She sighed. "I think it would have been fairer to get the whole scoop before marriage, so I could be prepared. I don't like surprises."

"Those are the kind everyone could do without. My poor Zack . . . I think he got one of those with me. He has to do a lot of the cleaning."

"I'll bet. I've lived with you, remember?"

"So what are you going to do with Mathieu?"

Marie-Thérèse grabbed her sister's hands. "Please don't think

I don't love him. I do, I really do. If not for this, I think we'd be perfect for each other."

"Like you were meant to be together."

Marie-Thérèse smiled. "For some reason that makes me think of Pauline and Emeri."

"I like that."

"I think they would, too."

Chapter Sixty

"But Josette just got here and we're going to eat. You can't leave now!" Louis-Géralde said to his parents in the entryway.

Ariana kissed his proffered cheeks, thinking how much he looked like his father. "Don't worry, we won't be gone long."

"Where are you going?" Marc asked. "I'm starving."

Ariana adjusted the strap on her purse. "We've been called down to the church for an interview with the stake president. We'll be back in a while. Grandma Josephine will put the finishing touches on the food, and we'll eat when we get home."

Zack grinned. "Uh-oh. I sense a new calling. Funny how you brought the family together on the pretense of receiving a calling, and then you're summoned to the church. Hmm, what a coincidence."

"Yeah, someone up in heaven has a sense of humor," Marc added.

"I'm sure he just wants to talk about some of the leaders at church," Jean-Marc said. "Since I was a counselor in the bishopric until a few months back, they'll want to know about the capabilities of our members. They did that when the last stake president was called."

"Sure, Dad," Marc said. "Dream on."

"Dream on," Louis-Géralde echoed in his high child's voice. Jean-Marc grabbed him and tickled his stomach.

"We'll be right back," Ariana said. "Tell the girls if they come out of the bedroom."

"They may never come out," Mathieu said. "Marie-Thérèse is mad at me." He picked up his daughter who pulled at his leg, asking for a drink of water.

Zack chuckled. "So you're in the doghouse, as we say in America. What happened?"

"It's nothing," Mathieu said, shrugging. "It'll pass." He took Larissa into the kitchen for a drink.

Ariana frowned at his retreating figure. She'd felt for some time that Mathieu and Marie-Thérèse were having problems—ever since last December, when Marie-Thérèse had belatedly mourned Pauline's death. Before that they'd always seemed so perfect together, but lately there was a distinct tension between them. She knew from past experience the torment of being in a bad marriage, and she couldn't help being worried. Even strong love couldn't hold a relationship together when other key elements were missing. She wished Marie-Thérèse would confide in her, but until she did, Ariana could only wait and give her love. The gentle probing wasn't working, but maybe prayer would.

At least Josette seemed happy. Now if only Marc could find someone special. Ariana's eyes went to the sitting room where she could see Zack's sister on the sofa, trying out her French on Grandpa Géralde. Brionney was very pretty with those beautiful blue eyes, and she seemed nice, which was more important. *Who knows? Maybe she's the one for Marc. We'll wait and see, I guess.*

Ariana came from the stake president's office, smiling at the dazed look on Jean-Marc's face.

"I can't believe it," he said. "I was pretty sure our bishop might be called as the new stake president—everybody thought that. But me, a bishop? That's something I never expected. What about you?"

"Well, I've known all along that you had the potential," Ariana said.

"Are you really willing to sacrifice the time it'll take?" he asked, taking her hand in his. "I mean, we've been talking about going on that extended trip this summer and spending more time together. Now the trip will have to wait, and . . ." He shrugged. "It's a big responsibility."

"It is," Ariana said, hugging him. "But you can do it, and I'll support you. We'll be fine. I think we've learned how to keep our family together by now, don't you? This'll be one more adventure."

Jean-Marc gave a short laugh. "Some adventure. But if you're willing to do it, then I guess so am I." His arms tightened around her. "I love you, you know. Just when I think I couldn't love you any more, the feeling increases."

"I love you too. So are you going to say yes?"

"Now, now," Jean-Marc chided jokingly. "He told us to go home and pray about it."

"But we already know, don't we?"

"Yes. So what we have to do now is to pray for me to be equal to the task." He grinned, and his green-brown eyes sparkled. "Just when I was getting comfortable."

Ariana laughed and hooked her arms through his. "Be careful of complacency—it'll get you every time. Come on, let's go talk to the children. He said we could tell them."

When they arrived at the house, the family gathered and Jean-Marc made the announcement. There were slaps of congratulations and good-natured teasing.

"Next time, you'll listen to me," Zack said.

"Does this mean I have to call you bishop?" Louis-Géralde asked.

Jean-Marc rumpled his hair. "No, it most certainly does not."

The boy sighed with relief.

"Well, I think it's about time we had our meal," Ariana said. "I don't know about you guys, but I'm hungry."

"I could eat a horse," Zack said.

Louis-Géralde laughed and followed the others into the kitchen, saying, "I bet I could eat an elephant. No, a whale. Maybe even a tyrannosaurus rex!"

Ariana noticed Marc and Brionney trailing the rest. "I guess it's up to me to show you Paris this weekend," Marc said to her, "since I'm the only one not married and boring. How about it? We could start after we eat. The night is still young."

Brionney's grin matched his. "Sure. But I want to see the Eiffel Tower first."

Marc laughed. "That is *so* American. You know, the only times I've even gone there have been with Americans."

"Get used to it. I'm going to be here all summer."

"I guess I can make the sacrifice." Marc didn't act like it would be too painful.

Ariana was glad to see him so content. He'd been too quiet since Josette had left for America. Maybe now that she was back, he could find his own happiness.

Chapter Sixty-one

*Z*ack walked in the door before five o'clock after a busy and satisfying day. He couldn't wait to share the details with Josette. "Honey?" he called. "Are you home?"

There was no answer, and he experienced the same letdown as he had on the other days she hadn't been there. He set down his briefcase and read the note she'd left on the counter.

> *Gone with Marc, be back soon. I'll bring dinner. I love you!*
> *Josette*

He poured himself a glass of juice from the refrigerator and sat down to wait. After almost two months in France, he'd made good progress. He had obtained a work visa and started a new job at a promising real estate firm owned by a business associate of Jean-Marc's, where he was becoming popular with their clients. The Parisians loved his American accent and were intrigued with his height and blond hair. Happy customers sent friends and family his way.

Eventually, Zack planned to open his own agency, but only after he learned the procedures and received the appropriate licenses.

One of the first things he'd done after securing a job was to find this small apartment, which was both inexpensive and an excellent investment. With only one bedroom, a bathroom, a kitchen, and a tiny living room where Brionney stayed when she wasn't out with Marc or Marie-Thérèse, it was the perfect size for a newly married couple, even one with a baby on the way.

At first Josette hadn't seemed to mind the small size of the apartment, but lately he wondered. Often she went out with Marc or her friends when he wasn't home. Zack found himself remembering with longing the closeness they'd shared in their house in Provo, when she'd been all his.

He frowned. Where was she, and why was she taking so long?

Not wanting to waste time, he opened his suitcase and pulled out some papers that needed his attention. Concentration didn't come easily.

Another hour passed before he heard Josette's laughter at the door. He arose quickly and ran to the hall to meet her. "Where have you been?" he asked.

Josette kissed him before replying. Zack could smell her familiar perfume. She was six months along with their baby, and he thought her more radiant than ever. Her hair lay loose around her shoulders, long and thick.

"Oh, Zack, we went to the cutest little place! It was an entire old-fashioned village in miniature. They had windmills where they actually ground real flour, a cobbler shop, a bakery, a pub. And so much more. There were even short castle walls surrounding the whole place. It was so cute. Wasn't it, Marc?"

Marc leaned against the door. "It really was interesting how they set it all up. We'll have to take you there. It's free to the public."

"I was worried about you," Zack said.

Josette looked puzzled. "I wrote you a note so you knew I was with Marc. And we had so much fun! It was better than sitting around here, wondering how many more days until I can't see my feet. Marc knew that, and since he had some time off from school, he came and took me away."

"I helped her wash the dishes first," Marc added with a grin.

"And we brought dinner." Josette shoved a white paper bag at Zack. "It's from the bakery at the miniature village—not from the miniature bakery, of course. From the real one they have there to sell to visitors. They have a pottery shop, too, with all sorts of stuff. That's how they make money to take care of the village. But go ahead, look in the bag. It's bread with meat inside. I tasted it already, and it's good. So let's eat!"

Zack didn't reply, and Josette made her lips pout. "Come on Zack, don't be upset. You know I'll always be careful, especially since I'm carrying our baby."

She turned a cute pink, and Zack's irritation vanished. He began unrolling the top of the paper bag. "Let's see what you have here. What? You call this a meal?"

"Try it."

Zack did. "Mmm, it is good."

"Well, I'll leave you to your gourmet feast." Marc moved toward the door.

"You won't stay?" Josette asked.

"No, I'm going to pick up Brionney at Marie-Thérèse's. I can't hang out with you old married folks all the time." He kissed Josette's cheek, gave Zack a salute, and went out the door.

"Poor Marie-Thérèse." Josette walked down the short hall, past the bathroom to their tiny front room. "All that ironing she's taking in because Mathieu can't control himself. I don't know how much longer I can stop myself from interfering."

"It's Marie-Thérèse's call," Zack said, sitting next to her on the couch. "You know as well as I do that Marie-Thérèse is enabling him."

Josette sighed. "Enabling. Such an ugly word. But I guess you're right."

"As long as she keeps making excuses for him and keeps scrambling to make enough money on her own so she doesn't have to depend on his earnings, things aren't going to change."

"She's started to clean apartments now, too. She usually can take Larissa with her, but sometimes she leaves her with Mom." Josette looked up at the ceiling as if remembering. "Marie-Thérèse always did the same thing with me when we lived together. Enabling, I mean. When I didn't want to clean something, she'd do it. Or when I wanted something, she'd find an excuse to let me have it. In fact, the only time she ever stood in my way when I thought I wanted something was when she and I both sort of liked Mathieu. Then she fought for him."

"He was important enough," Zack said. "I think as soon as she feels their problem is important enough, she'll put a stop to it. But it's really Mathieu's fault. I've tried talking to him, but it's like talking to stone. He just doesn't see what I'm getting at. I'm embarrassed that a priesthood holder can be so oblivious to the Lord's counsel to stay out of debt."

Josette slipped off her shoes and tucked them under her, cuddling up to Zack. "I'm glad we don't have problems like that."

Zack put his arm around her shoulders, thinking of his earlier aggravation at finding Josette once more gone with Marc. "Why do you like being with Marc so much?" he asked casually.

Josette looked surprised. "I don't know. We've always been together, I suppose. He makes me laugh when I get uptight. You know how he is, always joking around."

"Yeah. He's a great guy."

"He's promised to take me on a boat ride soon. But I'm a little nervous with the baby and all." She touched her stomach. "What do you think?"

"Give me a few days' notice, and I'll go with you."

"Oh, Zack, that would be wonderful! You're such a great husband." She turned around in his arms and began kissing his face an inch at a time. "I love you, did you know?"

Zack felt fire in his reaction to her touch. He kissed her back. "Yes. But I don't mind hearing it again."

"I love you, I love you, I love you." She kissed him each time she said the words.

Zack laughed, feeling content. Josette was happy as she'd never been in America, and he loved seeing her this way. Whatever challenges he faced in sharing her with family and friends, this move had been the right thing to do.

Chapter Sixty-two

Marie-Thérèse felt weary. Her arms ached from the extra ironing, and her heart felt compressed and heavy like a ball of steel in her chest. But then Brionney had shown up unexpectedly in the afternoon and helped iron a tall mountain of clothing. The tight grip on her heart began to loosen.

When Brionney skipped off somewhere with Marc, Marie-Thérèse went down two flights to apartment 2-A and spent between five and six-thirty cleaning for the widowed dentist who lived there. Larissa doubled the amount of time it normally took by getting into everything, and Marie-Thérèse felt happy the dentist was still at work and wouldn't fire her.

When she went back upstairs to make dinner for Mathieu, who usually arrived home at seven, she found two strangers waiting outside her apartment. "Madame Portier?"

Marie-Thérèse adjusted Larissa's weight to her other hip before answering. "Yes?"

One man whipped out a paper and handed it to her. "We're from Retrieval Incorporated, and we've been assigned to collect a bill for your new bedroom set. We've talked several times on the phone with you, and you have made no headway on your loan as promised, so I'm afraid we'll have to repossess the items in question. Of course, the company will keep what funds you've already paid for a usage fee. Now, if you'll be so kind as to show us the furniture?"

A sense of panic grew inside Marie-Thérèse as she cleaned out the drawers to the dresser under the men's impassive stares. Her face felt hot and embarrassed, and it was all she could do to hold back the tears as she watched the men haul out her bed. Where were the old mattresses her mother had given them? Gone to charity with all the other perfectly useful items Mathieu had replaced.

She sat down in the living room to fan herself. The heat was terrible, but she didn't dare turn on the air-conditioning because of the added electric charges. She was glad Larissa had missed her nap earlier and now lay sleeping on the couch opposite her.

Marie-Thérèse's body rested, but her brain flew at top speed. She wouldn't miss the bedroom set—she hadn't wanted it in the first place. But would the repossession make Mathieu take notice of what he was doing?

She doubted it. The increasingly frequent phone calls from bill collectors hadn't seemed to do a thing. The calls bothered her greatly, and her embarrassment grew each time she had to promise another person she would try to pay. It was impossible.

When the doorbell rang, she was almost glad for the distraction. "Hello, Madame Cerro," she said. "Your clothes are ready."

"Good, because I have to wear that purple dress tonight."

Even the thought of Madame Cerro looking like a human-sized purple grape didn't make Marie-Thérèse smile. "Well, it's done. Here." She handed the dress to the older woman. "And I guess just take it off the rent."

"Uh, you are already five weeks late. For the second time," Madame Cerro said. She looked uncomfortable, but her expression was rigid. "I feel I've given you ample notice, and I really just can't delay any longer. You know I have bills to pay, too."

Marie-Thérèse felt light-headed. "What are you saying?"

"I'm saying that you and your husband have two weeks to find a new place to live. I've found someone else for this apartment—someone more reliable. And I'll have to keep your deposit money to cover my expenses."

"I could ask my parents," Marie-Thérèse said. "They could help." She'd known they were overdue on the rent, but since it was the one thing Mathieu had still been paying, she hadn't realized just how late they were.

Madame Cerro drew herself up to her full height. "I would think you would have already asked them by now, before those men came to get your furniture." Marie-Thérèse colored, but Madame Cerro plunged on. "It's too late now. I've already promised the apartment. I trust there will be no problem getting out?"

"No," Marie-Thérèse said faintly.

After Madame Cerro left, Marie-Thérèse walked numbly through the house, searching for something that was missing, something she couldn't identify. The room she shared with Mathieu was now empty of everything but a pile of clothes and sheets on the floor against one of the walls. If the bed had been there, she might have thrown herself on it and cried out her anger and frustration. Instead, she simply stood in the doorway and looked at the jumble of her life, epitomized by the unorganized heap.

Oh, dear Lord, she prayed. *What now? I don't know how much more I can bear.*

When Mathieu came home a short time later, she was sitting at the kitchen table with a large pile of bills. "Hi," he said, giving her his winning grin. "What's for dinner?"

"I don't know yet. I've been busy."

"What's up? You look depressed." He kneaded her shoulder with a strong hand. "I must have sensed you'd be depressed, because look what I picked up for you at lunchtime." He took a little box and set it on the table, pushing it over to her with a flourish.

Marie-Thérèse thought she was going to be sick. Unwillingly, she opened the box. A pair of smooth gold earrings glinted up at her, as wide as her little finger.

"They'll match the necklace and bracelet set I've given you better than anything else I've seen. And I wasn't even looking for it. I was at the store to check out those candle holders we talked about, and when I passed the case, I saw them."

"You talked about them," Marie-Thérèse said.

"What?"

"*You* talked about the candle holders. I don't want them."

"Okay, we won't buy them."

"I don't want the earrings, either." She snapped the lid shut and tossed them back to him. Rage filled her, a desperate out-of-control feeling that she couldn't control. "I don't want you to buy me anything! I only want you to pay the bills you have. I don't want to iron anymore, or clean other people's dirt! I'm sick of it, do you hear? I'm not doing it anymore. You can do it yourself—at least for two more weeks until you're kicked out of this apartment."

Mathieu stared at her, amazed. "We've had this discussion before. You don't have to iron."

Marie-Thérèse had to stop herself from slapping him. "I want to eat. I want to feed my daughter. And I want to hold up my head when we're with other people."

Tears finally found their way to the surface, but Marie-Thérèse stalked out of the kitchen and down the hall to the living room. She picked up her purse and the sleeping Larissa and headed for the door.

"Where are you going?"

She stopped for a moment and faced him. "I don't like sleeping on the floor."

"What?"

"Go see." She pointed in the direction of their room.

"Wait right here," he pleaded. "Let me go look."

Mathieu took her silence as agreement. Marie-Thérèse waited until he was out of sight and then opened the door. Without another look, she turned her back and left the apartment.

When Marie-Thérèse arrived at Josette's apartment, she was happy to discover her sister there alone. Larissa, who'd awakened during the trip and was cranky and cross, brightened when she saw her Aunt Josette.

"I'm so glad you came to visit." Josette said, tickling the baby. "One of Zack's home teaching families called for a blessing. Zack wanted me to go along, but since I'm pregnant, I didn't want to risk getting sick."

"That's understandable."

"I thought so, but Zack is kind of different here. Possessive. Like he wants to know what I'm doing all the time. It's kind of cute, but sometimes it can be annoying."

"There are a lot of changes when a baby comes," Marie-Thérèse said mechanically. "A lot of men feel left out. There's so much they don't understand about us."

"I don't think Zack's problem has anything to do with the baby, but . . ." Josette's voice trailed off. "You've been crying. What happened?" She put her arms around Marie-Thérèse, whose tears once more came to the surface. "Look at me babbling on when you're so upset. I'm sorry! Come and sit down here on the couch and tell me what's wrong."

Marie-Thérèse let Josette lead her to the couch, where she let Larissa down to play. "I've left Mathieu," she said, starting to cry.

"You what?"

"I left him." Marie-Thérèse cried harder. "Men came to repossess our bedroom furniture. I had to clean out the dressers with them watching. It was so awful. All our underclothes and personal items heaped in a pile. They didn't say anything, just stared at me." She put her cold hands against her hot cheeks, trying to calm down. "Then Madame Cerro came to pick up her ironing and told me she's kicking us out of the apartment. She's tired of waiting to be paid."

"I'm so sorry!"

Josette's arms tightened around her, and Marie-Thérèse cried until her anger and frustration was spent. When she calmed, her sister went to the bathroom and returned with a wad of tissue.

"Here. Are you feeling better now?"

"A little," Marie-Thérèse admitted. "But I need someplace to stay. I'm not going back there."

"We'll need to get your clothes."

"I also have ironing I need to deliver to people, but I can't face Mathieu again. It tears my heart out to see him. I love him so much, but I can't live like this any longer."

"You could stay at Mom's," Josette said. "They have plenty of room."

"Can't I stay here?"

"Of course, but I was only thinking you'd be more comfortable there since we have only one bedroom and Brionney's staying in the living room. Plus, Mom would love having Larissa around."

"But I can't face her. Not knowing how badly I've failed."

Josette's eyes flashed. "How you've failed? You? You mean how Mathieu has failed. The only thing you've done wrong is letting it go so far."

Marie-Thérèse blinked in surprise. "Do you really think that, or are you just trying to make me feel better?"

"Oh, Marie-Thérèse." Josette hugged her tightly. "For an intelligent woman, you can be awfully blind."

"Why does Mathieu act this way?"

"Maybe he's trying to make up for the poverty he dealt with as a child. I think deep down, he just wants to take care of you, to give you all the things his mother didn't have because his father died and couldn't support them."

"I've thought that, too. I've even tried to tell him that, but he just tells me what a great job he has and how he'll pay for it. He keeps promising me we'll buy an apartment soon, but I think the credit companies are finally learning that he can't pay."

"Maybe they won't give him any more money. That'll actually be good."

"I wonder where he'll go," Marie-Thérèse said. "His mother lives too far away for him to stay with her and commute to work."

"He'll probably follow wherever you go."

"I don't want to see him." Marie-Thérèse grabbed her sister's hand. "Promise me you won't let him see me."

"I promise. But at least let me call Mom."

"She won't understand."

"Yes, she will. Mom's been through a lot, and I'll bet she knows more about what's going on than you think. It's easy to see that you're not happy."

Marie-Thérèse looked sadly at her hands twisting in her lap. "I thought love was enough, you know? Romance, love, being together. But there are other things, aren't there?"

"Well, yes, but I believe that whatever is wrong between you and Mathieu can be fixed with love. I mean, if he didn't love you and want to please you, then he wouldn't care. But he does."

"He listens, but he doesn't hear what I'm saying. Now we don't even have an apartment to sleep in."

"That old witch Cerro could have at least told you before you ironed her tent dresses," Josette said. "Talk about rude!"

Against her will, Marie-Thérèse smiled. "I don't want to iron anything ever again."

"So don't. Wrinkled is in, haven't you heard?"

Marie-Thérèse laughed. "I love you, Josette. Thanks for being here."

"Heaven knows you've pulled me out of enough trouble. Maybe I can finally help you." She rose to her feet.

"Where are you going?"

"To call Mom. She should be here."

Marie-Thérèse didn't object. Maybe talking to their mother was a good idea.

Before Josette could lift the receiver, the phone rang. Marie-Thérèse bounded the few steps to the small kitchen and stopped Josette from answering. "Let the answering machine pick it up," she said. "It might be him."

They waited until the message came. "Uh, Josette, it's Mathieu. I'm looking for Marie-Thérèse. I'm trying to find her, and I'm a little worried. She's not at your parents' apartment either. If you see her, ask her to call home. Thanks."

When their mother arrived less than half an hour later, Marie-Thérèse was already beginning to feel crowded in Josette's tiny apartment. Zack had returned, and he and Josette were discussing a boat ride they were planning with Marc and Brionney. Marie-Thérèse saw now that there was no way she could stay with them in this small space. There simply wasn't room.

Ariana must have sensed her feelings. "Why don't we take a walk together?" she suggested after greeting everyone. It's dark, but the streets here are safe."

"Would you watch Larissa?" Marie-Thérèse asked Josette.

"Sure. It'll be good practice, won't it Zack?" She patted her swollen stomach with a complacent smile.

"Take your time," Zack said. "As long as you need."

Marie-Thérèse felt a rush of gratitude. "Thanks."

As she went out the door, Josette squeezed her arm. "You'll get through this, you'll see." Trite as the words sounded, they made Marie-Thérèse feel better.

Marie-Thérèse and Ariana walked slowly along the cobblestone sidewalks. A few cafes along the street lit up the darkness with light and noise. "You and Larissa are welcome to stay with us," Ariana said quietly.

"How much did Josette tell you?"

"She said you and Mathieu were having problems and that you needed a place to stay tonight. That's all. She said you'd fill in the rest."

Marie-Thérèse stopped walking abruptly. "I left him, Mom, and I'm not going back. Not unless he changes."

Ariana put a hand against Marie-Thérèse's back and propelled her gently forward. "Tell me about it."

Marie-Thérèse found herself explaining the details of Mathieu's spending habits and her constant struggle to make ends meet.

Her mother nodded sympathetically. "Why didn't you tell me before? I could see you were unhappy, but every time I tried to ask, you would change the conversation."

"I'm embarrassed. This was never supposed to happen to me. I'm a finance major, of all things."

"An education in finance doesn't guarantee freedom from money problems."

"It could. I mean, Mathieu makes good money. If we were careful, in a few years we could have all of those nice things."

"Mathieu has to want to change."

"You're thinking I shouldn't have left him, aren't you?"

"Me? Heavens no! Maybe this is the wake-up call Mathieu needs."

"I thought you wouldn't be proud of me anymore."

Ariana gave a low laugh. "Marie-Thérèse, I've always been proud of you. And I know you tried everything before you left Mathieu. The next step is up to him."

They walked on in silence for a few minutes, and then Ariana said, "Your father left me once. Or rather, I kicked him out of the house."

Marie-Thérèse gasped in disbelief. "What?"

"It was before you came to live with us, when your parents were alive. Jean-Marc was spending too much time working, and I felt I was raising the children alone. I only had the twins and André then, but it was overwhelming. Jean-Marc was off starting a new branch for my father's banking firm, and I would sit home praying he'd come home early enough to tuck his children into bed. For their part, they didn't really know him or care when he cancelled promised trips. But once he promised them a ride on the Canal Saint-Martin, and when he cancelled for the third time, I'd finally had enough. When he came home that night we argued, and I repeated all the arguments I'd given him for months about spending time with his family. When he wouldn't listen, I gave him his suitcase. He was so angry that he packed and left."

"I can't see him doing that," Marie-Thérèse said. "He's so calm and understanding."

"He's come a long way. We both have. But at that time he had a tendency to run away from conflict, so when I confronted him, he ran."

"What did you do?"

"I cried, I ranted to myself, and I took the children on the canal ride without him. You and your mother came with us."

Marie-Thérèse thought for a moment. "I think I remember. Wasn't that about when my mom started to get sick?"

"Well, she'd been sick for a number of years, but it was right after the canal ride that we found out about the AIDS."

"So how did you and Dad get back together? Did he come back?"

"He only stayed away a couple of nights—I can't even remember exactly how many. But I do remember feeling so ashamed when my father pointed out to me that Jean-Marc hadn't left, but that I had kicked him out." Ariana laughed. "It's funny to me now, but at the time, we both really suffered. When he came home and we made up, he almost ran right back to work when I told him we had to be tested for HIV because of our close association with your parents. In the end, he stayed and we faced it together."

"So kicking him out was the right thing to do?" Marie-Thérèse asked doubtfully.

"That was the beginning of waking him up. Of course, we had

a lot of work left before we found a satisfactory compromise. We both had to give. For example, I realized that I as so competent with the children that often I didn't let him do things for them. Consequently their relationship wasn't close, and he buried himself in his work where he could find satisfaction. It was hard for me to relinquish control, but I did. I had to realize that things done halfway by Jean-Marc were better for the kids than me doing them all the way."

"And he got better."

"Oh, yes. With practice, he became a lot better at some things than I was."

"I have no control," Marie-Thérèse said bitterly. "Mathieu does whatever he wants."

Ariana was silent for a minute. "Perhaps you've let him off the hook too long." The words were gentle, but they bit into Marie-Thérèse's soul.

"Josette said the same thing. She's happy I left him." She looked earnestly at her mother. "But without me, I don't know how Mathieu will get by."

"Maybe that's what he has to find out. For now, why don't we get Larissa and go home? I'll call Mathieu and let him know you're all right. He called the house three times before I left, and he sounded very upset. I would have called him once Josette told me where you were, but I thought it might do him a little good to worry for a while."

"I don't want to talk to him—yet."

"You don't have to. I'll do it. Better yet, I'll let your father. That'll give him more practice as a bishop."

Marie-Thérèse smiled gratefully. "Thanks, Mom."

"Don't give up, honey. Not yet, anyway. Mathieu's a good man. He just has a few problems to work through. You take a rest and when you feel ready, then you can talk to him."

"Sometimes I'm afraid he'll never change," Marie-Thérèse admitted. "And it hurts so bad that I want to die."

Ariana put an arm around her. "I know that feeling well. But maybe I have an idea to help you. Think of Pauline and Emeri. I've seen no greater example of love helping someone to change. Pauline continued to love Emeri, never giving up, and that gave Emeri a chance to find his Heavenly Father."

Marie-Thérèse thought of Pauline and her brave refusal to marry the man she loved in order to share eternity with him. If Pauline was so courageous, then maybe Marie-Thérèse could also risk losing Mathieu temporarily, if that meant in the end their marriage could be saved.

Chapter Sixty-three

Two days after Marie-Thérèse left Mathieu, Marc took Brionney to a stake-wide dance for all members thirteen and older. He hoped Marie-Thérèse and Mathieu would both be there, and that maybe they would finally talk things out and life could get back to normal. Actually, Marc wished he could beat some sense into Mathieu, but he didn't think his sister would appreciate it.

"They're not here, either of them," Brionney said, reading his thoughts as she often did. Her sensitivity was one of the reasons he liked her so much. "At least I don't think so. I'm going to look for them."

As she left, Marc noticed that she was no longer the plump girl he'd met when she first arrived in France. Their morning skating outings, weekend hikes, and constant tourist visits had helped her lose the weight Marc knew she'd despised, though with her sky blue eyes and her white-blonde hair, he'd always thought her beautiful. Marc didn't know when he'd begun to feel attracted to her, but he knew the feeling was strong. Could she be the woman he was supposed to marry? Maybe tonight he would find out.

"You know that in less than one month she'll be going back to

America to attend BYU," Josette said, appearing beside him. "You need to find out how you feel about her before she leaves."

"Where's Zack?" he said, looking behind her.

"Parking the car. There's hardly any space left out there. But don't change the subject. Have you kissed her?"

"Not yet. I didn't want to rush anything."

"Not rush? You've been dating her two months."

"She's a good friend. I don't want to ruin that."

Josette sighed. "You men are impossible."

"Men? So what's Zack doing now?" Marc asked with a grin.

His sister sobered. "You've got to talk to him, Marc. I don't want to hurt his feelings, but he's smothering me. I love him, and I love being with him, but sometimes he acts suspicious about what I do in my free time. The other day I went out to lunch with some old school friends—all girls except Fábio, who's married to one of them. I didn't know Zack planned to come home for lunch. Then he waited for me to make sure I got home all right. He even missed an appointment." Josette took a deep breath and rushed on, "I've been wondering if . . . well, he knows I used to go out a lot. I'm worried that he thinks I'm going to, you know, fall into my old ways."

"That can't be it."

"No, I guess not. I'm truly different now, and I love Zack so much. He's a great guy."

"I'll have a talk with him when I get the chance," Marc promised.

His sister smiled. "Thanks. I appreciate it."

"What are younger brothers for?"

She laughed and slugged his arm. "For getting me more nieces and nephews. Now remember what I said about Brionney." She started across the room toward Zack, who had just entered the gym. As she reached him, she turned and made kissing motions toward Marc, and he knew exactly what she was trying to tell him.

He looked for Brionney and found her laughing with a group of young men near another door. He sauntered over and touched her arm possessively. "May I have this dance, Mademoiselle?"

Brionney nodded. "Mais oui." But yes.

Rebekka Massoni flew up to them. "Oh, there you guys are. Finally! Marc, you have to dance with me. You promised."

Marc smiled and patted the girl's shoulder. "Of course we'll dance. Don't we always?"

Rebekka's laugh tinkled through the cultural hall. She still showed the awkward edges of being thirteen, and though her body was quickly filling out into graceful curves like her mother's, Marc still saw the pesky five-year-old she'd once been.

"The two beauties of the ball." He placed an arm around them both.

"I concede him first to you, Rebekka," Brionney said with an exaggerated curtsey.

Rebekka nodded regally. "Thank you, Brionney. I accept." They both giggled.

Marc stifled his irritation at being interrupted by Rebekka. Tonight was supposed to bring magic for him and Brionney, but how could it with Rebekka in the way? He ended up dancing three songs with Rebekka, and he noticed that Brionney didn't sit on the sidelines but danced with some of the single men.

Marc finally extracted himself from Rebekka. "Come on, let's dance," he said, appearing at Brionney's side. "I got rid of the pest, at least for now."

"Rebekka's not a pest."

"No, but sometimes she can be persistent." Marc took her hand and led her out to the floor. Other couples crowded after them.

"Tonight is for us," Marc said nervously. It might have been the most romantic thing he'd ever said to her. His heart thudded oddly in his chest.

The music changed to a slow song and he took her into his arms, closer than he'd ever been to a woman. He guided them to one of the more secluded corners of the room and stopped dancing. His face was very close to hers.

This is it! he thought, stifling a sudden urge to laugh. The crowd of people faded, and he felt as if they were alone in the room. Marc's lips met hers, tentative at first, then more demanding. Brionney responded in kind.

A pleasant feeling spread throughout Marc's body. He waited eagerly for the fireworks and the rush of passion he expected would follow.

Nothing happened.

He faltered and drew away.

"I wondered when you'd do that," Brionney said. "I was beginning to think we were only friends."

"I-I-I," Marc stuttered. He wasn't sure how he felt or what to say. Maybe fireworks were overrated. He certainly enjoyed kissing Brionney, though it wasn't what he'd expected.

He scratched the raised scars on his arm, old markings from the dialysis treatments he'd received before his kidney transplant. Finally, he found his voice. "I see the relationships my sisters have, and my parents. I want that. I like you, Brionney."

He lapsed into silence and Brionney said, "I like you, too."

"I mean that I more than like you. I see your potential."

"You mean now that I've lost weight."

He snorted impatiently and took her hand. "It has nothing to do with your weight, but what's in your heart. You're beautiful, yes, but you're also a wonderful person. You have a strong testimony of the gospel, you're good with kids, and you're fun to be with. I'd like to get to know you better."

"I'd like that too, Marc."

Marc gazed into the dark room, pleased with her response, but not knowing what to say next. His eyes fell on Danielle Massoni, Rebekka's mother, who was dancing with her husband. Her auburn hair caught the lights. *She is beautiful as no other woman could ever be,* he thought.

"You're in love with Danielle, aren't you?" Brionney said quietly.

The realization that Brionney easily saw what he'd tried so long and hard to hide hit Marc like an iron fist to his stomach. He jerked his head toward her, his mouth open to speak. Then, without utterance, he shut it again, letting her hand drop.

"I didn't realize it was that obvious," he admitted after a long while. "I've loved her since I was fifteen."

"You saved her life in the bombing; it's natural you'd care for her." Brionney's words were soft but questioning, and Marc had to tell her the truth.

"Oh, Brionney, I wish it were that. How I've prayed for something like that!" He turned his head back in Danielle's direction. "But it's more. I've never admitted this to another person, but I really love her." He grimaced, feeling sick to his stomach. "Boy, do I feel stupid. Here I am trying to start a relationship with you, and I'm telling you that I'm in love with another woman."

"She's very beautiful."

With effort, Marc took his eyes from Danielle. "And very much in love with her husband."

Brionney studied the dancing pair. "I don't see why. He's handsome, but he can't take her to the temple. He seems a little arrogant to me."

"A little?" Marc said in amazement. "The guy's a complete idiot." He paused before rushing on. "No, that's not fair. He had a hard life as a child, and I think he's come a long way. He treats Danielle like a queen, and he makes her happy. Great, now I'm defending him."

"Defending him when you wish he'd disappear?"

Marc shook his head slowly. "No, she'd never look at me. I'm only a child to her. I gave up long ago any idea that my feelings would lead to a relationship. And I do want a relationship, Brionney." He took her hand again and continued earnestly, "I think we could try."

Brionney's eyebrows drew together in thought. "We're both looking for someone, and neither of us want to settle for anything that's less than what will make us happy. I really like you, Marc. But although I've tried to tell myself it was nothing, I've seen how you act around Danielle." She frowned, pulling her hand gently from his. "The truth is, I could fall in love with you all too easily, but I'm not ready to settle for a man who's in love with someone else. I want someone to love me and only me."

"I want to," Marc said. "I really do."

"I think you need to resolve how you feel about Danielle before you try another relationship. It's not fair. Not to me or to you. We might both end up getting hurt."

"So the answer's no."

"That's not what I'm saying. I'm saying let's go back to being friends. Some day when you're ready, maybe then it'll be time for us. With modern technology, America's not so far away, and we're both young—or at least that's what my parents keep writing me. In the meantime, I don't want to lose what we have right now."

"You've told your parents about me?"

She grinned, and the tight clench of Marc's stomach eased. "Of course. Since losing my brother and Josette to each other, you're the best friend I have."

"I know what you mean. I guess I can live with us just being friends—for now. But my family isn't going to be happy about it. They really like you."

"They'll get over it."

"Can I have just one more kiss? It might help me get over Danielle that much quicker."

"All right." Her voice held amusement. "But only one, and then that's it."

He kissed her again, and this time he didn't see Danielle in his mind. Maybe eventually the part of him that cared about Brionney could overshadow the part of him that loved Danielle.

Brionney drew away, something in her eyes catching the dim light. Were those tears? Was she as sad as he was that things hadn't worked out between them?

"There's just one thing, Brionney," he said. "In case . . . I mean, when you go back to America, don't settle for the first good-looking guy you see. Not unless he's like . . . well, what I'm trying to say is, don't marry a man unless he treats you right and you can be yourself around him. He shouldn't care what you weigh or how much makeup you have on. That stuff doesn't matter—only what's inside. Just be careful." He didn't know how to put it better. Sometimes she was so vulnerable, and he wished he could protect her.

"I will. But don't worry so much. I look back now and see how far I've already come. Once I would have jumped at the chance to have any sort of a serious relationship with a man as wonderful as you, but this summer I've realized what I'm worth as a person and as a woman. In part to how you treat me. That's a gift I can never repay." She smiled and added, "Who knows? Maybe I'll just wait for you."

Marc glanced once more toward Danielle, feeling desolate. Brionney grabbed his hands. "Come on, the music's changing. Let's go boogey."

"Boogey?" asked Marc. "Is that another of your untranslatable English words?"

"Yeah, come on. I'll explain."

Marc was relieved that the awkward moment between them was over. Now that they weren't in love, things could go back to normal between them. They danced for two more songs before Brionney began to limp. "I think I have a blister," she shouted over the music.

Marc picked her up and carried her to the row of chairs lining the gym. "I really should stick around and marry you," Brionney joked. "Not only are you really sweet, but then I might get to have twins."

He faked a wounded look. "You just want me for my genes. I hate to break it to you, but the tendency to have fraternal twins passes through the mother's genes, I think."

"Then, I guess you're off the hook. What a relief."

Marc grinned. "Just for that, I'm leaving you. There have to be some girls around here who don't have lousy shoes. Besides, I promised Rebekka on the threat of death that I would dance with her again." He hesitated. "Or would you rather I stay?"

"No, thanks. Now as my father always says, I'm going to go see a man about a dog."

"You Americans and your euphemisms. Can't you just say you need to go to the bathroom?" With that parting shot, he disappeared into the crowd.

Marc couldn't find Rebekka anywhere inside the cultural hall. Where could she be? He didn't feel much like dancing any more, but he'd promised to save at least one dance for her, and he might as well get it over with. In the hall, he passed laughing couples and families, but no Rebekka. When he reached the end, he wandered into the next corridor where the lights were off. The sound of soft sobbing came to his ears. He followed the sound and pinpointed the darkened room where it came from. "Hello?" he said, knocking on the door.

The sobbing stopped. "Go away," came a tear-filled voice.

"Rebekka, is that you?"

"No!" The door slammed shut.

Marc turned the knob, pushed the door open a crack, and peered through. On the other side, Rebekka tried to shut it again.

"Open up," he said.

"No."

"Rebekka, let's talk about it. Come on."

"I don't want to. Now go away and leave me alone!"

"I'm your friend, and I'm not going anywhere. If you don't open the door, I'm going to force it open."

The pressure on the door gradually released, and Marc swung the door inward. Rebekka slumped onto a chair in the middle of the room, her face turned away. "Don't turn on the light," she said. "Someone might come in. I don't want anyone to see me like this."

Marc crouched in front of her chair. "Okay, what's wrong?"

Even in the dim light coming from the door, he saw Rebekka clamp her mouth shut, her lips puckering stubbornly.

"Tell me, or I'm going to go find your mother."

The threat worked. "I saw you kissing Brionney." Rebekka's eyes filled with tears that spilled slowly over and coated her cheeks. "I guess now you'll be getting married. I hope you're happy together, I really do." Her voice rose on the last words, and she began to sob again.

Marc hugged Rebekka and stroked her hair. "You don't sound happy," he said softly. "But if that's what's worrying you, I should tell you that Brionney and I have decided we're just going to be friends." He felt guilty as he said it because he hoped someday he and Brionney would become more than friends.

Rebekka's lower lip trembled, and for the first time Marc noticed how much she looked like Danielle.

"You don't love Brionney?" Rebekka asked. "Really?"

"Really. Well, I love her as a friend, but that's all for right now. Just friends. Pretty soon she'll be going back to America to study French at BYU."

Rebekka smiled through the tears. "Her accent's better than when she first came."

"It really is. But if we did want to get married, why would that make you sad?" Marc had been sure Rebekka had quit having a crush on him at least a year ago.

Her expression changed to a wistfulness that belied her young age. "You think I'm just a little girl, don't you?"

Marc studied Rebekka. Her wavy auburn hair fell becomingly around an oval face. Her cheeks were streaked with tears and her eyes were more red than their usual striking gray, but the potential for beauty was undiminished. One day she might be even more attractive than her mother.

"You're a beautiful young woman, Rebekka," he said sincerely. "And I know you're beautiful right here, where it really counts."

He thumped his chest. "Some day you're going to find someone who loves you more than life, but don't be in such a great hurry. You have a lot of time."

He paused, not knowing if he should say more. "For the record, I do know what it's like to love someone who will never return that love."

Rebekka's eyes grew big. "Who?"

"I can't tell you. But now it's up to me to decide what I'm going to do with it. I think mostly I have to move on and find a way to be happy without her."

Rebekka touch his cheek, a light touch that was different from anything Marc had ever felt from her. "I'll help you."

He smiled. "I appreciate that. You can do that by dancing with me again. Would you?"

"Sure," she said, jumping to her feet.

Marc rose with her. "I guess I might have to share you with that bunch of boys I saw you with earlier. I'll bet they're still out there searching for the most beautiful thirteen-year-old girl in the stake."

"They do always want to dance with me," Rebekka said with childlike frankness. "But I don't like any of them as much as I like you."

Before Marc could reply, she grabbed his hand and pulled him to the door. When they neared the cultural hall, Rebekka slipped into the rest room. "Wait here," she ordered. "I have to make sure my eyes aren't red."

Marc decided to rest on the couch in the foyer while he waited. Zack was already there, moving his head in time to the music. He made room as Marc approached.

"Hey, what's up?" Marc asked.

Zack laughed. "Bathroom stop. Josette spends a lot of time there nowadays. Something about the added pressure on the bladder."

"Good, then she can help Rebekka with her face."

"What's wrong with Rebekka's face?"

"I think she still has a crush on me and is feeling a little neglected."

"She'll grow out of it," Zack said sympathetically.

"That's what I keep hoping." Marc sat without speaking for a moment before recalling Josette's request. "That reminds me—what's going on with you and my sister, anyway? Are you upset because she's been hanging out with me so much? I mean, I don't want to get in the way of your relationship, but she needs to get out."

Zack stared at him for a moment, as if debating what to say. "Well," he began, "now that you mention it, I guess it does make me a little . . ."

"A little jealous?"

"No, that's not it. Okay, maybe it is." Zack shook his head. "I don't know what I feel exactly, but I do want to figure it out before it becomes a big problem. I mean, look at Marie-Thérèse and Mathieu. Whew! What a mess!"

"So what do you think is wrong?"

"She's so happy."

Marc blinked. "What's wrong with that?"

"I don't know."

"Aren't you happy?"

"I am when I'm with her. When I'm not with her, I can't wait to get home so we can be together, but she doesn't seem to feel that way." He gave a frustrated growl. "What I mean is, she seems just as happy hanging out with you guys as she is with me."

"Ah-hah. You don't understand how she can be so happy when you're not around."

Zack shut his eyes and groaned. "That sounds so stupid when you say it out loud like that. Man, what an idiot I am! She wasn't happy in America, so I decide to move so she'll be happy, and now that she's with her family and friends, she is happy—and I'm jealous."

Marc stifled an urge to laugh. "You think that's bad. She's my sister, and I still felt betrayed when she went to America to marry you—and I even like you. But I couldn't believe she could be happy without me. Think about it. We grew up together. We've been everything to each other. Then in one day, she's your wife first and my twin sister second. That was a shock."

Zack grinned. "I see what you mean. So how did you get over it?"

"I found some hobbies, more friends, and when you came back, I kept going to see her. She's changed, but she's still my sister, and I know she loves me. I'd rather be second in her life than lose her completely. Besides, I keep hoping that someday I'll find a woman who will put me first, like Josette does with you. And she does put you first, I hope you see that. But that doesn't mean you should be the only important person in her life."

Zack ran a hand through his blond hair. "I love her so intensely. It's a feeling I never imagined I'd have about another person. It's an eternal thing—it's so huge."

As his friend talked, Marc knew that what he described was exactly what was missing in his relationship with Brionney. But that didn't mean it couldn't happen someday. He hoped.

"Sometimes I can't believe she's chosen me," Zack continued. "I think I'm afraid that one day she'll wake up and find I'm not the man she thought she loved. Look at Marie-Thérèse and Mathieu."

Marc snorted. "Mathieu's blind. You don't have that problem. Well, maybe you do. Would it help to know that when you're not with us, Josette always talks about you? It's Zack this and Zack that. She's crazy about you." Marc lowered his voice. "Just because she's beautiful doesn't mean she's going to leave you one day. Take Danielle Massoni, for example. She's beautiful and everyone knows how she adores her husband, even though he's not a member and a jerk most of the time." Marc hoped the longing in his heart didn't reach his voice.

"He treats her well."

"Like you treat Josette."

Zack sighed. "Except I'm rather possessive."

"Don't worry about it too much," Marc said. "That seems to be an emotion women are willing to deal with if it doesn't get too serious. They like being adored. Now, if you were in love with another woman . . ."—he made a chopping motion—"they'll cut you off in an instant. But possessiveness is definitely something you can work on." He forced a laugh to express mirth he didn't feel. He didn't want anyone to suspect how much Brionney's refusal to deepen their relationship bothered him, though he understood and agreed with her reasons. "I knew you had a tendency to be single-minded," he added. "In fact, looking back, I can see that's part of what made you such a successful missionary. Once you had a hold on those investigators, you never let them go. But I never knew that stemmed from insecurity."

Zack groaned. "Is it that obvious?"

"Yep, your secret's out." Marc slapped him on the back. "But how are you feeling about everything else? You've got to be missing your family. And that's probably a part of why you're holding to Josette so tightly."

"I do miss them," Zack admitted. "But with Brionney here, it's been all right."

"Does Josette know how you feel?"

Zack shook his head. "I promised myself I'd never let my homesickness affect her happiness. Sometimes it's not so much my family I miss, but America or some aspects of my life there. Not that I want to go back now," he added hurriedly. "Not with Josette missing you all so much. She needs her family, especially during this pregnancy."

"You should tell her your feelings so she can be there for you, like you were for her. You need to trust her. I don't think she'll let you down." He didn't add that once, years ago, she might have done just that. The Josette Zack knew and fell in love with wasn't the same person.

"I trust Josette," Zack said.

"Good."

Whatever Zack was going to say next was cut off by the return of the women. Or the woman and the girl, rather. Josette smiled and accepted her husband's proffered hand. "Sorry I took so long."

Marc glanced at Rebekka and was relieved to see no traces of tears. As she smiled at him shyly, he grabbed her hand and started for the cultural hall. "Thanks, Josette," he mouthed over his shoulder, but his sister's attention was focused on her husband.

As it should be, Marc thought. His step quickened. If he hurried, he might be able to talk to Danielle before the night was over. Maybe even dance with her.

To his delight, Danielle herself met him at the door. "Don't look now," she said, "but my cousin and your sister are both here and about to run into each other."

Rebekka clapped her hands. "Your plan worked, Mom!"

Danielle gave them a radiant smile. "All I did was ask Ariana if Marie-Thérèse was going to be here and then tell Mathieu. I hope that on neutral ground they can work things out."

Marc hoped so, too.

Chapter Sixty-four

Marie-Thérèse went to the dance only because she was sick of being cooped up in her parents' apartment, which despite its comfortable size didn't feel like home anymore. Of course she wouldn't dance with anyone other than her brother or her father, and even that didn't seem right without Mathieu there.

She missed him more than she wanted to admit—especially at night, when they had usually curled up together and talked about the future. Even though she'd started to consider most of his financial dreams delusions, it had still been a special time. They would talk about Larissa, and often about the gospel. At times the old sensations of love would fill her heart until they absorbed all the mistrust and anger.

Tears bit Marie-Thérèse's eyes. Maybe she should go home to Larissa, who was being watched by Grandma Josephine. All around her people joked and laughed as though the world was still turning, when Marie-Thérèse was sure it must have stopped the moment she left Mathieu. She made her way to the refreshment table and picked up a slice of sweet bread. Maybe eating something would settle her stomach.

The bread did make her feel better—until she turned and found herself face to face with Mathieu.

Her mouth opened, and an exclamation of surprise slipped out before she could clamp it shut. *Dear Father*, she prayed silently. *Please, please help me know what to do!* Mathieu had called her three times a day since he found out where she was staying. Yesterday, she'd let her mother take Larissa to spend a few hours with him. Marie-Thérèse hadn't felt ready yet to face him, but had wanted him to be able to see his daughter.

"Marie-Thérèse, I'm sorry," he said, a pleading look on his face. "Please come back."

She looked around at the crowd. "I don't want to talk here. Let's go outside."

Mathieu obediently turned and led the way. As she followed, Marie-Thérèse caught a glimpse of Josette on the far side of the dance floor. Her sister made a fist and punched it into the air. *Be strong*, was the silent message. Marie-Thérèse's resolve strengthened. She loved Mathieu and she would fight for him, even if her opponent was Mathieu himself.

Chapter Sixty-five

When they left the busy church, Mathieu took a deep breath of the fresh night air. Stars shone down on them from the night sky, giving him courage. "I want you to come home," he said. "I'll do anything you want. Anything! Please . . . I love you." In fact, the last few days had been the most miserable in his entire life.

"I love you too, Mathieu," Marie-Thérèse said softly. "That's not the problem. It never was."

He sighed with relief. "I thought maybe you stopped. I thought you were so angry that you would never want to see me ever again."

"I was angry. I'm still angry."

"I'm sorry about the bed."

Now it was her turn to sigh. "Mathieu it's not the stupid bed, it's the finances. I can't deal with it anymore."

"Then let me do it."

"I have." Her face tightened and turned red, a sure sign that she was about to walk away from him. He hadn't felt so desperate since the day she'd decided to submit her mission papers. He touched her shoulder. "Please, don't leave. Maybe there is a problem. I just don't know how to fix it. But I love you, Marie-Thérèse, and I do want to make you happy."

Her face relaxed, and Mathieu thought he had convinced

her, but her answer surprised him. "I'm not going back to that apartment, Mathieu, or to anywhere else unless you see a counselor about this."

"Tell our problems to a stranger?" He knew how much it would cost her emotionally to do that. For all her friendliness to people, Marie-Thérèse was very careful about sharing personal information.

"Why not, if it helps? I just want things to be all right between us again."

"We can work this out alone."

"No, we can't. We've tried."

"Just come back home, and I'll show you."

She shook her head and said abruptly, "I'm pregnant."

The news sent Mathieu reeling. "You are? But that's wonderful!"

"I wish I could be happy." Her voice was so soft he wondered if he heard her right. "One more doctor bill, one more mouth to feed, one more to buy clothes for." She glared at him. "Do you know how that makes me feel—to think that way about my own son?"

"Son?" Mathieu gasped. "You already know it's a boy?"

"Yes. I'm four months along."

"Why didn't you tell me?"

"Because I'm not happy about it. I don't want another baby."

His mind rebelled at what she was saying. "But it's not the baby, right? It's me—the money."

She nodded once, and silent tears began to trickle down her face. Mathieu wanted to make it all better, but he didn't know how. She looked too thin to be four months into the pregnancy. He remembered how sick she'd been with Larissa. Had it been better for her this time? Had she been eating well? How had she hidden it from him for so long? He longed to ask the questions, but didn't feel he had the right. But how could he live in the same house with her and not know? Was he that blind? What else didn't he know about her?

Another thought tortured him even more. If he'd been so blind that he hadn't recognized the obvious signs of pregnancy, then maybe he *was* blind to their financial situation as Marie-Thérèse kept insisting.

"Okay," he said, blinking fiercely to clear the tears from his eyes. "Who do you have in mind?"

She looked down at the ground and back up, hesitating. "My father. He's been the bishop for two months, and he works in banking. He cares about us both."

Mathieu would have preferred a more impartial counselor, but he didn't want Marie-Thérèse to suffer any more than she'd already endured. "All right. Let's do it."

She appeared relieved. "Okay, then."

They stood awkwardly for a few moments, then Marie-Thérèse said, "I should probably go. I need to stop by Grandma Josephine's and pick up Larissa."

"Give her a kiss for me."

"I will. Good night." She backed away for a few steps, then turned and hurried into the building.

When she was gone, he stared up into the night. "Dear Father," he prayed, "I don't know what I'm doing wrong, but I think I need to change. I want to for her, for Larissa, and for my son." Now that he was alone, Mathieu let the tears come freely. "Please, help me. Help us."

Chapter Sixty-six

Though her father had only been set apart as bishop for two months, Marie-Thérèse thought he fit into the role easily. Even when she'd first talked to him on the night she'd left Mathieu, he hadn't reproached her for not bringing it up earlier, told her it was nothing, or begun attacking her husband. The Lord had certainly chosen well. Marie-Thérèse didn't know if she could have been so open about their problem with someone else. The very thought made her stomach feel uneasy.

"Having money problems is nothing to be ashamed of." Jean-Marc sat himself behind the desk in his home office, which had once been Pauline's room, and indicated for Marie-Thérèse and Mathieu to sit in the two empty chairs in front of him. "A good percentage of couples have problems agreeing on how the money should be spent. In fact, it's one of the prime reasons for divorce."

"We don't want a divorce," Mathieu said looking at Marie-Thérèse, who nodded once, tightly.

"Of course not," her father said. "I know you love each other and that you value your relationship above all else. This is good, because we know that no matter what happens here today, there'll be no talk of divorce or similar ultimatums. So now we can get down to the heart of the matter."

He looked pointedly at Mathieu, but his words were gentle. "And there *is* a problem here, as I see it. I've prayed long and hard about the solution these last few days, and I think I may have hit on a few suggestions. But before we begin, I'd like to have a prayer. Mathieu, as patriarch of your family, would you be willing to offer it?"

"Of course." Mathieu reached out a hand to Marie-Thérèse and she held it tightly as he prayed.

Hope flickered in her heart. *Maybe now things could start being all right.*

After the prayer, Jean-Marc pulled a stack of money out of his pocket and laid it on the desk. "This represents your take-home pay each month. It sure looks like a lot this way."

Mathieu nodded confidently. "It's a good wage. And I like my work."

Jean-Marc said nothing, but turned to the pile of bills Marie-Thérèse had brought. "These are your debts, including tithing but not including food, odds and ends, or impulse buying. Let's see now. Mathieu, I understand that Marie-Thérèse usually pays the bills, and I think you're right to let her. She's always been very good with numbers. If Larissa hadn't come along when she did, I would have put Marie-Thérèse in charge of one of the banks I supervise. She has the education for it and the experience. But just this once, you pretend to make the payments."

Mathieu divided the cash among the bills. After doing so, there was plenty of money left over.

"Now, how much do you need for groceries, Marie-Thérèse?" Jean-Marc asked. "Take it out of what remains. Only that much? Come on. You can't possibly be living on so little. That's not healthy. Take some more. Larissa is eating now, too."

Marie-Thérèse obeyed, though it was more money than she'd

been using. Is that why she always felt she only scraped by each month?

"Okay now. This is what remains."

Mathieu eyed the small stack, his smile dimmer now. "We still have enough left for our needs," he said uncertainly.

"We haven't taken out for your weekly date," Jean-Marc said. He laid a few notes to the side. "I know you go out because we watch Larissa. Okay now, what about a fast offering? And diapers? Last I heard, Larissa wasn't potty-trained. Hmm, is that about right? Took out a big chunk, didn't it?"

Mathieu didn't say anything, but Marie-Thérèse began to experience the desperate feeling she normally got when doing the bills. She crossed her arms tightly over her stomach to stifle the churning.

"Now what can you buy with this?" asked Jean-Marc.

"Not much," Mathieu admitted.

"Certainly not enough to buy a hand-crocheted bedspread," Marie-Thérèse muttered.

Mathieu glanced at her quickly, but he said nothing.

"As I see it, there's no room here for impulse buying, at least not at the rate either of you might like." Jean-Marc didn't say any names or accuse anyone, and Marie-Thérèse was glad to see that Mathieu didn't act offended. Jean-Marc looked down at the pile of debts. "We have sixteen credit card bills here, besides the rent and utilities. Let's put together the money we ordinarily have to pay on those bills and see how much we have. See? This is how much you'd have if you didn't have to pay those debts. It would be enough to buy, say, one nice piece of furniture each month. It's a good sum of money—if it wasn't already taken by credit card bills.

"Now, as I see it, one of your main problems is too many debts. It's not as bad yet as some couples I've seen in my years working at the bank, but it's not a good sign since you've been married such a short time." He looked directly at Mathieu. "You cannot spend more than you make. You *must* not. Our prophets have counseled against doing so for as long as I've been in the Church. The situation you are in now calls for tough measures."

Mathieu squirmed uncomfortably. "Well, what do you suggest?"

Jean-Marc leaned back in his chair, leaving the money on the desk. "When I was serving my mission, I met an elder who would consistently run out of money the first week after receiving his stipend. It wouldn't matter how he tried not to spend it, he still did. Then he'd borrow money from his companion and church members to last out the month. Soon all his money was owed before he even received it, and he started borrowing on the next month's stipend. Finally, it got so bad that the president called him in for a chat. The president paid off all his debts and scheduled repayments for the missionary. Then he set up a system where the missionary wasn't allowed to buy anything unless his companion agreed. The missionary was able to pay everything back before he left his mission. It took some doing, but—"

"Are you saying I need Marie-Thérèse to approve everything I buy?" Mathieu interrupted, dropping Marie-Thérèse's hand. "That's ridiculous! I'm not a child. I earn the money, and I did pretty well before we met."

Marie-Thérèse slid down in her seat and wished she could disappear.

"I think Marie-Thérèse has worked pretty hard to earn money as well," Jean-Marc said, not showing any reaction to Mathieu's anger. "In fact, in my analysis of your finances, her earnings are actually paying for all your daily expenses—food, utilities, clothing, doctor visits. I repeat: her earning are paying for all your daily expenses. Plus, she has the primary care of your daughter. But it really makes no difference who earns the money. You know that. What matters is how you spend it together. Please, let me explain a bit further. Don't get angry. I want all your feelings in the open, but we need to be honest. Mathieu, I want you to look through these bills and tell me the percentage of the bills you ran up before your marriage."

Mathieu looked at the bills helplessly. "I couldn't begin to say. Maybe ten percent."

Jean-Marc opened a file on the desk. "Mathieu, I asked you to give me all your old statements."

"I know, I gave them to you yesterday."

Marie-Thérèse sat up straighter. She hadn't known about this.

"Well, I went through them today, and I found that over seventy percent of your debts were incurred before your marriage. So it seems Marie-Thérèse has had a good effect on your spending habits."

Mathieu's hands gripped the armrests on his chair. "I'm an adult. I can control myself."

"I think you will be able to, but first you have to understand the problem." Jean-Marc's brow furrowed as if he was thinking deeply. "I've got an example for you. What if Marie-Thérèse spent money without consulting you?"

"So? I know she won't go overboard."

Jean-Marc snapped his fingers. "There's the key. You know that and you trust her. But can she trust you in the same way? No, don't answer; I just want you to think about it. The fact of the matter is that when you get two people together, one nearly always takes on the role of spender and the other the role of saver—to differing degrees, of course—regardless of what they did before the marriage. Take two savers, for instance, and generally, one will have to become a little bit of a spender." Jean-Marc laughed. "This actually needs to happen to some extent, or even the couple's basic needs may go ignored. But in a relationship where the spending and saving habits start out vastly different, each partner tends to view the other person as wrong and will sometimes go to extremes to try to correct the problem. The more one pulls, the more the other pushes. I see that here. Mathieu, how do you feel about Marie-Thérèse's spending habits?"

Mathieu sent a furtive glance in her direction. "She never wants to spend money. I have to get her things, or she'd never have anything new. *We'd* never have anything new."

"And you, Marie-Thérèse?"

"He spends too much," she snapped. "I'm afraid I'll never have enough to even buy a china cabinet. Or—or enough food." Marie-Thérèse felt her face color as Mathieu's gaze riveted on her. Did he hate her for what she had said? Then she felt his hand stroking her arm.

"You don't trust me at all, do you?"

Marie-Thérèse didn't dare respond, but he read the answer in her eyes.

"I'm sorry," he whispered, his eyes filling with tears as they had when she'd told him about the baby.

She felt dampness on her own face, tears driven by her guilt and unhappiness. Her poor baby! Would her feelings of not wanting him right now affect him later? She couldn't let that happen. He had no fault in his father's compulsiveness.

"So there is a problem," Jean-Marc said softly.

Mathieu frowned and gave a sharp nod of agreement. "I love Marie-Thérèse and I want her back in my life. I'm willing to make a change."

"To really change, you have to be willing to do what I recommend."

"I am." Mathieu looked at Marie-Thérèse.

She wiped her face with a tissue her father handed her and smiled tentatively. "Me, too."

"Well, as Marie-Thérèse's father, I can get you a good loan at the bank that will pay off all these credit cards. However, I'll do so only if you promise to cut up all the cards and never use them or any others again. Ever."

"How will getting a loan help?" Mathieu asked.

Jean-Marc looked at her. "Do you want to answer that?"

"I've known we should do it, but I was afraid we'd just run up the cards again." Or afraid Mathieu would run them up again, but maybe she didn't need to point that out.

"Mathieu will promise not to do that, and I believe he's a man of his word."

Marie-Thérèse took a deep breath and looked at Mathieu. "If we get a loan from the bank to pay off all our bills, we could pay less overall and still pay it in the same amount of time because we'd be paying a lower interest rate."

"But doing so is only valuable if you don't get back into debt," Jean-Marc emphasized. "If you go back to spending at the same rate, you'll be even worse off." He gathered all the money on the desk that represented the amount they needed to pay the bills. "The goal is to get rid of all your debts entirely. You really would need only about half of this cash to meet the new loan payment. However, I suggest you keep putting seventy-five percent down to get rid of it faster. I would normally suggest putting one hundred percent of what you have been paying on the bills, but there is no way you can survive doing that. You'll need money for things that crop up, like car repairs, dentist bills, clothes, and so forth.

"Now, there are only two rules in spending the remaining twenty-five percent of this money, or any extra funds you may receive. Both of you must agree on how it is to be spent, and you do not borrow any more. Period. Let me repeat: you do not borrow any other money at all. That means absolutely no credit card debt. None. If you don't have the cash in your bank account, you don't buy it. And when you get raises or bonuses, you need to calculate what the overall increase is after you pay taxes and tithing, and put that on the loan as well. Paying off that debt must be your chief concern. After you get that paid off, you can focus on getting a mortgage—which is the only debt I'll ever recommend to any of my children, because it will increase in value—especially if you pay it off early and save interest charges. For the rest, even a vehicle, it's better to make do with what you can afford. So what do you think? Are you willing to do that?"

Mathieu sat back in his chair and sighed deeply. "I guess so, but it doesn't sound very fun."

"Oh, but I haven't mentioned the best part. Of the twenty-five percent you are now not paying on the bills, you each get a small portion." Jean-Marc counted some money onto the desk in front of them. "This is yours to spend in any way you wish, without consulting the other. You get this same amount each month. And you cannot ask the other what he or she did with the money, or in any way get an accounting unless it's voluntary. Consider it one of the monthly bills."

Marie-Thérèse stared at the money. "Anything I want?" she asked, fingering the notes.

"Anything," her father said. "Except in your case, I want you to promise that you will spend at least half of it on something for yourself. I make this stipulation only because I know you are too likely to spend it on the bills or on an outfit for Larissa."

Mathieu laughed, scooping up the money from the desk. "That's for sure. I guess I won't have much trouble spending my share."

"There's also a support group for people who have spending problems."

"Spenders Anonymous?" Mathieu asked.

Marie-Thérèse couldn't miss the humor in his voice.

"Something like that. I want you both to go."

Mathieu's brow drew in puzzlement. "But if we follow your plan, we shouldn't need to."

Jean-Marc pushed back his chair from the oak desk and stood, stretching his back almost imperceptibly. "It isn't going to be that easy, Mathieu. Perhaps it might be for the first little while, but after that it gets hard. With a support group it'll be easier, believe me."

"Are you saying that as a bishop or as Father?" Mathieu asked, coming to his feet.

Marie-Thérèse also arose, moving closer to her husband, hope in her heart.

"Both." Jean-Marc put an arm around each of them. "You

guys are good kids. I believe that with a lot of prayer you'll find your way. There are much more serious problems in the world. Just remember how much you love each other and begin giving a hundred percent of your effort to making this marriage work." He dropped his arms and walked with them to the door. "Now, I want you to go into that room down the hall, pack Marie-Thérèse's things, and go home to your own apartment. For the last week that it's yours, anyway. I hope you've found another place."

Marie-Thérèse shook her head. "I'll start looking tomorrow."

"First, I expect to see you both at the bank."

She opened her mouth to thank her father, but he shook his head. "Don't thank me now. In a few years when you're free from your debts, or most of them, then you can thank me. Believe me, it's a wonderful freedom you won't be able to find anywhere else. Of course, that won't let you out of the other problems life will throw at you—and this family has certainly had its share. You fall sometimes when you're hit, but as long as you keep getting up, you're not out of the game."

He hugged Marie-Thérèse before holding out his hand to Mathieu. "Uh, my money?"

Mathieu grinned sheepishly as he handed back the money Jean-Marc had given them to represent the personal money they were to spend each month. "I almost forgot."

Marie-Thérèse tried to return her share as well, but Jean-Marc pushed her hand back, also adding the money Mathieu had returned. "Fathers are allowed some privileges," he whispered in her ear.

Marie-Thérèse tucked the money into her purse. It was amazing how a little cash made everything look brighter. She watched her father return to his desk, and then grabbed Mathieu's hand. "We can do it, can't we?"

He pulled her into his arms, and she almost couldn't believe how right she felt at that moment. She knew her father had said that it wouldn't be easy for Mathieu to change, but she loved him and was determined to give him the chance.

Chapter Sixty-seven

The end of August came with record heat spells and a sad fare-well to Brionney, who left for America and her French studies at BYU. Even with her own concerns, Marie-Thérèse noticed Marc's regret when Brionney's plane left, and she wondered if he would go after her someday.

Marie-Thérèse and Mathieu had moved to a new apartment, a smaller, less expensive one, but it felt like home. They had left behind all of the old memories and as much of the expensive furniture as they could sell back to the stores. She could only pray that the peace would last. Mathieu brought home his paycheck and, other than his monthly allotment, didn't spend anything without consulting her. Sometimes she could tell that he was doing all he could to please her and that the effort didn't come without a cost. He did mention that they seemed to eat better now, and the small kitchen actually had more space without all the ironing and clothing rods.

In her spare time, Marie-Thérèse had taken up crocheting bed covers for extra money to put toward their large debt, but she didn't point this out to Mathieu because she believed he needed to feel that he was supporting their family alone. He was doing a great job, but Marie-Thérèse worried that he might experience a relapse into his old spending habits. When could she know that he was entirely safe? Or would that day never come?

As September passed, their baby grew and flourished inside her. She and Josette often spent the afternoons together talking and planning for their babies. Marie-Thérèse still felt guilty for wishing she wasn't expecting during those first agonizing months. How could she have not wanted this precious life? Her situation with Mathieu had been serious, but surely not so desperate as to reject the gift of a child of God. Mathieu did his best to convince her to let the matter go, and the doctor had assured her of the baby's health, but in the back of her mind the worry simmered that she had somehow damaged her baby with her negative emotions.

Each week Marie-Thérèse attended a financial support group with a reluctant Mathieu. It reminded Marie-Thérèse of the few times she had attended the AIDS support meetings with Pauline when André hadn't been able to accompany her. Only there were many more people, most of them older.

One night in mid-October when she was seven months pregnant, Marie-Thérèse and Mathieu took Larissa to Josette's and went to the meeting. As usual, the room was too warm, but a fresh evening breeze wafted through the open window. Marie-Thérèse listened as a man in the thirty-odd member group told his story to the rest of the compulsive spenders.

"I was eighteen when I received my first credit card application in the mail," the man said. "They talked about freedom and independence and all the things I could buy to bring me joy. Build up a good credit rating, they said. It'll make it easier to buy an apartment someday. I sent in the application, and then when the card came I went shopping and spent up to my limit. They were right, I was very happy. New clothes, a new look— perfect to go to my new college. But they had only told part of the story." Everyone in the group nodded, some in sympathy, some in contemptuous denial.

"Same as me," another man spoke up. "You had to get another card, didn't you? To keep the same feeling."

"Exactly," the first man replied. He wasn't new to the group, but it was the first time he'd spoken in front of everyone. His expression showed a mixture of relief and nervousness. "Pretty soon I couldn't pay, and that's when the court ordered me here."

"They hadn't told you the truth, that's for sure," someone from the audience said in a loud voice. Murmurs spread through the rest of the group as people began to offer advice, or to ask questions. Marie-Thérèse felt her attention slipping. They had been here almost an hour already, and it looked as though it might go for one more. While she appreciated the testimonials of these men and women, she was more worried about Larissa, who'd been acting cranky as she often did before coming down with a fever. Josette and Zack were competent baby-sitters, and they'd come over to her apartment to watch Larissa so she could go to sleep in her own bed, but that didn't put Marie-Thérèse's mind completely at rest.

Mathieu squeezed her hand. "Let's go," he said. "We'll come back next week."

Marie-Thérèse hesitated only an instant, then smiled apologetically at the speaker and slipped out the back door with Mathieu close on her heels.

"Did you hear anything new?" she asked.

For two months they had been coming to these meetings, and for the same two months she felt as though she'd been holding her breath, waiting and watching . . . and praying. Mathieu had followed her father's advice to the letter, but she felt there was some part of him that was not entirely happy about their new goals. He had shown a reluctance to attend these meetings, and even Marie-Thérèse had to admit that most of these people had problems much more severe than Mathieu's. In a way, knowing that helped her. But had the group helped her husband at all? Each time she asked him, and each time he said no.

She expected the same unenthusiastic reply, but today he looked at her differently, a smile playing on his lips. "Actually, yes."

"And?" She tried to hide her surprise.

Mathieu opened the car door. "I'll tell you on the way."

Marie-Thérèse remembered Larissa and hurriedly settled into the seat, buckling her safety belt. Mathieu started the engine and waited for a chance to pull into the heavy traffic.

"Well?" she asked, fidgeting with her hands.

He took one hand from the wheel and put it over hers, stilling their nervous movement. "When that last guy started speaking, I realized that he was telling my story. I remembered it so vividly—that incredible, exciting feeling of independence. At last I was a man and could do as I liked. I didn't have to wish for things as I had when my mother was too poor to take care of any but my basic needs. There was nothing before me but freedom and everything money could buy. I know they've talked about this at the group before, but it was only tonight that the Spirit told me that such an illusion of freedom is nothing more than a blatant lie Satan is using to entrap young people. It's every bit as dangerous as alcohol, gambling, adultery—you name it. It's another perversion he's using to make us miserable. Or even to cause divorce." He slammed one hand against the steering wheel. "It's so clear to me now—why didn't I see it before?"

"Well, if Satan's plan was that obvious, it wouldn't work now, would it?"

"You didn't believe him."

Marie-Thérèse snorted. "I'm a banker's daughter. I could add before I could read."

"That's a good thing for me." Mathieu gave a choked laugh. "You know, it's a strange thing, but as I was sitting there, suddenly I could see everything so clearly. You know, like the Spirit was talking directly to mine without having to go through the slow reflexes of my body."

Marie-Thérèse nodded to show she understood. She'd felt

the same thing twice before, once when she had decided to marry Mathieu and once after Larissa was born. "Like a pure understanding," she said.

"That's it. And now I know we're going to make it. I've felt a bit resentful and angry these past months, but now it's okay." He reached over and took her hand. "I thought you'd want to know."

The months of worry fade away in that moment. Marie-Thérèse squeezed Mathieu's hand and gave silent thanks to the Lord.

They didn't speak again until Mathieu drove up to their apartment building and opened Marie-Thérèse's door. He pulled her close and said in her ear, "Thanks for standing by me."

Marie-Thérèse met his gaze. "I guess that's what marriage is all about. You did the same for me when I kept wondering if I'd done the right thing by not going on a mission."

"You had me worried," he admitted. "Until Larissa was born."

They headed to the elevator, hands linked. When they arrived at their apartment, the door flew open before they could insert the key.

Grandma Simone's thin, wrinkled face grinned at them. "Thank goodness you're home. We've got to get to the hospital."

"Is Larissa okay?" Marie-Thérèse asked, feeling panic spread through her.

"She's fine. It's Josette I'm worried about. She's gone into labor. Imagine that—a week early. Come on. Let's get down to the hospital before we miss all the action!"

Chapter Sixty-eight

Josette had heard from nearly all the women she knew that labor and delivery were the most horribly painful experiences they had ever endured. Though she knew some women tended to exaggerate their experience, she'd been apprehensive enough to make sure Dr. Samain knew that she wanted an epidural when the time came. Her mother had suffered difficult labors, and the doctor had said that a woman's labor pattern often followed her mother's. Yet as the labor progressed, Josette noticed that Zack seemed to be more uncomfortable than she was.

"Some help I am," he muttered, when he had to sit down to avoid feeling light-headed.

Josette laughed. "You can't help it. And I'm fine. I'm just feeling a little pressure, that's all."

"You're about seven dilated," the nurse informed her. "Are you sure you don't want anything for the pain?"

Josette shook her head. "I'm not feeling any."

"Well, I think your baby will be coming very soon. The epidural may not have a chance to work anyway."

Josette couldn't believe this moment was here after all the

months of planning and waiting. To finally hold her baby in her arms—she could hardly wait!

Another nurse came into the room. "Your mother's here. Would you like me to send her in?"

"Yes, please. And my sister, too, if she gets here in time."

"Well, there's a crowd waiting out there, but I don't think anyone mentioned a sister. I'll go ask again."

"Her name is Marie-Thérèse," Josette called after her. A new contraction began; this time Josette did feel a little pain and had to use the breathing techniques she had been taught by the nurses.

"Here, I'll coach you." Zack's pale face made her want to laugh. How strange. She never thought she'd laugh through labor.

Her mother came through the door, obviously hurrying but not ruffled. "How are you holding up?"

"I'm fine," Josette said. "I guess I'm pretty lucky so far. But Zack's feeling kind of bad."

Zack looked at Ariana sheepishly. "Did I ever mention that I feel faint at the sight of blood?"

"There's no blood yet," Ariana told Zack with a smile.

Fifteen minutes later the nurses called the doctor, who instructed Josette to begin pushing. Now the pressure and pain grew worse, though it became more bearable when she bore down.

"He's out!" Dr. Samain said, a few minutes later.

Josette glanced at Zack to make sure the doctor had been talking about the baby and not her husband. But a battered and exhausted-looking Zack was still on his feet, even if he was being supported by Ariana.

"He's breathing well," said Dr. Samain as he placed the baby on Josette's stomach and began cleaning his little body. Josette couldn't believe how perfect their son was, and how tiny.

"Didn't even let out a peep," the doctor added. "If it weren't so bright in here and cold compared to what he's used to, he'd probably already be back to sleep. That was one of the easiest deliveries I've ever witnessed. Congratulations." He motioned for

Zack to come closer, but hesitated at the sight of his white face. "I usually let the father help wipe the baby a bit, but in this case, I think I'd better let the father rest."

The nurses giggled and Zack grinned. "Thanks," he said. "That's a good idea. He's so tiny I might knock him off the bed."

"It's you falling down on top of us that he's worried about," Josette teased. She was glad her delivery had been so smooth, since Zack wasn't much help, but her discovery of this latest weakness only made her love him more. At least he had been able to conquer his queasiness enough to stay in the room.

Zack sat next to Josette on the bed, and his color slowly returned.

"So what are you going to name him?" one of the nurses asked.

"Emery Terrell Fields," Josette said without hesitation. She glanced at her mother to explain. "For Emeri and Zack's father." She felt it appropriate to name her baby after good men, one who was unable to leave posterity in this life and the other, Zack's father, who had so lovingly supported their decision to move to France.

"I like it," Ariana said. She was smiling, but several tears escaped from the corners of her eyes. "It seems like just yesterday they placed you and Marc in my arms. I was so grateful for you both. Your dad was, too. It was one of the best days of our lives."

Marie-Thérèse came into the room then, followed by the rest of the family—Jean-Marc, Marc, Louis-Géralde, Mathieu, and the great-grandparents. They congratulated the new parents and waited for a turn to hold little Emery.

After a while, Josette looked pointedly at Zack and he began to usher the family out the door. "They're not releasing her until tomorrow," he said. "So you all might as well go home and sleep."

Only Marie-Thérèse still lingered when a nurse came into the room. "We'll need to take the baby for his bath and checkup. Would either of you like to come?"

"Yeah, I'll go," Zack said. "I think I might be able to handle that much."

"I'll stay with Josette until you get back," Marie-Thérèse said. "Mathieu's still talking to my parents in the hall."

Marie-Thérèse sat down heavily in the chair next to the bed. Although she looked uncomfortably pregnant, she radiated happiness, and Josette knew it was because Mathieu's problem with money was under control, if not completely conquered. She squeezed her sister's arm. "I'm glad it's working out for you and Mathieu. You're good together."

"I think we're going to make it. But I'm glad you're here and not in America. I don't know what I would have done without your support these past months."

Josette laughed. "There's one for the books. Me being supportive."

"You've come a long way."

"Don't let Zack hear you say it. He still thinks I'm perfect."

Marie-Thérèse shook her head. "I doubt it—not as long as he talks about earning enough money to get you a housekeeper."

"I'm learning." Josette wrinkled her nose. "I never realized how much you used to clean up after me. Sorry about that."

"So is Zack happy here?" Marie-Thérèse asked after a brief lull in the conversation.

Josette thought for a moment. "I think so. He hasn't said he isn't. And he's really trying to let me have my own space. He's taken to playing tennis with some of the guys at work. At first it was funny, seeing him running around the court, but he's actually getting pretty good. Several times he's urged me to go out alone with my friends. I think he's growing accustomed to non-missionary life here."

"Haven't you asked him if he misses his family?"

"I guess I'm afraid of what he might say. What if he's not happy? What if he wants to go back to America to live?"

"What if you're just making problems where there aren't any?"

Josette sighed. "You're right. I have to talk to him." She paused before adding, "It wouldn't be so bad, going back there now and staying. Now that Emery's here. I think I could get pretty wrapped up in him."

"It does make a difference, having a child."

"But I don't really want to go back."

"Maybe Zack doesn't either. Ask him."

"I will." If Marie-Thérèse could face her fears, then Josette would also find the courage. She couldn't bear to think that Zack had traded his happiness for hers.

Marie-Thérèse patted her large belly, and Josette remembered only too well the discomfort. "Your baby will be here in no time," she said. "It's so fun, both of us having boys two months apart. I bet they'll be great friends—like we are."

An odd shadow flitted across Marie-Thérèse's face. "I still hate myself for not wanting to have him. I tell him every day how much I love and want him, hoping to make up for those four terrible months. Mathieu thinks I'm a little crazy. He says the baby couldn't possibly know how I felt, and even if he did, he'd understand why. But I keep having this uneasy feeling like something's wrong."

Josette blinked at her in surprise. "Your baby's going to be fine. Don't you remember what Pauline said? She said she'd look after him till you got him. I wish she'd said that to me."

Marie-Thérèse grabbed Josette and laughed until the tears came. "Oh, I can't believe it! She knew I'd need this reassurance— and all this time, I've been wondering if she was hallucinating."

"Well, you never know," Josette said. "I'm just saying what I feel. She could have been guessing. I mean, with as many children as you've always wanted to have, you were bound to have a boy who would give you some worry or another, don't you think?"

Marie-Thérèse shrugged. "It doesn't really matter. I feel it's my answer. Now it seems so silly that I worried at all."

Josette was relieved to hear it. She'd been reading parenting books and one author claimed that some children acted up simply because their parents expected them to. She didn't want Marie-Thérèse's feelings of guilt to affect her son once he was born.

Zack returned with the baby, and Marie-Thérèse went to find Mathieu. It was only much later that Josette remembered to ask Zack the question. The room was dark and it was time to sleep, but they'd left the bed light on so they could watch Emery sleeping in Josette's arms. Everything was quiet in their part of the hospital, and there was a new closeness between them that gave Josette the courage to speak. "Do you regret coming here?" she asked. "I mean, to France."

Zack lifted his head to meet her gaze. "I miss my family and my country," he said slowly. "For a while, I think I tried to fill that void only with you—and that wasn't fair, especially to you. You didn't do that to me in America. You worked, you had school interests, a close girlfriend and more. You didn't expect me to be everything to you. That's a pretty large order for anyone. I'm sorry for that, and I hope you've noticed that I'm trying to depend more on myself."

"I did notice, and I appreciate everything you're doing. But I guess what I'm asking is if you're happy."

With a swift movement, he arose from the bedside chair and put his forehead against hers. She could taste his breath as it mingled with her own in the still air. The only sound she could hear other than her own rapid heartbeat was Emery's soft breathing underneath the arch of their joined heads.

"I told you we were meant to be together," he said. "I still believe that. I don't regret anything as long as I'm married to you. And yes, I'm very happy." His mouth met hers, and Josette knew he spoke the truth.

$\mathcal{R}$achel Ann Nunes (pronounced noon-esh) learned to read when she was four, beginning a lifetime fascination with the written word. She still reads everything she can lay hands on, from children's stories to science articles. She began writing in the seventh grade and is now the author of eighty published books, including the popular *Ariana* series, *The Huntington Family* series, *Eyes of a Stranger,* and *Saving Madeline.* Her novel *Before I Say Goodbye* won the 2011 Whitney Award in the general fiction category. *Imprints, An Autumn Rain Novel, Fields of Home, The Independence Club,* and *Line of Fire, An Autumn Rain Novel* were all Whitney Award Finalists.

Rachel also publishes mainstream novels under the name Rachel Branton and urban fantasy under the name Teyla Branton. To read about upcoming books or sign up for her newsletter, visit Rachel's website at http://www.RachelAnnNunes.com.

www.ingramcontent.com/pod-product-compliance
Lightning Source LLC
Chambersburg PA
CBHW071640260626
47170CB00001B/177